THE
NURSE

BOOKS BY JENNA KERNAN

THE
NURSE

JENNA KERNAN

bookouture

Published by Bookouture in 2023

An imprint of Storyfire Ltd.
Carmelite House
50 Victoria Embankment
London EC4Y 0DZ

www.bookouture.com

ISBN: 978-1-83790-746-5
ebook ISBN: 978-1-83790-745-8

For Jim, always

PROLOGUE

LAKELAND, FLORIDA

Another call goes unanswered, as the housekeeper continues into the luxury suite, uncomfortable about what and whom she might find. Management has sent her to check on this guest who has not responded to multiple attempts to reach her by phone.

In the living room area, she pauses, waits, listens as she glances about.

The first indication that the suite is still occupied is the pair of shoes, carelessly cast aside. The iconic golden triangle logo emblem bears a reminder of status, while the cast-off expensive footwear punctuates the casual disregard of someone who has too much and needs you to remember that.

The snack wrappers on the coffee table verify that this occupant has no problem overpaying for convenience.

Beyond the sliding barn-door, the primary bedroom is in ruin with open hard-shell suitcases spewing costly contents, and classy clothing scattered on the floor, bench, and coverlet. A stack of crates containing paperwork sits beneath a portable lockbox. She arches a brow at this unusual discovery. These aren't the typical contents of such a room, and she knows that the carry-on bag, dropped on the floor beneath a second flatscreen television, costs more than she'll make in a month, including tips.

Unease trickles within her as she realizes the luggage sits on a perfectly made bed.

No one has slept here.

Before the drawn curtains, she finds a possible reason. There, an open champagne bottle sits, submerged in the stainless-steel bucket, complete with stand. That is a lot of alcohol for a single guest, who might have gone out and found some companionship or might have passed out drunk in the bathroom. The ice that once filled the bucket has liquified to warm water, all signs of condensation reduced to a puddle on the laminate woodgrain floors.

The hotel staffer presses her fists to her narrow, aching hips, purses her lips, and scowls at the expensive designer suit abandoned in a crumpled mound before the closet.

She turns to the grand bathroom. In the outer room are twin glass basins, in the color of the Caribbean Sea, and the shower, with its choice of two showerheads. No water droplets cover the glass walls. There is no smear of toothpaste in the sink. The assortment of complimentary products are untouched. There is no toothbrush, but a travel bag sits on the counter. Her brows wrinkle at the irregularity. This guest does not appear to have used the sinks. Worried now, her gaze flicks from the closed door to the toilet and then to the one leading to the spa tub. Both are ominously closed, but on the floor leading to the inner bathtub, a puddle of gray silk gleams against the shiny marble tiles that show every single body hair and speck of dirt. The sash identifies it as a robe.

The last time this happened, the guest was dead on the toilet, his flabby body already going green at his generous waist.

Curiosity urges her on. Whoever wore that robe might still be here.

The housekeeper gently taps the edge of the plastic keycard on the bathroom door. There is no response. She taps again and calls out. "Housekeeping!" and opens the door.

No one is in the toilet, much to her relief.

Beyond the door to the spa, however, she stops, eyes on the white marble tile.

The horror of the scene before her brings some of her breakfast up in her throat. She tastes the bitterness as she swallows, forcing it down.

A ghastly corpse, gray and waxy, stares obscenely at her from cloudy sightless eyes. The water is red and dark congealed blood forms a grisly, clotting puddle on the marble tiles.

A shiver shakes her, and her hands and feet go numb. She gapes at the unnaturally still body, assaulted by her own heart beating in her eardrums like the repo man pounding on her door.

The body's arm lazes casually over the edge of the white porcelain, pointing at the clotting gore on the tiles and soaking into the bath mat just beyond. There on the white terrycloth rectangle, now stiff and saturated with dried blood, sits a shiny double-edged razor.

That blood is never coming out of the grout lines. They will have to be redone. She blinks at the absurdity of the thought. She dismisses the need to check for signs of life. That ship has sailed, and she is not tracking her clean white sneakers through this mess.

The tip of its index finger holds a congealed droplet of blood, a black useless scab dangling like an engorged tick.

The sound of her own labored breathing fills the quiet space, rasping like a saw through dry wood. She is with this person, only somehow alone. Whatever was there, it's gone, leaving a naked husk.

The air is heavy with the sweet sickening stink of a slaughterhouse floor. The gore is rising again. She clutches her stomach, wishing she hadn't looked. Feeling the walls closing in on her.

She'll never get this horrible stench out of her nasal passages. Never forget the sight of the stiff arm and drying crimson puddle.

With one hand clamped over her mouth, she backs out until her legs contact something and give way. Then she folds on the bed she has made a hundred times but never dared to sit upon. Now the uncontrollable shaking seizes her, making her jaw clatter and her body twitch.

She is surrounded by beautiful, expensive things.

Why would a person, with all this, take their own life?

ONE

Emily Lancing wasn't much to look at. But she had the advantages of height, brains, and a soft-spoken manner that professors and employers thought pointed to compliance. In fact, she was a fighter who had to juggle part-time jobs and take on student debt just to finish her nursing program in two years.

Most people took three.

Emily carried her weight and anyone else's that needed carrying. Her shock of curly red hair, the glasses, and her height made you notice her. Her tractable manner let you easily dismiss her. Meanwhile, she was clever, smart enough to pass all her classes with high marks and reach the top in her graduating class.

She didn't need glasses but wore thick blue frames with clear lenses because that, and the hair, gave people convenient handles to identify her.

Today, she scrubbed her pale skin until it glowed pink, subdued her wild hair by tugging it back into a tight bun and secured it with a dull Number 2 pencil. The navy skirt, flats, and a simple white blouse, she hoped, would give the impression of a professional, instead of a recent graduate who had yet to earn her first dollar from her brand-new nursing degree.

From the kitchen of their two-bedroom, ground-floor apartment came the sound of her roommate filling the coffee carafe. After two months together, she knew Jennell Green was a light sleeper, loved fuzzy, pink girly things, and that her YouTube recommends included more cavorting puppies than true crime investigation.

But she was kind, thoughtful, serious, and—a bonus—funny.

Jennell's tightly coiled hair hung loose about her shoulders and her light brown skin gleamed from a combination of good health, youth, lotion, and a very hot shower.

She turned at Emily's appearance. Without the cat-eye makeup, and dressed in leggings and a baggy T-shirt, she looked more like a high school freshman heading for cheerleading practice than a twenty-five-year-old hotel assistant manager.

"Did I leave you enough hot water?" Jennell asked in what she called her hotel voice. It was that calm, competent tone she used when speaking to guests with questions like, "How was your stay with us?" and "Was everything to your satisfaction?"

Their arrangement was that Jennell got up first, showered, and then knocked on Emily's door, to tell her the bathroom was clear. But after one too many cold showers, Emily complained.

"Fine today."

"Oh, good."

She pointed a manicured finger, tipped with acrylic, airbrushed silver nails, and rotated it in a circle, encompassing Emily's outfit.

"And remember, the closest exit may be behind you."

Emily's shoulders sagged. "Oh, no. Flight attendant?" she asked.

Jennell giggled and poured the water into the coffee maker, then slipped the empty carafe into place.

"I was going for competent professional."

"Flight attendant," said Jennell again, her smile generous and her expression mirthful. "But seriously, is this the hospital posting?"

"No. Personal nurse. Job interview. Second round."

Behind Jennell, the coffee machine chugged and then gasped, drizzling the last of the black brew.

Jennell lifted her brows. "Well, you are a firecracker. The ink must still be wet on your diploma."

"I know, but this prospect asked for me specifically."

"You? Why?"

"Well, not me exactly. He asked for their top graduate."

"And that's you!" Jennell grinned. "All that hard work paying off."

"I hope so. And next month, I might be able to pay my rent from a paycheck instead of my student loan." The amount of that bill frightened Emily, and she tried very hard not to think of the total.

"Super."

She and Jennell had not known each other long but were a good fit so far. The apartment, though situated in a crappy part of Winter Haven, had got her out of a crappier part of Lakeland, where she'd been raised.

"Well, good luck."

"Working days again?" Emily asked, collecting her bag. Jennell's schedule at the boutique hotel was erratic.

"All week." She lifted the mug and blew on the steaming brew.

Emily glanced at her phone. "I have to run."

Jennell wiggled her fingers in farewell and Emily headed out.

The sunshade over the front step was no match for the Florida heat and humidity. She pushed a red corkscrew curl off her damp forehead and groaned.

Before she finished walking the fifty feet to her car, parked on the street, her clothes clung to her damp skin and beads of sweat rolled down her back. There was no chance she'd show up looking anything but flushed and sweaty.

Nerves over her success in this call-back interview made her stomach churn and her palms sweat.

This day, this first impression, this job—they were everything.

The hard part wouldn't be the work. The challenge would be convincing this power couple she was honest, trustworthy, and reliable. Rich people were particular about who they let in their homes. And from her internet search of their residence, Dr. and Mrs. Roth lived in a fortress inside a walled kingdom out of bounds to all but residents, guests, and the help. Houses started at three-quarters of a million and that was without a pool. In a few minutes, she'd see what they kept behind those guarded gates.

At her 2009 dented black Toyota Corolla, she opened the door and waited for the blast of hot air to dissipate as she removed her blazer and tossed it and her purse onto the passenger seat. With a sigh of resignation, she dragged the towel off the steering wheel and climbed into the driver's seat. The scalding temperature of the vinyl seat made her wince. There she folded the sunshade covering the windshield and drew on her sister's old driving gloves that allowed her to touch the superheated steering wheel without burning her hands. The heat, humidity, and violent afternoon thundershowers in June were enough to drive most visitors back up north. The rainy season took practice and some special gear.

Finally, she twisted the key and prayed the engine turned over.

The "Go ahead and laugh, it's paid for" bumper sticker, which her sister had placed on the used vehicle when Emily was twelve, had faded to a gray and pink, flaking, unreadable rectangle on her rear fender. But she couldn't bear to remove it.

The memory of the day her big sister peeled off the backing and swept her hand over the message to the world brought a tug of sorrow and a glimmer of pride.

This vehicle had become Emily's after her sister's death. She recalled the freedom this car had symbolized, at first, before the beater became a means for her sister to get to her job and a constant burden of repairs she couldn't afford. Little had changed, except Emily now sat behind the wheel and prayed that nothing broke or fell off.

Once Emily had been a little sister and the younger daughter. Who were you when your family was all gone?

The black smoke behind her announced to the world that her car burned oil. Thank God Florida didn't require emissions tests or inspections of vehicles.

During her first semester of community college, her gigs driving for food delivery and grocery stores had ended when her car ran out of gas on route and all the frozen food had defrosted in her trunk. They didn't pay her enough to fix her car, or to pay her rent. The jobs were more like living in a leaky rowboat with a small pail for bailing. She was still sinking, but the descent was slower.

Once her practicum began with the required minimum of eight hundred unpaid hours, and she could no longer manage the part-time jobs, her finances really got tight, and her loan ballooned.

Getting a real job would be a blessing.

But while completing her nursing degree and then taking her licensure exam, she hadn't had time to apply for jobs. She didn't worry. They weren't scarce. Since the pandemic, there were plenty of vacancies. The trick was finding a good job without crushing overtime, low wages, an impossible patient load, or all three.

The exam itself had not been as grueling as all the unpaid practicum hours she'd clocked to be eligible. She'd known she'd passed before leaving the testing site and received her scores within the week. Like her GPA, her results were high enough to impress any prospective employer.

Student life, with her impossible schedule and moth-eaten safety net, meant she'd skipped meals and nearly run out of gas a few too many times.

Just once she'd like to get ahead of the game. She'd told this to her advisor at the career center at school, who seemed unimpressed, reminding her that recent graduates started at the bottom of every pay scale, and unless she was ready to move up to the frozen north, where the money was better but the living expenses prohibitive, she'd better be prepared for several more spare years.

"We have more than enough postings. If you're not picky."

She *was* picky, but tell that to her empty gas tank.

Her savings were exhausted years ago. Since walking beneath her mortarboard cap, she could add a hefty student loan payment to her living expenses. Currently, she couldn't even cover the interest on her credit card. The crush of debt and anxiety seemed unending.

This job might change all that. It was the ripe peach in an orchard of hard green fruit.

When the career center phoned and explained that a prominent local psychiatrist approached them wishing to hire their valedictorian, Emily was elated. She was nervous, of course, but so absolutely ecstatic that her hard work and planning might pay off. It was everything she wanted. Experience, a good salary, benefits, close to her apartment, and her patient load would be *one*. Just imagine that!

Emily had leapt at the chance. Even before their preliminary interview, she already knew Dr. Roth because of her practicum hours in the hospital in Lakeland. Everyone at the hospital liked him. He was charming and upbeat, but that was his public persona. He might be different in private.

If she got the job, she'd soon find out. And also, the answer to the bigger question, why did he need a private nurse for his wife? In their preliminary interview, he'd been vague, using the meeting only to get to know her better. And she'd cleared that hurdle and was on to the next. Meeting and getting the green light from his wife.

Luckily this interview was right here in Winter Haven because the drive to his offices in Lakeland had brought her dash gauge to E. She was nearly out of gas.

It would be worth it, she reminded herself. *Just wait. It will all be worth it.*

Getting this job would be like hitting the Powerball Jackpot. She had her heart set and her mind fixed. This had to work.

The air conditioner was slow to cool the interior. Sweating, she rolled onto the three-lane thoroughfare, thrusting her arm out the side window and merging into traffic. No one else was using their arm as a turn signal.

For the last ten minutes of the drive, she kept expecting the engine to gasp and run dry.

How many days could you ignore that yellow illuminated empty gas icon on the dashboard or the needle that now sat below the E?

The gas station before her mocked.

"Okay, fine."

She pulled in and flipped open the tank.

Sticky. All over sticky and hot. She plucked at her blouse, trying to drag the sodden fabric from her moist skin. Blowing dust adhered to her face as she made her way into the station, side-stepping to avoid the melting wad of blue gum on the blotchy sidewalk before the door.

Inside, the woman behind the register arched a brow.

"Pump cut out on you?" she asked. The attendant was fifty-ish, too tan, and too thin. Both her rasping voice and the crinkly texture of her loose skin would have been enough to announce her as a heavy smoker if the stale stench of cigarettes had not. The yellow stains on her finger and thumb and the ash on the counter confirmed Emily's suspicion.

"No. It's fine. Five dollars of regular, please." She held out her last ten.

The attendant pressed her thin lips together and nodded sagely. If Emily had to guess, she'd say this weathered woman earned her "Been there, done that" T-shirt many years ago.

The cashier accepted the bill and counted out change. Back at the beater she drove, Emily wondered if a gallon would last until she had another paycheck.

June 1st already. Thirty days before the rent came due again. This job would give her that and more.

Back in traffic, she found the highway was full of the normal impatient drivers swerving around her as she clung to the right lane, putting along, conserving gas.

Winter Haven lay east of Tampa and southwest of Orlando, making it convenient to the Gulf waters and close to the assortment of theme parks, but far enough to discourage visitors to either beach or park from staying there. By design, it had the sort of attractions that didn't lure tourists off the most dangerous highway in America, though the constant crashes of tired, lost, and distracted drivers along I-4 kept the paramedics and fire department busy and filled the hospitals with out-of-state trauma patients.

Their closest neighbor, Lakeland, had plenty of lakes and turtles, black clouds of biting insects and roaming alligators. This included the eight-hundred-pound gator recently spotted sunning itself on the sidewalk outside the local middle school. Trapping alligators came with the territory for the Polk County Sheriff's Office. Emily found the reptiles less irksome than the out-of-state invaders, the snowbirds—which were not birds. Snowbirds was the term for the elderly guests who rented for three to four winter months, escaping the most brutal cold weather in the northeast by flocking to the southeastern and southwestern states. They also filled the hospitals with elective surgeries, doctor visits, and medical emergencies.

The affluent visitors and residents lived in the more exclusive parts of Winter Haven, which was why she felt a certain triumph at arriving at the gated community, in her beater of a car, without encountering the local police.

She'd been pulled over before for the infraction of driving while poor. But she reached her destination without interference, rolling beside the high barrier wall that enclosed the gated community like the feudal castles of old. The landscaping popped with ornate vegetation and the smaller versions of ornamental palms, neatly trimmed, of course. What she did not see was a sidewalk. The private, gated community did not encourage pedestrians, unless they were also residents.

A wide swatch of pavement provided the guard a clear view of anyone turning into the property and allowed for two resident entrances and one for guests. This one directed visitors to the left where a gatehouse sat in the median beside a lowered barrier arm.

This seemed the opposite of welcoming.

The main entrance gatehouse was bigger than her bedroom.

Emily didn't belong here, would never belong in a neighborhood like this, except as hired help.

But if this went as planned, and she was prepared to do whatever it took to see that it did, she'd have everything she needed to begin looking forward, instead of back.

Emily slowed beside the gatehouse window to suffer the sweeping scan of disapproval from the female attendant seated on a stool before a computer inside a glass box. The guard wore a navy jacket with the property logo stitched on the breast pocket. Her hair, an unnatural blond with dark roots, hung limp beside her narrow face as she stared from red-rimmed eyes seated above puffy bluish bags. She slid open her window allowing a blast of arctic air to reach Emily and offered no greeting or smile, just a look of sullen apathy, suitable to a woman trapped in a glass cage just outside Elysian Fields.

A black Jaguar cruised through the residents' side of the main entrance, followed by a bright blue Corvette. The guard did not even glance at the status rides.

"Name?"

"Emily Lancing."

"Who are you here to see?"

"Dr. Henry Roth."

The guard glanced at her computer screen and began tapping keys.

"Emma?" she asked.

"What?"

"It says Emma Lancing."

It appeared that Dr. Roth did not know her name. She went with it.

"Um, yes. That's right." It wasn't. But correcting the computer entry might just mean a call to Dr. Roth or worse, bar her entry.

"License?"

Really? This was worse than the TSA. Or so she assumed. Unlike her mom and Emily's sister, nine years her senior, Emily had never been on a plane.

She handed over her ID.

"Says Emily."

"Yeah. That's my legal name. Friends call me Emma." They didn't, but if that was the name Dr. Roth had given the gate, then that was her name. Emily offered a welcoming smile to her lie.

Satisfied, the woman passed back her license.

"Drive through," said the attendant and slid her window closed.

Emily tucked away her license. When she had passed her

driving test and received this most important proof of adulthood, her older sister baked her a cake, in one of those silly kids' pans in the shape of a firetruck because they didn't have a car-shaped one. The pair had different fathers, different complexions, and different personalities. Her sister—well, half sister, though Emily rarely thought of her that way—had been full of kindness and joy, while Emily was not, which made them the perfect yin and yang.

The gate lifted with tedious slowness.

"You have a nice day," Emily said and waved her hand at the closed window. She felt as welcome as a homeless person at a country club buffet.

Emily put her car in drive, rolling past elaborate, gilded street signs and ornate landscaping on smooth roads that had neither potholes nor garbage in the bike lanes. Generous, sinuous sidewalks sidled along, allowing two women in athletic gear to stroll side by side with cheerful golden retrievers tethered on nylon leashes, one hot pink and one royal blue. Farther on, a French bulldog waddled before a thirty-something guy on a skateboard wearing baggy, artfully ripped jeans, an untucked yellow polo shirt, and a fanny pack with a neon orange strap, slung over one shoulder. Emily would have bet the guy still lived in his parents' spare bedroom.

Her head was on a pivot as she tried to take in everything at once. Sunlight glittered on ponds where mallard ducks drifted beside fountains that turned their perpetual spray into dancing rainbows. On the shore, benches clustered beneath huge oaks draped with long streamers of Spanish moss. She passed a huge empty playground with bright blue and gold climbing walls, platforms, swings, and inviting slides. Here, the shade over the groupings of benches and the equipment was provided by large blue triangles of canvas. Next came the tennis courts filled with women in brightly colored outfits, flitting back and forth like exotic birds in the bright sunshine.

Her phone directed her to turn here and there until she was thoroughly lost. The homes grew grander, the lots bigger, and the walls higher. In some places, the landscaping was so lush it was impossible to see past the dense tropical foliage, and others offered only a tantalizing glimpse of what lay beyond, like professional strippers.

Emily's nerves continued to rattle, along with her muffler.

The phone navigation app alerted her that she had reached her destination.

If she got this position, she'd have the job she wanted more than any other. That seemed like a dream compared to working at the hospital and bouncing from patient to patient like a chewed tennis ball gnawed by a Labrador retriever.

She turned into the drive and was met with a locked metal gate and a call box positioned just outside her window. There was a red button to the left of the speaker.

It was so tempting to press the button and order a cheeseburger, fries, and a Coke. Instead, Emily gingerly pushed the button, heard a buzz, and waited.

"Emma?" the voice was male and as clear as if he stood beside her open window. She recognized this as Dr. Roth.

"Yes. It's Emily." She hoped for a cheerful chirp of a voice, but thought her inflection sounded more desperate, like a drowning woman who is about to go under but still insists she's fine.

"Great. Drive on up."

The wrought-iron gate rolled back behind the wall, and she had her first look at the Roths' private residence.

"Holy mackerel," she whispered.

The laugh came through the speaker.

"You can use the front door," Dr. Roth said.

It hadn't occurred to her to use any other one. But it should have. It would have occurred to her sister, who had worked as a housekeeper and later as a household manager, while their mother cleaned houses and later hotel rooms, hoping the tips gathered from pillows and side tables would be enough to keep them fed.

She closed the window and inched up the circular drive of pale gray paver stones, past the pristine tropical landscaping of royal palms, wide-leafed traveler palms, mature pink and green bromeliads, and yellow hibiscus bushes that ringed the putting-green of a lawn. Something told her not to park before the main entrance, so she rolled by and passed three huge arching windows. Was that the main bedroom? Creeping along, she turned the corner and discovered that, no, those ornate windows were not for the main bedroom but for the garage, which had four huge carriage doors.

"Wow." She'd never even seen a garage that big.

How much did a man like Dr. Roth charge per hour to afford this sort of luxury? She was so curious about him. What was he like when not at work and what was his wife like?

Elegant, she was certain, well educated, she knew from a web search, and stunning, if their engagement photo, published in the paper over twenty-four years ago, was any indication.

Just beyond the last bay door was a parking area with room for two vehicles. Before her was a high hedge of pitch apple with lime-green, paddle-like leaves that prevented her from seeing the side yard or the lake, which she knew, from the map application, lay beyond. All she could see was a little sidewalk, which led to a utilitarian rear door to the garage.

Emily exited her vehicle, praying that when she returned, it would start again. She didn't even care if she only made it outside the private gate, so long as the Roths didn't see her old car run dry.

On the hot pavers, she tugged down her skirt and ignored the oppressive humidity that enveloped her. After debating, she left her purse, tucking away her car keys and taking only a simple notebook and pen. She could not bear the thought of putting on her blazer, so she just looped it over her damp fore-arm, like a towel. Lifting her chin, she headed back past the ornate bay doors, hurrying along the walkway between twin royal palms flanking the columned entrance. On the landing, she paused before the two massive lead-glass double doors and the digital doorbell to slip into her blazer. Surely the gatehouse and her conversation through the speaker alerted Dr. Roth that she had arrived.

No pop-in, drop-by visitors in this neighborhood. No, sir. Not unless someone wanted to get fired.

She had the most irrational urge to abandon this opportu-nity, turn tail, and run. Then she remembered her mission, pressed the digital doorbell, and stepped back.

TWO

From inside the Roths' lavish home came the echoing chime that reminded her of a clock tower bell. Emily stood on the sweltering landing of the Roths' residence, trying not to fidget because she wanted the video doorbell to relay an image of a confident young woman instead of a trembling girl who might be about to jump into a situation way over her head.

Despite her confidence in yesterday's interview, she didn't know if she could do this.

She glanced upward, finding a huge wrought-iron lamp hanging above her head. A side-step took her out from under the massive light.

The door swept open, and there stood Dr. Roth, greeting her with a warm, encouraging smile and an off-putting eagerness in his expression. He rubbed his hands together as if he didn't know what to do with them or perhaps didn't wish to shake her hand.

Henry Roth might be in his forties, judging from the deepening of the lines beside his eyes and flanking his wide mouth, but he was attractive, and his trim figure made him appear younger. The psychiatrist was lean, fit, and freckled, with silver sideburns and golden-brown hair, just a tad too long and curly to be stylish. His eyes were the color of the top-shelf whiskey she used to serve to rich frat boys in her short-lived bartending job in Daytona. His features were regular and appealing, if you could look past the white caps on his unnaturally straight teeth. Roth looked like what he was—important.

He was tall enough to look her in the eyes, making him at least five-eleven. His athletic build, flat stomach, and muscular body all confirmed what he had told her, about his love of biking and running. The man put in the time and had avoided the midriff spread so common in men his age. Where did he find the time? He'd told her he had completed more than one marathon, including Boston and New York City, during a humble brag over coffee at the hospital cafeteria and she'd pretended to be impressed. Emily ran, too, for buses, to her car with hot food deliveries, and from patient to patient at her practicum in the hospital. But recently, she'd also started jogging on a treadmill in the air-conditioned gym at school. She was up to five miles now and the runs almost felt easy.

She knew Dr. Roth had the biggest psychiatric practice in the region. And she knew from the career center that he was among the area physicians who hired graduates of their nursing program. The first time they'd bumped into each other at the hospital cafeteria had been orchestrated by her. But he'd approached on the second. She'd talked about her practicum hours here at the hospital and he'd asked about her grades. When she'd gotten the call from her college's career center with the offer for an initial interview, she'd assumed she'd made a good impression, but had been told Dr. Roth had requested, not her, specifically, but the valedictorian, as he had done in the past. It was her grades, not her charm, that landed her this chance.

"Oh, good! You found us."

"Of course, good old nav program."

He glanced toward the place where her car was hidden.

"Does it have one?" he asked, his tone doubtful.

"My phone," she admitted.

"Well, I'm so glad you're here. With your grades, I'm certain we are not your only offer. Am I right?"

She tried for a confident smile, but it felt forced.

"I'll just have to make my offer irresistible then."

He grinned, unashamed that the world generally gave him exactly what he asked for. Surprisingly, it was also exactly what she wanted, though she suspected she was more used to disappointment.

Now here she was on her second interview, with fingers and toes all crossed that this would work out as she hoped.

"Nice to see you again, Dr. Roth," she said, offering a warm smile and readjusting the large glasses that had slipped down her slick nose.

Should she tell him it was Emily, not Emma, or let it slide?

"You look so different. With all that hair pulled back. You know?"

So, he had been noticing specifics. Wandering eye or just detail oriented? Time would tell.

"You look professional, as always," she said.

He wore a perfectly fitted dove-gray shirt, a matching thin silken tie, pressed dark gray trousers, and a black leather belt. His loafers looked both new and expensive.

"How was the ride over? Good? I knew you'd made it to the gatehouse. Any trouble finding us? The roads can be a bit of a maze."

"No trouble."

He clasped his hands together, squeezing. "Fine. That's great. All finished with your practicum at the hospital?" he asked.

"All finished up. I had to have that completed to take my exam."

"Oh, lovely."

Emily had done her homework, filled her internet browser with searches for Dr. and Mrs. Roth, but located very little on his wife. Their wedding announcement was published in 1997 and told of Sabrina Katherine King's engagement to a young medical student beginning specialization in psychiatry. Nothing about Dr. Roth's family who, oddly, were not mentioned. The bride attended an expensive boarding school and elite colleges in the northeast, but it did not say she had graduated from any.

The accompanying black and white photo showed a professional image of an exceptionally well-groomed and impeccably dressed couple, who might have been models for Bergdorf Goodman, had it not been for his slightly crooked teeth and the expression of confusion on her pale face. He looked eager, she looked uneasy as if the photographer had used the sort of noise-making toys designed to make a baby look in the correct direction. They appeared to Emily like an image of a Labrador puppy marrying a rescue cat.

Next came a birth announcement one year later. A girl. No photographs, just the parents' names, hospital, and the baby's weight and name: Taylor Lee. The only other article about Sabrina Roth, other than ones touting her work in charitable organizations, reported her vehicle's involvement in a traffic fatality in 2013, ten years ago.

Emily struggled not to fidget, resisting the urge to strip out of her blazer and streak into the inviting coolness billowing from the open door of his home. But she waited as sweat dribbled down her back with the consistency of a leaky faucet.

"Come in. Come in."

She stepped onto buff-colored tiles, laid to create the pattern of an ornamental carpet. The cool air brought her the aroma of fresh brewed coffee and the sharp bite of his after-shave, which was so overpowering she could taste it in the back of her throat. The foyer was bigger than her kitchen. A glance told her just how much of a fish out of water she would be in this country club estate.

Emily swallowed back her apprehension. She wanted this. And she could do this. She *would* do this. If she just kept repeating that, it might become true.

The walls were a soothing tan that made the white moldings, baseboards, and chair rails pop. Through an archway to her right were two closed doors, one small and the other impressive, with a gold latch handle. To the left, she saw a tray ceiling and a walnut table surrounded by eight coastal chairs backed with rattan on a wooden frame with upholstery seats in a pattern of broad green banana leaves. In the center was a large bouquet that she assumed was artificial. It wasn't. The fresh arrangement held two dozen raspberry-colored dahlias and pink rosebuds with occasional sprigs of gray-green sage. She'd seen smaller, less elaborate wedding bouquets.

On the buffet was a crystal decanter, half full with amber liquid, empty silver candlesticks, and three large buttery yellow candles that had never been lit. Before her, a white leather sectional held royal blue accent pillows and was low enough not to interfere with the view outside the massive wall of sliders. The pool and screened cage only partially distracted from the lake, which seemed a long walk from here. The Roths were doing very well for themselves with a pool, whirlpool, lake view with a dock, boathouse, and at least one boat.

"Wow," she breathed. "This place is huge."

He chuckled. "Only four acres, thirty-seven hundred square feet. One level. Four bedrooms, five full baths, plus the powder room."

Five bathrooms. Emily's mind flashed her a perfect image of this morning as she and her roommate juggled time and counter space in their single bathroom.

"Oh, and a small apartment over the boathouse. Vacant now. But it used to be our daughter's favorite teen hangout."

How nice for teenage Taylor Lee.

"But our daughter is grown and married now. Living over in Tampa. Her husband is just starting his residency."

"Another doctor?"

He grimaced, but whether it was because he didn't like his son-in-law or for some other reason, she was unsure.

"Yes. Hopefully."

That sounded like he lacked confidence in his son-in-law.

He pointed at the two doors off the foyer where they now stood.

"My office and a powder room," he said. "Beyond the kitchen is a family room, guest bedrooms, Taylor's old room. That's our daughter. And the bonus room my wife commandeered for her studio."

She wondered if that was a photography studio or yoga, perhaps. Dance, maybe. Or was Mrs. Roth some kind of artist?

He scanned the empty living room, and when the pause stretched a little too long, she asked, "Will your wife be joining us?"

His warm smile slipped, and he cast a worried glance toward the sliders. His Adam's apple bobbed before he answered.

"Bree will be with us in a bit." Then he rubbed his hands together again, as if in anticipation, but she thought perhaps it was a nervous habit he used to introduce transitions.

"Would you like something to drink?"

She was so thirsty her tongue stuck to the roof of her mouth, but she said, "Oh, no. I'm fine."

"What about some coffee?"

She could smell the enticing aroma of brewing beans and the offer was nearly too good to refuse, but her sister taught her to say "no, thank you" until she was asked a third time. And her intuition told her that "the help" did not drink coffee during job interviews.

"Maybe later on."

"All right then." His disarming smile was back, and he motioned to the left. "This way."

He led her from the foyer, through living and dining rooms, to the kitchen. Here he paused, having regained his relaxed bearing and air of composed grace.

"Just had it redone. Walnut cabinets, puck lights, granite countertops. Stone comes from Brazil. I've added a wine cooler, just a small one, because Sabrina doesn't drink, of course."

She stared at the wide counters and breakfast bar and wondered about that little "of course" tucked at the end of the sentence. If his wife didn't drink white wine with fish and red wine with pasta, she suspected Sabrina was either in recovery or on some conflicting medication.

Yesterday he'd told her that his wife had some medical condition that made him feel she needed a nurse's supervision. What exactly her challenges might be was a question that had been driving her crazy.

"Have you used one of these?" he asked, motioning toward a high-end espresso machine.

"Yes." She nodded. Before her mom got sick, Emily had a second part-time job in a coffee shop and had even picked up a shift on weeknights after finishing her classes.

"Lovely. Feel free. Whatever's in the refrigerator or cupboards is fair game. Oh, and you can add anything to the weekly shopping that you'd like."

Her brow furrowed at that offer. She was applying to work for them, not live with them.

"One little quirk." He tugged open a drawer. "Sabrina will insist you wear gloves when touching or preparing food."

"That's fine. I'm used to wearing gloves."

"We've been having groceries and some meals delivered. But she might like you to go pick it up from here on."

"I'd be happy to." Thrilled was more like it. But then came the jab of panic because she knew her beater might not make it to the store and back. She hesitated, not wanting to appear incompetent or to disclose that she was too flat broke to fix her vehicle's many and increasing problems. "Um... would I be using one of your vehicles?"

"Yes, of course. Sabrina has a full-sized SUV. Would you be comfortable driving that?"

She nodded, though she'd driven nothing larger than a compact car.

"Great." He paused and his polite smile slipped. His gaze drifted as his focus moved beyond her. He opened his mouth, snapped it shut, and continued the tour.

What had he been about to say?

Emily trailed behind him past the refrigerator adorned with wooden paneling to match the cabinets. The dishwasher and microwave were tucked under the counters. The range had six gas burners.

She thought of their battered electric stove. That and the microwave encompassed the total of her cooking appliances.

The stone counter breakfast bar held a wrought-iron fruit bowl of blown glass balls and more fresh flowers. Purple tulips in a blue glass vase.

She followed him to a breakfast table for four, in case the eight empty chairs in the dining room were not enough. Whimsical place mats circled the table. Two on one side, two on the other. They were the quilted cloth kind with tropical patterns of flamingos on a turquoise background. Only two had pink cloth napkins, neatly tucked in clear acrylic rings. The pink was a dead ringer for the highlight color on the flamingos' long curved necks.

"Laundry and pantry are that way, between the garage and

kitchen. Cleaning stuff is in there and under the kitchen sink if you need to mop up a spill, but Rosalind does the heavy cleaning."

Emily glanced in the direction he indicated.

"In addition to your nursing responsibilities, you might need to do a little tidying up and some food preparation. Will that work?"

"Of course." She nodded, but he wasn't looking at her.

She got the feeling he didn't hear the word "no" very often. His respected position as a psychiatrist, his wealth, and his charm ensured it.

"That archway leads to the family room, secondary bedrooms, and studio. Also, the pool bathroom is down that way and accessible from the hall or the pool deck, of course."

Of course. She wondered if the pool bathroom was also bigger than the one in her apartment.

"We'll meet out on the lanai with Bree. But I wanted to go over a few things first." He pressed his lips together and motioned to the dining room. She trailed him back the way they had come. "Why don't we sit?"

He indicated a side chair but did not pull it out for her. It was heavy and made a scraping sound as she dragged it back against the floor tiles.

She sat, and he took his place at the head of the table adjacent to her. His chair had arms. Hers did not.

He pinned her with a steady stare, his expression no longer welcoming.

"So, why do you want this job?"

THREE

Emily resisted the impulse to clear her throat.

"My practicum let me try a number of departments at the hospital. And, although I learned a great deal, I'm not sure working in this sort of enormous facility is for me. The patients come and go so quickly and there's not really time to make a personal connection."

"That's important to you?"

"Oh, yes. I'd like to work in a doctor's office or in a small private care facility. One where I have a chance to develop relationships."

Dr. Roth gave her a grin and a nod of approval.

She shouldn't need it, but it helped reassure her. Emily smiled back.

"And though I enjoy the practicum, being a private nurse is appealing. It would give me more of a chance to make a real impact and have my total focus on the health and well-being of just one person. You know?"

"That's very well put, Emma. The patient load at the hospital can be onerous," he said, pausing to cradle his smooth chin in the palm of his hand, thinking. "Our former nurse left us in a lurch. We're hoping that you will be more reliable."

"I'm very reliable." She sounded too eager. Emily cautioned herself not to appear desperate. Nothing was as repellent to the rich as desperation.

"Wonderful."

And if she got this, she'd make enough to pay her share of the rent and utilities and she'd get to know more about them. The temptation of looking into the personal lives of this wealthy couple made her nearly giddy. She should be ashamed of herself. But she wasn't. Belatedly, she added, "And the career center has been wonderful about helping me with my job search." That wasn't wholly true, but nothing made a person as appealing as knowing she was wanted elsewhere.

"You're in high demand."

Emily flushed and looked away. "Yes. I think so."

"Good to know." He rubbed his fingertips over his smooth jawline, regarding her, looking unsure. Then he spoke. "You've seen the job posting but let me just lay it out for you. We need you here five days a week. That's a minimum. And you cannot call in sick or be a no-show."

"I would never do that." But how did a person promise never to be ill, she wondered.

"I'm not allowed to ask, but I think I assumed you were older."

"I'm twenty-three."

His smile returned. "Oh, very good." He nodded for so long she felt uncomfortable again—still.

Was she doing all right? She thought so, hoped so.

"All right. Also, I often get called to the hospital for emergencies. Would you be able to get here in the evening, on short notice?"

"I could. Yes."

His nod told her this answer pleased him. "And would you

be available on the occasional evening if I have an emergency or a function to attend?"

"I could be."

His approving grin showed the caps were on both top and bottom. He'd cleaned up since that engagement photo. He now looked more *Best in Show*, rather than *an adoptable puppy*.

"Shall we go over the position?"

She drew out her pad and pen, ready to take notes.

"This nursing position will be different than others you may have experience with. You will have nursing responsibilities, specifically overseeing my wife's medications, and monitoring her mental and physical health. But in addition, we want you to be a personal assistant. You must be a responsible person, dependable, conscientious but still flexible. Sabrina can be rash at times. You should step in, when necessary, without being overbearing. I need you to be a companion for my wife and you can't do that if you're too dictatorial. She needs guiding, persuading, you know? Without a heavy hand. You would also be doing the shopping, or receiving food deliveries, and preparing meals during the day, lunch, sometimes dinner. Nothing fancy. Most of what we order is already prepared. Just needs to be reheated and so on. Then clean up. You know?"

She wrote in list form: *Medications, Mental & Physical health, Driver, Deliveries, Shopping, Meal prep (gloves), KP.* When he stopped speaking, she lifted her head and found him studying her list. Their eyes met and he cleared his throat, then continued.

"You'd place orders from the restaurants. Menus are in the drawer beside the refrigerator. There'll be some laundry, light housekeeping. The gatehouse will text if there are deliveries. Between eight and five, they'll contact you, instead of me. Pick them up at the end of the drive. Don't let the trucks past our gate. I don't want that lot of misfits driving delivery trucks inside our walls. Understand?"

THE NURSE 31

"Of course." She'd once been one of those "misfits."

"There'll be some tidying up after Bree, as needed. Errands, of course, like dry cleaning pickup, pharmacy, deliveries, and driving Bree to all her appointments. Hair, nails, massage, personal trainer. What else? Well, to the art store. She's there nearly every week. Oh, and her golf league on Wednesday mornings. Remember to load her clubs."

He paused and glanced toward the sliders from the kitchen to the pool. The sound of the humming air-conditioning ceased, and the birdsong reached her.

"Does that all sound agreeable to you? Something you can handle?"

"Yes, it does."

"Do you have other family in the area?"

"No. Just me now."

Her dad had lived in Arizona. Emily regularly checked on him and his happy other family via social media. That's how she recently found his obituary: "In lieu of flowers the family requests a donation to the American Cancer Society."

Having two parents die young of cancer should have made her fatalistic. Instead, it gave Emily her superpower. If you believed you would live a short life, you had the freedom to do things a more reasonable person would not.

"Me too. Bree and our daughter, Taylor, are my only family."

She wanted to ask where he came from and how he had managed to hook up with a woman as rich as Sabrina King, but this wasn't the time or place.

"And since you are a new graduate, I assume you are unincumbered but I wanted to ask, do you have any other jobs or commitments?"

"Not currently. No."

"Excellent. I'm optimistic. Just to clarify, you have no family responsibilities that might interfere with your ability to do this job?"

"My mom was sick, and she needed me. But not anymore, unfortunately."

"I see." He didn't seem to be listening, just waiting for her to finish so he could continue with his demands.

Emily set her teeth and exhaled. Her mom had been gone now more than two years after a horrific battle with cancer sucked away her lifeforce like some cosmic parasite.

"How is your mom now?"

"She's passed, unfortunately."

"Oh, how sad. I'm so sorry for your loss." He didn't look it. In fact, he looked relieved that they'd have all her time and attention without any interference.

And she'd already told him this at the hospital. Over coffee she had said that she'd been raised by a single mother and her older sister. He'd asked if her mom and sister had the same red hair and she'd told him they didn't because she and her sister had different fathers and hers was the redhead. Her sister had gotten their mother's blond hair and she had her dad's crazy red curls. He'd seemed interested when she had revealed that she'd lost her sister in tragic circumstances several years ago and that her mother had recently passed after a long battle with cancer. Clearly he had not been paying attention because he'd actually made that exact response the last time she'd told him.

Her high opinion of him dipped and Emily narrowed her eyes, but said, "Thank you."

"Is that where you developed your desire to become a nurse, in caring for her?"

"You could say that. Yes."

He moved on.

"You'll see the yard people on Fridays, usually, depending on the weather. Pool guy is Monday, and Rosalind, our cleaning lady, comes Tuesdays and Thursdays. You'll meet her." He glanced at his watch. "You might meet her today. Her English is, well, it's terrible. You speak Spanish, by chance?"

"Un poco," she answered.

"Very good. I'd like you either with her or within earshot while I'm gone."

"Really?"

"Yes. Your career counselor said you have a calm, confident demeanor. And I already know you can be charming. I feel that's just what we need here. Bree is very smart, and she prefers a companion who can keep up. You seem relaxed in conversation with..." His mouth twisted.

Had he been about to say with her betters?

"With people of different backgrounds," he said, but the effort to amend his first thought was obvious and the pause stretched. He filled it a moment later, picking up the thread as easily as an experienced seamstress. "You live in Lakeland?"

"I did. But now I'm in Winter Haven."

"As I said, we didn't expect to lose Bree's nurse. Bit of a scramble now."

Was this going to happen?

She bounced her leg until she realized the repetitive motion was visible above the tabletop. She would have agreed to anything. She needed this for so many reasons and hoped his wife would like her.

Of course she hoped for many things. A better life, better than the crappy place she lived, better than the cancer diagnosis her mother had drawn from a random universe, better than the early grave she now occupied beside Emily's older sister, and better than an absent dad who had provided only his name on her birth certificate.

If she *could* get her hands on a little extra cash, she might afford the headstone for her mother's grave. Right now, all that marked her resting place was a mound of collapsing sandy earth and a small plastic sign with her mother's name and the name of the funeral home that arranged the burial. But after two years and four months, the writing had faded and the edge of the paper sticker curled away at the corners. How she was going to pay for a headstone was the gnawing kind of question that kept her awake at night.

Her mom had left the contents of her apartment, six hundred dollars in the bank, and over nine thousand in credit card debt that Emily was relieved not to be responsible for. But she was still on the hook for the burial, tipping her credit card toward its max.

"Frustrating because we've had her for several years." He shook his head and his lips pressed tight.

She'd missed something.

"Your wife's former nurse?"

"Yes. Just unacceptable. Her problem... well, I'm not telling tales to say we are both so disappointed. I've missed therapy sessions and..." He shook his head. "My wife needs a nurse, assistant, and companion. And, as I've said, someone who'll take on other light responsibilities."

The list was not light, despite what he might think.

He no longer looked easygoing and earnest. Now his brow sank, and his expression turned stormy. She felt she was seeing a different man, just a glimpse behind the mask. Which was he, the affable loving husband or the harried, overburdened one?

She meant to find out.

"That's unfortunate."

"Bree needs consistency."

"I'm very responsible." She grinned and his expression popped back to the one he most often flashed. Charming. Successful. Carefree.

But she'd caught sight of the other.

"Emma, are you familiar with patient confidentiality rights?"

"Yes. It's required to understand HIPAA regulations." Her cheeks burned from holding her smile.

"And you'd be willing to sign an NDA?"

"An..." She'd heard that term but wasn't sure what it meant.

"A non-disclosure agreement?"

Why did he need an NDA? What was he afraid she might reveal?

"That..." She hesitated. Her confident smile slipped like melting ice cream from a sugar cone. "Would be fine."

"Excellent."

He pivoted in his seat to retrieve a folder from the buffet, along with a very expensive-looking pen; hers was the kind where the cap was constantly falling off and getting lost.

"I have it right here. You read it over and we'll have a chat. Then I'll tell Sabrina we're about to begin the interview."

Her heartbeat was pounding behind her eardrums as he opened the folder and drew out a single sheet. At the top of the first page, in large bold type, was written: NON-DISCLO-SURE AGREEMENT. Below that was the date and the Roths' full names, and below that was her name.

"Here we are." He pointed. "Did I get that correct?"

The type read: Emma Lancing.

She nodded. "Yes, but it's Emily."

"Could I see your identification? A valid driver's license?"

Which she'd left in the car. The sinking sensation dragged at her confidence. Why hadn't she brought her identification with her? This was not the behavior of a conscientious, dependable, and mature caregiver.

"Oh, yes. My purse is in my vehicle." Her smile felt forced, but she held the mask of competence.

"No trouble. You can go out through the garage and the side door. I'll print another one of these."

She pointed. "That way?"

"Yes."

They stood in unison. Emily headed into the kitchen and opened the door he indicated. Beyond that was a huge laundry room with a utility sink and closet opposite a walk-in pantry. Before her, another door led to three stairs and a garage. The huge arching windows illuminated the cavernous space.

"Switch is on the right."

She didn't need it but clicked it on anyway and gasped. The rows of lights popped on, revealing a black and white checkerboard floor and a line of vehicles. In the space beyond the cars' front bumpers was a large open area and a kind of stylized booth that looked as if it had been stolen from the 1950s. The red vinyl seats, Formica table, rimmed with stainless steel, and the personal jukebox all confused her. Did Dr. Roth come out here and listen to 45s while drinking an egg cream? Or perhaps while he polished his cars?

And who put a vinyl floor in a garage? Most people in this state had to settle for a carport and Emily had been fighting for off-street parking for as long as she'd been driving.

Meanwhile, the Roths' garage looked like a 1950s soda shop with three occupied parking spots and one open one before two double garage doors reinforced with huge aluminum bars.

Emily scanned the vehicles.

Farthest away was the black full-sized Mercedes SUV. Next was a large gray BMW sedan. And nearest was a two-seat, silver Mercedes-Benz GT. Beyond that, hanging with the front wheel up, was a sleek silver racing bike with a frame so thin it looked incapable of holding a man's weight.

Emily gawked. Then remembered her mission and hustled between the luxury vehicles and the diner booth, past the matching counter and custom cabinets, to the steel door, which was unlocked.

Outside, the humidity enveloped her as she hurried to retrieve her bag. Then she retraced her steps, pausing as she realized the floors of the garage were cleaner than the hallways in the hospital. The immaculate order of a space that was usually chaotic troubled her. But she wasn't clear why.

Returning to the kitchen, she set her bag down and retrieved her wallet.

Dr. Roth was waiting, having moved the folder to the kitchen counter.

"I left the door unlocked," she said.

"It's always unlocked. That way, Rosalind can get started on the garage before we're up."

"I see." But she didn't.

Now she wondered how late Mrs. Roth slept or how early Rosalind arrived.

Emily offered her identification.

"That's great. Mind if I make a copy?"

She did mind, but she shook her head. "No, of course."

"You go ahead and read that."

He left her at the counter, seated on one of the high barstools before the vase of purple tulips, the blossoms heavy on the arching green stems. The contract had wording like "in connection therewith" and "remain in full force and effect." She was clever but didn't understand legal gibberish.

She scanned to the second page and didn't like the part that said "the agreement shall survive change or termination of the parties herein."

But she needed this to work, and if keeping the Roths' private life private got her through that ornate gate, then that was fine and dandy. Besides, she had a superpower.

She signed and printed her name, added her address, the date, and left the title blank.

"There," she said. "Done."

That's when she realized she had yet to meet his wife, the only remaining hurdle in the road between her and her goal.

Dr. Roth returned with her license, passing it to her.

"Oh, already signed. That's lovely." He turned the page in

his direction and added his signature and other details. "I'll give you a copy before you go."

Emily returned her license to her wallet and dropped the bag to the floor. Then she laced her fingers tight in her lap and willed herself not to fidget.

"So, before you meet my wife, I wanted to go over a few of her special needs."

FOUR

Dr. Roth took a seat beside Emily at the breakfast counter, one barstool away from the one she'd chosen, leaving the remaining two empty beyond him.

He rested his hands on the stone, fingers laced, with one tapping, like a tiny echo of a heartbeat, on the opposite knuckle.

"Where to start?" He flexed his fingers and then laced them tight, pressing his palms together. Finally, he drew a long breath and said, "When I first met Sabrina, I was taken by her wit and charm. Beautiful, of course, but more than that, she seemed in such command of every aspect of her life. It was more than poise, she was charismatic, blindingly so. People were drawn to her, strangers noticed her, everyone wanted her on their committee or in their club. I was no exception and we clicked. Looking back, I might have been dazzled by the world she inhabited as much as in her. I was riveted by her and she seemed attracted to me. I can't begin to tell you what an ego booster that was for the young scrapper that I was at the time. I had no family, and she was the daughter of an industry giant. Kent Bale King, her dad, was a success by every measure. She's proud of him, even kept King as part of her legal married name.

Honestly, I had a time convincing her to use Roth at all. Anyway, her parents took me in as if I was a native son, encouraged us and, well... I'm getting ahead of myself."

He must have felt like a mustang adopted by thoroughbreds, Emily thought.

"Back to my wife. When we first met, she positively glowed with self-assurance. Sabrina, Bree, I call her, was and is extremely bright, but what I didn't see then were the clues that she was perhaps too confident and too sheltered. Those two factors helped disguise her emerging mental health problems. For example, her ability to hide her depression fooled me because she didn't display the textbook symptoms."

She found herself leaning forward, interested now that he finally was coming to the reason or reasons that Sabrina King Roth needed a nurse.

He lowered his head, staring sightless at some point between them as his shoulders rounded.

His despair rippled from him like a heavy stone dropped in still water. She stifled the urge to reach out and rub his back.

"My wife often thinks people are after her. This can cause her the impulse to flee. She thinks I am having an affair, and this means anger and tears. Accusations." He shook his head wearily as if the weight of his wife's condition was a heavy, impossible burden.

Pity, tight and pulsing, awakened inside her chest.

"I'm so sorry."

"The tragedy is, if someone believes a falsehood, no evidence or explanation will change their minds. I know this and yet, I keep hoping that with the right combination of medications I can, well, if not fix her, bring her peace."

Admirable, she thought, smiling.

He lifted his head and met her gaze. She hoped he saw compassion there.

"This must be very hard for you."

That seemed to take him by surprise. He hesitated and blinked like a raccoon caught by the unexpected illumination of a floodlight.

"Yes." His reply was automatic and then he said it again, slower, sadder, and with a slight nod. "Yes. Sabrina and I, well, it was so different early on. Everything delighted her. She was like a cut crystal, all sparkle and rainbows cast in every direction."

Emily's smile was genuine. She could picture them, young, rich, madly in love. He, the driven, up-and-comer, ready and eager to prove his worth and earn his place, and she the model of wealth and southern charm, comfortable with her influence and status. A power couple with nothing ahead but possibilities.

"And I was in such awe of her and her parents. They were well-off, of course, but they used those resources to do so much good and to enjoy their lives. I thought Bree and I would continue her parents' legacy." He glanced at the ceiling as if he expected it to come crashing down on them. "We were so happy. And I knew she was driven. But that seemed like a good thing. I didn't see that as the start of her current mental health problems. The anxiety and depression."

His pain dragged on his broad shoulders, making them sag.

Emily set her jaw and swallowed, struggling to find the right balance of empathy and professionalism. She reached toward him, then drew back, pressing her fist to her mouth for a moment as she gathered her thoughts.

"I'm sorry to hear that."

"My wife struggles with moods. She obsesses on the bad things. Reliving them. She experiences a type of PTSD. It's called co-morbid PTSD, if you care to do some research. And suffers related symptoms, including anxiety and panic disorders. Flashbacks too, unfortunately." He cast a deep sigh and then drew a breath to forge on. He seemed in a hurry to get it all out there. "Also, insomnia. And depressive disorder. She's full of fears. Luckily my profession is helping people with these sorts of issues. But helping her... It's been a struggle."

He ended by rubbing his temples with his fingertips.

"She's lucky to have you."

"I do my best. We both do. She's trying, too. Fighting it. Sometimes she wins. Other times..." He shook his head, lips pressed tight as his gaze slid away. "But I can't always be with her. That's where you come in."

"How present should I be?" It was important to see just how serious Mrs. Roth's problems were.

"She doesn't need constant supervision if that's what you mean. Give her, her privacy. Be available to see to her needs."

"Of course." But Emily knew this ambiguous directive, being there and present while giving his wife her privacy, would be a very difficult line to walk. The magnitude of this undertaking caused her skin to prickle a warning. Was she getting in over her head?

He pivoted toward her, resting an elbow on the table. His confident posture slipped, and seemed to hunch around some invisible weight. When he spoke, his tone was more intimate and quite sad.

"Early in our marriage, it became clear to me that a childhood trauma was leaking into her present. I thought we had it handled but she regresses at times. She had a little incident recently and I've been struggling to find the right medications to keep her happy but also coherent. Still a work in progress, unfortunately."

"I'm sorry to hear that." Emily stomped down her curiosity, which was quickly overtaking her compassion. What childhood trauma? She rolled her lips between her teeth and kept silent.

"The mood stabilizers seem to have resolved some of her issues."

"That's encouraging."

"Yes, but the struggle is to get all the various medications right. Each has side effects, of course. It's unavoidable."

Emily broke eye contact as her breathing accelerated. "I'll be on the lookout for anything out of the ordinary."

"I had to put her on anti-anxiety medication. But she has a lot of shame about the anxiety and her paranoia. Her family was very resistant to admitting any mental weaknesses. She was expected to just buck up. Not all of us can. So, if you would, please don't ask her questions about her past. The normal things you might ask, like where she was born, how she grew up, does she have any family. All of that brings her tremendous stress."

"I won't." She felt sorry for him, trying to help his wife and assuage her pain. He was a good husband, admirable. And as for Sabrina Roth, she had yet to make up her mind.

But now that she could not ask about her upbringing, she was more curious than ever.

Was Sabrina Roth so mentally impaired she couldn't be held responsible for her actions? It was another question Emily wished to answer. An important one. Just how competent was his wife?

He blew away a breath and stared at a spot above Emily's head, his eyes going out of focus. She felt sorry for Dr. Roth, burdened with a wife who faced such challenges and had the feeling that this litany of ailments was just the first brick in the wall.

She waited.

Finally, he spoke, but he wasn't looking at Emily.

"We have been focusing on keeping her out of the dark places. And away from reliving traumatic life events. I oversee her medications to deal with the treatable aspects of her condition."

"Treatable?"

"Not all mental disorders respond to intervention. We're working on the depression. Obsessive behaviors, too. Tapping, drumming. You'll see those, especially when she's agitated. And her drawings come to mind."

Her new charge seemed extremely troubled, and she tried to imagine the weight of responsibility that fell on him and how difficult Sabrina's reality must be for them both.

"She's an artist?"

"Once. Now she draws. Doodles to calm herself." His mouth went tight, and he was silent for a few moments. Then he met her gaze and continued. "And my Bree has faulty memories of things, memories of events that didn't happen, along with an unshakable belief that they happened or *are* happening. It's called paranoid organic delusional syndrome. That means she has these misconceptions in a *normal* state of consciousness."

The non-disclosure agreement now made a lot more sense.

Emily's brow furrowed as she tried to absorb all he had shared with her.

"So... her version of events can't be trusted?"

"She mixes in events that never happened or changes them to fit her version of reality. And no amount of evidence or reasoning can shake her conviction."

Her eyes rounded, not really understanding what that all meant.

He scrubbed his smooth cheeks with his knuckles and then let his hand drop.

"Confusing, I know."

She felt sorry for this man being saddled with such a dysfunctional wife.

"Bree feels guilt for things that never happened and is also terrified of the consequences."

"Consequences?"

"Yes, imagine you believed, were convinced, that you'd committed serious crimes and had never been caught. How paranoid would that make you?"

Emily thought about that. It wasn't a pleasant scenario.

"What kind of crimes?"

He shook his head. "It varies. She has built a series of complicated delusions, stemming back to her childhood. The point is, she thinks '*they*' are coming after her."

"Who is?"

"That's unclear. But she is terrified that these 'bad people' are out there watching. FBI, sometimes. Other times the police. She hyperventilates if we just pass a cop car. For a time, she was afraid her parents wanted to harm her."

Emily had already known Sabrina's father had been very successful. Lots of articles on him online. Business and mergers and charity events, endowments too. Then the obituaries four years ago for Kent Bale King, heart failure, and, soon after, his wife, Michelle Horton King, "a short illness."

"The point is, my wife is certain some shadowy individuals are following her and just waiting to hurt her for what she believes she's done. Like all delusions, it's very complex, and no matter what logic you present, she explains it away."

"I'm so sorry." This poor man, having to deal with a wife who was so paranoid and broken.

"Yes. It's difficult." He scrubbed his mouth with his palm. "Perhaps obviously, she has no close friends but many, many acquaintances. Her Wednesday golf league, for example. She's driven most past attachments away. Her parents are gone, which is a mixed blessing. No further harm but no resolutions, either."

Emily knew that feeling well.

"She believes strangers are working for the authorities she thinks are pursuing her. I've tried to introduce her to colleagues but invariably she thinks they are watching her. Can you imagine? Always believing you're being followed by these unknown entities."

"Won't she think I'm one of them?"

"I hope not. I believe, between the two of us, we can get her to accept you."

"What do I do if she thinks someone is following us?"

"Just tell her she's safe and get her home, if possible."

Emily pictured all sorts of frightening public breakdowns. Driving Mrs. Roth might be a terror for them both.

Confidence shaken, she tried to appear capable.

"All right. I can do that."

Now Emily wondered what would happen if Mrs. Roth didn't accept her. If Mrs. Roth pegged her as one of the "bad people," she'd be lucky to last the week.

And if Mrs. Roth fired her? She'd be back to job hunting and eating off the dollar menu.

She gulped back the cherrystone of worry rising in her throat.

"Dr. Roth, is she, you know, mentally competent?"

"Well, that's difficult. In many respects, yes. But her delusions make it a challenge for her. Knowing what and whom to believe."

"What if your wife... I mean, what if she doesn't like me?"

"We'll face that challenge if it arises. In the meantime, I need you to give this your all."

"I will." And he need not worry on that one. She would cling to this job like a baby opossum to its mama's back.

"The less medication she takes the worse the paranoia becomes, but even with everything at optimal levels, they never go away. And she may harm herself or others while reacting to the delusions. You understand? We need to keep her calm to prevent that and under no circumstance should she be allowed to drive. This is a major point."

"I understand. No driving."

Emily wondered how Mrs. Roth would feel about being toted about like a child. Or would she view the experience as more suggestive of a celebrity or VIP zipping past paparazzi en route to some gala opening?

"What if she insists?" asked Emily.

"She won't insist. But she may try to get hold of the keys."

Emily's brows lifted at this news. Did he mean Mrs. Roth might steal the keys to a vehicle?

"I keep the fobs locked up, to be on the safe side. You should, too, because Sabrina sometimes forgets she can't drive. She's had a driver for a while. She's adjusted, so you don't need to worry about that."

Something wasn't right. Either she could handle her own affairs, or she couldn't. Dr. Roth seemed to want it both ways.

Emily, always curious, loved puzzles and this was a doozey.

She did have second thoughts. She wanted this job but was uncertain that it would give her what she needed. Her doubts must have shown on her face.

"You'll do fine," he assured. "It's less work than you think. Just be sure she isn't alone out in public. Shadow her. And when she tells you about some grizzly event, remember to assume it didn't happen."

"My goodness."

Shadowing her sounded like following her. Had her last nurse done that? If so, no wonder Sabrina thought she was being followed.

And if his wife had so many problems, why hire a recent graduate with little to no experience? It wasn't to save money. The posted hourly wage proved that.

So, what was the real reason?

"What about here at her home? Can she be alone?" Emily glanced about the empty kitchen, worried where Sabrina Roth might be and what she might be doing.

"As I said, give her, her privacy. She's never had an episode in our home. She can be alone in the bathroom, bedroom, her studio, and the pool area. But not on the lake. Rule of thumb, if she is likely to meet strangers, you need to be there."

"I see." She didn't. What would happen if she met a stranger? "What might I expect if she has an episode?"

"Weeping, angry outbursts, hostility toward them."

"She might attack them?"

"It's possible." He tried and failed for a reassuring smile. "That's why you do the errands, or we have things delivered and you accompany her to appointments for hair, nails, massage, doctor, and so on."

"Golf?"

"She knows those women. Has for years. They are very helpful and accommodating. They're used to her claims that the groundskeeper is watching her." He chuckled. But it wasn't funny.

"What if she leaves while I'm running an errand?"

"I have the keys in a lockbox, so that's not a problem."

"Where's the lockbox?"

"Garage. I'll give you the combination."

Dr. Roth drummed his fingers on the counter as he studied her. Then he checked the NDA. Finally, he said, "Before we go out there, I need to tell you about something disturbing."

FIVE

Dr. Roth rested his palm flat on the NDA as he spoke to Emily.

"Several years ago, my wife's driver was in an auto accident. Bree was a passenger when her assistant struck a pedestrian. Since that time, she got the incident twisted in her mind. She thinks she was driving. That she caused the crash. Her delusional thinking, flashbacks, and her prescription medication, well, any one would be reason enough not to allow her behind the wheel."

"I see." That did make sense. "Do you mean the traffic fatality involving her driver?"

His brows lifted and he paused, studying her.

"You read about that?"

Emily shrugged. "Preparing for this interview."

Ten years back according to the article. Emily waited for more information.

He held her in a critical gaze a moment longer, then looked away. "I see. Well, it's public record, isn't it? I'm sure it pops right up on any search engine. What was your source? Newspaper article?"

Emily nodded. That, among other things.

He waved a dismissive hand.

"Was your wife injured?"

He gave a nod, along with another exhalation of breath, as if he found the subject trying. "Broken wrist. Broken nose. And as you mentioned, the pedestrian was DOA."

"And your wife feels responsible? She thinks she..." Her throat closed for a moment and her words trailed off.

"She believes it. Convinced of it. She knows I don't, that no one else does. Mostly she tries to avoid bringing it up. But the depression, the emotional issues, make it very clear that she still is convinced she caused the accident."

"But she was a passenger."

"She was. And, as you might have read, the pedestrian was a young mother."

Emily pressed a hand to her chest, feeling her heart thrumming faster than normal. "How tragic."

"Indeed."

He lifted his gaze to the tray ceiling above the breakfast bar. "So, you know this happened years ago."

"Ten."

He smoothed his hand over his silky necktie, pausing with his hand flat on his stomach. "At first, Sabrina was very depressed about the entire thing."

"Didn't I read that the driver later claimed your wife caused the crash?"

He flicked his attention to her, displeasure clear from the way he glared from beneath his lowered brow. He lifted his hand to the table and locked it under his opposite one. "That's true. She did claim that later on. But who can believe a suspect who changes their story?"

"I suppose."

"Predictable attempt to avoid a charge of vehicular homicide."

Vehicular homicide. Emily's face felt hot and her pulse thrummed through her veins.

Emily kept her opinions on injustices in the legal system to herself. No reason to contradict her would-be boss because nothing good ever came from that.

Despite the challenges, and perhaps because of them, she still wanted this job.

"The accident exacerbated her existing difficulties originating from some additional tragedies."

She hoped he'd elaborate but he did not. Additional tragedies? What else had happened? He'd mentioned childhood trauma. Was this what he referred to?

He hurried on, as if anxious to get it all out there. "So nothing I or anyone says will dissuade her. And no treatment we've tried has done anything to change her beliefs. The important thing for you is to listen but then repeat the facts. She didn't do this. She's not cursed or culpable and no one is after her."

"I can do that."

But could she?

Sabrina Roth's troubles were way more serious than she'd anticipated. Doubts descended like storm clouds bringing the flashing lightning of insecurity. Handling this position would be the biggest challenge yet.

"Good. Very good." He rubbed his palms together as if washing in air. "Just be calm. Reassure her that she's safe."

"I'll do my best."

He retrieved another sheet of paper from beneath the NDA and pushed it before her.

"This is her medication list. She knows what to take but loses track of the time. Her watch should remind her. Times are here. Seven in the morning, noon, and seven at night. Be certain she takes them when scheduled. All down here on this. I've labeled the pill bottles with letters, so it will be easier. See?" He opened an upper cabinet and withdrew a large rectangular plastic container. Inside were so many pill bottles that her eyes bugged.

How would anyone keep track of all that?

This was why he needed a licensed practical nurse. As an LPN, she was qualified to dispense medications.

"Just to be clear, you oversee her medication, but she generally is self-sufficient enough to handle taking her pills when it's time. I've set her smartwatch."

He lifted one of the larger bottles.

"This one is a benzodiazepine, for anxiety, a new one, for now. We've made some recent changes after... a recent relapse. You understand? But what's important for you is that it has a capital letter A on it. So, according to the list..." He pointed. "She takes it twice a day, morning and evening, and so you don't need to give her one of these unless I'm delayed."

"Does that happen often?"

"More than I'd like. I'm on call for psych emergencies at two hospitals, here in Winter Haven and also at General, so..."

She hadn't realized he had privileges in two hospitals. The chance he'd be called away would be greater.

"Is there anything else that might cause her anxiety?" Emily tried not to let her own anxiety bubble to the surface.

He gave a mirthless laugh.

"That's a long list. She doesn't like loud noises. She is afraid of bugs, needles, blood, lightning, planes, crowded places. That's why we have most everything delivered. She thinks all shellfish are either laced with bacteria or just disgusting. Calls them sea-bugs." He laughed. "Dogs frighten her. All sizes, all breeds, well, all animals, really. Flying, strangers, law enforcement, doctors, germs, and the sound of breaking glass. Sometimes she worries people are poisoning her food. And she generally leaves the house when Rosalind vacuums. The loud noise again."

"That is a long list."

"Oh, here's a big one... germs. So, she might ask you to wash your hands before you prepare any food for her or before you touch anything she needs to touch or before you handle any of her medication. But I've already told you about the gloves."

"Yes."

"It's possible she won't eat what you prepare. It's that suspicion of being poisoned again. The germaphobia or both."

"That could be a problem."

"If it is, we'll have meals delivered. She might want to watch you reheat things, be sure you don't add anything. So do not add salt or mustard. Nothing. You understand?"

Now Emily was getting anxious. Of course this job and the hourly wage were too good to be true. There had to be a catch.

The gentle nervous flutter of butterflies in her stomach changed to the frantic flapping of a trapped bat.

"Just oversee the list of her noon medications. I'll go over it with you again before you start. And if she won't eat, give her something sealed, like a yogurt or protein shake."

"Um..." She couldn't verbalize her apprehensions, but they were there like the smoke that preceded a fire.

"You'll just be sure she takes the right ones and at the right time. All right? Supervise is all."

She considered abandoning her plan and preparing to cut and run. But she couldn't. Responsibilities pressed down on her.

Emily pictured having to tell Jennell she didn't have her half of the rent. It wasn't about what she wanted to do or might be able to do. She needed to do this for so many reasons.

"Supervise. Got it."

As if sensing her rising apprehension, he reached across the table but stopped short of touching her. Instead, he gave her an encouraging smile. His whiskey-colored eyes held a touch of desperation, and she felt the strong compulsion to help this man all she could.

"Emily, will you look after her while I'm away? Can you do that?" He held her gaze and she pressed down her anxieties.

"Of course."

His smile widened and he sat back in his seat.

"That's great." He put the medication container back in the cabinet. "Just spend some time reviewing this. Okay?"

She nodded.

Emily accepted the list and scanned, seeing antidepressants, sleeping aids, and some she didn't recognize.

"You can hold on to that copy but keep it secure. Familiarize yourself with the color and shape of the medications. It's all on there."

"Okay." This would be like cramming for a test.

"Run the dishwasher every afternoon before you leave. We generally just pile the dinner dishes in the sink, so you can add them in the morning. The kitchen needs a light clean every morning."

He continued with instructions, cleaning products, how things were done. Finally, he ran himself out.

"Quick orientation tour and a few additional tasks. Right?"

He stood, collected the folder, and she followed as he motioned to a closed door.

"You've been through the laundry, pantry. You know how to run this sort of machine?"

"I can Google the manual."

"Great."

"That's the garage and the way you'll come in from now on."

The help did not use the front door. Her big sister had told her that when she dragged herself home from work, as usual. Emily, hungry and cranky, having again walked home and let herself into the apartment to spend the evening alone, didn't appreciate the effort it took for her sister to make her a late supper and check her homework. They'd watch TV before bed. Emily loved horror movies and had probably seen every one out there. Meanwhile, her sister watched them through her hands clamped over her eyes. She was usually asleep before her mother came home from the hotel. In the mornings, her mother was already gone. It was always her sister who woke her, fed her breakfast, packed her lunch, and dropped her at the AM keepers program with the other kids whose parents needed to be at work well before school began.

Her sister told her to stay in school. Make something of herself. But then her sister had done that terrible, irreversible thing and was gone. Emily tried to stay in school. But when her mother got sick, it was impossible. Emily had dropped out of high school to care for her mom, then studied for and passed her GED. Four months after her mom's passing, she'd enrolled in the nursing program. Would her nursing license be enough to lift her from poverty? She was proud to be the first in her family to graduate from college, but really, she was now the only member of her family and there had been no one there to congratulate her after the ceremony or pose for photos with her. Just her and a piece of paper in a padded, ornate folder.

Still, she hoped her mother and sister would be proud. She'd done it all for them.

Dr. Roth paused in the foyer and Emily stopped as well.

"I'll leave the side door to the garage open. This one stays bolted until we expect you. So, if you arrive early, you might find it locked. Don't worry. You can't trip the alarm when the door is closed."

"Alarm?"

"Yeah." He pointed to a small sensor fixed to the door above eye level. "The dead bolt will keep you from tripping it. When I'm up, I'll turn off the system and unlock that."

"What about the gate at the end of the drive?"

"I'll give you the code."

She opened her notebook and lifted her pen.

He chuckled and waved a hand. "You don't need to write it down. It's the year minus ten. I change it on New Year's Day."

"So, 2013?"

"Exactly. The lockbox for the key fob, in the garage... did you see it?"

"No."

"I'll point it out. It's near the side door. The one you came in. That one is secured by a padlock. Code is the year plus twenty. 2043. Just rotate the numbers and spin them when you lock it."

She nodded, feeling that uncomfortable crawling sensation on her skin. Spinning numbers and locking things was what you did when you needed to keep someone out, like a teenager after liquor or an addict after drugs. The prickling unease warned her that Dr. Roth's control over his wife might be excessive, even if it was intended for her own good.

He motioned to the French doors in the kitchen. "That leads to the patio and an outdoor firepit, just check in the morning that we didn't leave any bottles or glasses out there. We're going this way." He motioned to the archway leading out of the kitchen.

They crossed through the dining room holding the enormous floral arrangement and the artificial ficus in the corner. The wall art was pastel, abstract, and original. The draperies were a soft gray, simple, and there were Bahama shutters on the windows for good measure. No sense in letting the sun fade your furnishings after all.

The chandelier was modern and tasteful, suspended perfectly over the center of the table.

"Flowers are delivered weekly. Just arrange them in any of the vases in the pantry. One bouquet here." He pointed to the center of the dining table. "One in the kitchen, one on her nightstand. One in her studio."

"I've never arranged flowers."

"Arrange is the wrong word. They come wrapped in four bundles. Just plunk them in water and place them. Easy."

He led her into the cool living room where the views of the outer greenery and blue waters of the lake seemed to flow into the indoor space with its green potted ferns, blue accent pillows, and beige floor tile. The custom cabinets were glossy white and held a massive television, some artfully arranged books, and a few interesting sculptural pieces. Another tray ceiling presented an abundance of glossy molding, a massive chandelier, puck lights, two huge fans, and accent lights turned this way and that.

"Just tidying in here." He lifted the afghan that lay on the floor and returned it to the couch. "As I said, powder room is off the foyer, and my office is beyond the entry." He pointed. "I'll just put this away. Excuse me a moment."

She waited as he disappeared, glancing up at the chandelier suspended on four cables above her head. She imagined that when the power was flicked on, it might rival the star on the top of the Christmas tree in Rockefeller Center.

Dr. Roth reappeared, his smile still tight as he pointed toward a doorway on the right. "And that direction leads to the master suite. Oh, I'm not supposed to call it that now. Had you heard? It's now the primary bedroom or main bedroom."

"Really?" Of course she knew, but she'd never lived in a house with a main bedroom, only a shitty bungalow with stained beige carpets and avocado-green bathroom tiles held to the walls of the shower with globs of clear caulk and gray duct tape.

She followed him to the couple's bedroom.

"Flowers on her nightstand, pick up any clothing you find. Hamper or hang back up in her closet. When it's full, do a laundry load, but watch her stuff. Some is *dry clean only*, so read every tag."

"I can do that." She was beginning to think she needed to write a list to remember all this.

"She often leaves the slider to the pool unlocked. Leave it so she can come in here from the lanai."

"Of course." Emily gazed at the three-panel sliding doors that gave views of the furniture arranged on the lanai, the pool cage, and the firepit beyond. She stepped forward and glimpsed the lake, sparkling blue in the sun.

What would it be like to wake up to this view every morning?

Her current apartment had two small bedrooms, each with an undersized closet and window. Her window had bars on it because it was at ground level and facing the alley. Jennell's, also barred, faced a wire fence that separated their apartment complex from the one behind it.

"And that way?" he asked, testing her.

"Family room?"

"Right. Bree loves to watch her British comedies in there."

Emily stifled a groan. She hated British comedies, the humor of awkwardness and embarrassment. It was more uncomfortable than funny. Meanwhile, Emily devoured every legal thriller, police drama, and true crime series currently streaming.

Dr. Roth continued the tour, his gait relaxed and his voice calm.

"We have two guest bedrooms. They share a full bath with a Jack-and-Jill bathroom between, and one additional bedroom beyond with a private bath that could function as a mother-in-law..." His words tapered off.

Emily wondered if it was because neither had a mother that would need care in elder years. The sorrow at her own losses pressed on her shoulders with a heavy hand.

"That one was Taylor's when she was a kid. You shouldn't have much to do in these rooms but have a look each day. Check the pool bathroom for wet towels and swimsuits. Our bonus room is down there past the family room. Bree uses that one as her studio. So, flowers in that room, as I said. You'll spot them. She likes a particular vase, so keep using it for that room."

Dr. Roth rubbed his hands together as if scrubbing up for surgery. "Shall we go meet Bree?"

SIX

"Ready?" Dr. Roth asked, preparing to make the introductions.

"I'm looking forward to it." She thought she almost sounded convincing.

Despite her own doubts and insecurities, Emily needed to make this work.

He smiled, his expression indulgent, as if he knew what was coming and she had no idea. It gave her the kick in the pants she needed. Emily lowered her chin and prepared to do battle. Over the last two years she'd handled her course load, homework, and hands-on training, plus hundreds of practicum hours with hellacious nursing supervisors, and patient loads that would have sent a less tenacious person running. But she was on a mission and, hell or high water, she would make this work.

Then he opened the slider and stepped out carrying along a breeze of cool air that dissipated as he closed the door.

Before them was yet another table. This one with six chairs.

Ahead, the kidney-shaped pool glistened, inviting and out of reach to "the help" on this and every other day. The gurgle from the waterfall added to the illusionary tranquility.

Under the roof in the lanai a grouping of upscale teak patio furniture clustered about a large coffee table holding a lantern. Above them two circular fans stirred the muggy air. To her left an empty outdoor kitchen seemed unused, in fact the grill still had the protective plastic covering the lid. She spotted two under-counter refrigerators, a sink, and custom cabinets. Across from the sink, grill, and stovetop, a stone counter and four stools created the perfect spot for entertaining.

But based on what she now knew, the Roths did not entertain. She cast a sideward glance at the doctor, certain that his life was not turning out the way he'd imagined when they purchased this house.

It was heartbreaking that Dr. Roth couldn't invite colleagues over for barbeques or to watch the games. And he'd said that Mrs. Roth had no real friends, so the ladies didn't sip white wine while they gossiped out here beside the pool. This house was empty and hollow as a scooped-out avocado.

Between the kitchen and seating area sat a Peloton bike. Did he find it easier to work out here because he did not like to leave his wife alone?

Outside the lanai sat a large green ceramic smoker, also seemingly brand new. She tested her theory.

"Do you do a lot of entertaining?" she asked.

"Not anymore. Crowds," he said by way of an explanation.

At her count, the Roths had outdoor seating for eight and indoor seating for ten, not including the family room she had yet to see. And they used only two in the kitchen. That seemed so sad, and Emily, whose own dining table seated two, felt sorry for Dr. Roth all over again. Despite the lingering air of entitlement, he seemed a nice, genuine sort and, clearly, he loved his wife.

Many men would have cut and run years ago. Like her father. Emily absorbed the gut punch at bringing him to mind.

Was it her? For years she'd believed that, despite her mother insisting his leaving had nothing to do with her. But just like

Mrs. Roth, Emily believed herself to blame because a man doesn't leave his pregnant girlfriend to call a do-over with someone else if something isn't wrong.

Outside the pool cage, beyond the sloping hill and perfectly manicured lawn, the lake glistened in the bright sunlight, sparkling like sequins on a couture gown, shimmering across the water.

Tucked off to the left, within easy access, but positioned not to obstruct the view from the pool deck, a boat dock stretched out from the shore. Two boat lifts sat beneath the boathouse. One of them held a large motorboat.

This place resembled a luxury resort more than a private home.

"That's the boathouse. There's a studio apartment above. Taylor used to love it out there. Had friends over constantly. In and out of the boats and we had a Jet Ski back then."

She glanced in the direction of his gaze at the small structure above the side-by-side boat lifts. Empty, now that their daughter and her teenage friends were grown and gone.

Had her daughter loved it out there or used it to escape the stress of a mother with mental illness?

What had growing up in this house, with this woman as her mother, been like?

Somehow a clubhouse for your friends seemed less important than an adult who was present and there for you, as Emily's sister had been for so much of her childhood.

She was certain most people would think Taylor Lee Roth was lucky and blessed, but Emily knew that she had been as well.

On the shore, four brightly colored kayaks sat upended on racks, paddles leaned against the watercrafts and floatation vests hung from the end posts, because obviously none of these neighbors were going to steal your stuff.

The Roth family had all the toys. How often did they use them? As often as they used the outdoor kitchen?

Emily glanced about, thinking the only thing that looked well used was the exercise bike.

He noticed the direction of her attention.

"Do you ride?" he asked.

"Not anymore." Riding was harder without a front tire. She grimaced. The way her car was acting, she might need a second set of wheels and made a mental note to prioritize getting her bike fixed.

Jennell had offered her bike. If she didn't fix her car or replace the bike tire, Emily might take her up on that. She figured her apartment and the Roths' home were separated by hundreds of thousands of dollars and about four miles. She could walk that, in a pinch.

What would the lady at the gate think of her if she showed up at her guardhouse window without her car?

"Too bad," said Dr. Roth. "Biking is a great way to stay in shape. Though I prefer running."

"You mentioned that at the hospital. Marathons. Right?"

"I used to. Nearly impossible, at the moment. The training takes a huge time commitment and I'm needed here." His smile turned brittle, but held as his gaze swept to the lake and then the boat that she suspected he rarely used.

She reflected on all the many pursuits he must have shelved to be here for his ailing wife. This kind of silent heroism lifted him up again in her estimation. But did he really know what was wrong with his wife? He was an expert after all. If he couldn't figure it out, how would she have any hope to do so?

"I'm sure it's difficult to make time."

"True. But I do use the stationary bike. And the racing bike in the garage. Sometimes. But with you here, maybe again in the future." A half smile quirked his lips, but his eyes were vacant and his gaze distant.

Another point in his column. He had given up something he loved to be there for his wife. Admirable, she thought.

"Qualified for the New York Marathon again," he said.

"Oh gosh! That's a big deal. Wonderful. Congratulations."

He stood a little taller. He had that wiry runner's body, all efficient muscle, low body fat, and arrogant disdain for the rest of the non-running world.

"Thanks."

They shared a smile. Maybe his was genuine. Hers was not. Recreational exercise was for rich people. For them it was tennis, golf, rowing, and the like.

Of course Dr. Roth wouldn't describe himself as rich. Instead, he'd say they were secure, well-off, or comfortable.

When Emily was old enough, her sister would bring her along on house cleaning jobs. The work was physical, mopping floors, cleaning bathrooms, and then she'd do her homework in the car as they drove from one place to the next. Later, after her sister was gone, and her mom got sick, Emily took anything with flexible hours. But no longer. Now that she had her nursing license, she needed to get her feet back underneath her, pay some bills, fix her car, and buy that headstone. But first, she'd be picking up wet towels, doing laundry, and driving Sabrina Roth to her spa treatments.

Emily balled her hands to fists and tried and failed to slow her rapid breathing. She was so nervous about meeting Sabrina Roth.

Dr. Roth's smile fell away as he glanced about for his absent wife.

He raised his voice. "Bree?"

Emily turned in the direction he had but saw no wife.

What she did see was the pool. The huge, magnificent kidney-shaped pool that included both a hot tub and waterfall. The crystal blue water, of the pool she would never swim in, sparkled, a lovely reminder of the line between the owners and the help.

For just a minute she had the silly thought that *he* was the one with organic delusions, like he was married and had a wife, when Bree was actually a German shepherd.

"Bree?" he called again, this time with a slight edge of panic in his voice.

Where was she?

SEVEN

"Lately, mornings are hard for her," said Dr. Roth, explaining away his wife's absence. "She isn't sleeping well and the medicine she's taking to handle that makes her a little spacy. I'll go over the side effects with you later. But one of them blurs her vision."

"Is it safe for her to be walking around out here alone?"

There were undoubtedly water moccasins, coral snakes, and possibly a large gator or two in that lake.

"The medications don't make her incoherent. She knows what's what. And she loves it out here. Plus, exercise and sunshine are good for her."

Meanwhile, he craned his neck, restlessly checking for some sign of his wife. His body language told her instantly he was worried, despite his reassurances. The grim slashing line of his mouth confirmed it.

His voice now crackled with concern. "She was sleeping when you arrived."

He'd just told her she could be left alone at home but not with strangers.

Emily was a stranger. Her face began to tingle as she prepared to meet Sabrina Roth.

"You may notice a facial tic. Squeezing her eye shut or a half smile. That's the medicine. She's not smiling." His gaze wandered off again with his thoughts. He looked troubled, as if his wife smiling was a bad thing.

Another silly notion. The only medications she knew that gave facial tics were for Parkinson's or antipsychotics.

Was Mrs. Roth psychotic?

"Which medication is causing the tic?"

"Unsure. Antidepressants are my best guess."

Guess? She didn't like the sound of that, although Emily conceded that getting so many medications in the correct balance was as much art as science.

Dr. Roth motioned to the waterfall. "There's an exit to the yard and lake back there. We store some floats and things on the lower level so they don't blow into the lake. She might have gone out that way."

He raised his voice. "Bree, honey?" He shoved his hands in his pockets and turned to Emily. "Did you bring your car keys inside with you?"

Odd question, she thought. "Yes. They're right here." She patted her front right pocket.

"Good. That's good." He called again. "Sabrina?"

"Over here." The sound was low and melodic, like a trained voice actress.

Emily followed the direction of the sound, straining her neck to catch a glimpse of the wife that needed twenty-four-hour supervision.

Sabrina Roth emerged from behind the waterfall, rising on stairs that Emily had not noticed.

He blew out a breath. His jovial expression returned as he bounced on his toes.

Sabrina Roth held one hand on the crown of the floppy straw hat as she ascended. A black gauzy beach cover up fluttered about the gold one-piece bathing suit that hugged her curves. She had a stunning figure, petite, with long tan legs darting out of the coverlet as she descended from the top of the waterfall to ground level, like Venus emerging from her scallop shell.

This woman would be a shoo-in for the contributor pages for any or all of the area's nonprofits. *Mrs. Sabrina Roth at the opera gala. Dr. and Mrs. Roth at the botanical garden's masquerade ball, ribbon cutting, groundbreaking, dedication.*

Clearly Sabrina Roth had not felt the compulsion to dress for the interview, though Emily judged Mrs. Roth's swim attire to have cost more than anything in Emily's shoebox of a closet. Once on level ground, the woman walked with the swaying confident grace of a fashion model on a Paris runway. Emily admitted to herself that, if she had the funds, she'd buy whatever Mrs. Roth was selling.

The ticking resentment at witnessing all this couple had, and owned and enjoyed, made Emily grind her teeth together until her molars squeaked. Why hadn't she even given a thought to the possibility that being surrounded by so much casual wealth would be a struggle for her?

Dr. Roth moved to intercept.

"Bree, honey, I want you to meet someone."

Emily heard no resentment in his tone as he spoke to his wife, only genuine warmth and tenderness. Now, with Sabrina at his side, he hid all traces of sorrow.

Dr. Roth extended a hand toward Emily as he spoke. "Darling, this is the new nurse."

Sabrina released her hat and turned her attention from her husband to Emily, slipping her large, designer sunglasses to the end of her pert nose revealing silvery gray eyes. The lady of the manor inspecting the help.

"Is it that time already?"

Emily tried to judge her potential patient's condition, but with the pleasant smile and huge sunglasses, she could see little. She did note that she took her husband's offered elbow and leaned against him. Both her coordinated stride and appropriate question pointed to a woman who seemed lucid, despite all the medications.

"Yes, nearly eleven."

"Good heavens." She squinted back in the direction of the house. "I can't see a thing."

"Come say hello." He took hold of her hand, now draped on his elbow and escorted her forward.

Emily squared her shoulders as Mrs. Roth gazed up at her. The general inspecting her troops.

"A giant. I can see that much." The corner of her mouth jerked in a quirking smile that lasted less than a second.

Had she not been warned, Emily would have taken the expression as disapproval.

"Why don't we sit. Shall we?" Dr. Roth motioned to the outdoor table. Upon the surface was a collection of candles and a stack of upscale magazines on fashion, beauty, and home decor, fanned out as if for a real estate showing.

Emily compared the picture of effortless style and wealth to the cinderblock bungalow where she'd grown up, sharing a bedroom with her older sister, while their mother worked eighteen-hour shifts. Often a nightmare sent Emily scurrying across the room she shared with her sister. The covers would flip back, Emily would slip between them and tuck in close to her sister's warm body where she was safe from all monsters, real and imagined.

Mrs. Roth removed her hat, tossed it toward a lounge chair, and missed. Picking it up would soon be Emily's job. *If* she were lucky.

Her husband drew out her seat and Mrs. Roth perched. Her sable-brown hair was either wet or slicked back with gel. Her makeup was flawless, and Emily had to admire both her full red lips and the precision of its application. Her eyes were again covered with dark glasses, but her tanned skin, golden reflecting powder, perfect nose, and arching brows were all visible.

How was she not sweating? Despite the fan spinning tirelessly above them, Emily felt the back of her head growing damp and her bra sticking to her skin.

The doctor sat next to his wife, on the opposite side of the teak table. Both stared up at her as if expecting a puppet show. Mrs. Roth began drumming her index and middle finger on the tabletop.

Emily realized she was still standing.

Should she sit or wait for an invitation to do so? Her sister would know what to do. She was used to working for such people. Emily felt lost, grasping her notebook before her so tightly that her knuckles cracked.

"Please have a seat," said Sabrina, waving a manicured hand briefly over the table.

Like a trained schnauzer, she sat.

Mrs. Roth lowered her glasses again, taking a good long look at her.

"Is that a natural color?" Sabrina asked, her attention fixed on Emily's coppery red hair, twisted into a tight, utilitarian knot off her face. Despite best efforts, some of her shorter bangs had escaped to adhere to her sweating forehead and temples.

"Yes, ma'am."

"And green eyes and apple cheeks. Charming." She turned to her husband. "Isn't she pretty, Henry?"

"I hadn't noticed."

She made a sound of mirth in her throat and then leaned conspiratorially toward Emily.

"Because men so rarely note a pretty face or slender figure."

Anxiety made Emily's smile slip. She'd had female bosses before but had yet to deal with a husband-wife dynamic.

This was about to go sideways.

"How did you find her?"

Sabrina Roth stared at Emily as Henry answered.

"She's this year's valedictorian, top of her class, and she's passed her exams."

"Is that right?" Her smile never faltered as her cat eyes flicked from Henry back to Emily. "Do you have a resume or something?"

Emily handed it over. Sabrina Roth accepted it and then placed it on the table, without glancing down.

"But such fair skin. Do you burn?"

"Constantly." Emily offered a smile that was not returned. "I wear plenty of sunscreen, so working outside isn't a problem."

Sabrina nodded, seeming to approve of this answer.

"Skincare is very important."

Her face ticked again, lifting at the corner for just an instant.

"My Henry burns as well. It's a pity. I'm brown as a nut. Just think women look better, healthier, you know, with a tan."

Medical studies to the contrary, Emily thought, and she nodded her apparent agreement.

"So," Sabrina glanced at the resume. "You're Emily Lancing." There was that jerking half smile again. It was disturbing, as if some unseen force was tugging the corner of her mouth with an invisible fishhook.

Dr. Roth said, "That's right." At the same time, Emily said, "Yes, ma'am."

She sat awkward and uncomfortable, sweating through her blouse.

"May I call you Emily? Fine," Sabrina said, not waiting for an answer. "And you can call me Mrs. Roth, dear."

So far, this woman seemed right on track for what Emily expected, except for the facial tic. But her air of superiority, haughty expression, and condescension all checked out.

Emily let her gaze drop and landed on Sabrina's upward thrusting breasts. There was a certain disturbing, gravity-defying uniformity to them. If those breasts were real, she'd eat the pencil holding up her bun.

"Are you from..." She waved a hand. "Here abouts?"

"Yes, ma'am, er, Mrs. Roth. I grew up in Lakeland, but I recently moved to Winter Haven."

"Better location. But I detect an accent. Where are you from originally?"

If she had an accent, it was a gift from her Irish mother. But Emily thought it more cadence than accent, a certain way of skipping your words along like a song.

"I was born here. Plant City. Grew up in Lakeland with my mother and sister."

"Lovely. And a Floridian," said Mrs. Roth. "Goodness, we're as rare as hen's teeth, aren't we?"

"With all the new residents from the northern states, I guess you're right."

Mrs. Roth continued to stare at her husband. "She's got the first rule already, always agreeing with me."

Her chuckle made Emily's insides tug in a way that she didn't understand.

"Of course I was born here. But Henry's mother, a single mother, came from Chicago."

"Cincinnati," he corrected.

"Oh, that's right. My memory."

Sabrina Roth tilted her head and smiled up at her husband, who covered her drumming hand with his.

"You're adorable," Dr. Roth said. "Don't make yourself out to be—"

"Crazy?"

His smile grew brittle. "I was going to say forgetful."

The mouth tic fired in a double and Emily tried not to stare.

"How old are you?"

"Twenty-three."

"Education?"

"I'm a licensed practical nurse with an associate's degree in nursing."

"Emily told me she'd like to someday become a nurse practitioner," said Dr. Roth, injecting himself into their conversation again and repeating a detail from their initial meeting.

Sabrina laughed. "If you try that with an associate's degree, you'll get arrested."

Emily did not appreciate being mocked, but you'd never know from her affable smile.

"Good one," she said.

"College is expensive. And the debt," said Mrs. Roth. "You'll be forty, a spinster, and still living in a studio apartment to pay down your student loans. Better just work hard and you'll do fine."

And what would this woman, dressed in a bathing suit in the middle of a weekday morning, know about working hard?

Sabrina King Roth came from money and Emily would bet a month's rent that neither Roth had ever scrubbed a toilet. These two had the kind of wealth that corrupted the worldview and gave people a sense of superiority over their fellow humans. The kind that thought nothing of offering career advice to an interview candidate trying to land a job.

Emily hid her disdain beneath a benign look of blank stupidity. This one she had learned from her mother.

Never let them see you thinking. It makes them nervous.

Sabrina raised her chin, the lady of the manor regarding her chattel.

"So Winter Haven? Where abouts?"

Emily told her and Sabrina grimaced. She didn't blame her. Even great places to live bumped up against the bad ones.

"Are you married?"

"Darling, you're not allowed to ask that," said Dr. Roth.

"Why not?"

"It's against the law," he said.

"Fiddlesticks."

"I'm not married, ma'am," Emily said.

"Children?"

Dr. Roth's expression turned grim. "Darling—"

"Just me," Emily answered.

Dr. Roth blew out his frustration in a long, suffering breath.

"Ah, that's lovely. Freedom to come and go as you please."

Or free to be on call twenty-four seven and come running whenever they demanded. Without children, Emily would never be a no-show because her toddler had a fever. And a bonus, she lived only a few miles from their elegant double doors.

"And nothing to tie you down."

Except debt, earning a living, and her agreement with her roommate. Other than that, she was free as a bird, which was lucky because her car might not even make it home. Maybe she could just spread her wings and fly. Most days she felt more roadrunner than eagle.

"We're tied by Henry's practice and the dreadful on-call hours. And our daughter. She's grown, of course, and married to a doctor."

"Resident," corrected her husband.

She cast him a smile and nod before continuing. "Yes, working as a resident. We just bought them a house."

"And they're expecting," added Dr. Roth.

This time Emily was unsure if the facial spasm was the tic or a grimace. Sabrina clamped a hand over her forehead as if dreading the impending arrival of a grandchild.

"Twins," said Dr. Roth, positively beaming. There was no need to guess how he felt about becoming a grandfather.

"Congratulations on your first grandchild. Or grandchildren," she said, confused about Mrs. Roth's facial expressions that were so disjointed and out of sync with the conversation.

Sabrina scowled. "Twins. Ugh. And a grandmother, at my age."

Silence stretched and Emily felt another bead of sweat roll down her spine.

"You have a little apartment?"

"Sharing an apartment. I have a roommate."

"This must be a change then."

"Your home is beautiful." Over-the-top, eat-the-rich beautiful, Emily thought.

Her prospective employer toyed with the gold necklace about her throat, lifting it and then dropping the heavy rope back in place in a repetitive motion. It draped over the blade of her collarbone, only to be lifted and fall heavily again, conforming to every curve and hollow.

"Henry picked our place. Close to the hospital and room for all his vehicles. Well, most. We store the others in his collection off site. My Henry loves anything with an engine." She slipped her hand from beneath his, and he clasped it, then brought it in for a kiss. Mrs. Roth smiled.

How many vehicles did they have? Emily masked her scorn behind the bovine look of idiocy. It was their money. Who was she to judge?

Without only a child who had flown the nest to support, all the doctor's income could go to toys with an occasional charity auction thrown in for appearances.

"Henry said you're an excellent driver."

During their initial interview, she'd given consent for Dr. Roth to run a background check. He'd also requested a copy of her driving record, which had taken her half a day at the DMV, but she'd hand delivered it to his receptionist late yesterday afternoon.

Emily pushed the unease back down into her already-churning stomach as she imagined what her credit check revealed.

"And your record is clean. That's important. So no run-ins with the law," Sabrina clarified. "Did Henry tell you he has friends on the force here? Quite a few." She beamed up at him. "Isn't that right, dear?"

That news gave Emily an unexpected jolt of anxiety. She didn't know why. Her record was perfect, driving or otherwise. Her mother's fear of police had always popped up like the occasional sewage smell from a drain. Normal for a naturalized citizen who grew up in Northern Ireland as a Roman Catholic, Emily supposed.

"She's an excellent driver," Dr. Roth said. "Not even a speeding ticket."

Emily glanced at Dr. Roth, who did not meet her gaze.

She flicked her attention to Mrs. Roth to see what effect this new endorsement might have and spotted the first smile that lifted both sides of Sabrina's red, full lips. Emily felt the opposite of encouraged. Something about her expression was disturbing.

How did a person make a smile appear threatening?

"That's excellent," Sabrina said. The glee ebbed to nothing.

Mrs. Roth stopped speaking now and just stared at Emily with an expression that grew harder by degrees until her mouth turned down and she was shaking her head.

"No," said Sabrina, suddenly flushed and panting. She lifted a finger, shaking it at Emily. "I've seen her before. She's one of the ones following me."

Emily sucked in air and held her breath, glancing to Dr. Roth for rescue.

"Bree, she's not with them."

Sabrina tilted her head and whispered to her husband. "Then why has she been following me?"

Emily gaped as she struggled to recover.

"Wore a wig. Right?"

"She hasn't." He glanced at Emily. "Have you been following my wife?"

"No. No, sir. I have not."

"Of course she'd say that! Find someone else."

EIGHT

The change in Sabrina Roth had been as fast as a streak of lightning. She'd gone from a lucid and welcoming sophisticate to a spitting, red-faced combatant, eager for confrontation. She glowered at Emily as she blasted air in and out through flaring nostrils like an enraged animal.

What was happening?

Emily's mouth opened but only a strangled, pathetic little squeak emerged, as if someone was choking her. Her skin tightened, lifting each tiny hair follicle on her scalp. The sensation of bugs crawling on her neck made her shoulders do an involuntary shake before she could rein herself in.

Sabrina's eyes narrowed as if this involuntary reaction was some sort of confirmation, but Dr. Roth didn't notice Emily's ungainly spasms, as his eyes were only for his wife.

"I can't, Bree. I can't find someone qualified on such short notice. She's the best of the bunch."

This was a tone of voice Emily had never heard. Dr. Roth's words rang with frustration. The note of command had Emily straightening in her seat.

"You don't believe me." His wife seemed bewildered by the

abandonment of her fiercest defender. Confusion etched her brow, and she looked as lost as a small child finding herself suddenly alone in the grocery store. She blinked, twitched, and her mouth yanked back as if tugged by some invisible force. Then she shook her head, gaze dropping, head dropping, as her breathing continued, fast and panicky.

Emily's emotions ping-ponged between worry for her chances of landing this job and concern for the obviously troubled woman. Mrs. Roth seemed so bewildered.

"Henry, please," Sabrina whispered. "Get rid of her."

He was not deterred and gave his head a slow shake. Emily looked back to his wife, feeling like a spectator at a tennis match following that fuzzy green ball.

"This is part of your illness."

"She's a spy."

Henry never let go of his wife's hand. It was sweet, the way he supported her through the storm of her animosity.

"She's qualified. And she's available." He softened his voice and patted her hand, while still holding it with the other. "Do you trust me?"

There was a slight hesitation before she said, "Yes."

"Then let me hire her. She's top of her class. Reliable. She's here to help you. Not trap you. And she's never worked in law enforcement."

Odd thing to list as a qualification and the possible reasons tickled Emily's curiosity.

Dr. Roth's glance flicked to Emily. "We were left in a lurch. We need someone right now."

"That woman should be ashamed," said Sabrina, her face flushed with emotion. "She deserves whatever she gets."

Emily's brows lifted, but she didn't ask about her predecessor or what she might "get" as a result of disappointing the Roths.

Henry patted his wife's hand. "I agree."

"And after you bought—"

He cut her off. "That's enough now."

Emily really wanted to hear the rest of that sentence, but Sabrina's lips were pressed tight as she turned to glare.

"She was scared... you know. And they think *I'm* paranoid." She made a condemning sound through her teeth.

Emily fidgeted, wringing her hands in her lap as sweat trickled down her back like rain on a windowpane.

"She agreed to work the occasional evenings, Bree."

Now Mrs. Roth's pretty face turned sharp and her expression cold. Sarcasm dripped from her words.

"Well, aren't you quite the little saint? Saint Emily. No vices at all. But everyone has nasty little secrets. Don't they? And yours is following people."

Henry wrapped an arm about his wife. She lowered her glasses to cast him the kind of look that made Emily's skin flush. "My little pet," she said, stroking his cheek. He leaned into her touch.

Emily got a definite vibe that things in the bedroom at the Roths' might tip toward the unconventional.

Sabrina replaced her shades, and her expression was now pleasant and welcoming. The speed of transition gave Emily whiplash.

Sabrina expelled a little breath and gave another tic. "All right. But if I catch her spying..."

"No one is spying on you."

She made a harrumphing sound. Then she turned to her husband and gave a dismissive wave. "You'll work out the details?"

"Of course."

Why was it his job to handle those details? Mrs. Roth didn't seem to have a lot to do if you didn't include tanning, avoiding shellfish, and intimidating the help. And she seemed, extremely paranoid, and that belief that she was being followed might be seen as delusional, but to Emily she seemed very capable. Of what, she wasn't sure.

"We'll see you Monday, Emily. Blouses, solid-colored skirts, no slacks. Conservative. No shoulder, midriff, or cleavage. And don't you dare show up wearing those horrid little hospital scrub things. If you have tattoos, cover them. Understood?"

"Yes, ma'am." She'd need a trip to Goodwill because this was her only skirt. As a full-time college student, she'd mainly worn leggings, cut-offs, and shorts. Her only other attire were the scrubs she bought to wear at the hospital and treatment facility, which Mrs. Roth just forbade her to wear.

Why? Was it so her golf buddies wouldn't know that Emily was not just an assistant but also an LPN? Or was this a fashion thing?

"Ta-ta." Her hostess wiggled her fingers in farewell. "I'd shake your hand, but I don't shake." She wrinkled her nose as if shaking hands was as abhorrent as shellfish.

After what they'd all been through with Covid, shaking hands had become universally less popular.

Sabrina lifted a magazine from the expensive collection before her.

Dismissed, thought Emily.

Dr. Roth motioned her away.

"I'll be inside shortly to walk you out."

She exited through the door he indicated and found herself back in the kitchen between the table and the lanai door to the patio where a ring of Adirondack chairs circled a pristine firepit. Yet another unused gathering place, she realized. She glanced through an archway, seeing a long hallway that he'd said led to the family room, guest bedrooms, and a studio. She resisted the urge to go exploring. Plenty of time for that if that prickly, unpredictable woman didn't change her mind.

Through the glass, she watched Dr. Roth return to his wife, squatting beside her seat.

Emily wondered why she had closed the door behind her. It made listening nearly impossible. Hurricane windows, she realized. Thick and strong.

She cracked the door open until there was a gap. Sabrina had been right. She *was* spying on them.

"She'll work out. I'm giving you my word."

"You always say that."

"It's difficult, Sabrina. I need to know you're safe or I can't work."

That was actually very sweet. Henry appeared to be a concerned and loving husband.

"Fine, fine. If it will give me some peace."

What did that mean? Peace from his nagging or from having him at home with her? He had to get back to work and it seemed he didn't dare leave her unattended.

Other than the stench of superiority and the tic at her mouth, Sabrina Roth appeared to be the perfect, self-serving, cold ice queen of a wife.

But then Emily remembered how fast she went from smiling and appropriate to rage.

And Sabrina bounced from appearances of controlled normalcy to so very not. It wasn't hard to spot that something was wrong with his outwardly perfect spouse.

Keep your opinions and your questions to yourself, her mother had advised before her very first job interview.

Dr. Roth stood and Emily eased the door closed and darted back to the space between the granite counter and the six-burner stainless-steel cooktop with matching steel hood.

He spotted her immediately and paused.

"That went very well," he said.

Had it?

"I don't think she likes me very much."

"That will take time. When you grew up like Sabrina, you

don't trust people very easily. Her illness has only made her less accepting of outsiders, as I explained."

She wanted to ask what about her upbringing made her less accepting, but he was already standing in the foyer with a hand on the knob.

Keep your opinions and your questions to yourself.

It seemed obvious Sabrina had used her privileged upbringing and her beauty to hitch her wagon to a very successful doctor, who had a thriving practice. Shielded by her wealth and his position, she was protected from tiresome inconveniences like getting a job or paying rent.

He cupped one hand to his neck and seemed momentarily lost in thought. Finally, he dropped his arm back to his side.

"Well, I'm satisfied. Can you start right away?"

The smile splitting her face was genuine. This was everything she wanted.

"Of course."

"Great. Anything else?"

She could hear her mother's voice again. *Keep your questions to yourself.*

"I can't think of anything."

"Ready?"

She nodded, as if her head were on a toggle. Yes, was the only direction she could move. Yes, sir. Yes, ma'am. Yes, and yes again.

She followed him to the foyer.

Dr. Roth paused inside the front doors. "Oh, remember. During a dissociative episode she needs to stay where she is safe. That means she must not have access to an automobile. So, the key fob for Bree's car is either with you or locked up after she's gone in the house."

"Got it." She wished he'd added some instructions on what to do, instead of only what not to do. Both Sabrina's medication and her mental health problems would impair her judgment, and her cognition. Naturally, she should not drive. But apparently, she still wanted to, including when having a dissociative episode or, perhaps, because of it.

"Seven this Monday. Okay?"

"Just give them my name at the main entrance and use the code for the gate?" she asked.

"That's right. Park where you did today. Come in through the side door and grab Bree's car key from the lockbox. Hers is the Mercedes SUV. Be sure to lock the box afterwards. She has something to do almost every day. So, you'll be busy. She'll tell you where to go. Just get her there safely. No speeding. All right?"

She pictured herself standing in the laundry room for hours waiting for them to remember she was there. Oh, but the gatehouse would make certain that never happened.

"Yes. I understand." But she didn't really understand leaving several hundred thousand dollars of automobiles in an unlocked garage with the keys in a lockbox she suspected she could open with a bolt cutter. She knew the gatehouse kept out most unwelcome guests, but there were ways around such security measures.

"Then we'll see you on Monday."

"Yes. Have a nice weekend."

"Oh, Rosalind parks over on that side of the garage, too, so leave some room for her."

"Sure. I will."

"Bye, Emily."

He opened one of the front doors, and she hurried across the landing. When she turned to wave goodbye, she found him closing the door behind her.

Dismissed.

But he'd hired her! She got it. The job was hers. Whether she could keep it was another question.

Perhaps things were finally working out. That was if Sabrina didn't decide to fire her come Monday.

Emily determined to be whatever this couple needed. She'd kept more than one job by being indispensable and she'd do it again.

She walked out onto the drive, and reached her broiling car, baking in the sun. Emily stripped out of her blazer and tossed it, with her notepad, on the passenger seat, then slipped behind the wheel and dragged on her driving gloves. Finally, she inserted the key, prayed the engine would turn over, and gave a twist.

NINE

Her roommate was off on Saturday, so they hit several yard sales together, in Jennell's little Honda, because she had gas in her tank. They were still looking for a small coffee table for the living room to replace the wooden pallet that currently sat on the plastic tubs of Emily's mother's belongings.

Jennell wanted all the details on the Roths' home, furnishings, wardrobe, vehicles. Emily shared general details because of the NDA she had signed, and which Dr. Roth had neglected to give her a copy. She was usually jovial and even-tempered but the subject of the uber rich brought out a witch's cocktail of envy and distain. Like her, Jennell had been raised by a single mother. Unlike her, she had Caribbean roots, and her mother, three brothers, and two sisters all lived close by. Tomorrow, Jennell would invite Emily to church and the weekly gathering of her family for brunch at her mother's place. But sometimes it was easier to just stay home with memories of her mom and sister and binge watch *Bosch*, *Luther*, or *Criminal Minds* on her laptop.

She didn't understand why spending time with Jennell's

large, rambunctious family always left her feeling melancholy, unless it was just grief.

They didn't find the coffee table but came away from a church sale with two mint-green ceramic seashell lamps with yellowing drum shades that had endured since the eighties, and at the cost of four bucks each, including working lightbulbs.

On Sunday, Jennell was off to church with her family, leaving Emily to wash her car and make a thorough search of the interior. She was rewarded with three dollars in loose change, which she was prepared to spend on gas. But her hunt for a gas can, in the landlord's abandoned shed, yielded an ancient red, plastic container, still half full.

Jackpot.

Their landlord had replaced the tiny front lawn with crushed shell and wrinkly Astroturf, and removed the lawn-mower, which was no longer needed, before Emily even moved in. She was confident he would not miss a gallon or so of gas.

Sunday night, Jennell arrived smelling of nutmeg and cinnamon and complaining about her mother's efforts to intro-duce her to yet another nice young man.

"She just wants you settled," said Emily.

"He's bald and three inches shorter than I am."

"But he has a job." Emily knew this because Jennell's mom carefully vetted all candidates.

"I gave him my number. Hope I don't regret it." She flopped on the couch. "You still seeing Brian?" she asked, referring to the guy from the lab at the hospital Emily had seen a few times.

"On and off. He wanted me to go to some biker rallies, but I needed the weekends to pick up practicum hours. So, he's kind of pissed about that."

"Well, that's over now."

"Yeah."

She had her degree and a job. Everything was working out, so why did she feel slightly sick to her stomach?

* * *

On Monday, Jennell woke her right on time announcing she
had finished in the bathroom. Emily set her phone alarm, of
course, but her habit of hitting the snooze or just switching it off
had proved a problem when she was late to her practicum at the
hospital more than once. Jennell's knock had become a sort of
"last call" alerting Emily to force herself out of bed if she wasn't
already up.

Today, she was waiting for her turn in the bathroom. She
rushed her morning routine and was out the door with time to
spare.

Once past the guardhouse and through the Roths' security
gate, she found the garage side door was open, as promised, but
the door to the laundry room locked. The gatehouse would have
already alerted Dr. Roth of her arrival, so she didn't add another
text. Instead, she simply explored the garage, finding the
lockbox mounted by the side door. She succeeded in getting the
padlock open and tried the likely fob. The Mercedes SUV
chirped locked and double-chirped as the locks opened again.
Emily tucked the key ring in her front pocket and replaced the
padlock.

Next, she familiarized herself with what was stored in
those lovely dark custom cabinets and on the pristine wire
shelving, finding tools, gardening equipment that looked brand
new, flower pots, new again, golf gear, and holiday decorations.
There was an entire cabinet dedicated to car-washing para-
phernalia and a shocking number of wash and wax products.
The rest seemed to be sporting equipment she suspected had
been abandoned by their adult daughter. She located no security cameras in this area and so she sat in the cozy little diner
booth, flipping through the small jukebox offerings from the
'50s through the '80s. The coin slot made her wonder if the
system worked. But she didn't have any quarters to spare and

doubted the help should be blasting oldies before seven in the morning.

From somewhere inside the house came the mechanical announcement that the security system was off. Emily could have turned it off herself since she had access to the lockbox right here in the garage. The alarm fob on Mrs. Roth's key ring had three settings: On. Off. And Panic. That seemed clear enough.

Their security system had some major holes.

She reached the laundry room a moment before the dead bolt clicked from the kitchen side and gave a tentative knock.

Dr. Roth opened the door as if this was a totally normal way of admitting the help. Perhaps it was. The psychiatrist was dressed for work, smelling of coffee and a spicy aftershave. A navy-colored mini dot tie was draped about his neck and a tiny bit of tissue stuck to a bleeding spot on his jaw.

"Oh, hey, the early bird this morning. Were you waiting long?"

"Just a few minutes."

"Key?" he asked.

"Got it."

He glanced past her to the secure lockbox.

"Great. They texted me from the gate that you were here, but I was shaving and didn't see it until I grabbed my phone. Did you mind waiting?"

"Not at all."

"That's fine."

"I didn't want to be late. The morning traffic is unpredictable."

"Better early than late. I have appointments at my Winter Haven office today beginning at nine. If you aren't here, I have trouble."

"You have more than one office?"

"Lakeland and here in town."

"I see. Don't worry. I'll be here."

"Discreet and reliable. That's what your practicum super-visor said. 'Never late.' We certainly are lucky to have found you."

Found wasn't really the right word.

"Did you pick up the papers?"

The momentary flash of pride withered like yesterday's hibiscus flowers.

"The what?"

"End of the drive. Should be the *Times*, *Sun*, and *Wall Street Journal*. You bring them up. Didn't I mention that?"

"No. I'll go get them."

Emily retreated through the garage at a trot. Of course, when she reached the end of the drive, the papers were on the opposite side of the closed gate and the call box was outside. She tried and failed to slip between the upright bars, just as the gate moved. She leapt back as the gate retracted. Emily grabbed the papers and then hurried back as the gate closed behind her with a click.

Winded, she reached the kitchen.

"Here they are."

He took them and laid the *Times* and *Sun* out at the break-fast table, sticking the *Journal* in his satchel.

"Bree insists on having these waiting for her when she has her coffee."

"Got it."

Sweating, Emily pushed her glasses up her damp nose and swept her moist hands over the same old skirt. The gesture was more about nerves than wrinkles, since the synthetic fabric was impervious to the sort of rumpled appearance of expensive linens and fine silks. She'd borrowed the pink blouse from Jennell, but the color, which looked so fresh and lovely against her roommate's light brown skin, only made her florid face pinker. It was a color most redheads avoided but beggars can't be choosers. Her hair was tugged back in a pompom pony, as she usually wore it for work.

"Am I dressed all right? Your wife said skirts and blouses."

He gave her a quick once-over and the corners of his mouth tugged down.

"I'm sure that will work." He didn't sound sure as he cast a worried glance over his shoulder. "You're sweating. Grab a paper towel."

She did, and noticed the kitchen sink piled with dirty dishes, food drying and crusted to the plates. More bits of food scattered near the refrigerator. Someone had spilled cereal and then crushed it by walking over the flakes. Turning to mop her brow, she glimpsed the breakfast bar, which was also a mess of paper scraps, food containers, mail, and some kind of fluid.

Emily turned a full circle looking for the trash.

"Garbage?" she asked, holding the used paper towels.

"Drawer." He pointed.

She found both a garbage and recycle bin where he indicated. The recycle bin included two empty wine bottles. Sabrina couldn't drink. Not with her list of prescriptions. Was he drinking that much alone, or did he have company after the Mrs. went off to bed?

"We're having a rough morning. Bree has been up since two."

"Oh, I'm sorry to hear that."

"Actually, it's been a tough weekend. Her new medicine isn't working as I'd hoped. Before it gets in her system, she's agitated. Afterwards, well, it helps with impulse control and the restlessness, but she's out of it. Not ideal."

Impulse control? That was not one of the problems he'd mentioned. That made her wonder which of his wife's impulses Dr. Roth was trying to control.

"She's still okay to have her privacy?"

"Yes. Just be nearby, in case she needs something. She'll text when she wants a pickup. Try to get her to ride in the back seat. She doesn't like it, but I feel it's a safer place for her."

Another assessing glance showed he was again immaculately dressed and his hair was styled and combed, though still damp. But there were deep circles under Dr. Roth's eyes. The bags were puffy and greenish brown. He was going to work after being up half the night. Admiration mixed with compassion. He was such a good husband.

Emily didn't understand how he'd picked such a troubled woman. He'd said she'd once been charming, as well as beautiful. And rich was usually enough of a qualification to overlook certain obvious flaws. Had there been any flaws or had this mental illness emerged only after they tied the knot?

She could picture that: her with the allure of all that wealth embodied in the sophistication and the assurance of one's place on top of the societal food pyramid, and he with ambition, brains, and the compassion of a physician.

They made a good match, financially.

Still, Henry Roth couldn't have anticipated the emotional cost.

Those connections had come with a hefty price tag. Did he have buyer's regret?

But she didn't really know much about Dr. Roth. No parents listed in the engagement notice. How did he get from Cincinnati to Winter Haven? Was he born to wealth or was he one of those fabled self-made men? It wasn't the sort of question you could ask directly. But she'd figure it out, given time.

Time, the one thing she was not guaranteed. Answers required time.

"Unfortunately, the delusions are now more problematic. You'll see soon, I'm certain. She is fixated on the accident and what came after. But anyone with Bree's many traumas would likely develop problems."

"Many?"

TEN

In answer to Emily's question, Dr. Roth bobbed his head, reminding her of a walking pigeon.

"Unfortunately, yes. But the first, and most devastating, was the death of her brother."

That did sound tragic.

"Oh, I see. I'm so sorry."

How had she lost him? Emily didn't ask. She wanted to, but the moment passed.

She'd had no delusions about what it would be like to work in the home of a rich couple because she'd worked with her mother during the summer recess. The ones she'd known were careless with their things, but she'd never met anyone like Sabrina.

"Bree likes the arts section," he said, tapping his knuckles on the *Times*.

A white coffee mug whizzed by and smashed on the tiles.

"Spider!" The voice a screech, female and sharp as roofing nails.

Dr. Roth hurried to his wife, seated at the dining room table, and Emily followed. Mrs. Roth pointed at the buffet, the other hand pressed to her mouth. Dr. Roth lifted a cloth napkin and swung at nothing. Then he turned to his wife.

"It's gone." His voice was calm and reassuring, but the tense muscles at his jaw contradicted his composure.

Sabrina sat in satin gray pajamas with a distrustful expression on her face as her eyes darted between the closed buffet and her husband. Finally, she nodded and returned to the assortment of pill bottles. Below the table, Emily glimpsed a bare foot, with carefully manicured toenails and one scuff on the other. Her hair, which had been so sculpted on Thursday, was a crazy knotted tangle. She wore no makeup and now looked older with that unfathomable aura of crazy that often made Emily cross the street to avoid drug addicts or disturbed individuals. There would be no crossing the street today.

Sabrina spotted Emily and her face flooded with color as she screeched, "Who the hell is this?"

"This is Emily Lancing. You met her on Thursday." He spoke as if to a child, quiet tones and cool reassurance. His gaze flashed to Emily, and he arched a brow, then motioned with his head.

Emily stepped closer, feeling like she was playing some silent game of Red Light–Green Light.

"The hell I did." Sabrina pointed toward the dining room. "Get out!"

Emily backed up, pausing in the kitchen doorway. Had she really thought she could do this? How stupid was she?

Mrs. Roth now aimed her finger at the new help. "I don't want her. Where's Clare?"

Emily wondered if she should retreat out of sight or say something. But what?

Dr. Roth approached his wife, squatting beside her.

"Bree. We talked about this. She's our new housekeeper."

Housekeeper? The job posting had said the position was for a nurse and personal assistant.

"I don't need a babysitter."

"Of course you don't." His voice now held the first tones of stress but he still placated.

"And I can drive myself."

Here he did not instantly agree, and his voice changed to one of authority. "No. You can't. You don't drive. Not anymore."

She dropped her chin, looking repentant. "I know that."

His mouth went tight as he seemed to be grappling for control. His breathing came in full, fast exhalations, and a vein in his forehead pulsed as the stress became clearer. What a toll this kind of moment-to-moment emotional roller coaster must take on him. It was like having to constantly defuse a bomb that kept resetting itself.

"Now let's have Emily fix you another hot cup of coffee and we will sort out your pills."

Emily watched the bizarre exchange, trying to tamp down her anxiety.

Sabrina's cheeks flushed as she glared at the invader in her kitchen. Did she really not remember meeting her?

"She's staring at me," said Sabrina, chin down and scowling up at Emily from beneath a furrowed brow.

Emily turned to the counter and tried to control her percussive heartbeat and flash of heat burning her cheeks and neck.

Which of those medications was giving her short-term memory loss?

Dr. Roth helped his wife to her feet and guided her to the kitchen, seating her at the breakfast table. He was so calm, and his voice held only reassurance. Emily admired him and told herself to mimic his behavior. Even his movements were deliberate and slow.

She studied the high-end coffee maker that included a grinder, espresso, and coffee features. It was so like the one at the coffee shop she'd once worked at, she felt a tiny shot of relief. Here was something she was good at.

"How does she take her coffee?" she asked Dr. Roth, who was collecting the plastic containers of medications and a bottle of sparkling water.

"*She's* right here," snapped Sabrina. "Latte, one sugar."

Emily held her smile and returned her attention to the coffee maker, then rummaged through the closest cupboards for the larger cups but located only the clear glass espresso versions.

"Oh, for God's sake, over there! With the glasses." Sabrina's voice was sharp, like a lash.

Emily scurried in the direction her employer indicated, collecting a large cup and saucer.

"Why is she so sweaty?" whispered Sabrina.

"Hot outside." Dr. Roth opened bottles and set out a line of brightly colored pills and capsules.

"Three more," he said. "Not that one. You took that one already."

Emily turned to watch this slow-motion trainwreck. He'd said she only needed a reminder when it was time and supervision while taking her prescriptions. This scene before her made it obvious that was not the case.

When her mother said rich people have their own problems, Emily had not understood what she meant.

Emily placed the fresh beans in the grinder and hit start.

The scream from behind her made Emily jump. She held her heart as she noticed Dr. Roth frantically motioning toward the grinder. Beside him, his wife clamped her hands over her ears and continued to scream.

Emily yanked out the plug to the grinder and it whirred to a stop.

"No beans. I do that before she's up." He gave her a slow shake of his head and a look as if she were the stupidest creature alive. "I told you about the loud noises."

He had, and still, she'd just... It had slipped her mind and that was unacceptable.

The doctor slung an arm around his wife's shoulders and rocked with her, murmuring assurances, which Emily doubted Sabrina could hear beyond her hands, still pressed over her ears. His eyes were squeezed tight, accentuating the crow's feet, and his expression was drawn and weary. She wondered if the rhythmic sway and encouragements were as much for him as for his troubled wife.

When Sabrina dropped her hands to her sides, he opened his eyes, glancing in Emily's direction. He spoke in a low, quiet voice intended for his wife, but the words were for his wife's new nurse, who was making a very bad start.

"I keep the ground beans in the refrigerator. Please don't use the grinder."

"I won't. I'm sorry."

She retrieved the glass jar of ground coffee and busied herself tamping them down and then setting the machine to brew. She hazarded a glance at the couple. His attention was on his wife, who now hunched over the shiny reflective glass that covered the walnut table.

He offered a pill and watched her swallow it. Meanwhile, Sabrina lifted her gaze to stare daggers at Emily. This was not going well.

As the coffee dripped into the large white ceramic, Emily filled the metal cup with milk and then glanced at Dr. Roth. He nodded and she frothed the milk, added one sugar to the coffee cup, and stirred. She finished with a heart created of hot milk on hotter coffee and carried it to Sabrina.

The woman looked down her perfect nose at the offering.

"She's not wearing gloves."

Emily's stomach dropped. How had she forgotten?

"I'm not drinking that." Sabrina pulled her sleeve down over her knuckles and then pushed the cup away. When she spoke, it was to her husband. "Where did she work before this, a homeless shelter?"

"She was a nursing student. I told you that. But she has experience as a barista and waitress."

Had he memorized her resume?

"Probably gave them all food poisoning. I'd like to speak to her supervisors."

"I did that for you."

Sabrina cast him a wicked side eye and downed the final pill.

Her husband exhaled his relief and then collected the medications, stowing them in a bin and then in the cupboard. How many of those medications were controlled substances? He tucked two containers in his blazer side pocket, piquing her curiosity.

"Emily can help you with cleaning, laundry, even get you dressed."

"I'm not one of your psychos, Henry. I can get myself dressed." She aimed a finger at Emily. "You stay out of my way. I don't want to see you until lunch."

"Yes, ma'am."

"Call me Sabrina."

Emily tried not to show her surprise at this. Thursday she'd been told to call her Mrs. Roth.

"Well? That's my name."

"Yes, Sabrina. When do you take lunch?"

"At lunchtime." She looked at her husband. "Is she stupid or just being difficult?"

"She's trying to make a good impression, I think. Now, what would you like her to fix for lunch?"

"You too! God, I haven't finished my breakfast yet. Am I going to have to play twenty questions all day? I'm exhausted already." Here her voice became a whine. "I don't want you to go to work."

"I have to, Bree."

"As if we needed the money. You just want to get away from me for a few hours."

"That's not true."

"You're seeing someone."

"No. I'm not."

She folded her arms and refused to look at him, as if she were a child.

He stood, refusing to be baited. His ready smile looked forced. "Emily can take you anywhere you like. Why not book a massage. Maybe lunch out?"

This sounded like a terrible idea. Emily could just imagine the scene Sabrina could make in public. Why was he even suggesting it?

And would she sit with her or sit in the waiting area? The logistics of being a personal nurse were lost on her.

"Yes, lunch out with your little spy. Sounds perfect."

Dr. Roth's smile tightened. With practiced ease, he knotted his necktie and kissed his wife.

"I've got rounds and then patients. But will see you at suppertime."

She glanced up with imploring eyes. "You're leaving me with a stranger?"

Emily wanted to ask the same question.

"You've met her. This is Emily."

Sabrina made a harrumphing sound in her throat, crossed her eyes, and stuck out her lower lip. Emily half expected her to hold her breath. This wasn't just a disturbed woman; this was a spoiled one.

Dr. Roth rested a hand on his wife's shoulder. "See you later. Have a great day." He bent and Sabrina lifted her chin, accepting the kiss.

Both women watched him collect his satchel and blazer,

then disappear toward the garage. Once out of his wife's line of vision, Sabrina turned and narrowed her eyes on Emily.

Emily glanced toward the hall. From her place beside the coffee maker, she could see out into the laundry room where the doctor motioned for her to follow.

"Excuse me a moment. I think I left something outside."

Emily followed Dr. Roth into the garage.

He handed over the two pill bottles he'd pocketed.

"Keep these on your person. If she is still anxious in an hour, give her one of these. Just one and no more. I'll give her another before dinner."

"What is it?" Emily glanced at the label, recognizing a powerful sedative. The kind used for the most troubled patients or ones prone to self-harm.

"For her OCD. Calm her down. Only if she's agitated."

"Has she expressed a desire toward self-harm?"

"No. Nothing like that." He had his hands up, rebuffing the very idea, but his denial sparked doubt.

He wiped his face with both hands and then raked his fingers through his hair in a gesture of frustration as clear as his expensive watch.

"Lately, her mind tracks in a downward spiral. She has many consuming fears and a lot of irrational guilt."

"Guilt about what?"

"Mainly the death of her twin brother, Julian," he said.

"You mentioned that she'd lost her brother. I'm so sorry."

"Yes, when she was just a toddler."

Emily pressed a hand over her chest, absorbing the shock at this information. "What happened?"

"Drowned in the family's pool. Common down here. Unfortunately, too common."

It was.

"Oh, that's terrible." Her sympathy now turned to Sabrina Roth. How tragic.

"You have no idea." He pinched the bridge of his nose and exhaled. "It dropped a bomb in the family dynamic. Her mother never got over Julian's death. Broke her mother in some fundamental way. Really... disturbing."

Emily's brow knitted together. "I don't understand."

"Michelle, that's her mother, developed some irrational beliefs, following her son's death. My experience with her was that she was never what I'd describe as a warm woman. According to her husband, afterwards, he was quite disturbed to see her become less affectionate, and more critical, toward her daughter. Bree could do nothing right. Eventually, Michelle formed the opinion that Julian's death was somehow her daughter's fault. She told me this more than once."

"Why would she think that?"

"Because Bree didn't save him. And she didn't call for help. As a three-year-old she couldn't understand that he wasn't swimming any more than a child that age can understand the permanence of death."

"She was there when he went in the pool?"

"When he fell in. Yes."

"But your wife wasn't responsible for that."

"I know that. But her mother told her it was her fault, regularly. In her mind, Julian was the good one and she the bad. He was the loved one and she was unlovable."

"How terrible." Emily could not help herself from feeling sorry for the poor little rich girl with the ice queen mother.

"Michelle really did a job on her." Now his voice was weary. "I could write a book on this one. Her mother was a cold, bitter woman. After Julian's death, it appears her mother withdrew her affections toward Bree. At least that was her father's take on the situation. Once, I overheard Michelle telling her daughter that she wished that it had been Sabrina who died that day."

A tight fist contracted around her heart sending a painful

pulse of empathy thrashing through her bloodstream. She gave an audible hum of sympathy on a long exhalation of air. Still, the aching twinge endured, gripping her chest.

How tragic. Emily could only imagine what kind of mental instability the double-whammy of the loss of her twin and her mother's love might cause in a child.

Dr. Roth glanced at his gold watch. "Listen, I'm late. You'll be fine. Bear in mind that her memory is unreliable because of the organic delusions. What she believes to be true just isn't, despite how adamant she might become. It's part of her coping mechanism."

She would brush up her knowledge base on organic delusions at her first opportunity.

He turned to go.

"Should I confront her misbeliefs or..."

"Try distraction, change the subject. You aren't qualified to confront them."

"She seems very upset to have me here."

"Not for long." He tugged at his cuffs.. "The medication should be working shortly. She won't be any trouble. Promise. Good luck."

If she wouldn't be any trouble, why would Emily need good luck?

"Dr. Roth? My copy of the NDA?"

"Oh shoot. I remembered after you left." He rifled through his blazer and handed her an envelope. "Your copy."

"Thank you." She folded the envelope and tucked it in her back pocket.

He headed to his luxury sedan, parked between the enormous SUV and the silver convertible.

His work car was shiny, bluish gray, and spotlessly clean.

The garage door trundled up, the brake lights flashed, and Dr. Roth abandoned his wife into Emily's care.

She turned, then startled to see Sabrina standing in the open door to the garage.

"I didn't hear you," she said, one hand over her thumping heart.

Sabrina smiled, as if that pleased her.

"I remember you," she said.

"Yes. We met last Thursday."

"You've been following me."

Emily shook her head. "I haven't been following you."

"You think I wouldn't remember?" She cocked her head. "I don't recall that hair. But it was you."

"Would you like a latte?"

Sabrina hesitated, then nodded. Emily went back to the kitchen and Sabrina returned to the table, flipping through the news.

Emily brought her coffee, this time wearing gloves.

"Get me a pencil," she said.

Emily did and drank the latte her employer had rejected, while decluttering and mopping clean the breakfast counter. Sabrina sat in her satin pajamas, ignoring her, as she scanned the local news page, one foot tucked up on the chair, and her knee resting against the table's edge.

"Would you like some fresh coffee?"

"No." She turned to the crossword puzzle and set to work. Not what Emily expected from an overmedicated mentally ill woman. Something had changed.

When her coffee mug was empty, Sabrina rose and pushed away the paper. "I'm getting dressed. Toss that out," she said, indicating the folded paper.

She turned and sauntered away, the hems of her silky pajamas whispering over the tile.

As her stomach growled, Emily gathered the two coffee cups and cleaned away the shattered one Sabrina had hurled at the imaginary spider. From the pile of dishes dumped haphazardly in the sink, she guessed that the collection was from last night's dinner and perhaps the weekend as well. She transferred the contents of the sink to the dishwasher, finally reaching the bottom of the deep farmhouse sink to find several more cups. Had this mess been sitting here since Thursday? The pods for the dishwasher were under the sink. She dropped one into place and started the full load.

After sweeping the floor, tossing out the food packaging from the countertops, and cleaning the grit and sticky spills from the surfaces, she ran her hand over the smooth, clean stone and smiled. The grain was lovely and now glowed. Next, she checked what was in the pantry and refrigerator, taking photos to record the brands and food that the Roths kept on hand. Her stomach's growling became more insistent, so Emily made herself toast, lavishing on the butter and peach jam. She ate standing at the window facing the lake. The butter was salty, and the jam loaded with lovely bits of fruit. Such a luxury.

After her meal, she picked up the clutter from the breakfast table and cleaned that as well, then she repeated this with the dining room table. As Dr. Roth predicted, the living room needed straightening. She made sure the pillows were arranged, the afghan artfully draped, and the contents of the coffee table organized.

The kitchen floor was sticky, so she mopped it.

With nothing more to do, she turned to the unfinished crossword puzzle, located a pen, quickly filled the empty boxes, and then realized Sabrina had been gone quite some time.

Anxiety needled, sharp as a thorn.

Emily set aside the paper and hurried to check on Mrs. Roth. She headed through the living room, thumping the couch pillows into order on her way past.

Personal photographs adorned the wide hall leading to their bedroom. She paused to examine the images of a bright-eyed little girl changing, photo by photo, into a woman until finally there she was beside a tall young man framed with a wedding invitation. *Taylor Roth and Seth Parker request the honor...*

Emily continued along to the primary bedroom.

The door was closed. She pressed her ear to the surface and did not hear a shower or any movement at all.

Her light knock yielded no answer. She knocked harder. Still, nothing.

Now her heart was pounding in her throat. What if something had happened to Sabrina? Then everything would be ruined.

Her knock became more insistent, mirroring her rapid heartbeat. Her knuckles became a woodpecker—tapping, then pounding.

She called in a high quavering voice threaded with notes of alarm, "Mrs. Roth! Are you all right?"

Emily's heart slammed around in her chest, making her dizzy. Her skin went damp and the buzzing in her ears rose to the roar of a jet engine. Mrs. Roth had locked herself in her bedroom and would not respond to her polite knock, turned frantic open-palmed pounding.

"Mrs. Roth! Please open this door!" Her strangled voice sounded as if someone were choking her.

Her new medication might be doing anything. Dr. Roth had said they were changing things. That could cause any number of horrible scenarios.

Images of Sabrina Roth unconscious on her bathroom floor filled her mind. EMS at the gate. Paramedics filling the house.

She stepped back, preparing to kick the door open. Instead, she lifted her phone from her back pocket.

Should she call Dr. Roth's office or 911? She glanced up, trying to think past the cacophony of fear. This was not the plan. Not at all. How had everything gone sideways so fast?

ELEVEN

Then Emily spotted it, a tiny little brass-colored ring poking out from the molding above the door and smaller than a dime. She lifted on her tiptoes and hooked her index finger in the loop. The ring was fixed to a narrow tool, something like a key but with only a small single bend and an end that looked more like a tiny screwdriver.

She inserted that end into the hole on her side of the locked door with shaking hands. The metal tool caught something, and she twisted, hearing a satisfying click. The knob turned.

Emily called out as she opened the door.

"Mrs. Roth? It's Emily Lancing. Are you all right?"

Before her was a huge king-sized bed, unmade, with a rumpled blue and white coverlet squatted on a pale hardwood floor. Sitting in a rocker on the opposite side was a collection of expensive-looking, jointed teddy bears and two glassy-eyed porcelain dolls. The grouping gave her the creeps.

To the left were both a door to the pool and a window seat. She rounded the bed and discovered an empty sitting area anchored with a blue rug beneath a love seat and cream-colored low-profile barrel chairs. The room smelled of vanilla and chlorine.

Reversing course, she hurried to the primary bath, passing discarded gray pajamas beside the single slipper and a satin robe.

Was Sabrina really all right in there by herself?

She spotted the second slipper between a huge soaker tub and walk-in steamer shower large enough to park a Harley inside. She paused to arch a brow at the heated towel rack unit. Heating towels in Florida seemed beyond extravagance.

Between the twin columns, and above the tub, sat high naked windows allowing views of the tops of palm trees. No reason for window dressing when you had this kind of privacy.

What she didn't find was Mrs. Roth.

Turning, she faced the wall of mirrors above the double basin sinks sitting on a sugary white marble counter upon more walnut cabinets. Between the shower and sinks was a double louver door.

Toilet? She crept forward and knocked.

"Mrs. Roth?"

The doors were not locked and contained a linen closet. Beside that, a toilet and bidet sat in a private alcove with a view of a framed impressionist print of a woman in her bath.

Hurrying out, Emily realized that *she* was now the one with the anxiety.

Rushing into the living room and through the foyer, she discovered the front door locked. Could Sabrina have done that from the outside?

Emily turned a full circle. Where was she?

Her bedroom door had been locked. So, she *was* still in there.

She ran back to the bedroom and dropped to her knees to peer under the bed, seeing nothing but a discarded sock.

A tiny thread of jealousy peeked past the panic. This

couple had so many things she knew would never be part of her life. If she had this right, these two had three living areas and a boathouse.

She turned back to the bed, seeing the dresser and the huge television mounted on the wall. Beyond that was an arched doorway she'd missed the first time she'd come in.

This was the entrance to two huge walk-in closets. His was copiously neat and smelled of leather and aftershave. Hers smelled like the perfume counter at a high-end department store and was also empty, if you did not count the shelves of designer bags, huge central ottoman, racks of clothing, and a collection of shoes of every variety, with some repeats in different colors. There was also a wall of drawers in increasing size that she had no time to explore. Emily shook her head in frustration. If you counted things as the currency of happiness, Sabrina should be the happiest woman on the planet.

"Oh, God, the lockbox! She's in the garage."

Reflexively she patted the pocket holding Sabrina's key fob. She'd locked the padlock. Hadn't she?

The part of her brain that remembered details was drowned out behind the voice shouting for her to find Mrs. Roth.

How long had she been in the kitchen, cleaning up? An hour? More?

Emily darted from the closet and happened to glance out the door that led from the main bedroom to the lanai and pool deck.

She carefully dragged back the heavy drapery and stared out past the outdoor kitchen to the pool. The slider was unlocked.

Sabrina had come this way. Emily followed and spotted something pink floating in the turquoise, chlorinated waters.

Her charge dragged a hand in the pool as she drifted naked on a pink floating lounge with a nylon mesh base and adjustable headrest.

"Mrs. Roth?" Emily's voice had a hard edge. "There you are."

Sabrina didn't lift her head and her eyes remained closed. From the lack of bathing suit lines, Emily believed this behavior might have been normal, but didn't dismiss the possibility that the woman was unconscious, instead of just a jerk.

"Took you long enough. If I'd been face down, you'd be looking for a new position. Honestly, it's been hours. Do you know how quickly a person can drown?"

She didn't. But Sabrina Roth most certainly did. Emily thought of her poor little brother and Sabrina's nasty, bitter mom and some of her resentment melted.

"I'm so sorry. I didn't know you wanted me out here with you."

"I don't. But I should fire you." Mrs. Roth shaded her eyes.

The threat sent a jolt of panic squeezing her belly. Emily made no reply. But even from here she could see Sabrina's lips curl upward. Was this fun for her? Hiding from the help? Threatening their livelihood?

There were some conditions that no amount of medication or childhood trauma could remedy. Egotism among the rest.

Emily folded her hands before her and kept her opinions to herself.

"I don't need a babysitter, Ellie. Why don't you just shove off."

"It's Emily."

Sabrina opened one eye and stared up at her. "Just go. Be back at four-thirty if you like, before he gets home."

Tempting, but no. He likely would check on them and he'd fire her for sure. Then all this would be for nothing.

"Why were you in my room?"

"Thought you needed me."

"Doors lock for a reason."

Sabrina rolled into the water and out of sight. She swam to

the deep end and emerged for a breath, her dark hair now swept back as it had been the first time they'd met.

Emily left the lanai and moved out into the bright sunshine, squinting at the glare off the pool.

Sabrina swam for twenty minutes while Emily watched, acting as lifeguard for a nude woman who seemed to have no modesty. Her charge glided through the water like silk over warm skin, leaving barely a ripple in her wake. She was fit and lean and, Emily had to admit, beautiful. She could see what Henry had seen. The tragic figure. Did he think he could fix her?

Likely, she decided.

Had he? Or was she irrevocably broken?

Finally, Sabrina climbed the stairs.

"Towel?" she said, standing, arms extended, like Cleopatra waiting for her slaves to wrap her damp body.

Emily darted inside to grab a towel and returned, holding it out.

Sabrina tugged the thick terrycloth about herself and sank into a lounge chair.

"This isn't a beach towel. Don't you know the difference?"

She did but she'd been in a hurry and hadn't seen any beach towels.

Emily realized the pool and deck, as well as the house, sat on a rise, well above the lake, giving them both a full view of the water and privacy from any boaters who might pass the back of their property.

Unless you were standing naked beside the pool. Then, anyone and everyone might see you.

"Go away, Morgan. I'll call when I want something."

Who did Mrs. Roth think Emily was this time? Or was she playing this name game on purpose?

She took a step toward the door and hesitated. "Would you like something now? Ice water?"

Her answer was an angry growl. Emily retraced her steps, collecting the discarded pajamas and robe and depositing them in the full bathroom hamper. She spent the next hour checking labels, sorting clothing for dry cleaning, and starting a wash for what she could. She located a stack of zipper bags with a store logo on them. A web search told her these were provided to customers for delivering dirty items to them. So, she tucked the delicate and special care items inside one.

Periodically she checked Sabrina sunning herself naked on one of the chaise lounges. No wonder her skin was so tanned. The woman had quite a body.

From the kitchen, Emily saw Mrs. Roth rise and move to a chaise lounge in the shade of the lanai. She stepped out to check on her after she settled and heard her new boss snoring. Dr. Roth had expected this. Told her that his wife would not be a problem. Was this what he meant, that after her antics, she'd be narcoleptic all morning?

That didn't seem healthy or like appropriate care, but at least she wasn't threatening Emily's job.

Next, Emily unloaded the dishwasher and checked on her charge from behind the safety of the living room glass sliders as Sabrina Roth slept poolside. She fixed herself a cup of coffee. While it brewed, she sorted the damp clothing, sticking what she could in the dryer and hanging the rest in the laundry room to dry.

When she returned to the kitchen, it was to a cold cup of coffee.

Before noon, she collected the midday medications, carefully checking the list and lining up the pill bottles on the counter.

She glanced around for something else that needed doing, but found nothing. So, she decided this might be a fine time to do a little snooping. After all, Dr. Roth had said his wife did not need constant supervision.

Besides, this was an easy, interesting way to get to know her new employers. If there was a person on earth that babysat or was a housekeeper that didn't look inside medicine cabinets and bedside drawers, she didn't know one.

People kept secrets tucked away behind closed doors. It did not take long for her to make her first interesting find.

TWELVE

Emily began in Dr. Roth's freakishly clean study, which was right off the foyer, beyond the powder room. The skylights in the large sloping ceiling made for a bright inviting space, with shelves filled with medical texts. The comfortable seating area, in shades of sage and gray, and the private entrance made her wonder if he'd seen patients here during the pandemic.

She wanted to learn all about the Roths, and more about Sabrina and her medical issues. Keeping this job was important for many reasons, among them the chance to make that first student loan payment to avoid yet another bombshell exploding in her credit. But before she could pay any of her debt, she needed enough to pay her bills and buy some food. Yeah, food and gas. Then the headstone and if there was anything left over... There was never anything left over. That sinking, "iceberg right ahead" feeling was back, dragging at her like a heavy invisible load. The ballast of river rocks that tugged downward. But Emily stubbornly held her nose above the waterline. As long as she kept kicking, it would stay that way.

It all seemed impossible.

Upon an impressive wooden desk were the usual items: a

laptop, expensive fountain pen, closed leather portfolio, and a digital recorder. The lamp was modern and stood sheltering two framed photos. One was of a much younger version of Sabrina, glowing with youth and happiness as she held a chubby-cheeked toddler. The second was of Dr. Roth walking a tall, veiled bride down the aisle. His daughter, Taylor Lee, she assumed.

A quick check of the closet revealed several designer name cardigan sweaters on hangers, two filing cabinets, cardboard boxes on shelving, and a large safe bolted to the floor.

The dryer buzzed and she collected the clothing, carrying them back to the primary bedroom.

Putting away the clothing took more time than expected, as she had to figure out what was to be placed on hangers and what went in which drawers.

In his closets, she recognized the spicy tang of Dr. Roth's cologne in the air and clinging to the soft expensive fabrics of his enormous wardrobe. As she hung his polo shirts with the others, arranged by color, she counted seven yellow dress shirts alone. They both had way too many articles of clothing and a stupid number of accessories. He even had a watch drawer that illuminated when opened, and she had one holding dozens of scarves nested like songbirds in their special compartments.

"Oh, brother," she muttered, wondering if she should wake Mrs. Roth for lunch.

She returned to the bedroom and the sliders facing the pool, flipping open the curtain on the lanai. Mrs. Roth now lay face down on the lounger, arms folded and cheek resting on her hands.

Emily stepped out and Sabrina opened one eye, then waved her off with the two visible fingers. She withdrew as Mrs. Roth closed her eyes and relaxed like a sunning alligator.

Time for a quick look around that bonus room, she decided.

She ventured into the unfamiliar wing of their home,

coming first to the family room to find a television large enough to use as a home theater. At least the furniture here sagged in places and seemed comfortable in a well-used navy and red nautical sort-of-way.

This gathering space had yet another adjoining full bathroom with a gleaming clawfoot tub.

Through an arched doorway and down the hall beyond, she discovered a neatly decorated, spotless, unremarkable guest bedroom. From the doorway she sensed the stagnant, hollow feel of unuse. She moved through the room to the semi-private bathroom, trying not to envy the twin sinks, as she crossed from it into a second bedroom. This one added a touch of the surreal with several more female dolls perched atop a trunk and seated in a row beneath the window. Emily squinted at the glassy-eyed babies, knowing this was a stare down contest she could not win.

She crossed back into the hallway and then into the next bedroom, this had been Taylor's room and held some of her belongings and a private bath.

The final room, described by Dr. Roth as Sabrina's studio, lay just beyond with a wide doorway that lay open.

Once in the bonus room, Emily paused. Even with the electricity switched off, the space was full of light from the wall of windows that rose twenty feet from the angled ceiling. The lake sparkled and Emily enjoyed the view from the comfort of the air-conditioned bonus room. The bonus room, as if with all this, they deserved a bonus.

No gaming area or Ping-Pong table here.

Unlike the rest of the house, painted in sedate pale shades of blue-gray and warm whites with shiny enamel molding, the walls here were a sunny yellow. This room held the scent of ink and charcoal. Like every other space, it was a mess. But Emily instinctively felt she should not move anything or clean here.

Piles of drawing paper sat stacked on all surfaces, including the stool, the drafting table, and a desk. The desktop also held a large antique crock filled with an impressive variety of drawing tools.

Dirty, misshapen erasers congregated beside the canister on a fine porcelain tray that seemed to have escaped a tea table somewhere. She lifted one that looked like gray putty, another resembled grimy yellow rubber.

From atop an antique wardrobe more creepy antique dolls stared down at her with critical, unblinking eyes. Beside this, she spotted the kind of cabinet architects used to store drawings and cartographers used to hold maps. On top sat a stunning bouquet of cascading sprigs of fuchsia bougainvillea branches, ornamental grasses, ferns, and upright crape jasmine. She could smell the jasmine from across the room and took a step closer to examine the black and gold Japanese lacquer vase holding the arrangement. This looked old and expensive, like the sort of Asian antiquity she had seen in museums in the decorative arts displays. Were those dragonflies made of real gold?

She shook her head in wonder. If she had that vase, she'd use it in her room as well. It was elegantly, sedately expensive without too much flash.

The map cabinet intrigued her. She drew open the top drawer and found several sketchbooks with paper no bigger than an average printer sheet. On the cover was the kind of quick, carefree sketch that Emily could only dream of crafting.

At the desk she turned over the top page. Her brow furrowed in confusion. The page was black. Pencil shading covered nearly the entire surface. Only the finest sliver of lines remained. At first, she thought this might be a sketch Sabrina hated and had scribbled over. The pencil lines were so violent that they indented the paper in places. The tiny white threads that remained uncovered seemed an oversight. But the more she looked the more she thought this might be a spider's web, or some nightmarish asymmetrical version of one. In the center was something that could have been a white spider. It looked almost like a star or a bullet hole.

She couldn't make anything out of it. An abstraction, perhaps.

Emily flipped over to the next image, a nearly identical one. And yet another. All of them, repeating the same strange dark image, over and over and over again.

The drawings gave her a chill. There was something dreadful and dangerous about them. Was this what she drew back here in this sunny studio with views of blue skies and green water?

These were not the drawings of a woman with anxiety. These images seemed sinister reflections of a haunted mind.

"Clare? Where are you?"

Emily's head jerked toward the door. She bolted upright as currents of panic sizzled down her spine.

That was Sabrina, who either couldn't remember her name or was doing this for kicks.

Emily quickly returned the drawings to the pile and was halfway to the door when she was confronted by Sabrina.

"What are you doing in here, you little snoop?"

"Getting oriented." Her words came out in a singsong cadence, as if she'd just announced she was making chocolate chip cookies.

Her false cheerfulness did not fool, judging from Sabrina's scowling face and tightly pressed lips. Emily held her stupid smile as her stomach crimped itself into a series of vicious little knots because she could think of no other option. Sabrina had both caught and cornered her.

"Stay out of my studio."

"Yes, ma'am." She swept past her and back to the kitchen, the only suitable place for the likes of her.

Sabrina stormed after Emily, her angry face radiating disapproval laced with a whiff of malice.

"It's time for my medication. My watch beeped. Perhaps if you did your job instead of poking around in my private spaces, you could keep track of such things." She shook her head, arms folded tight and mouth ticking like a tiny, malevolent heartbeat. "Or I could just fire you." She lifted a hand to tap her index finger in the indentation above her upper lip, thinking. Drumming. Tap. Tap. Tap. "From the look of you, you need the money." She swept a critical eye down her body and back, making Emily feel naked. Her mouth ticked. "Is that the same skirt you wore here last week?"

Lie or the truth? "Yes. I only have the one."

That made Sabrina laugh, as if having so little were funny. It took Emily several seconds to shove down the rage that roared to life like a tropical storm.

"My medicine?"

"Yes. I have them ready." Emily motioned to the row of medication bottles that she'd arranged earlier on the breakfast bar.

Sabrina eyed her, waiting.

"Well?"

Now Emily waited.

"You have the list. Get them out. He puts them all in that." Sabrina pointed at the bin containing her medications. There among the plastic pill bottles was a finely carved rosewood stash box shaped like a sleeping cat.

Emily dragged on gloves, removed the lid to the ornately crafted cat effigy, then tapped out one pill after another into the bowl's smooth curved interior. This done, she retrieved a green bottle of sparkling water from the refrigerator.

Sabrina seated herself at the receiving side of the wide expanse of colorful stone, watching. Emily placed both bowl and water before her employer who accepted the offerings.

There she twisted open the cap and downed the pills now correctly presented in the finely carved bowl.

Meanwhile, Emily grappled with her rising distaste. She didn't like Mrs. Roth and didn't need to. It wasn't a requirement of doing this job or getting some answers.

"Didn't I tell you to throw that away?" said Sabrina, indicating the morning copy of the *Times* now before her at the breakfast bar.

"Yes, you did." Emily reached for the paper, folded open to the crossword that Sabrina had failed to complete, but Emily had not. Her bold blue lettering looked like a jagged invader amid Sabrina's looping pencil script.

Sabrina's brow quirked with interest. "You finished it?"

Emily nodded, her stomach contracting at the accusation in Sabrina's tone.

"Yes. I'm sorry. I thought you had finished." She thought so because Mrs. Roth had told her to toss it. Why she hadn't done so after filling in the darn puzzle was just carelessness.

"Let me see," Sabrina demanded.

Emily felt a moment of regret. Why had she done this? She was here to find out all she could about Sabrina. Not the other way around. And she'd filled in all those blanks that Mrs. Roth could not.

Reluctantly, she passed Mrs. Roth the paper.

"Clever girl and in ink. Not a single mistake."

Sabrina was wrong about that. The mistake was doing the puzzle in the first place. It was the sort of error her older sister would not have made.

This job was important for many reasons, and she'd do whatever it took to keep it.

"You should be a professor. But wait, you said you want to practice nursing."

She remembered that?

"Nurse practitioner. I already am a nurse, a license practical nurse," Emily corrected, causing Sabrina's forehead to wrinkle and Emily to break eye contact.

Correcting her employer was another mistake. That, and Sabrina's unexpectedly recalling their brief discussion about Emily's ambitions disconcerted, as if this woman and the one she'd met this morning were different people. Did the medications account for that? She didn't know.

"But you advised against it," said Emily, off-balance now and unsure where this was going and if it might produce some outburst. She waited, watchful.

"If it helps you become independent, do it. Nothing is more important for a woman."

Surprise lifted her brows at both the advice and Sabrina's coherence. "You said I'd be a spinster."

"There are worse things. A bad marriage is worse than none."

Did she mean her own marriage or, perhaps, her parents'? From appearances, she had a good marriage and was very lucky that her husband was such an obvious support. It wasn't the sort of question Emily could ask, so she waited, holding her smile and trying to exhibit the kind of calm Dr. Roth seemed to easily manifest.

"I'm lucky. Henry indulges me and he helps keep me on track and safe. If you find someone like that, you should grab him with both hands."

They were having a conversation. Their first.

"If you pursue an advanced degree, will your parents be helping or do you hope for a scholarship? Henry got loads of scholarships. Poor as a church mouse, that one."

"My parents are gone."

Sabrina sat forward, suddenly interested. "Oh, you mentioned that. Recently?"

"Well, my father, yes, though he left when I was a baby. My mother has been gone a little over two years now. Three in February."

"I'm sorry for your loss."

It was a perfunctory reply delivered by reflex, rather than emotion, leaving Emily to wonder if Sabrina was sorry her father abandoned his family or that her parents were dead. Both, she thought, either.

Emily's reply was equally unthinking. "Thank you."

"My parents have also passed on. And my brother."

"I'm so sorry."

"He was my twin, you know?"

"Dr. Roth mentioned it."

"And my mother says, oh never mind." Sabrina's eyes blinked heavily. "She just hated me from the moment they found him, is all. Never could be good enough or mind her the way she expected."

Emily hustled the bottles away and shoved the box out of sight.

When she turned back to her charge, she discovered Sabrina had her head on the stone counter, the one that had come all the way from Brazil, as one hand still gripped the green plastic water bottle.

"Are you all right?" Emily asked.

She thought most people would have felt some empathy. But Emily experienced only a tingling wariness, concern mixed with distaste.

"Just waiting for them to get into my system. They work faster on an empty stomach."

"Does it take long?"

"No. But they don't work, either. Not completely. Because I still see them."

The tick of her mouth made Sabrina's words appear insincere.

"Them?" Did she mean the people she thought were following her? Or was this something creepier like her dead mother and twin brother?

"I don't understand."

"He calls it a form of PTSD, you know, flashbacks and... what happened afterwards, it just shreds me."

Did she mean losing her brother, the traffic fatality, or something else? Emily was afraid to ask.

Sabrina lifted her head, then drummed her fingers on the stone counter. Her mouth jerked at the corner.

After a few moments, she noticed her own drumming fingers and locked her hands together, then stared at the ceiling.

"Nothing helps," said Sabrina.

"Have you tried talking about it with a therapist?" Emily said, trying to draw out the conversation.

"Of course I have. I married one. Doesn't help."

The shoemaker's children go shoeless. It was an odd thing to remember, her sister saying that after Emily had commented that a classmate always brought the exact same lunch, peanut butter and banana sandwich, apple, and three Oreos to school, though his father was a chef.

Emily qualified for free lunch, but at least it changed daily.

Sabrina straightened, closed her eyes, and exhaled. "I'm tired. Get me to my room."

She hadn't eaten anything. The medication list still lay before her, and Emily read: Noon medications *after* lunch.

Oh shit, she thought. If Sabrina zonked out again, without eating... Well, that was bad.

"How about a sandwich?"

"I'm not hungry."

Emily retrieved a yogurt shake promising thirty grams of protein.

"You have to take those last ones with food." She raised the drink, offering.

Sabrina motioned her forward like Neo in *The Matrix*. Then she guzzled the drink, relieving Emily of the worry over not feeding her.

"Get me to my room. I want to read."

Emily helped her up, surprised at how slight she was, like a bird. Her employer leaned heavily as they made their way to her bedroom.

"Couch."

Emily struggled past the bed, half dragging Sabrina and thinking that carrying her would be easier. Then she deposited her in the adjoining seating area facing the lanai. Before her employer, on the coffee table, lay more magazines including Vogue, Country Living, Real Simple and the UK version of Town & Country. Emily knew, from the bookstore, that each cost between fifteen and twenty-five dollars, except for one that had a price in British pounds.

"Perfect." Mrs. Roth waved her away. "Nothing more."

Emily withdrew, silent as an English butler, leaving Mrs. Roth staring at a vacant sky with empty eyes.

The woman was a zombie, her condition much worse than Emily had anticipated. It was hard not to feel sorry for her. And even harder to figure out if she was competent to make decisions for herself. But what had Emily expected?

Everyone she'd met while working her practicum at the hospital liked Dr. Roth. Although, that was his public face, and here, at home, she was catching a glimpse of a much different person.

One burdened with a dysfunctional wife. But how dysfunctional? Emily wanted to know if Sabrina's mental illness was the kind easily managed, like insomnia, anxiety, and mild depression, or the upheaval sort, like dementia or paranoid schizophrenia. The latter were the kind of illnesses that could make Sabrina Roth unable to understand the consequences of her actions. In other words, was Sabrina legally competent?

From her law dramas, she knew that if Mrs. Roth were deemed incompetent, she would never be held legally responsible for her actions.

Back in the heart of the house, Emily made herself a sandwich on a kaiser roll with some of the Boar's Head roast beef. Then she selected a flawless Anjou pear, poured some pretzels from a bag onto her plate beside a few kalamata olives. She enjoyed every delicious bite and the luxury of fresh, expensive ingredients.

After cleaning up, Emily checked on Sabrina, finding her not reading, but snoring. The reason for her thinness was obvious. She wasn't alert long enough to eat.

She left the room and headed to the opposite wing, ignoring Sabrina's warning for her to stay out of the bonus room.

Back in the studio, she retrieved from the stool a sketchbook, which fit in her hand. The pages of this one were filled with dark scribbles, but oddly on the back of each sheet of paper. Most of each page was thick black lines, but there were also a series of gray forms that looked like tiny horseshoes, or thumbs?

Emily turned to the next. One seemed to be slightly larger. Flipping to the last pages, she saw what the shape was, gravestones. And finally, just one gravestone. Upon the raised mound of earth was a single lily.

"Whose grave?"

Was it Sabrina's twin?

She let the book close and noticed something, this was a flip-book. Beginning at the back and moving to the front, this was a walk through a graveyard, ending at one particular grave. And there was the name on the stone, faint but legible.

AVERY NELL THOMAS

THIRTEEN

On Tuesday, Emily stood a long time in the laundry room waiting for admission to the Roths' residence. She glanced at her watch, seeing it was already twenty minutes after seven.

Each minute added to her anxiety. Would Sabrina not remember her and start screaming again?

Finally, Dr. Roth appeared, his dress shirt unbuttoned, and his pink paisley tie looped around his neck. Yesterday evening, he'd quizzed her on her impressions of Sabrina's ability to function. Emily had been selective with her words, but had conveyed that Sabrina had been agitated in the morning, then slept poolside and was progressively sedated for much of the afternoon.

His furrowed brow suggested he seemed concerned at this news. She could not imagine how hard it was to get such a complicated amount of medications correctly balanced for a woman as small as Sabrina Roth.

"We're just about to have some breakfast."

She followed him to the kitchen where the sink again overflowed with dishes, greasy take-out containers littered the counter, and several shattered plates made walking on those expensive tiles a challenge.

Here was more indication of the crushing burden, not only of battling his wife's condition and outbursts, as evidenced by the ruined flatware, but at her absence from the duties of running his household. Tectonic plates grinding together, sending tremors through this outwardly tranquil household.

Sabrina was already dressed in a floral one-piece sleeved dress, Emily recognized the designer by the signature pink and green floral pattern. Dr. Roth returned to his seat beside his wife to continue feeding her pills, one after another. Finally, he mixed a paste in a plastic shot glass using a tongue depressor.

"Based on your report that she slept all yesterday morning, I've reduced the dosage. She shouldn't be so sedated today. You'll have to tell me if she's calm or if she gets overanxious. I need you to order some groceries. I made a list. Call Howlands."

Emily accepted the list, familiar with the high-end, gourmet grocery, but having never shopped there.

"The gate will text you when anyone's arrived. They know the usual suspects. Rosalind has the gate code, too. You'll see her sometime after eleven. Meet all deliveries at the gate by the road. You carry the bags from there. I don't want anyone but you and Rosalind in the house. Oh, and the flowers come today. Morning, sometime. I think that's all. If Bree wants to go out in the afternoon, just take her wherever and then be available."

"Yes, sir."

At the sound of Emily's voice, Sabrina looked up from her seat at the breakfast table and narrowed her eyes at the intruder.

"Who the hell is that? Are you having an affair?" screeched Sabrina.

Emily stiffened and stepped back.

"That's your nurse, Emily."

Sabrina glared at her with bloodshot eyes, swaying slightly in her seat.

"Puzzle girl."

"What's that?" said Dr. Roth.

"She knows," she said, challenging Emily with a fixed stare.

He turned to his new employee, brows raised.

"I finished the crossword after Mrs. Roth was done."

"I see." He shook his head. "Don't do that."

Emily's stomach clenched at the rebuke. Trying hard wasn't always enough.

"Would either of you like some toast or eggs?" She thought food might be a good pairing with all those chemicals.

"None for me. I've got rounds." Then to his wife. "Almost done. Just this last one."

Sabrina opened her mouth and accepted the gritty paste from the tongue depressor like a baby bird being fed a fat worm from its parent.

"That should help." He glanced at Emily. "She's had another bad night."

"I'm sorry to hear that."

"I can't sleep because I hurt people. Bad girl," said Sabrina in a matter-of-fact tone.

Dr. Roth dropped his chin. "You didn't, Bree." Then to Emily, he said, "She's been obsessing over the accident."

This time she didn't ask which one.

When his wife had finished her medications, Emily decided to find out what each one of them did. No harm in comparing what she'd been told with what she could dig up, was there?

* * *

A bit after nine, a text chimed on Emily's phone. The guardhouse was alerting her to a floral delivery. How could she open the gate from the inside?

Sabrina was reading the paper and directed her to the

button beside the front entrance door that sat below the security alarm and next to the row of light switches.

The gate retracted and she waited for the truck, only remembering when it stopped beyond the gate that Dr. Roth didn't want delivery people on the property.

She hurried out, accepted the delivery, and felt guilty she didn't have anything to give the driver as a tip.

"Have a good one," he said. Then hopped back in his truck.

She carried the bouquets inside, closed the gate, and filled a pot with water, resting the flowers together inside as a temporary holding area. Did she just throw away the perfectly good flowers already in vases?

It seemed so wasteful.

From the pantry, she collected three various empty vases and placed the bouquets for bedroom, kitchen, and dining room on the counter, feeling as if she owned a floral shop. Meanwhile, Sabrina carried her coffee and papers to the dining room.

Emily had never seen so many flowers.

Luckily the intended rooms were indicated on the tags in each wrapped bundle. This week the arrangements for Sabrina's bedside table were white roses, white lilies, and blue hydrangeas. Emily chose a small, square blue glass vase for that grouping. The roses and lilies smelled amazing. The dining room received pink lilies and dark pink roses. She chose a crystal-cut clear glass for that. There were green orchids and red roses for the kitchen, now seated in a ceramic vase that resembled bamboo. The magnificent arrangement of tropical blooms and succulents intended for her studio included white plumeria, bird of paradise, and something with dark maroon leaves she could not identify. That one needed to be arranged in the lacquer vase now in use in Sabrina's studio.

She fussed with the three bouquets in the kitchen. Satisfied, she set the first on the counter, then carried the second to the dining table. Sabrina glanced up as Emily set the bouquet in place but said nothing. Emily retrieved the lilies and hydrangeas, now properly set in a vase, and carried the fresh flowers to the main bedroom, returning with the old arrangement, passing Sabrina, flipping through the paper. In the kitchen, she found the empty lacquer vase on the counter beside the final bundle of flowers.

Had Sabrina retrieved it? She must have.

"I'll put that one back," she said without looking at Emily.

"Of course."

Now the kitchen counter had three perfectly good-looking "old bouquets" and the final cluster of blooms.

Emily arranged them in the vase, running a finger over one of the raised gold dragonflies gripping a bending stalk of grass, all exquisitely painted by a skilled craftsman she assumed was long dead.

"Mrs. Roth, I wondered what I should do with the existing bouquets."

This caused Sabrina to lift her head from the paper and stare.

"Well, I won't be pressing them in my scrapbook. Toss them. What else?"

"Yes. Of course."

Emily did not have the heart to throw away perfectly good fresh flowers, so she sorted them into two piles, tucking the fresh ones in a large freezer bag of water inside a kitchen garbage bag and the rest went in the full kitchen garbage. She delivered the fresh ones to her car en route to carrying the trash to the bin with her apologies.

When she returned, the flowers she'd arranged in the Japanese vase were gone.

A trip down the hall showed Sabrina working in her studio. Behind her sat the fresh flowers in their proper vessel.

The woman was quick as a cat.

* * *

The food delivery arrived, and Emily hauled the bags, four at a time, up the long driveway and into the kitchen. An unfamiliar chime sounded, and Emily stepped to the dining room to look down the drive. She saw the gate open and in rolled a battered Honda Accord that was missing the flap to the gas tank and sported a scrape that ran from the passenger-side door to the rear fender.

Rosalind. The only one allowed past the gate.

Emily continued to the kitchen, unloading the groceries. A few moments later, the door from the garage to the laundry room opened and in stepped the house cleaner. She carried nothing but a canvas shoulder bag, which she placed in the closet above the cleaning supplies. She was short, solidly built, with thick black hair wound into a bun the size of a cinnamon roll. Her faded capri jeans revealed strong calves and the shape-less pink T-shirt showed muscular brown arms. On her feet were plain white canvas sneakers with rounded toes and perfect bows on threadbare laces.

Emily judged her to be fortyish, with threads of white at her temples.

"Hello," Emily said.

The woman startled and spun, hand going to her heart. Her dark eyes went wide. A fringe of bangs curtained a wide fore-head, framing a square face, devoid of even the least makeup, including lip gloss.

She fixed Emily with a direct stare. She wore the smallest gold studs in petite earlobes and a gold crucifix about her neck.

"I'm Emily. You must be Rosalind."

"Yes. Hola, Emily," she said, smiling. The gap beside her front teeth showed the kind of neglect that came with not having the money for bi-annual cleanings, root canals, and caps. She did not offer her hand but nodded a greeting.

"Dr. Roth said you would be here Tuesdays and Thursdays."

She hesitated. "Sí."

"Would you like some coffee, Rosalind?"

Her thin brows rose in surprise.

Both hands went up and waved in refusal. "Oh, no. I have to clean."

"Yes. Please let me know if I can help you."

She nodded, her brow descending over her narrowing eyes. Clearly help was not something Rosalind expected.

"Or if you'd like some coffee later on," she said.

The woman pressed her lips into a slashing line, and said, "I'm cleaning now."

Rosalind reached into the closet, dragged out the vacuum, and hustled down the hall to the Roths' suite.

Emily brought a fresh cup of coffee to check on Sabrina, who now sat in her studio, a sketchbook open and ignored before her. She rocked as she turned her coffee mug in circles while humming an unfamiliar tune. The morning medication had kicked in and she was glassy-eyed but still upright.

Sabrina accepted the coffee, looking from one mug to the other.

"Two?" she asked, clearly confused.

Emily scooped up the old one with a gloved hand.

"This one has gone cold."

"Ah," she said and nodded as if her head was on a slow-motion setting.

Sabrina began tapping her finger on the mug's handle as if hammering out a message in Morse code.

"Rosalind is here."

Sabrina groaned, stood, and carried her coffee outside, settling at the teak table with Emily trailing behind.

"How about some toast and a bowl of fresh fruit?"

"I'm not hungry."

Emily bit her lip. One of her jobs was making sure Sabrina ate. Sabrina was already slight, and it was a short hop from slender to gaunt.

"Yogurt? Protein shake?" she offered, remembering what Dr. Roth had said. These items would be sealed and therefore more difficult for Emily to tamper with.

Sabrina's eyes blinked closed. "Nothing now."

Emily caught movement from her periphery. From the living room sliders she saw Rosalind staring at them. The moment she was spotted, the woman closed the drapes and the vacuum roared to life.

What had she witnessed over the years?

* * *

By week's end, Emily was settling into a routine, proving with time you could get used to anything.

The Roths didn't cook so much as select ready-made, or nearly ready-made foods.

When anything was delivered, the gatehouse sent a text.

Today, they alerted her that a delivery driver was on his way. Emily opened the gate and walked to the end of the drive to wait. He pulled up in a gold Buick with duct tape completely covering the space where a side rear window had once been. He unfolded from the seat and popped the trunk.

The guy was tall, young, painfully thin, and had both a nose ring and black rubber plugs in his elongated earlobes. His forearms and neck were covered with blue ink.

He lifted four bags and started for the entrance.

"Stop. I'll take them."

"Oh, yeah. I forgot."

He placed the bags on the gray pavers.

He returned to the trunk, removed the remaining bags, and set them with the others. "That's it. You be careful."

"You as well." It was an odd farewell.

Careful of what, she wanted to ask, but he was already trotting toward his car.

Emily carried the groceries inside and started unpacking.

Tonight, the Roths would be having forty dollars' worth of grilled salmon, premade Caesar salad with the dressing waiting in a sealed little bag beside two others of both shaved and grated cheese, garlic bread that needed only to be baked in the oven a few minutes, and for dessert, tiramisu, from the bakery department. Emily could have bought an entire dinner for two on what Sabrina spent on the Parmesan cheese the pair would shave over the ready-made mix which already included cheese.

Emily compared the lukewarm pizza from last night to this bounty and shook her head. Her favorite meals included potatoes in any form, from potato skins with bacon to overseasoned curly fries. But she had yet to see a single potato in the Roths' home. Neither did they have Emily's second favorite food group, chocolate, so she'd taken to bringing some along to help her through the day.

She fixed a plate for Mrs. Roth's lunch. She was getting the hang of what she liked. Cottage cheese on a crisp piece of butterhead lettuce that she never ate. Fresh sliced tomato, salted. Pasta salad with vegetables or chicken but no shellfish. Fancy crackers with either Brie cheese and fresh pear or apple slices or foie gras which Emily found disgusting.

Sabrina didn't eat so much as nibble as she worked. Meanwhile, Emily took the opportunity to eat anything and everything she liked, which today was leftover rotisserie chicken because Sabrina had confessed that her husband refused to eat leftovers.

No wonder they spent five C-notes a week on groceries.

Emily brought the plate to Sabrina, along with an iced tea and the noon medication. After lunch, Emily cleaned up the kitchen as Sabrina changed into a swimsuit and stretched out in her favorite napping spot, a lounge chair on the pool deck.

After checking to be sure Sabrina didn't need her, she headed for the doctor's office to do some more snooping. The wall of sliding glass doors from the lanai made a distinctive whoosh when drawn open on their rollers and each entry door caused the security hub to chime an alert, so Sabrina would not get by her unaware.

Emily's first discovery was the medical records for Sabrina's hospitalization after the auto accident a decade earlier. That was a long time to keep medical records, especially since they were all digitized and available online anytime. According to the discharge from the ER, Sabrina had broken her nose, suffered an abrasion on her cheek, lacerated her lip, and sustained a fracture of the distal radius of her left wrist. There were follow-up appointments and physical therapy for her broken bone. She'd also had plastic surgery on her nose to correct a deviated septum.

When Emily's phone alarm sounded, she startled, her heart revving into a painful staccato. Fumbling, Emily silenced her phone and pressed a hand to her chest, slowing her breathing to quiet the anxious beating of her heart. Once the pulsing in her neck slowed and the heat left her face, she tucked away her phone and then returned all the medical records. The ringing sound had broken the absolute silence of this house and had given her a start, triggering her guilty conscience. At this point she knew how long Sabrina generally napped and set the alarm because she did not wish to get caught snooping again. The quiet, and her calm restored, she headed out to the pool to wake her boss.

Sabrina roused slowly, groggy as usual from sleeping so soundly and possibly from the cocktail of drugs that would now be circulating in her bloodstream.

Despite being ill at ease in this opulent home, Emily had an obligation that went beyond Dr. Roth's expectations. She had heard his instructions and read his notes, but she intended to use her own eyes and judgment to form her opinions as to his wife's condition. She wasn't going to let anyone, or anything, stop her from doing the job she came here to do.

Here in their home, there was less charm and more heartache. How much of it was of their own making?

Emily sat in the shade as Sabrina waded down the steps and into the warm water. She used a pool noodle to kick around for about twenty minutes.

She thought Mrs. Roth would get more exercise loading the dishwasher or cleaning the enormous house they owned. Mopping, dusting, and vacuuming made a full-body workout. Nearly as much work as emptying bedpans and changing sheets.

Sabrina required Emily to hold open her beach towel as she exited the water. It was stupid but seemed to make her happy. Thankfully she required no assistance changing, unless you counted picking up the sopping bathing suit she routinely left on the floor in either her closet or the primary bathroom. That was when she wore a bathing suit.

Sabrina led the way to her bedroom, then dropped her towel and vanished into her walk-in closet. Emily scooped up the towel and carried it to the bathroom and hung it on the towel warmer.

"That's all," said Sabrina from the closet.

Emily glanced at the cabinets beneath the twin glass basins that served as sinks, noticing something she hadn't before. One side had a keyhole. She checked the other side, finding Sabrina's electric toothbrush and an assortment of facial creams.

Then she tried the opposite side, the side she assumed held Dr. Roth's things, and found all the drawers locked.

Who locked a bathroom cabinet?

FOURTEEN

Over the next two weeks, Emily collected the newspapers each morning. Accepted deliveries from pharmacies, food services, grocery stores, dry cleaning trucks, and the flower shop, all at the end of the driveway. On the second Friday, she collected her first paycheck and began to see some improvements in Mrs. Roth.

That weekend, she and Jennell had found two serviceable vases at yard sales so they could each have a bouquet, in their bedrooms, of the Roths' weekly discards. Emily had kept her eyes peeled for a wagon to help her carry things up the drive, which now seemed less elegant and more extremely long and in full sun. Unfortunately, she struck out on the wheels.

Sabrina's medication list changed slightly, and she grew more alert, less snappish, and less consumed with grief. It appeared Dr. Roth had determined the best combination of chemicals.

Now, in the start of Emily's third week in the Roths' home, she prepared to take Sabrina on today's outing to have her nails done. Emily pulled the SUV out of the garage and up to the front entrance, as usual, where Sabrina waited. The woman remained on the top step, staring down at Emily.

This had baffled her at first, but now she knew to switch off the SUV, then open the rear door for Mrs. Roth. Only then would she descend the steps.

But today, she hesitated at the open door. She lowered her designer shades and pursed her lips, now the color of the pearly coral inside a scallop shell. Then she opened the front passenger door and swept into her seat, waiting.

Emily shifted, awkward at Mrs. Roth's sudden decision not to ride in the back, which, up until now, she had been doing on each trip, without objection.

"Your husband asked that—" She never got the rest out.

Mrs. Roth's chin lifted, and her voice was clipped and cold as their infrequent frosts.

"That I ride in the back like a toddler. I'm neither child nor celebrity and shan't be treated as one. In addition, the obstructed view makes me nauseous. From now on, I ride up front."

It wasn't a question but a declaration. And the challenge was clear in the hard lines bracketing her mouth.

Emily deliberated what to do, and then closed both doors. She wasn't prepared to drag Sabrina from the seat or force her into the back. Her only other choice was to refuse to drive her or, worse, tattle on her to her husband.

Off-balance and worried about keeping the job she so needed, she rounded the front of the vehicle and slipped back behind the wheel of the Roths' imposing, full-sized Mercedes SUV. Emily waited for Sabrina to buckle up, then she put the boat of a vehicle in gear and off they went.

When Dr. Roth returned home, Emily told him about Sabrina's new choice of seats and he pulled a pained expression but said only, "Fine."

And from then on, Sabrina always rode in the front seat.

This week, Sabrina had turned from sedated to sedate and had been able to do some unnecessary shopping. When driving Mrs. Roth, Emily spent most of her time waiting in Sabrina's car, reading, scrolling various feeds on her phone, or walking around the parking area. On Wednesday, Mrs. Roth returned to the ladies' league for golf. Emily walked back and forth along the hot sidewalk, edged with prolific pink and white impatiens, punctuated with pygmy palms as she waited for the text to collect Mrs. Roth from the clubhouse because Sabrina did not want to be "hanging about, waiting for her driver" when all the other women in the league simply drove themselves off in their luxury cars.

Sabrina did a better job on the crossword now, nearly finishing with only one or two wrong answers. Every morning, Emily secretly finished the crosswords, correcting Sabrina's decreasing mistakes and then tossing the paper in the outside recycling bin beside the garage.

After the crossword, Sabrina often read much of the paper and occasionally clipped something that went with her to her studio.

Emily fell into a routine. She arrived with the papers and collected the keys, got Mrs. Roth to eat breakfast, then handled the dishes, picked up around the house, cleaned the surfaces and floors, carried out the garbage and recycling, collected scattered garments, towels, and wine bottles from the outdoor areas. Gathered the newspapers, when Sabrina was done clipping, reading, or scribbling on the news. Then, when Sabrina was usually engaged in her studio, Emily did the remainders of both puzzles, from the *Sun* and then the *Times*. Laundry went in before lunch, dry cleaning was placed in a bag and collected at the gate on Monday and Thursday afternoons, returning on Tuesday and Friday mornings just after Dr. Roth left for work. More than half their wardrobes went in those fancy zip-up pouches. Emily suspected their dry cleaning bill rivaled her monthly rent.

As Dr. Roth had suggested, Sabrina liked to venture out daily, often in the afternoons. Sabrina patronized several nearby, high-end stores. She shopped for things she already had too many of, like shoes, bags, scarves, and clothing. Sabrina's closets burst with unworn blouses and skirts that still held the tags.

Henry Roth had been right about another favorite stop: the art store, where the owner greeted Sabrina by name, as the favorite customer she no doubt was. Mrs. Roth never came away empty-handed.

She had her nails done every two weeks, her hair cut once a month, and often had a blowout when she was going out to dinner with Henry.

Sabrina seemed almost normal, except for the facial tics and the apparent exhaustion at the start of every morning.

Mrs. Roth spoke to Emily infrequently and usually to issue an order. On the bright side, she no longer suspected Emily of spying or threatened to fire her. Baby steps, Emily thought.

Rosalind would now speak to her in English with some Spanish thrown into the mix, and they often drank coffee and chatted together before the cleaner went to work.

Rosalind had a husband and five kids. They lived in Lakeland, and her younger three kids went to the same elementary school Emily had attended. Rosalind's older daughter dropped off and picked up the younger ones, just as Emily's sister had once done.

They both had older sisters, only Rosalind had seven, two of whom were here in North America, and one of whom lived with them, along with her sister's two teenage children. All in all, the three-bedroom apartment now housed ten people. It was what happened when housing prices and rents soared, inflation rose, and wages stagnated.

Both she and Rosalind had old, unreliable cars and spent time comparing problems, repair costs, affordable mechanics, and the impossibility of affording a newer vehicle. The cleaner's English was better than she'd first let on and she was funny.

"If mine was a horse," said Rosalind, about her car, "I'd have to shoot it."

That made Emily laugh and she'd said, "Horses are expensive, hay burners."

"Yes. But I had a mule in Guatemala that was less trouble and he used to bite."

When Rosalind spoke of her husband, she beamed with pride and her voice changed, holding a little hitch of excitement or, perhaps, pride.

"My husband works nights at a nursing home, he makes all the food preparations for the meals. I get the kids ready for school. My daughter takes his car and drives them to and from school. I go to work, and he comes home to sleep, then he is there when they are done with school. When I come home, my Miguel is off to work again. It is hard. But we do it."

"You sound very busy."

"Yes, but on the weekends we go to the state park, the one with the springs, and we spend all day by the water. We all love the water."

"The natural springs are beautiful."

"Like a miracle. Cool and fresh, the color of turquoise. And so much water. We bring inner tubes and float along. My boys like to use the mask to see the fish and turtles."

"I love the springs. Rainbow was my favorite." But Emily hadn't been in years because it made her too sad. The memories lurked there, in the lovely clear water.

"Do you go to the springs with your sister?"

Emily dropped her gaze to the empty coffee cup. She had mentioned her sister, but not that she had died. The grief

squeezed her heart and dragged on her shoulders, but she told
Rosalind of her loss.

"My older sister passed away when I was sixteen. She took
her life. A suicide. And my mom died when I turned twenty-
one. Cancer."

Rosalind crossed herself and kissed the crucifix that hung
from her neck. "I'll say a prayer for them both."

"Thank you. I miss them so much. My sister was much
older. She basically raised me. When I was very little, I thought
she *was* my mother, that I had two mothers. Back then, I
thought she was all grown up but she was only fourteen.
Seemed very adult to me. She was the one who walked me to
school, picked me up afterwards, like your daughter."

"It's good to have a big sister. My Jasmine is a very good big
help to me. She now even cooks sometimes."

"My sister used to make me after-school snacks. Use cookie
cutters on my cinnamon toast, turning them into dinosaurs or
cheese slices into stars."

That made Rosalind smile.

"My kids all like empanadas after school. I make enough for
the week, on Sunday, then I sneak vegetables in with the meat
to make them eat some." She laughed. "I wish I was home when
they finish school. I am missing so much."

"Like my mom. She had to make a living. She also cleaned
houses. I used to work with her sometimes during school vaca-
tions. Later, she worked as a maid in a few hotels."

"Hard work, hotels. Laundry, change the bed. Vacuum.
Again, and again." She placed her hands on her back, in a way
that reminded Emily of her mother, stretching the tired
muscles.

"Yes. It wore her out."

"I understand." Rosalind turned her own hands over, stared
at her palms, and balled them into fists. Then she met Emily's

stare. "I've been here a long time. Seen many, many nurses come and go."

"How many?"

Rosalind lifted both hands. Ten.

Before she could fully absorb this disturbing revelation, something captured Emily's attention, a feeling something was wrong. The hairs on her neck prickled. Her first action was to look for Sabrina, but she lay on her stomach in a lounge chair beside the pool.

Then she spotted it. The glowing red light of the security camera above the sink.

Someone was watching them.

Emily lifted her cup. "Well, we'd better get to work."

* * *

Emily headed to the pool, knowing Sabrina had a manicure this afternoon and needing to know if she would have lunch here or out after that.

Mrs. Roth turned over at her approach and her phone chimed with an alert.

"Rosalind is here?"

"Yes."

She glanced at the other alerts on Sabrina's phone, two from the doorbell cam recording Rosalind's arrival and one that someone had turned on the live view in both the kitchen and patio.

Sabrina waved toward the lanai. "Hello, darling."

It was an odd way to greet her.

Sabrina turned to Emily. "He's got the pool camera on." She pointed to the security camera mounted above the sliders. The light was glowing red.

Emily waved as well, feeling foolish. The light flicked off.

"Does he do that often?"

"Constantly. Reassures him to see me. One day I'm going to cover them all with black tape."

"Do you find his check-ins invasive?"

"As terrestrial termites."

Another glance at her phone. "I'd better get moving. Emily, would you like to try lunch at Evangeline's?"

"I'd be happy to bring you there."

"I'm asking you to join me for lunch. My treat."

Emily hesitated, both surprised and taken back. This was something new.

"Oh, that would be lovely."

Sabrina waved a dismissive hand. "I was meeting someone, but she had to pick up her daughter at school. Some bug going around. She stood me up. I hate eating lunch alone in restaurants. You'd be doing me a favor."

It was the sort of ladies' lunch place Emily could only dream of visiting.

"I'd love that."

Mrs. Roth glanced at her assistant's black skirt and white blouse and rubbed her forehead.

"Hope they don't mistake you for the wait staff."

Emily shifted, and folded one arm over her middle, grabbing the opposite elbow as she reminded herself not to fidget under Sabrina's scrutiny.

"You'll need a sweater. It's cold as a morgue in there."

"I'm afraid I don't have one."

"I'll lend you one. Something to cover up that blouse and a scarf."

Emily pressed her lips together, feeling the prick of the criticism of her wardrobe. Mrs. Roth waited, an expectant look on her face.

"Thank you." Her reply was obligatory and still stuck in her throat.

Judging from Mrs. Roth's arching of one carefully sculpted

brow, Emily's words, and perhaps the tone, did not hold the correct outpouring of gratitude.

"Thirty minutes. Right?"

"Yes. Fine."

Sabrina stood and headed into her bedroom via the sliders, leaving her empty drink glass, magazine, beach towel, hat, and sunscreen scattered about.

Emily collected all the discards and headed inside where Rosalind waited in the kitchen.

Rosalind glanced toward the security camera before speaking. Then she asked, "You have her keys?"

"Yes." Emily patted her front pocket.

"Keep yours with them, too."

"Why?"

"She took mine from my purse."

"When?"

"Just before you started. I called Dr. Roth and he came home and got them back."

This was concerning. Dr. Roth had told her that his wife's delusional episodes could trigger her need to escape and that, at such a time, the car mustn't be an option. But stealing keys didn't sound like a delusional episode. It sounded... premeditated.

"All right. I'll keep a close eye on them. Thank you for telling me."

"I have them here now." She pointed to her own front pocket. "Never in my bag."

Was this the reason for the medication readjustment Dr. Roth had mentioned when Emily started here? He'd mentioned a recent incident, but stealing Rosalind's keys didn't quite seem to qualify.

She wanted to ask if the cleaner might know but Rosalind had already collected the carrier of cleaning products and headed for the pool bathroom.

Sabrina appeared with a sweater and scarf in her hand, tossing them to Emily. The angora knit was soft as a cloud and pink as a baby blanket and the scarf was awash with Monet-inspired waterlilies.

She slipped into the offerings and waited.

Sabrina nodded. "Better. Ready?"

Emily drove Mrs. Roth to her nail appointment, waiting in the vehicle for fear of sweating on the sweater and scarf. Afterwards, she drove them to the high-end department store where Evangeline's was located, and dropped her lunch partner at the entrance, as requested. Then she parked and hurried back to find Sabrina nowhere in sight. A stop at the cosmetics counter for directions got her on her way. Upstairs, she arrived, sweating, panting, and flushed. Sabrina scanned her from top to bottom and then rolled her eyes before proceeding into the lunch venue.

Inside the chic entrance, Emily paused as Mrs. Roth spoke to the hostess about their reservation.

The woman, young, thin, with a posh updo and perfectly applied cat-eye makeup, collected the large menus and wine list, then ushered them forward past widely spaced tables, and the chairs all upholstered in white leather. A wall divider held a series of white faux candles on a walnut structure that resembled an empty bookcase backed with a gauzy white curtain.

The patrons were largely well-dressed, older women poking at colorful salads and sipping white wine as they held on to trim figures like grim death. The expressionless, smooth faces resembled, in no way, the veiny, liver-spotted hands and crepe-paper skin visible above their designer necklines.

Gold seemed the preferred color for jewelry, preferably studded with gemstones. One of the women, with thinning, unnaturally red hair, noticed her and gave Emily a once-over. Suddenly, Emily was glad for the borrowed designer silk scarf.

At the center table, she wondered if she'd have to worry

about Sabrina drinking, which was not advisable with her medications. But Sabrina told the young lady to take that list away.

The menus were placed between the knife and fork and the hostess quickly removed the wineglasses. Emily waited for Sabrina to choose a seat, then took the one opposite, gazing down at the menu. The single page lay in a leather-like holder and was printed on quality ivory paper, like a wedding invitation. There was not a stain anywhere and Emily wondered if they printed these up each day.

After they were seated, they were told their server's name and that she would be right with them, when, in fact, she was right behind their hostess and introduced herself before rattling off the specials. Emily heard all she said but understood only the words not given in French—lobster salad, beef, pork.

What was a pommes frite?

Emily chose something recognizable and at the lower end of the prices. Still, twenty bucks for a chicken salad sandwich seemed high. Though when it arrived, she saw why. The fragile plate in no way resembled the paper wrapping that usually surrounded her lunch.

Sabrina, meanwhile, ordered the Fifth Avenue Steak Sandwich, with a side salad.

Once the server left them, Emily offered Mrs. Roth her midday medications. Sabrina cast her a look of annoyance but took the pills in rapid succession.

While they waited, Sabrina ignored Emily's attempts at conversation, preferring instead to pay careful attention to all meals being delivered to other tables with increasing annoyance.

Their server added more water with lemon to Sabrina's glass and then returned with their meals.

The sandwich was delicious, with curry dressing, cilantro, a very crunchy toasted bread, and a lovely crystal glass dish of the kind of fruits Emily never purchased because of their price. She saved the huge red raspberry and chunk of fresh pineapple for the last bite.

The lunch venue was wonderful, the menu magical, and her dining companion an absolute nightmare. It wasn't her place to be embarrassed when Sabrina sent her salad back because it was overdressed or her steak sandwich because it was too rare. But she was.

"If she thinks I'm leaving a tip, she's out of her mind," she said to Emily. "Terrible food. Terrible service."

Emily had never even worked in a place this nice, let alone eaten in one. She sat like Cinderella, in the clothing provided by her fairy godmother who currently seemed more wicked witch.

She struggled to conjure sympathy from what Dr. Roth had said about Sabrina's overbearing mother and awful childhood and failed.

They left the restaurant after Sabrina answered the hostess's polite question about how everything had been with a litany of complaints. They adjusted her bill, and Emily walked beside Sabrina through the high-end department store. On the lower level, Mrs. Roth paused and extended the shopping bag.

"Go get the car, Emily." Then she peeled off to look at shoes. Emily lifted an ordinary-looking brown loafer. The tag read $465. She replaced it and headed out into the oppressive heat. After collecting the vehicle, she pulled before the store, in view but out of the crosswalk.

Sabrina did not appear.

Should she text her or wait?

Wait. She drew off the sweater and scarf, fearing she'd sweat all over them. The air conditioner drove off the sticky blanket of humidity. To the east, huge clouds billowed, promising scattered thundershowers in the afternoon.

Emily occupied herself rummaging through Sabrina's

center console and glove box but found nothing but the usual items.

Then she toyed with the large touchscreen on the dash. The vehicle had a carputer, internet, and tons of apps. In fact, it seemed an accurate copy of Sabrina's own phone.

Emily went right to her contacts, scrolling. Next, she checked the navigation program and pulled up Sabrina's favorites. There were a lot of them.

She caught movement and glanced at the glass doors. Sabrina exited, gripping another bag. Emily closed the nav app and returned to the Spotify app, then drove to the front entrance where Sabrina waited under the portico.

Unsure what her role was, having morphed from lunch date to employee, Emily exited the running car to open Sabrina's door. Her client extended the bag and then swept into the seat, accustomed to this sort of service.

Emily stashed the bag with the other one and returned to the driver's seat.

Once inside, she felt a cold flash of panic as she realized she'd let Sabrina into a running car while she was outside, stowing shopping bags. Rosalind's warning popped into her mind. Would Sabrina take off in her own running SUV?

Emily wiped her palm over her face, pressing down the disquiet. Nothing had happened. They were okay.

Then she noticed Sabrina craning to look past her toward the store entrance.

"He's back again."

"Who?"

FIFTEEN

Mrs. Roth peered out the windshield at a man who had paused on the sidewalk to consult his phone. She aimed a polished nail in his direction.

"That guy. He's been watching me. Avery's husband." Her voice was a harsh, conspiratorial whisper, as if she were simultaneously agitated and afraid to be overheard in the closed cab of the SUV.

Emily recognized the name Avery from the image of the gravestone but did not think she needed to reveal that to Sabrina.

"Who?" asked Emily, following the direction of Sabrina's fixed attention. The guy was tall, with a precision haircut, long and highlighted on the top and shaved to stubble at the back. He wore a short-sleeved navy polo shirt, open at the collar, gray slim-fit chinos, and stylish canvas loafers. He dragged his designer shades down a narrow nose and peered over them at his cellphone. To Emily, he looked about as dangerous as a baby seal.

"The woman I killed. Her family has been watching me."

This appeared to be Emily's first encounter with Mrs.

Roth's delusional thinking. But Avery was the name on the headstone on the sketch she'd found in Sabrina's studio. Could she be right?

"Look at his car. Government plates. Explain that, why don't you?"

Emily looked in the direction Sabrina pointed, to an older model Cadillac, faded with a patchy hood. The plates were one of several dozen choices available from the Florida DMV for an additional cost. This vehicle's plates were red, white, and blue and below the American flag were the words: "Florida Salutes Veterans."

Emily could see no connection between the man by the entrance and the vehicle parked across in the handicapped spot Sabrina indicated. But she did know the name Avery. And if Sabrina was correct, this was the name of the woman killed by Sabrina's car. But Mrs. Roth had not been in the driver's seat.

Dr. Roth's explanation of the cause for his wife's issues seemed more believable.

Organic delusional syndrome. Emily had checked her medical texts and searched online for additional information. Then she'd looked it up in Dr. Roth's manual of mental disorders. The organic part meant Sabrina's issues did not stem from alcohol or drug abuse.

The question was, did Avery's husband follow her or was she having one of those delusions now?

"We'd better hurry on home then."

"Yes. We have to go."

Emily followed the route she knew but Sabrina objected.

"Not that way. Keep going. Owner's entrance."

She did as she was told and came to a similar gate, minus the guardhouse.

"How will we get in?"

Sabrina pointed to a small sticker, a barcode, affixed to the lower left corner of the windshield.

At their approach, the gate opened.

"Anyone can go out this way. Even you. But only owners can get in."

They rolled past mature bougainvillea bushes, awash with bright orange blossoms cascading to the ground. Next, they circled a large pond where white swans sat on the lawn at the water's edge.

En route, the phone rang. The touchscreen on the dashboard reported it was Henry.

Sabrina tapped the large screen.

"Hello, darling," she said.

"Are you in the car?"

"Yes, nearly home."

"How was Lilly's?"

"Evangeline's," she corrected. "And Abigail stood me up last minute. Courtney is sick but she has help. It's just, I don't know. Rude."

Sabrina made no mention of the man she had believed was following her. That was odd, Emily thought. Had she forgotten?

"You went alone?" he sounded concerned.

"Emily joined me. You're on speaker."

"Hello, Emily. Did you enjoy lunch?"

Everything but the company, she thought. "It was wonderful."

"Lucky you. That place is swank."

"Very."

"All right. I'll see you at home, Bree. I have an intake and will be a bit late. Is that okay with you Emily?"

Sabrina whined her disappointment.

"Yes, sir. Just fine."

"Do be quick. Reservations tonight," reminded Sabrina.

Emily didn't think she'd ever in her life been out for both lunch and dinner on the same day.

"I'll make it in time."

Back at the Roths' home, their private gate swept away at their approach. Emily paused before the main entrance for her passenger to disembark. Sabrina marched toward the front door, leaving Emily to park the car in the garage, collect the bags, and come in through the back door. She noted, as she pulled into the parking spot, that Rosalind's car was gone.

Inside the kitchen, she was greeted with an unfamiliar beeping.

Next came the repeated insistent doorbell chime, echoing through the house.

Had someone else followed them through the gate?

She hurried to the door, surprised to find Mrs. Roth there.

"I don't have my keys and she locked me out," said Sabrina, red-faced as she swept inside. "And she armed the system." Sabrina held out the phone as proof.

"I don't understand." Emily had never lived in a place with a security system that extended past a baseball bat near the bed.

Sabrina rolled her eyes.

"Rosalind armed the system, and you have my house keys."

Emily stared, confused. Sabrina extended her hand for the keys. Emily reached for them and then stopped, remembering Rosalind's warning.

"Well, we're inside now."

Sabrina's mouth hardened and her nostrils flared, but she dropped her hand.

"What's the beeping?"

Mrs. Roth pointed upward. "Ninety seconds and the alarm... Never mind." She retrieved her phone and began tapping. The beeping ceased as her phone rang.

"Yes, it's Mrs. Roth. Yes, I tripped it. It's Julian."

What was Julian, Emily wondered. Or rather, why was her twin's name necessary information to convey?

Mrs. Roth continued speaking to the alarm company representative, her voice growing more assured and less frantic by the second.

"Thank you. No, not necessary. Thank you for checking." She disconnected and then took another call. "I'm fine. Rosalind set the alarm." A pause. "Please speak to her about it." Another pause. "I just got off the phone with them. All right. No, I'm fine." She pressed a finger to her opposite ear. "Yes, see you soon. Love you, too."

Emily looked at the key fob in her hand. The alarm fob was there as well. On. Off. And a red button that tripped a panic alarm. She shoved the keys back in her pocket.

Sabrina tucked her phone away and let her designer bag slip to the floor beside the alarm control pad. Then she pushed the button to close the private gate. Sabrina pointed at the garment bag of clothing Emily carried.

"Put those things in my closet and send my sweater and scarf to the dry cleaner. I'm going to my studio. Bring me some water." She headed down the hall to her workspace.

Emily followed as far as the kitchen, dragged on a pair of gloves, and carried a bottle of water to Mrs. Roth.

Sabrina hunched over her drafting table furiously scratching at the paper with a nub of a pencil. She glanced up. "There you are."

"How is it going?" She placed the unopened bottle of water on the coaster on Sabrina's workspace. If it was sealed, she generally accepted the drink.

"Did you put away my purchases?"

"Not yet."

She lowered the bottle and quirked a brow.

"Well, I don't need you now. Go unpack them."

"Mind if I sit in your studio afterwards? Keep you company?"

Sabrina paused and gave her a long cool stare. "We aren't

suddenly friends because we shared a meal, Emily. You were a substitute, and a poor one."

"I'm sorry."

"I don't like people watching me work."

"I could sit outside the door."

"Like a proper little jailor. Are you one of them?"

It was as if entering the house had flipped some kind of switch. She'd been polite and conversational at the restaurant and rude to the help, and now, back at her home, Emily was again the underling.

"You know what, let me get your new things taken care of."

"Wear a different pair of gloves."

"Yes, ma'am."

Emily withdrew, pausing in the foyer to scoop up Sabrina's purse and shopping bags, then headed to the main bedroom. There she busied herself unpacking the new purchases. The sweater and lovely scarf she had borrowed went in one of the dry cleaning bags.

The smaller bag held a lipstick called Flamingo in a black and orange box, and a red lipstick in a gold case. They cost fifty-eight dollars each. Emily placed the small white bottle of hydrating serum, which cost over three hundred, in the bathroom drawer beside two identical unopened ones and tucked the makeup in a different drawer on her side of the bathroom cabinets that held both open and sealed products. In the second bag, she unwrapped silver pumps that cost more than Emily would make this week.

Rich people know the cost of everything and the value of nothing, her mother had told her. Emily put the shoes on a shelf with the other silver shoes.

Then she returned to the bathroom to have another look at the lock on Dr. Roth's side of the cabinets. She tried a nail file in the keyhole but did not manage to get it open.

A check on Sabrina found her sitting on the overstuffed chair in her studio, head back and eyes closed.

"How are you doing?" she asked from the doorway.

"I feel like my head is wrapped in cotton," she said. Her eyes remained closed. "My ears are ringing. Can you hear it? It goes eeeeee."

"Could be one of the noon medications," Emily said.

"It should help. He said so. But it doesn't. I just feel weird. Stoned, you know? Like my muscles ache and simultaneously are melting. It's terrible."

"I'm sorry."

"They've been pumping me full of drugs since I was a kid."

Emily was shocked. Then she wondered if she could accept this as the truth and decided she just didn't know.

"Didn't help much then, either."

"What happens if you stop taking them?"

Sabrina waved a dismissive hand. "I get... It's bad. I wreck things."

Was this one of the organic delusions or was this real? Emily had no way to judge. Getting answers was proving harder than she'd anticipated.

"What kind of things?"

Sabrina got a faraway look in her eyes and her expression morphed to regret. But she didn't answer.

"Mrs. Roth, I'm trying to understand. If you did something bad, and you have delusions, then you aren't responsible."

"I *am* responsible."

"Are you?"

Sabrina shrugged and forced herself up, cradling her head in her hands.

"Not according to Henry or the police. To them, I'm not responsible for anything."

Emily took a step into the room, wondering what to do.

"I can't draw when I'm a zombie."

"You're not a zombie."

"My tongue feels funny. What if it's just too much again? What if it gets worse?"

"What?"

Sabrina straightened, drumming her fingers on her knees. "I need to go somewhere. I need my keys."

A shiver danced up Emily's arms at this. The entire conversation was like speaking to someone who was sleepwalking.

"I can't give you your keys."

"I need them. Just for a little while. I can't think of anything else."

"Anything but what?"

Sabrina snorted and glared at Emily, like a feral cat noticing another feline encroaching on her territory. "I'm not telling you."

"You can."

There was a long pause as she stared out the window at the blue sky. When she spoke, her words were quiet, as if only for herself.

"Do I believe my memory or what he tells me?"

* * *

Emily left Sabrina and returned the key fob to the lockbox, double-checking the lock.

In the kitchen, she poured herself a glass of water from the dispenser in the refrigerator, drank it, and then washed and dried the glass.

Sabrina had been doing so well. She seemed much more alert and functional over the last week, then she had this little backslide. Trying to get her keys and seeing people following her.

She'd have to tell Dr. Roth.

Should she share with Rosalind about Sabrina demanding

her keys? The cleaner and she were just starting to develop a relationship.

In time, they might be friends.

This week, Sabrina's pattern had been churlish behavior and cutting sarcasm on Emily's arrival, increasingly coherent after Henry left, apparently normal as the morning progressed into the afternoon. Here she displayed an even temper while she was busy with various appointments, with occasional cruel remarks toward Emily. In the late afternoon, after returning from various outings, and perhaps when the medication was fully working, and Henry's return approached, Sabrina grew increasingly agitated and restless, with more drumming and obsessive behavior, like her scribbled drawings. Henry surely saw the worst parts of Sabrina's day. How she behaved in the evening and overnight, Emily did not yet know.

Emily glanced at the security camera mounted in the corner of the kitchen, remembering the triggered entrance alarm. That beeping had been disconcerting.

She decided to do a little research on her phone on the Roths' brand of security system, watching several videos on installation and operation with her ear buds. The *Away* setting meant the system was fully armed, the cameras all recorded any movement, and any trigger, glass break, motion, entry sensor, tripped the alarm and the beeping began. Owners had ninety seconds to disarm with the fob, phone, or keypad. After ninety seconds the siren sounded, and the owner was contacted. At this juncture, Sabrina would have had to give her secret word to confirm her identity and that she was safe. The company then refrained from calling law enforcement. If the owner did not disarm the system in the allotted time, failed to give the safe word, or was unreachable, police were called.

Emily thought back to what Sabrina had said on the phone.

The only word that was out of context was *Julian*. Was her

twin brother's name really her safe word? That discovery gave her a chill.

Dr. Roth said all his wife's problems began with her twin's death and that her mother had blamed Sabrina. It was hard not to feel sorry for this cold, snappish woman who had suffered mental anguish as a little girl.

Returning to the alarm company's FAQs, Emily discovered that all the cameras were shuttered, for privacy, unless an owner accessed them remotely or an alarm was tripped. Then the camera provided a live view online or could record activity. The exception was the doorbell camera which was never shuttered and recorded all movement always. Red lights indicated that the camera was on "live view." According to Sabrina, Dr. Roth used that function a lot.

Rosalind had armed the system before leaving. Of course she had.

It would have been irresponsible not to. And Emily had not known to press the off button on the alarm fob before entering from the laundry room to kitchen.

The holes in their system were obvious. Since there was no entry sensor between the garage door and the one leading to the kitchen, any intruder could enter, jimmy the lockbox, and deactivate the alarm with the fob, open the gate with the button in the foyer, and steal the cars, leaving the Roths with an empty garage and a doorbell recording of the theft.

It didn't matter. She had not been hired to analyze their home security system, so she kept her observations to herself.

Emily returned to her research project, heading to Dr. Roth's study. The red light of the camera remained off, so she scanned through Dr. Roth's reference book on Sabrina's list of prescription medications. The book had the advantage of leaving no digital trail and still giving her a very good idea of all the drugs Sabrina ingested daily and what they might be doing. Every one of the drugs before her seemed to be useful for a person with delusions, agitation, or depression. One listed its main indication was in the treatment of schizophrenia.

Sabrina's claim that she'd killed Avery and that the woman's husband was watching her sounded like delusional thinking. And schizophrenia could cause delusions.

Was Sabrina schizophrenic?

SIXTEEN

Emily did report Sabrina's paranoia outside the department store to Dr. Roth and that she'd expressed a desire to have her keys back because she needed to go somewhere.

The next day, Sabrina was back to being a mess, falling asleep sitting up and spacy for much of the day. She'd missed her Wednesday golf league because she couldn't even dress herself.

Whatever he was giving her now, was kicking her butt. Emily felt partly responsible, because it was her observation that had caused him to up her dosage again.

At lunch, Emily set out the medications as always and Sabrina just stared morosely at the collection of gel caps, capsules, and odd-shaped pills. Then she began to cry.

Emily felt the first real pangs of guilt over what she was doing here. This wasn't right.

"Mrs. Roth?"

"I can't take them."

"But you have to."

"They don't help. Just numb everything, cloud it. But oh, God, it's still right there. It never goes away. I know someone is following me. He won't believe me." Sabrina used the fingertips of both hands to wipe away the tears streaming from the corners of her eyes.

What was there to say? No one believed her but that didn't make her believe it any less.

"Make me seem crazy. It's not crazy to want things." She pushed the ornate little rosewood dish away.

What kind of things, Emily wondered, but focused on calming Sabrina.

A nagging part of her wondered what this woman would be like without the chemicals blasting around in her brain.

"Please take them."

"No," Sabrina said.

Emily would not try to force her or trick her into taking them. But she made a mental note to tell Dr. Roth about this refusal to take her medication. It felt wrong, like tattling, but she was Sabrina's healthcare provider, and her husband was her treating physician. The situation raised some red flags on its own. Many professional organizations discouraged physicians from treating their direct family except in the case of emergencies or sudden illness. But Emily knew that it was not illegal here in Florida.

No one had asked her opinion, but she thought a husband was too close to maintain objectivity when treating his wife.

"I'll have to tell your husband."

"I don't care." Sabrina glared at Emily, her mouth set in a stubborn line, lips pursed. "You don't believe me, either. Do you?"

"About the medicine making you crazy? I'm not sure. But if you're unhappy, couldn't you just leave him?"

Sabrina stilled.

Emily's skin prickled as she realized she'd overstepped. They were not friends. Emily was the Roths' employee. She felt sorry for Sabrina, but it was not her place to advise her. She knew it, but couldn't seem to stop herself.

"I'm sorry. It's not my business."

Sabrina did not seem to have heard her.

Her voice was now dreamy and distant. "My father picked him for me. He made me promise."

Emily frowned at this revelation. Her father had picked Henry Roth? That by itself was so strange. Why would he do that? Also, why would Sabrina agree?

"But your father is gone. Isn't he?"

"Are you seriously suggesting I leave Henry?"

This could backfire on her like a live round exploding in the chamber. Emily cautioned herself to do an about-face.

"No. Absolutely not. Though, you have wealth. You're smart, attractive, and your attorneys could help you. If you need help, I mean. And if you want some medical assistance, they could arrange it."

Emily squeezed her hands together, entwining her fingers and twisting as if intent on removing one. If this conversation was repeated to Dr. Roth, she was getting fired. But her first responsibility was not to him.

"That's not the deal."

"What deal?"

Sabrina was shaking her head, slowly back and forth, again and again.

"He's poisoning me."

"Dr. Roth?" That was a serious accusation.

Emily weighed the possibility of delusional thinking against the possibility that this was really happening. That conflict-of-interest problem rose up again. She had only Dr. Roth's word that Sabrina had delusional thinking. This could all be a lie and the medication was prescribed to... what? Make his wife appear mentally ill? Keep her from leaving him? Allow him access to her wealth?

Or everything he told her might be true.

Which?

"If you think that, you should call the police, or if you think he's tampering with your medication."

She snorted. "They won't believe me. No one believes me. He's seen to that."

Emily admitted to herself that this was true. Everything Sabrina said was suspect, if only because of the heavy doses of mind-altering chemicals now in her system.

"Mrs. Roth, if you feel threatened, you need to go to the police."

"You don't get it. My word is worthless. And without him, they'd find out. Eventually, they would because I can't do what he does." Her eyes were wild now and her breathing came in fast shallow gulps.

"Find out what?"

In answer, Sabrina pinched her lips tight and shook her head.

"What do you mean you can't do what he does?"

"He keeps me safe. And if I leave, he'll tell them. He said so. We have an arrangement. An old one. I stay. He stays. I... Well, he helps me through."

"Through what?"

"My problems." Her face ticked, a momentary spasm that made her bunch up her lips and grimace. "I can't stand this. But if I call, they'll arrest me. Not him."

"Why would they arrest you?"

That made Sabrina laugh. It wasn't a sound of mirth. It was a crazy, hysterical kind of sound that set Emily's teeth on edge.

"Because I killed Julian. My mother said so."

It seemed again as if Dr. Roth was the one who should be asking for a divorce. This woman was a lot.

"I'm not leaving him. And he's never leaving me. I'm

worried. If... if it gets out again, I mean, eventually they'll figure it out. Come after me. I can't hide forever."

"Avery's husband? Is that who you mean?"

In answer, Sabrina tucked her fingertips into her mouth and began gnawing.

This conversation was slipping away from Emily. Trying to understand was like trying to build a sandcastle in dry sand. The element holding the structure in place was absent. Her emotions tumbled and her stomach contracted to a hot, tight ball as she grappled with what to do. She knew what she wanted to say, but the overstep and the possible repercussions both immobilized her. After several deep breaths, she spoke in a quiet, tentative voice.

"Mrs. Roth, do you think, maybe, your husband is, perhaps, overmedicating you?"

Sabrina's eyes went wide.

"He's trying to help me. Keep me safe. It's what my father wanted. What he asked him to do."

"Of course. Yes, of course he is."

Sabrina's eyes were shifting from side to side. She lifted the drawing and tore it into two pieces.

"He can't stop me. He's trying. Almost feel sorry for..."

Emily thought of the skiers on the television who started an avalanche with just a little shovel full of snow. The slide engaged the rest and soon the entire mountain was tumbling downhill.

Had she just done the same thing to Mrs. Roth?

At first, Emily believed Dr. Roth was the victim, a man to be pitied for his troubled wife. But what if she had this all wrong? Mentally abused by her mother after her brother's death and treated for mental illness from an early age, perhaps Sabrina was the real victim.

Perhaps Dr. Roth was the one responsible here.

Was Dr. Roth doing his best to help his troubled spouse or was he just controlling her for his own benefit?

He was either a very devoted husband or an unscrupulous one.

Emily needed to figure out which.

SEVENTEEN

Emily worried about Sabrina over the weekend. She wondered if Mrs. Roth was all right alone in that big house with only her husband and her medications. When Dr. Roth checked in, Emily reported only that she'd been sad about her part in her brother's death and left the rest of her meltdown to herself.

By Monday, July 3rd, Sabrina seemed to be calm but too sedated to enjoy the pool, do any pointless shopping, or work in her studio, which Emily found upsetting.

Sabrina's confused outburst, first alleging her husband was harming her and then protecting her, still bewildered Emily. Was that all just the gibberish of a confused mind?

This entire puzzle was turning out to be more challenging than she'd expected. Why had she thought discovering if Mrs. Roth was competent would be easy?

* * *

Emily was off on Tuesday for the Fourth of July holiday. After sunset, she and Jennell sat on a blanket, lakeside, doused in bug spray and watching the fireworks with a few friends from the hotel. They'd drunk too much wine but wisely refused to take the party to the pub afterwards because they both needed to be up early on Wednesday for work.

They stopped for fast food and now the Honda's interior smelled like the residue from the sparklers they'd lit mixed with fried food. Traffic leaving the lake was heavy and they inched along in a sea of flashing brake lights, slowly munching on salty fries, still crisp and delicious.

The pressure of her concerns weighed on Emily. She wanted this job, was fascinated by every detail of the Roths' lives, but Sabrina's increasing lethargy couldn't be overlooked much longer.

Finally, she voiced her concerns, eyes on the pimped-out pickup with the turquoise undercarriage lights trying to force its way into the left lane.

"Lately, she's more unconscious than sleeping," she told Jennell.

"Maybe that's why their last nurse quit," said her roommate, flicking on her blinker and nosing into the lane to their right.

"I don't think she quit because Mrs. Roth said she hoped she got what she deserved, and Dr. Roth said only that they hadn't expected to 'lose' her."

"Well, she didn't wander off," said Jennell, waving to the driver who left her room to merge.

Emily said nothing.

"Can you track down the last nurse?"

"I'm sure I can."

Jennell lifted a fry and used it to orchestrate her next idea. "Or maybe get her tested or something?"

"I can't just walk her into an urgent care center and ask them to draw blood."

"Why not? You've got the keys."

"I'd get fired."

"Save you from quitting," said Jennell. "Otherwise, she's going to OD and they'll haul your ass into custody."

Emily swallowed her dread at that possibility. Whatever she did, she needed to do it soon.

"Should I confront him?"

This caused Jennell to whip her head in Emily's direction.

"You did not say that." She harrumphed. "You never go at people like that from the front!"

* * *

The day after the Fourth, a late cold front paired with an easterly breeze swept away the oppressive humidity. Taking Sabrina to her golf league was a pleasure when the air was so crisp and the birds all singing cheerfully in the trees. Emily sat on a bench watching the members practicing their putting before setting out on the course.

Just before lunch, Sabrina's group returned to the clubhouse and Emily returned to the car. Mrs. Roth preferred her out of sight until she was ready to leave.

The text arrived twenty minutes later, and she picked up Sabrina, who ordered her home and off they went.

As always, Emily dropped her at the door and then swung into the garage. Sabrina headed off to shower and change and Emily prepared her lunch.

Lately, Sabrina ate alone in the dining room, sometimes with a sketchbook beside her.

She'd been working at the Roths' for nearly a month and Sabrina had begun slowly to rely on her. She wasn't sure if she trusted her enough to listen to any more of Emily's theories or suspicions. What she needed, what they both needed, was proof that Sabrina was correctly diagnosed and that her medications were appropriate for her condition.

If she pressed her theories, Emily would have to be very

lucky for Sabrina not to reveal Emily's suspicions to her husband this time. Jennell was right about avoiding confrontations with Dr. Roth. But confronting Sabrina could inadvertently lead there.

If push came to shove, Emily might rely on his wife's unreliable memory and her delusions as an out. Just deny anything Sabrina said and blame it on her troubled mind. That sword cut both ways, as Mrs. Roth had pointed out. And her willingness to go there made her ashamed.

Today, she made Sabrina a fruit parfait with Greek yogurt and fresh blueberries with a balsamic raspberry reduction for lunch. Since starting here, she'd stepped up her game, visiting gourmet grocery stores and searching online recipes that might tempt Sabrina. And she knew that after golf, Sabrina preferred something light.

Finally, she tapped out the growing number of tablets, capsules, and pills into the only acceptable container.

Not knowing where Sabrina would like her lunch, she waited in the kitchen for her return.

She arrived in a high-necked, body-conforming floral sheath dress covered with baby-blue seashells and tied with a matching fabric belt at the waist.

"Mrs. Roth, would you like your lunch on the lanai, dining room, or your studio?"

"Kitchen will be fine."

Emily paused at this. Sabrina did not eat in the kitchen. The kitchen was for her morning coffee, but lunch and dinner were elsewhere.

Sabrina sat at the breakfast table and Emily presented her lunch to no comment.

When she finished, she called Emily to clear. But today, when Emily removed the plates and silverware, Sabrina asked a question.

"I thought about what you said, about overmedicating. How would I go about checking on that?"

Emily straightened, trying to decide what to say and knowing that the conversation could backfire right in her face.

"Well?" said Sabrina, casting her an impatient look.

Apparently, she waited a little too long. She swallowed the tight lump in her throat down far enough to allow her to speak. If Sabrina was the victim here, it was her job to help her.

"You could go see a different doctor," she suggested, the unnatural high pitch of her tone belying her attempts to seem calm. "Have some blood work drawn. Review your prescriptions."

"I mean, what could I do right now?"

"Mrs. Roth, do you ever go to a general practitioner?"

"No. Henry does my checkups."

She didn't like the sound of that. It smacked of conflict of interest or something worse.

"So, he's the only physician you ever see?"

This question caused Mrs. Roth to glower at Emily.

"Yes. But I did go to the ER recently." Sabrina tapped the eraser of her pencil on the table, thinking. "When was that? March, after... That was the most recent."

"Lakeland or General?"

"Here in town. I'd taken the keys. Henry gave me something to calm me down. But then I couldn't wake up."

She wanted to ask whose keys. Was that the time Rosalind mentioned? Instead of asking, she stuck to the topic at hand. Those test results.

"Did they run any tests in the ER?" She cocked her head, waiting. This was data, and data was useful in proving wrongdoing.

"I think so. They took blood."

"Did you see the results?"

"Henry saw them. Said they were fine. Adjusted something. I don't know."

Oh, did he? Emily pressed her mouth tight, then tried for a calm she did not feel.

When she spoke, her tranquil façade had evaporated like morning mist leaving only exasperated annoyance. "*You're* the patient. You're entitled to the results."

She wanted to get a look at those results, but more than that, she wanted Sabrina to want to see them.

Emily withdrew to retrieve a bottle of water and the carved wooden dish, setting it on the table before Sabrina. They both stared in silence at the colorful collection of pills.

Finally, Sabrina said, "Get my laptop."

Emily retrieved her computer and placed it before her. When she returned, the medication was gone and she realized her mistake. She had no idea if Sabrina had taken any of it.

Sabrina opened the laptop and tapped in a numerical password.

"How do I see my blood work?"

"From the hospital? You'd need to go to your patient portal."

Sabrina pushed the laptop to her left. "Show me."

Her charge was most clearheaded in the morning as the regime of medications began to wane and before the noon round sent her back into a semiconscious stupor.

Emily knelt beside Sabrina and navigated to the hospital site, the patient portal, and the registration page.

Sabrina provided the details and Emily typed and entered data until they gained access.

"There it is. Lab work." Emily pointed.

Sabrina drew the laptop before her and began clicking her way into the reports.

"That's the one." Emily tapped the screen, opening the lab results and scanning for anything out of order.

"There are a lot of them, aren't there?"

"But most of these are old. This one would be that ER visit. March 2023. That's four months ago."

Sabrina leaned in, peered at the screen for a while, and then threw up her hands.

"Well, that's all gibberish."

"Let's have a look." Emily studied the report. "This up here is just patient ID, age and so forth. It says the specimen was blood. See there." She pointed. "Down here are the tests on the left and the results and then the reasonable limits. So, for this, hemoglobin, you had a 12.6 and the normal range is twelve to fifteen."

"That's fine."

"Yes. But down here are the positive findings."

Sabrina rolled her index finger in a circle indicating Emily was losing her limited attention.

"It says 'Positive findings for the following compounds.' That means these were in your blood."

"I know what positive means, Emily."

Emily read her the list as Sabrina Roth nodded to each one.

"That's all?" asked Sabrina.

"Yes. What were you expecting?"

"Narcotics. I told him I'd never take them. He promised. But I know. I just know..." Sabrina rubbed both temples with the pads of her fingers.

"Know what?

"He's putting something else in there."

Emily gave a half shrug. "Not according to this."

"Well, it's wrong, is all. I need a new test."

Emily pressed down the worry over this obvious disconnect between what was and what Mrs. Roth alleged. According to her husband, no amount of arguing would change a belief and no amount of evidence.

"I don't think that will change the results."

Now she watched Sabrina to see her reaction. Was she even cognizant enough to understand what was happening to her?

"It must be the wrong—" She pounded her fist on the table. "He's changing them. I need to test somewhere they don't know me or him. And he promised me. No more narcotics. They're addictive! They're like poison."

Emily gasped, one hand pressed to her chest. She'd never heard Sabrina use this shrieking hysterical tone.

"He promised you?"

"Yes! He swore he'd never prescribe them. The liar!"

At this reaction, Emily sank back, wary as a stray cat, eyeing a potential threat. Her heart was thumping, and she was alarmed at the scarlet color of Sabrina's face. What was the right thing to do?

"But there are no narcotics showing." Why was she still trying reason, rationalizing against the irrational? One thing was certain. . . well, two. Sabrina hated the idea of taking narcotics and she did not trust her husband.

"They're in there!" Sabrina snapped. She drummed her manicured fingers on the tabletop, then pointed at the screen. "Print that!"

Emily wanted to do what was right. But she also needed to do that without putting herself in the middle of a potentially violent domestic dispute. And she certainly wasn't going to admit to Dr. Roth that she'd mentioned that Sabrina could leave him.

"Are you going to confront him?" Emily needed to know. To prepare herself for the possible dangerous or violent reaction of Dr. Roth once he discovered that his wife was irrationally certain he was giving her narcotics despite evidence to the contrary.

"That's not how this works." Sabrina's voice had dropped and turned icy. "Henry is a hound. I'm a fox."

"What does that mean?"

"It means don't tell Henry."

Relief at the temporary reprieve lasted only a heartbeat. Emily had to tell Henry because he was not just her husband, he was her attending physician and Mrs. Roth was becoming irrational.

Emily already dreaded the conversation and began to worry about Mrs. Roth's future plans.

When Dr. Roth returned, Emily asked him to walk her out. He lifted a brow in speculation and then nodded, trailing behind her as far as the garage. She turned, facing him and told him about his wife's beliefs, their conversation, and the examination of her blood tests. All the while his face grew redder and redder. Finally, she finished and waited for his reply.

EIGHTEEN

Thursday morning, Emily left for work as the rain poured down in gray sheets. She tossed a poncho over herself and her bag and dashed into the deluge, carrying more than a little water into her car with her. It was not until she was underway that she remembered her wipers were old, cracked, and missed a three-inch arching band on each pass. En route, the rain ran off the poncho and filled the floor mats.

The retaining ponds and lake were brimming, and a group of mallard ducks swam happily in the full ditch between the east and west lanes of traffic.

There was just nothing to compare with the volume of water dumped by a summer thunderstorm in Florida. The rain fell in sheets so heavily that the windshield wipers could no longer clear the water. She slowed, hunching over the wheel, peering at the blurry abstraction beyond the windshield and relying on the flash of brake lights before her as her guide.

The person at the guard booth took pity on her and did not ask for her license. Before she reached the Roths', the rain stopped as if someone had flicked off a tap, and sunshine poured down. Steam rose from the road and ducks bobbed happily in newly formed waterways.

She pulled into the driveway a few minutes later, but instead of taking the roundabout, she stayed left and parked on the wide swath of paver stones near the garage side door.

Emily switched off the engine and took several deep breaths, reluctant to encounter Dr. Roth again after yesterday's dressing down. He had not taken the news well that his wife wanted her blood test results or that Emily had "encouraged her" by retrieving her report. She'd left off her remarks about Sabrina's option to leave her husband and Mrs. Roth's tangent about her belief that the police would arrest her for the death of her twin, Julian. The first she'd omitted because she feared that comment would get her fired, and as to the second, he'd already told her she felt responsible for her brother's accidental drowning.

"It's delusional thinking. I explained this to you," he had said, speaking with a strained tone of frustration combined with a condescension she found insulting. "No amount of rational argument or physical evidence will change her mind. And the more you try, the more she obsesses on her misbeliefs. You can't change it. So, stop trying."

She apologized. He'd repeated that his wife's OCD and paranoia made her linger on such thoughts. In illustration, he'd reminded her that his wife was convinced that bad people were following her and added that Sabrina often alleged that wait staff and servers were spitting in her food. This new conviction that he was slipping dangerous drugs into her prescriptions was just more of the same.

"Just don't encourage her. Repeat back what she believes. Tell her the truth and move on."

Easier said than done. The obsessive part of his wife's condition made it impossible really for Sabrina to move on. Her paranoia was a huge Achilles' heel.

Emily left the safe, dry interior of her vehicle and dashed through the rain. The side entrance was unlocked, as usual. Once out of the torrent, she wiped the water off her face, dropped the backpack, and dragged off the sopping poncho. She hung the dripping plastic garment on a rake handle and retrieved a damp towel from her bag, thankful she'd packed it today.

She dried off and finger-combed her wet hair, then coiled it into a bun and secured it tight, but the hem of her skirt was soaked. Before leaving the garage, she collected the car keys, unsure if Sabrina would want to venture out for her appointment if it was pouring. She locked the box and left her bag near the door and headed up the five steps to the laundry room, hesitating inside.

Had Dr. Roth spoken to Sabrina about her blood work or the prescriptions? Had Sabrina moved on or was she still fixated on this fear? Emily hated not knowing what she was walking into, but she summoned her courage, twisted the knob, and called a greeting as she entered.

Dr. Roth answered with "Good morning."

She paused in the entrance to the kitchen and sucked in a breath. She'd been gone less than a day but the room was a disaster of dirty dishes, garbage on surfaces, and open food containers. Coffee grounds littered the floor. A spill or something worse, she wondered.

She spotted him chugging coffee while standing at the sink as if there was nothing disturbing about his surroundings. Today, he wore a gray pin-striped suit, black shoes, and a welcoming smile, the one glimmering sign of order in this chaos.

He toasted her with his mug.

"There she is. Right on time. No doorbell alert."

"I didn't use the roundabout. Just pulled along the side of the house."

"Ah, well, no matter. The gatehouse sent a text." He waved

his phone and then slipped it into his front pocket. "And our gate, of course. Can't sneak up on us."

Emily held her forced smile. If he noticed the water soaking her collar or dripping from her hair down her face, he said nothing. Rain didn't bother people with garages and covered parking.

"How's she doing?"

He grimaced. "She's up and dressed. Seems improved today despite the gloomy weather."

"Did she mention the blood test results?"

"No. But I brought it up and she feigned ignorance." He shook his head. "If she gets agitated, give my office a call. They'll track me down."

Or he could give her his personal cell number. But she didn't ask.

"Of course. I will," she said.

"Otherwise, she seems more engaged. I think the latest switch is finally showing promise, despite the increased paranoia. Some of those medications take a while for the body to build a threshold."

"I'm glad you're pleased."

"Not pleased, exactly, but satisfied." He gave an up nod, lifting his chin. "She's in there. Dining room."

Emily avoided the coffee grounds and walked in soggy shoes to the archway between the kitchen and formal dining room, trailed by Dr. Roth. The heads of the yellow roses, in the china vase, had begun to bow without opening and petals littered the table. Sabrina sagged as well. Before her the *Sun* lay open and she slowly scribbled on the newsprint, the familiar spiderweb already in evidence. Just moving the pen seemed difficult, as if she pushed something very heavy.

This was an improvement?

"Well, I'm off. See you." He pressed a kiss on Sabrina's dark head. "Dinner out tonight. Okay?"

Sabrina nodded, repeating the name of a restaurant Emily knew of but had never entered.

Henry dropped his empty mug by the coffee maker and headed out the same door Emily had come in through.

She turned back to the table in time to see Sabrina spit a mouthful of medications onto the newspaper.

"What are you doing?" asked Emily.

"I thought about what you said." Sabrina wiped her mouth on her sleeve, then lifted the cloth napkin and wiped her tongue. "About him keeping me here. And my father is gone. He won't even know if I leave Henry. And I *am* smart enough. I can do this on my own."

Emily's swallowed back the dread. She hadn't said any of that. And if Henry thought she had, well, at the very least, Dr. Roth would fire her, and she still didn't know if Sabrina had the conditions he'd alleged or was even capable of making such decisions for herself.

But it seemed it wasn't up to her. This was happening. Her choice now was to help Sabrina or alert Dr. Roth.

Suddenly, she felt the gut-wrenching fear of someone who's discovered she has lost her way. Which direction should she turn? Should she encourage Sabrina or pacify and backtrack?

Which was safer?

Which would give her the answers she sought?

Sabrina's eyes were flashing fire. "I think he is still tampering with my medication."

Spoken like a person with paranoia, Emily thought.

"There's no evidence of that."

Sabrina waved away the observation.

"What will you do?" asked Emily.

"Well, I've stopped taking them and I just acted spacy this morning. Hopefully he won't figure it out. But my mind was never so clear. I can see everything now."

This seemed like a different kind of problem.

Emily had wondered what Sabrina Roth was like off her meds and she was about to find out. She gulped back the apprehension.

What would she do if Dr. Roth discovered Emily knew that his wife was not taking her medications? That was her job. Her most important job.

Keep her safe, keep her medicated, and keep her from driving.

"No more pills. If I don't take it, he can't sedate me."

"He can if he finds out. Or runs blood work or if any of your previous existing difficulties develop."

"They won't. Not for a while anyway. I've done it before."

"You have?" Emily wondered again what Sabrina Roth unmedicated would be like and her curiosity was not entirely benevolent.

"When?"

"March. Before that..." She tapped her chin, thinking. "Around Christmas." She cast Emily a cheerful smile. "All this time, I thought he was protecting me. Well, he's not."

"You don't think you need *any* of your medication?"

"Oh, no. I do need it. But I'm done taking it."

"I don't understand."

"I just don't want to take them anymore. All right?" Sabrina was shouting now. "I need a break. I need... You wouldn't understand."

Emily held a hand over her chest as her heart slammed against her ribs.

"I understand." But she didn't. Not even a little.

Mrs. Roth was no longer lethargic or glassy-eyed. She was alert, agitated, and imposing. Seeing her like this sent a chill of dread through Emily because she understood that there was no way to control a smart, self-aware version of her charge.

"He says your thinking is... confused."

"*I'm* not confused. I know what I've done, and I know they're after me."

That was a giant red flag popping into what had seemed to be a lucid conversation. Sabrina was back to thoughts of the mysterious people she believed were following her.

Paranoid delusions, Dr. Roth called them, and he would say this was a real example.

"Leave me alone. I have to think."

"Should I call your husband?"

"Henry? No way."

"Your daughter?"

"Ha. She hates me. Says I ruined her wedding, which *I* paid for."

This was a revelation. But was it real?

"What about your attorney?"

"Just leave me alone."

She did as Sabrina asked, thrilled to leave the room. The woman scared her. More and more. Were these withdrawal symptoms or was the real Sabrina emerging?

Emily didn't know. But it troubled her.

Gradually, her racing heart decided she was not in mortal peril and quieted back to a normal beat. She still felt slightly nauseous. Confrontation was hard. Draining.

She headed back to the kitchen to tackle the mess while Sabrina sipped a latte and worked the crossword puzzles. When she finished, she headed to her studio and Emily straightened the dining room, gathering up fallen petals, abandoned condiments, breakfast dishes, and the discarded papers. She glanced at the crossword puzzles, finding both complete and the answers all written in pen without a single error.

* * *

After Rosalind had come and gone and noon approached, Emily worried what would happen if Sabrina ceased taking all her prescriptions. It took some persuading, but she convinced

Sabrina to take everything but the capsules, arguing that her husband couldn't easily add anything to the film coated tablets. Mrs. Roth agreed.

"Can't tamper with those," said Sabrina.

That afternoon, Emily tried to stay out of her way, busying herself with laundry, folding, putting clothing and towels away. All the while she worried what would happen when Dr. Roth returned.

Around three o'clock, Emily headed to the studio with one of Sabrina's usual afternoon snacks. This was presented on an ornate plate with a gilded edge. The offering consisted of one of three types of cheese, crackers (always the same brand), prosciutto, walnuts, or smoked almonds, and three figs. She wore her blue latex gloves as she knocked at the studio door.

No answer.

She opened the door and found the room empty. This time she didn't panic, but she patted her pockets to ensure she had her keys and Sabrina's set. Then she hurried to the garage, leaving the plate in the kitchen on her way past.

The lockbox was secure, but she checked it anyway. Dr. Roth's sports car fob was still on its hook. But the contents of her bag had been dumped on the floor. Alarm bells chimed a warning in her mind. Instantly alert, her body hummed, alive and aware of the potential problems this mess might cause.

"Are you looking for the keys?" she asked the bag as she tried to puzzle out what Sabrina wanted. Then she stooped to collect the contents.

She wasn't sure if she was now a nurse or Sabrina's opponent.

When she returned to the kitchen, she found Sabrina at the breakfast counter eating her snack and flipping through a photo album.

Funny, Emily didn't recall seeing anything like that in Sabrina's studio, bookshelves, or closets. Such a personal item would have been kept in a private place. But Emily knew most of their private places as well. Where had it come from?

"God, my skin itches." Sabrina lifted a cracker, topping it with cheese and one half of one walnut.

"Is everything all right?" To Emily, Sabrina seemed enlivened and her emotions chaotic. Something about her frantic little motions, as she prepared each cracker just so, gave Emily the creeps.

"Mrs. Roth, why were you in my bag?"

This caused Sabrina to freeze as if Emily had used a tractor beam. Then she chuckled and returned to her squirrel-like fussing over her crackers. When she met Emily's gaze, her eyes held a cold glitter.

"I wasn't."

Emily waited, thought about challenging her, reminding her that they were the only two in the house and Emily had not upended her own bag. Instead, she broke eye contact, surrendering her challenge and deferring to the lady of the manor.

"I need to look at this."

"Where did you get it?" Emily stepped closer to get a look at the photo album but Sabrina slammed it shut.

"Not for you," she said. "It's private."

Which only made Emily more curious. She'd get a look inside that book eventually. That much was certain. But for now, she deferred again, stepping back.

Sabrina ate her crackers in rapid succession, barely chewing before cramming the next one in her mouth. She spoke with full cheeks, so unlike the elegant woman Emily had dined with last week. This one looked like a half-feral animal.

"I'm finished." Sabrina pointed at the gilded plate. "Take that."

"Yes, ma'am."

Emily hand washed the plate. This one was too old and too

fine to go in the dishwasher. Sabrina told her that it was from her mother's china.

Emily's mother's china consisted of store seconds. When the plates were stacked, you could see a little ripple of the uneven edges. But when they weren't stacked, you could hardly tell.

Sabrina collected the album and left the room, with her bare feet slapping on the stone tile. Emily trailed her back to her studio. There Sabrina sat at her drafting table, studying her album.

"Close the door," she said without looking up.

Emily closed the door. Then she did a quick check of the Roths' bedroom, finding everything in the order she had left it. As an afterthought, she checked his office. The closet was open, and papers and folders littered the rug.

This was troubling. Should she clean them up or leave them?

One more step and Emily saw the large floor safe now stood open.

Emily's internal alarm jangled to life. Certainly Dr. Roth would not like his safe turned upside down. She was now also sure where Sabrina had found the album.

Why lock up a photo album?

Was it some kind of trigger?

Files, folders, and scattered documents littered the plush, cream-colored carpet. Emily set her teeth together. This was an opportunity, a dangerous one. She weighed the risk of getting caught against her need to know more about this couple. She fisted her trembling fingers and accepted the opportunity fate provided, knowing she might never have a chance like this again.

Inside the safe were several boxes, the sort for jewelry and beside one was a ring of small keys.

His bathroom cabinet?

Possibly.

Emily stooped to gather the closest document, a bill of sale for a blue Prius.

Was this for their daughter? She couldn't imagine any daughter of the Roths zipping around town in anything but a status symbol.

Puzzling, she thought.

Emily drew out her phone and snapped a photo, capturing the VIN number.

Who drove that car?

She tried out possibilities, rejecting their daughter and wondered if Dr. Roth had a mistress. You could hardly blame him. But she did. And that belief took the last of the shine off her initial impression of the perfect spouse and silent, suffering husband.

The papers lying all about were too much of a temptation for Emily. She checked each one.

Closer to the wall lay a legal document in a long folder. Having seen her mother's will, she knew what legal documents looked like. They were longer than standard paper and stapled at the top. That's what these were.

She lifted the first and read: *prenuptial agreement*.

The others included the couple's wills, healthcare proxy, and Sabrina's parents' wills. There were folders marked Financial, House, Insurance, Auto. She scanned as she stacked.

Then she sat on the plush carpet and lifted the prenup. Rather than reading, she took out her phone and began photographing each page. She got their wills, prenuptial agreement, and healthcare proxy. Should she photograph their financials? A move like this wouldn't just get her fired. She'd get arrested.

Emily had no business taking these photos, but she did. If Sabrina was a victim here, she needed to get the proof and her gut told her that the answers were scattered on the floor.

"But why won't she leave him? And why won't he leave her?" she whispered to the quiet room. Even the intentionally serene interior design did not quiet her rapid breathing. "What am I doing?" she whispered.

But she knew. She was getting answers to those pesky questions. What was really wrong with Sabrina Roth? What was her husband really up to?

And what was "their deal" that Sabrina mentioned.

Sabrina had admitted she was ready to circumvent her husband and his treatment plan for her. Doubts were such destructive things.

When she'd finished, Emily put everything back in the safe, except the keys, glad she still wore her latex gloves.

She checked on Sabrina, sitting on her studio floor, hunched over the album.

"Everything all right?" Emily asked, her voice tentative as she craned her neck to see something of the mysterious book. This section of the album held newspaper clippings, each mounted on a page.

Sabrina slapped the book closed. "What time is it?"

"A bit after three."

She hugged the album to her chest. "Then I still have time. Tell me when it's four."

Emily, dismissed, remained where she was. She cleared her throat, to regain Sabrina's attention. Mrs. Roth glanced up, waiting, as her nurse rocked uncomfortably from heel to toe.

"Mrs. Roth, about the things from the safe..."

"Put them back. Lock it."

"What about the album?" she asked, certain now that this was what Sabrina had been searching for and still wondering why it had been locked up and what was inside.

She shook her head. "I'm keeping this."

Emily lifted her brows. If she kept it, Emily could later find it. She withdrew.

In the primary bathroom, she tried the smallest key and the lock released. She opened Dr. Roth's top drawer and found ordinary items, like his razor, toothbrush, deodorant, and dental floss. The next drawer had some over-the-counter medications. She tried the last, largest drawer.

"Oh my God," she said, shocked at the contents. "No wonder you're locking this one."

NINETEEN

Back in the kitchen, Emily dragged out a stool and sat, still stunned and off-balance by what she'd found. Everyone had secrets, but Dr. Roth's had the potential to derail his career.

A quick check for Mrs. Roth found her madly pedaling on her husband's exercise bike as if training for the Tour de France.

Emily sat in the living room, facing Mrs. Roth's back and the sparkling blue lake beyond. She opened her phone and then her photos, retrieving the pictures she'd snapped of every document she'd found scattered by Sabrina before the safe. The images were clear, and by zooming in and scrolling side to side, she could read every word, starting with the prenup.

By the time she finished, her ears buzzed and her throat was sand.

"This is unbelievable."

But one thing seemed obvious. Sabrina's father thought she needed looking after. But from what she'd seen in Henry Roth's bathroom, Sabrina's father might have backed the wrong horse.

Regardless of his competence or the wisdom of choosing him, this was proof that Dr. Roth had ample reasons to keep his wife incoherent.

That album was a mystery. Sabrina did not have it with her and had not returned to Henry's study. Emily had looked for it but came up empty. If Sabrina kept the book hidden nearby, on the lanai or vicinity, she might be preventing Emily from searching. Temporarily, at least.

Later on, the guardhouse attendant phoned Emily about a delivery and she waited at the end of the drive, but the box was huge. The contents were right there on the cardboard, wrapped with nylon straps. Another exercise bike. How was she supposed to manage this?

The driver loaded the box onto his dolly and started up the drive. She didn't stop him but ran back through the garage to open the double door. Then she walked him out and closed the gate from the control box.

Back inside, Sabrina was still pedaling away on the old bike. It took some doing to get Sabrina off it. Finally, Emily resorted to reminding Sabrina that she needed to be dressed when Henry came home because he was taking her out for dinner.

"You're all sweaty. You need a shower."

"I'm not done yet."

"He'll be home soon. If he sees you like this, he'll know that you are off your meds."

"I'm taking some of them."

Not the ones for obsessive-compulsive disorder, Emily thought. And clearly not the sedatives. Hyperactive didn't begin to cover it.

Sabrina dismounted and headed for her room. Emily headed for Dr. Roth's safe, to return the small key to its place.

Soon after, the gate alert chimed on Sabrina's abandoned cellphone. Since he was an owner, there was no notice of arrival from the main gate.

A few moments later, as the garage door rolled upward, Sabrina emerged, dressed in an elegant black faux-leather halter top and crop pants with a metallic floral leaf pattern in copper on black. In high heels, Sabrina almost reached Emily's chin and looked stunning in full makeup and a bright red lip.

"Beautiful," said Emily.

"Thank you." Her purse was a crystal clutch loosely gripped in one hand. She gathered her phone and glanced at the screen. "Perfect timing. He's home."

She slipped the phone into her clutch.

The laundry door opened and Dr. Roth appeared, shirt unbuttoned and tie draped around his neck.

He looked at his wife.

"Wow!" His grin was appreciative as he walked forward and leaned in to kiss Sabrina on her powdered cheek. "You look amazing."

"Thank you," she said with a self-satisfied expression as if this adoration was her due.

Emily wondered how long Sabrina could fool him. Eventually, she'd need another plan. But what that might be, she wasn't sure.

"Let me just put this in my office," he said, lifting his shoulder satchel. "And then I'll change. All right?"

He was going to his office. She cast a glance at Sabrina, who was fiddling with her phone, unaware or unconcerned.

"Emily, could you come to my office. I'd like a word."

Emily held her smile but heat flooded her face and the hair on her head tingled. This could not be good and opened a host of possibilities. Did he know about the safe? About her opening his bathroom drawers?

"Of course."

She followed him, pausing as he reached his office and put his satchel in the closet beside the safe. Emily clasped her hands together, sure he knew Sabrina had been in there. She squeezed her stomach tight and struggled to control her erratic breathing.

"You got a package today. A big one. It's in the garage."

"Yes, I know. Listen, I need to speak to you about

something."

Despite the hard lump in her stomach and the heat flooding her face, she managed to look perplexed.

"All right."

"I told you that I didn't want delivery people past the gate."

The delivery he mentioned had been a huge box that she couldn't possibly carry. She'd allowed the driver to wheel it into the garage, where it now sat.

"Oh." How had he...? The doorbell cam, of course. It recorded everything that happened in front of the house.

"I'm so sorry. I couldn't manage it alone."

"Then leave it inside the gate. No delivery people past the gate. I could not have been clearer."

Her eyes widened. This wasn't the way he spoke to her. He explained and instructed and guided. But this was a harsh reprimand delivered in a tone of thinly veiled anger.

Unsettled, she took a step back as she tried to explain. "He just wheeled it to the garage. I didn't ask him."

"I know and I've called the company. That delivery person won't be back."

Did he get a guy fired for doing his job? Was he about to fire her? Emily gaped, unable to think of anything to say.

Why did people like this expect everyone else to follow the rules that they ignored?

"No one past the gate. Do you understand?" Those last three words were delivered with slow emphasis, as if she was too stupid to comprehend. Her shock and alarm were drawing in, contracting into indignation. She snapped her mouth closed and let the resentment pulse through her, knowing she was incapable of pointing out how unreasonable his instructions were. Not if she wanted to keep working here. Instead, she sucked in air through flaring nostrils as he waited, glaring as if she were the stupidest thing alive.

"I do, yes." Emily's eyes burned. She hated being reprimanded. Hated that she cared and that her anger appeared as hot, remorseful tears, when inside the anger burned like a forge furnace.

At least he wasn't wise to the safe—yet. And push come to shove, she knew what he kept in his bathroom cabinet.

She smiled.

"Then I should not have to explain again that you are not to let a flunky, who looks like he's escaped from a circus, inside our home."

She was about to point out that he'd only been in the garage but hesitated.

When you find yourself in a hole, stop digging. Her sister's adage had not made sense when she'd said it. But now it did. Emily kept her mouth closed and her head lowered, staring at the carpet. Then she saw the single silver paper clip she'd missed during cleanup. The panic smothered her humiliation as her heart slammed against her ribs.

"Will this happen again?"

"No, sir," she whispered past the lump growing in her throat like a hot ball of wax.

"I didn't hear you."

Emily sniffed and choked out a reply.

"No, Dr. Roth."

"If it happens again, you will be very sorry."

"It won't."

Because now she knew he was watching her, at least as far as the doorbell camera could see. And he was using the others to check in as well. She recalled the red light on the pool camera and knew that he was. But there was no camera in the garage or any of the bedrooms. She knew because she'd checked.

Her body jangled with the effort of remaining here instead of fleeing the threat before her. Her muscles ached and her head ached. But she stayed rooted to the floor like his personal whipping post, hoping he was done.

She wouldn't tell him about the safe now. Or about that weird photo album or that Sabrina had rifled through her purse and his papers. He'd broken something between them and she doubted he even realized it. But Emily did and she would treat him with the same respect without revealing that she was now a double agent, gathering intelligence, a foreign body living in his home like a virus in his bloodstream.

Emily needed to be aware of that little red camera light popping on while she was working in this terrible house.

The anger seeped through her like poison in a sponge cake, soaking to every molecule. He shouldn't treat people like this. He shouldn't treat her like this or his wife.

How had she ever felt sorry for this man? All this time, she'd thought he was the one burdened by a spouse that didn't deserve him but actually Sabrina had a controlling husband and the impossible living situation. Mrs. Roth needed her help to get away from this calculating man. Then, perhaps, she could move on to face whatever it was that haunted her.

But even after all this time, Emily was still unsure if Mrs. Roth had any understanding of the consequences of her actions. Was she mentally fit or was she incompetent? It was a question Emily needed answered because everything depended on it. If Sabrina was not of sound mind, then this needed to go differently. It was more complicated than opening the door of a birdcage. Domestic birds had no hope of surviving in the wild and a mentally ill woman needed looking after. Once she knew Sabrina's understanding, she'd have a clearer course. Either she could find her the appropriate care or, if she was able to care for herself and understand the consequences of her actions, Emily had other intentions.

After reviewing all the documents she'd photographed, she knew that what Sabrina had said was true. Oddly, her medical proxy had been assigned to an attorney, Gabriel Rottach, who also oversaw the King family trust.

Mrs. Roth was an heiress, and if she was deemed incompetent or institutionalized, her family trust would engage, and as best as Emily could make out, that meant that Dr. Roth would get nothing except his actual income and would assume all debts he incurred over the previous decade. And that took him back to medical school, purchase of this home, and who knew what else.

Sabrina's allegations seemed correct. Henry could not maintain a home that, five years ago, was worth eight million dollars, according to an online realty site.

If Sabrina were institutionalized, he'd lose this lifestyle, this house, and everything else accumulated by the Kings' trust. And if his wife did anything that brought her to the attention of the courts, this was a real possibility. That meant that Dr. Roth had yet another very good reason to keep his wife at home under his care.

"I need to tell you something," Emily said.

His brows rose as he gave her his attention.

"She's not taking anything in a capsule. Refused to take them."

"Afraid I'm adding something?"

Emily nodded, relieved he understood.

"Fine. I'll get them switched to tablets. In the meantime, dissolve the capsules in water or put them in her food."

Emily blinked, pushing back her shock at this. "But that plays into her exact fears. And if she figures that out—"

He cut her off. "Your job is to ensure she takes them. So see that she does not figure it out."

Dr. Roth's phone rang. He glanced at the screen and swore under his breath. Emily smiled. After getting chewed out, she enjoyed seeing him look stressed.

He took the call.

He asked a few medical questions about status and level of agitation. From the snippet she heard, she felt it was not one of

Dr. Roth's patients calling, but the hospital or inpatient facility contacting him with a problem. The voice on the phone was female. When he ended the call, he took a moment to scowl at his phone before tucking it away. Then he turned to her.

"There's a medical emergency at the hospital. Could you stay?"

"Right now? What about dinner reservations?"

"Cancel. You'll have to stay."

First he handed her ass to her and then he issued orders.

He had warned her that this could happen. She'd been so looking forward to getting the heck out of here.

"Well?"

Emily didn't respond.

"If you're upset because I reprimanded you, I can't apologize. I'm very protective of my wife."

Was that true? Or was he just protective of his wife's fortune?

"Of course. I'll stay and cancel your reservations."

"Order in for Sabrina. Get yourself something, too, within reason."

"Thank you."

He nodded, accepting thanks for providing her with a meal, within reason.

"I'll be home as soon as I can, but plan on about ninety minutes." He glanced at his expensive gold watch. "Maybe order me something, too. Let Sabrina pick for me."

"I will."

"Okay. Feed Sabrina. I'll see you later. Good luck."

Why was she going to need luck? And that was when she realized she had never been with Mrs. Roth at night—or without her afternoon medications. She knew only what he reported. That she had not slept, had slept poorly, or was up from four in the morning.

Dr. Roth didn't linger. He was back out the door to the

garage in a flash. A moment later came the sound of his sports car's high-power engine and the garage door rumbling down.

Interesting car to take to the hospital for a medical emergency. He usually drove his sedan.

Suspicions prickled like nettles over her skin.

Was he going where he'd claimed or was he meeting someone?

Again, she weighed the idea of him having an affair. It was possible. His wife could clearly not meet all his needs. It was likely, she decided.

Was she babysitting so he could cheat on his wife?

Emily found Sabrina listening from the opposite side of the living room, in the hallway that led to her bedroom. Could she hear a conversation in his office from here? Her question seemed an answer, of sorts.

"Is he gone?"

"Yes."

She glanced beyond Emily to the empty living room, every pillow in place, the chenille throw blanket artfully draped over the back of one panel of the sectional. Everything in this house looked just perfect. But it wasn't.

Sabrina swept past her, heading for the kitchen, and Emily followed. Once at the large stone island, Mrs. Roth paused.

"He thinks I don't know."

"About what?" Emily had suspicions but that was all.

"He's got another girl. One of his receptionists, I think."

Emily picked up on the reference to "another," as if this was a normal, annoying aspect of their relationship.

"Oh, Mrs. Roth. I'm so sorry."

Sabrina waved a hand. "I used to care. Even did the hiring for his office, for a while. Only hired men or the sort that he wouldn't find attractive. But he just looked elsewhere. *Can't keep the bull in the pasture*—that's what my father would say. It was exhausting."

Sabrina seemed more and more coherent by the day.

"Then I had an epiphany. He needs his outlets, just as I need mine. Can't blame me if he's just as guilty."

Guilty was an interesting choice of words. And Emily was positive Sabrina was not having an affair. So, what was she guilty of exactly?

Unsettled again, Emily frowned, trying to make sense of this new line of thought.

"You don't need to stay with him," Emily said, floating the idea again and watching for Mrs. Roth's reaction.

"Careful now." Sabrina went to the drawer holding the take-out menus and shuffled through them.

"If he's cheating and you feel he might be tampering with your medications, why not leave him?"

"He's not tampering. He is giving me what I need. Just not what I want."

"I don't understand." Every muscle in her body felt tight with the strain of the confrontation with Dr. Roth and now this bewildering conversation with his wife.

"I can't think or feel when I take them. But I need him —afterwards."

Afterwards? That was a strange turn of phrase. The bewilderment changed to disquiet, settling between Emily's shoulder blades.

"After what?"

Sabrina waved away the question like an annoying gnat.

Emily tried a different tact. "You could hire more help. As much as you wanted."

"Some jobs can't be farmed out. I can't delegate what Henry does."

Now her curiosity overcame her apprehension, like oil spreading over the surface of a mud puddle. "So, you'll stay?"

"As long as he protects us. Yes. It's fair."

Protected them from what?

TWENTY

By the following week, Emily suspected that Sabrina was somehow off her meds, at least some of them. The capsule easily dissolved in Sabrina's coffee, but Mrs. Roth's behavior had changed. Her husband saw nothing of her agitation or that frightening glitter in her eyes because those "tells" only appeared after his car left the driveway. Sabrina was a very good actress.

The twitch was gone, though she'd seen Sabrina do a very good imitation for Henry's benefit. Whatever her natural mental condition, it was emerging day by day. One thing was clear, even to a novice: Sabrina Roth was the opposite of depressed. Manic was more accurate.

After her golf league, Sabrina wanted to go for a drive. The destination was hazy, with Sabrina ordering her to stop at random locations and then finally directing Emily to bring her home. It seemed like a drive to nowhere. But Emily remembered some of these spots were the addresses programed into Sabrina's favorites.

But why?

Back at the Roths' home, she dropped Sabrina at the door.

Some part of her noted the rush with which Mrs. Roth entered the house but she thought that just meant she needed a bathroom. Emily continued to the garage. Once inside the home, she searched for Sabrina, finding her in the poolside bathroom.

"You okay?"

"Fine."

"Ready for lunch?"

"Yes."

"What would you like?"

"Surprise me."

Emily paused, blinking at that odd answer. Up until this minute, Sabrina Roth had dictated every detail of her meals. Sabrina didn't like surprises. She liked getting exactly what she wanted.

This attitude of adventure or of caring very little suggested she had other, more important things on her mind.

But what?

* * *

When Emily arrived on Thursday, she again waited for Dr. Roth to mention finding the safe contents out of order, that they had been tampered with, or noticing Sabrina's album missing. He didn't. Only asked if Emily had gotten the contents of the capsules into Sabrina's food.

She had, though she thought that was not the sort of surprise Sabrina had expected when she'd told Emily to surprise her yesterday.

Surely he'd eventually notice papers in the office safe were not as he'd left them? He certainly would, because he was meticulous, and Sabrina had tossed the documents about like confetti. Emily had done her best but... would he just blame his wife?

If he noticed, Emily hoped he assumed, correctly, that

Sabrina had been in there. But then he should also have guessed who would have put everything back.

Why had Emily tucked everything inside? He'd know his wife would have left things like a passing hurricane.

Should she tell him she'd been in there after Sabrina scattered the contents or wait?

She decided to wait. Because she should have told him when it happened, not days later. She'd just wait and hope he didn't go in that safe very often.

Never confess even when confronted. Especially when confronted.

Her big sister had told her that. Words to live by, she thought, and Emily kept her mouth shut.

* * *

On Friday, Emily accepted the dry cleaning at the gate and put away all the garments. She wished she'd made a copy of that key to his bathroom drawers, but then recalled she'd photographed it. Was it possible to make a copy from that? It was a flat key, like the kind used for luggage.

Why hadn't she photographed the contents of that drawer?

Sighing at the missed opportunity, she returned to the kitchen and her routine cleaning, and then slipped into her rubber gloves to begin lunch preparations.

It didn't take long for the little voice in her head to finally break in and sound the alarm. What was it her mother used to say about it being too quiet?

Something was wrong.

Emily cocked her head to listen to the deafening silence. The house felt empty.

Her ears buzzed a warning as her skin prickled with an electric charge. The sweat on her body turned cold as the home's cooling unit pushed frigid air at her from an overhead vent.

Emily hurried to Sabrina's studio.

"Mrs. Roth?"

She found her in the poolside bathroom. Emily tried the door, surprised to find it unlocked. Inside, Sabrina stood at the sink with the bin of medications Emily had not seen her take from the kitchen. She stood at the green glass basin, the open bin at her elbow on the black granite countertop.

"What are you doing?" Emily asked.

Sabrina startled and spun.

"Nothing. Go away."

At her elbow was a bag of confectionery sugar and the empty pill casings.

"Are you filling those with sugar?"

"These are the only ones he can tamper with. I don't want him to know I'm not taking them. He watches me. So, I have to do this."

Emily watched in silence. Had she been dissolving sugar into Sabrina's coffee all week? It explained the change in behavior. The alertness and high levels of agitation in her nervous energy. Emily needed to alert Dr. Roth that Sabrina was off some of her medications despite their efforts.

"Sabrina, listen, your husband prescribed every one of those for a reason."

"Yes. But perhaps not the reason you think. And he stands to gain by keeping me... pacified, which complicates things. Does it not?"

It did, but Emily did not take the baited question.

"He told you I'm hallucinating, right?"

"Something like that." Delusional thinking wasn't the same as hallucinating, but they could share some characteristics.

Sabrina motioned to the pills. "This is why. He knows I have my album. That I'm reading it again. He's giving me something. Like he did with morphine after he caught me with it the last time. Clare told him. We fought. I said if he gave me narcotics again, I would leave him. He promised. Swore to God, he would never. But he's doing it again or something like it."

Had their former private nurse told Dr. Roth something that caused him to douse Sabrina with enough morphine to render her unconscious? Is that why she ended up in the ER in March? Or was this more delusional thinking? There had been no morphine in her blood test results.

"He's trying to keep me calm because he's afraid."

"Of what?"

"Of me. Of me leaving him. Of losing everything." She balled one hand into a fist and shook it at the cool, circulating air. "These are the only ones he could use. You said so."

Sabrina had managed to open six capsules. The medication now lay in tiny white mountains in the sink. Clearly this ongoing certainty that Henry was dosing her with opioids was a long-standing and deeply held belief.

"Let me get you some lunch. We can talk about this."

Sabrina nodded but remained standing before the large oval mirror with the gilded frame to match the fixtures.

"Shall I call Taylor?"

"She hates me. Always takes his side anyway. She won't help."

"I can call Henry. Ask him to come home."

Sabrina shook her head. "I need to know what's in these." She pointed at the white powder on the sink. "Help me with that."

Emily blinked, watching the train skip off the rails.

She fell back to Dr. Roth's advice and repeated Sabrina's concern, letting her know she heard and understood. Then added, "But there is no evidence that it's true."

"Are you going to help me or just keep parroting me like an African gray?"

"What do you want me to do?"

"Get it tested. And without my name being associated.

Then if it comes back clear, I'll believe you. Otherwise, I'll tell Henry you're not working out."

Emily's first reaction was to stand up to the threat. But then she remembered Rosalind saying that Mrs. Roth had many nurses. They didn't stay long. Now she knew why.

"We can take it to the hospital for analysis. Figure this out together."

Sabrina shook her head. "It will be like the blood work. The lab is working with him. They'll just falsify the reports."

This sounded like an elaborate rationalization. Dr. Roth had told her that delusional thinking was rigid and that reasonable explanations were dismissed.

This seemed a fool's errand. If the results were good, Sabrina could claim the lab tampered with the findings because it seemed Mrs. Roth had already drawn her own conclusions.

And if they showed tampering? Well, that would be... surprising. What would Sabrina do if her suspicions were confirmed? Would Sabrina leave Henry? Seek an outside opinion? Call her attorneys?

"Well?" asked Sabrina. "Are you helping me or shall I tell Henry to give you the ax?"

Emily thought that this entire screwed-up situation was much more than she could handle. It was very possibly a great time to bow out.

But she couldn't. Not yet.

So, how could she turn this to her advantage?

"I know it's happening," said Sabrina, "it could be Henry or it might be the bad people."

Emily felt a sinking dread.

"They want me dead because of what I did."

"Who does?"

"The bad people. I've seen them watching me. Her family. The others. Following me. They've never forgiven me. They know. They know it was me."

Emily remembered what Dr. Roth had said. Her delusions centered on her childhood trauma, when she'd lost her twin, and had been exacerbated by the pedestrian fatality. Now her misbelief was that she'd killed a woman in the vehicular accident.

The mind was such a complicated place. Emily hesitated for only a moment before slipping into Sabrina's reality, uncomfortable but determined.

"Why don't the bad people go to the police?"

"Oh, it's too late for that. Case is settled. Henry said so."

"The police can arrest them, the bad people. Following you is illegal."

"They can't. Aren't you listening? It's *them*. Her family."

"Whose family?"

Sabrina rubbed her upper lip, muttering to herself. "No, no. Not them. But it could be part of a conspiracy. They set this up to trap me. My parents might have done that. She always hated me. Sent her running and then..." Now she was rubbing the side of her face with her fist.

Sabrina's beliefs disturbed Emily. It was disconcerting, the way she flipped from so normal to so paranoid. Unsettling and creepy. She fought her instinct to get away from the woman and tried to defuse the situation by diversion.

"I think you need a break. Let's get you fed."

"But what about this?" Sabrina motioned to the pills.

"I can finish them for you."

"Really?"

"Sure. I'm here for you."

"So, you'll test that powder, so I know if he's still helping me?"

"Would that make you feel better?"

Sabrina nodded, seeming to have forgotten her earlier threats of having her newest nurse dismissed.

Emily flicked some powder onto a bit of paper and tucked it in her front pocket.

Despite herself, Emily was so fascinated by Sabrina's version of reality. Whose family did she think was after her? And who was it who hated her? Did she think her parents, long deceased, were after her?

Emily decided to learn all she could about the Roths and the current state of their marriage. And while she was at it, she might do a web search to see if there was any valid reason or some kernel of truth that could have triggered Sabrina's belief that dangerous persons were lurking about, devoted to exacting revenge.

She guided Sabrina to the kitchen table and, with a gloved hand, set a sandwich of Brie, peach compote, and slices of green apple before her. Then she added the unopened sparkling water. Sabrina, now seated, scrolled through her phone. Emily finished making a cup of fresh tropical fruit so ripe they filled the air with their sugary fragrance and coated her gloved hands with sticky juice.

Emily set the cup beside Sabrina's plate.

"Did you put them in there?" she asked, pointing at the fruit cup of fresh mango and pineapple.

"I don't understand."

"The medicine in your pocket. Is it in my food?"

Wow, that really did sound paranoid.

"No. It's just food."

Sabrina examined the plate, peering inside the bread and at the bottom of the bottle, which she herself had just opened.

"Show me the powder."

Emily did so.

Finally, she began to eat. Emily sat quietly at the counter out of Sabrina's line of sight.

After finishing, she lifted her attention to Emily.

"I have drawings to complete."

Emily collected the plate as Sabrina left the table. Her water was nearly full, so Emily carried it to her.

Sabrina didn't glance up as she placed the green plastic bottle on a coaster nearby.

The current drawing filled a large sheet of paper. Nearly every inch of the page was filled with angry scribbles, yet some of the places were intentionally white or a soft gray.

It seemed an abstraction, but Emily would need a better look, perhaps when she had finished.

"That's a big one."

Sabrina pointed at the door. "Go away."

Emily withdrew, worry churning like a weathervane in a tropical storm. She patted the pocket holding a single capsule and loose powder.

Was she really thinking of doing this?

TWENTY-ONE

On Saturday, Emily had been up early, as usual, to get a quick five-mile bike ride in before the heat turned from oppressive to ridiculous. Her repaired bike now sported a new front wheel and a sturdier lock. She was back and in the shower before Jennell had crawled from the covers.

Her roommate liked to sleep in on Saturdays, when she could, so it was not until eleven that they were both showered and heading for the gym. Driving, of course, at Jennell's insistence. Inside, all the machines were purple and they had free bagels on Saturday until one. Afterwards, Emily would head home, and Jennell would hit some yard sales.

"Probably more calories in than out," said Jennell, adding cream cheese to her sesame bagel.

There was raisin cinnamon with peanut butter. They sat on Jennell's blue yoga mat as if it were a picnic blanket. Emily told her roommate about Sabrina's mysterious photo album.

"You can't find it?" asked Jennell, and then used her index finger to redirect some cream cheese from her cheek to her mouth.

"Nope. She hides it."

Emily had not mentioned that it had come from their safe or that she had read the documents, and photographed them, or what she'd found in Dr. Roth's bottom drawer. The NDA prevented her, though she was tempted.

Jennell fanned the air. "Rich people are extra weird."

"Right?"

From what Emily had read, if Sabrina left him, he would get nothing. If she was institutionalized, he also would get nothing. Divorce? He got what he came to the marriage with, which, as far as Emily could see, was nothing much. And if Sabrina Roth died, he owed the estate for all benefits his marriage provided, specifically mentioned, vehicles, real estate, personal property, his education and loans to establish his medical practice including the purchase of the office building.

In any of those circumstances, he'd owe a bundle.

Jennell finished the first half of the bagel and dug into the second. "But wait a second. Maybe it's porn."

Emily stared, shocked, and then Jennell broke out laughing.

Jennell's chin hovered inches above her stylish black sneakers as she stretched. She sat near the free weights neither of them had any intention of using, dressed in black leggings with a transparent side panel and an acid-green crop top. A tiny smear of cream cheese marred the otherwise perfect plum color staining her full lips.

Emily wished she found all this chaos funny. But it was anything but.

Jennell sobered.

"I think working for that couple is admirable, even if they aren't."

"Thank you." Nothing she had done, was doing, or planned to do was admirable. That was certain. Emily considered her need to share with Jennell against the likelihood revealing something personal would get her in legal trouble because of that document.

Jennell noticed the long silence and said, "Okay, spill."

"I'm not supposed to."

"I'm not talking."

She gathered herself and a full breath of air, tinged with the tang of sweat and rubber.

"Okay. It occurred to me that he has a really good motive for keeping her... um, subdued."

"Oh shit. You think that?"

"She takes a lot of mood-altering drugs. I'm worried."

Jennell jumped right into the crux of the matter with her next question. "Is that to keep her from leaving or to keep him from having to have her committed?"

"I'm not sure. And I still don't know if Sabrina is even mentally capable of making such decisions or caring for herself without, you know, serious mental health intervention."

"I read that, in the fifties, men could just commit their wives for hysteria if they caused them any problems."

"Now you need a diagnosis."

"Which he's given her. One that won't draw too much attention or get her committed."

"Exactly."

The pause stretched as each contemplated the situation.

"He might just be trying to help her," said Jennell.

Emily shook her head, her dismissal of that idea obvious.

They finished their breakfast and decided to return for more orange juice.

"Treadmill or StairMaster?" asked Emily.

Jennell snorted. "I'm too full. Let's just use the walking track."

"You can walk outside."

"In this heat?"

"You just want them to think you're here to exercise."

Jennell laughed but did not deny it. "I'll take bagels over barbells any day."

They headed for the rubberized track.

"There's a sale at the UU Church. Want to hit it on the way home?" asked Jennell.

"Sure. Maybe they'll have a toaster oven."

"I nearly had one last week, but some lady picked it up before I could get there. I kept waiting for her to change her mind." Jennell walked at a speed just fast enough to look like exercise. Emily knew from experience that she'd do a few laps, satisfied that the trainers were not wise to her real reason for visiting, and then head back to her car.

"So, Em. Are you going to quit?"

TWENTY-TWO

On Tuesday, when she and Rosalind sat down for coffee, Emily kept her attention on the security camera. It remained off and Emily began to relax. Ever since she mentioned to Dr. Roth that his wife had been dumping out the contents of her capsules, he'd been turning those cameras on constantly.

Emily didn't pepper the woman with questions, though she wanted to. Instead, she asked about her kids and listened to all they had been up to. They chatted about Emily's first dentist appointment in a year and Rosalind's son's upcoming seventh birthday. Before Rosalind announced it was time to work, Emily needed to steer the conversation to the questions that troubled her.

She wondered why the Roths bought that Prius. It seemed like a payoff or bribe. Something stank about that transaction. And the sale was in March, when Sabrina said she'd visited the ER after Clare had told on her. Told what?

She was trying to decide if she should ask who drove a blue Prius, or if Rosalind had any reason to suspect Dr. Roth might be having an affair, or if she had ever seen Mrs. Roth with a photo album. But the woman surprised her by asking a question of her own.

"You like working here?" asked Rosalind.

The astonishment must have shown on her face because Rosalind waved her hand. "Never mind. It's okay."

"No. It's fine. Well, most days are all right. Not lately. She's been..." She thought to say "kind of a bitch" and changed course. "She's been more agitated. And some strange things are happening."

Rosalind nodded as her jaw went tight and her gaze drifted. Had she seen this pattern before?

"Did they make you sign a paper?" Rosalind asked.

"The NDA? Yes. They did."

"My husband is so mad that I signed that. He wants me to quit but they pay very well. I didn't tell him what I see here because I'm afraid of that paper."

"Well, I've signed it, too. You can tell me. I can't tell anyone, either."

Rosalind's lips pinched tight, and she glanced toward the dining room.

"She's in her studio drawing."

The woman relaxed a bit.

"I saw her push the pool boy." She extended her hands in a gesture to demonstrate. "Like this. And he goes into the deep end. He just poured in the yellow bottle, a gallon of the bleach. When he came up, he was so mad."

Emily had seen the pool guy but only exchanged a word or two with him.

"Really?"

"She told him, 'You fell.' And I hear her tell her husband on the phone, 'He fell,' but I saw the push."

"Why would she do that?"

"Because she is loco." She lifted both open hands, showing calluses on her palms and speaking so rapidly, her accent made it hard for Emily to keep up. "She comes inside and calls the company and says she caught him swimming in their pool and she wants a new pool cleaner. And they do it!"

"That's terrible."

"Then she tells Dr. Roth that the next new man is watching her. So, she gets another man to clean this pool. And another." Rosalind throws up her hands in disgust.

Emily's stomach tightened and she felt sick.

"Once when we were shopping, she thought she saw someone watching her," Emily said.

Rosalind frowned and shook her head, a doleful gesture.

Emily glanced toward the hall. "She seems a little better."

Rosalind gave a mirthless laugh at that. "She is like the roads in Guatemala, up and down and up and down. Now she is up but soon she will be a devil again."

"Mood swings?"

"I don't know. But if she is down..." Rosalind sucked through her teeth and waved a finger. "Stay away. If she start acting crazy, she calls the police."

"The police? Why?"

"Because people are watching her. That's what she says. The police don't even come now. They call him and he comes."

"Dr. Roth."

"Sí." Rosalind lifted her crucifix and rubbed it between her thumb and index finger. "I never go out there when she is like that. I can't swim."

"Good to know."

Rosalind rose and carried her mug to the sink, signaling the end of their chat, but she turned back. "You see my bar lock on the steering wheel?"

Emily had not. She shook her head.

"That's not for thieves. That's for *her*. You should get one." She thumped her mug in the sink with unnecessary force. "Or maybe they just buy you a new one."

What did that mean?

"I don't understand."

"Her last nurse was Clare."

"Yes." She knew that much.

"She and I talk." Rosalind motioned between them. "Like this, every week about her car troubles."

"What kind of car?"

"Brown, no front fender. Mazda, I think. Yes, Mazda because she went to a special mechanic that works on foreign cars." Rosalind gestured with both hands. "Anyway, one day she has a new car. I asked her when she bought it, because she was telling me she can't afford to fix the old one, and now here is a new one. That doesn't make sense." Rosalind touched her head. "And she doesn't want to talk about it."

"So, she quit?"

"No. She got the new car and she keeps working for another three months, but now she is as nervous and crazy as Mrs. Roth. And one day she's gone, and you are here."

"What happened?"

Rosalind leaned in, whispering. "Arrested."

"For what?"

"I heard Dr. Roth tell Mrs. Roth that police found drugs in her car."

"Really? Was she stealing from the Roths?"

"Drugs?" Rosalind turned and scrubbed her mug clean. Now her face was flushed and her breathing was fast. "I don't think it is her drugs," she said, thumbing toward Sabrina's studio. "The paper said it is narcotics. But *I* never saw signs Clare uses drugs."

"Then what do you think happened?"

Rosalind gave her a look of confusion, looking worried and lost. "Maybe she needs money to pay for the new car?"

"Maybe."

Finally, she tugged at her T-shirt and announced, "I have to work now."

"Yes. But one more thing. That new car. The one you mentioned. Was it a blue Prius?"

The woman's brows lifted, and she gaped.

"How'd you know?"

TWENTY-THREE

PALM CREEK VILLAGE, LAKELAND, FLORIDA

Clare Eastman had a malleable face the color of melting peach ice cream. She stared at the world from behind the bunkers of her cheeks through weary eyes, waiting for the next bad thing to happen. And it did, arriving moments after she flicked on the kitchen light.

Clare tugged the cardigan sweater tight at her neck as she regarded the bold woman inhabiting her doormat as if she paid rent.

She judged the woman to be slightly younger than she was, perhaps twenty-five. She didn't like the arrogant slant of her chin, her mirrored glasses, or her arrival at six in the morning, just as Clare was preparing to leave for her new job at an urgent care center. Sunglasses hid much of her narrow face, which was framed by a fringe of straight black bangs and hair cropped at the collar.

There was only the lopsided screen door between them, which should have been enough, but something about the woman put Clare on guard. A glance showed the lock was engaged.

"Mrs. Eastman?"

The woman on her stoop looked all business in a blazer, dress pants, practical, lace-up black shoes, and a white dress shirt. Tall and fair skinned, the most distinguishing thing about her was the pink, fluorescent Band-Aid fixed over what she could see of one brow, as if she were a prize fighter.

And then Clare recognized what had set off warning bells. There was something under the jacket, like padding. This woman wore a flak jacket or body armor. And then it clicked. She was another cop.

Clare's life had derailed with a drug arrest. When they'd pulled her over, she was sure it was about the Prius, but they'd searched her car.

She still believed that cop had planted the drugs they found. There was no other explanation.

After the last six weeks of hell, she was finally home until the trial, and her license was under review. If she was convicted, her lawyer said that review could turn into a suspension. And there could be prison time. Even if she did not go to jail, and if she kept her nursing accreditation, an arrest for narcotics by a local nurse would be memorable. If she managed to get out of this, she'd need to leave the area.

And now here was more trouble.

"Ma'am. Are you Mrs. Clare Eastman?" repeated the woman.

"Yes." She tightened her grip on the sweater.

"I'm Detective Lucille Flint with the special crimes unit."

The officer flashed a gold badge, confirming Clare's fears, then tucked it away, providing a clear look at the shoulder harness holding a handgun beneath her left arm.

On the street, behind her, sat a shiny black unmarked car.

"Could you step out, please?"

Clare sighed and flicked open the flimsy door lock, opened the screen, and stepped outside, forcing the woman back to the sidewalk. From her stoop before the double-wide trailer, the sky that had seemed dark from within revealed that dawn crept across the sky in bands of apricot light. The humidity hung heavy in the air forecasting another hot, sticky day.

Behind her, cool air leaked out until she closed the door to her mother's place. God, she swore she'd never come back here. But here she was.

"Yes?"

"It's about your vehicle. The tan Mazda?"

That news struck with the stinging of a slap. Despite the assurance that this day would never come, it had arrived.

She'd known this would boomerang back at her. Could feel it in her bones like a change in the barometer.

She stole a quick look at the new blue Prius squatting in her carport like an accusation. Clare forced her attention back to the threat before her.

Here she was, Clare's worst fears made flesh.

"You found it?"

Her stomach twitched. This was never supposed to happen.

"Some of it. Enough."

Clare gathered her sweater to her throat, choking it against her neck, as she tried to keep herself from revealing the wild panic thumping through her like the percussion section of a marching band. Her mouth was as dry as burned toast. Belatedly, she remembered to look surprised.

What if they knew? What if they already knew? She'd been promised that it would be all right, but was it?

"That's... that's good," she said, stammering past the panic. Except it wasn't.

He'd fired her and had no reason to protect her. Whatever this was, she was on her own.

"Why didn't you report it stolen?"

Clare blinked stupidly as the thinking part of her brain struggled against the numbing shock. Was this how the chicken felt before the ax?

Say something, the little voice shouted. But she couldn't form a sentence, much less a coherent thought.

"Because it wasn't. I just took it off the road."

"Really? Where is it?"

"I don't know."

"Did someone borrow it?"

"No. No, I just took it off the road." She was babbling now.

The woman cocked her head and her mouth tipped down. "You know it's a crime to lie to the police?"

Clare cut her gaze away. She couldn't do this. Why had she thought she could?

There was no way she could even look at the detective. She was, and always had been, a terrible liar. The tears already leaked down her flushed cheeks and her face was on fire.

All she could do was sweat and pant and try to keep from saying anything incriminating.

"Clare." There was impatience and threat in the detective's tone. "I'm going to ask you again. Who used your car?"

TWENTY-FOUR

August arrived with more daily downpours. At the end of a long day, Dr. Roth rolled out of the afternoon thunderstorm and into the garage in his shiny luxury sedan. Emily tried and failed to slow her galloping heart.

This was silly. Wasn't it? Dr. Roth wasn't dangerous. Greedy, possibly, but he wouldn't hurt his wife.

Or drug her?

Or detain her?

Emily realized she no longer could convince herself because she had seen all those legal contracts and what he kept in that secret locked bathroom drawer. She had cut herself a copy of the key from the photo and it had worked. She'd had another look just to be sure that the double-edged razor was among the least dangerous things inside.

She believed that he'd been intentionally overmedicating his wife and now she knew why. Without her here, at home, under his care, he'd lose everything. Henry needed to ensure she didn't get arrested, institutionalized, leave him, or die. Her coherency was insignificant, her well-being a secondary consideration.

What to do about it was a more serious question.

The door to the laundry room opened and in stepped the doctor. He was dry, despite the afternoon torrent. He would have used the hospital walkover, taken his car from the covered garage, and then pulled into his own little sanctuary. How lovely for him that he didn't have to fight for a spot on the street, sometimes circling the block in ever-expanding orbits, then running through the rain, leaping puddles to get inside.

"Roads are flooding," he said, by way of a greeting. "Maybe you'd better wait a bit before heading back."

She wasn't doing that. She was getting in her car, and getting clear of this house and this man, because she no longer trusted him.

"Any trouble today?"

"Normal day," she lied. Then, because she could not stop herself, she asked, "Dr. Roth, does she really need all those medications?"

He went instantly on alert. "Is she taking them?"

"Yes."

"All of them?"

"With some coaxing, she is."

His shoulders sank and the relaxed expression returned. He was hiding something. His culpability, certainly.

"She needs them. More than she knows."

Emily no longer believed a word of that.

* * *

On the first Thursday of August, just after the dry cleaning delivery, Sabrina announced that they were going out for a caramel macchiato. Emily didn't understand why, because the machine in their kitchen did nearly everything a commercial one might do. But apparently, the coffee machine, espresso machine, and French press were insufficient to the task at hand.

Emily pulled the SUV out and waited for Sabrina, opening the car door when she descended the stairs, clad in a pressed khaki-colored linen dress with large opalized shell buttons running from neck to knee, designer shades, and carrying a small woven rattan handbag. Around her neck, a scarf was artfully tied and draped to display the orange poppies covering the fabric. On her feet were gold sandals that revealed her pink polished toenails.

Once the vehicle was in reverse, Emily flicked her attention to the huge monitor for a crystal-clear picture of the world behind the bumper. The circular drive made reversing a snap. She was now accustomed to her new higher perspective from the elevated seat. It was easier to look down on people from up here.

As they left the gated community, Emily tried not to think of yesterday's exchange with Dr. Roth. She failed to repress the shudder at the recollection. It was grating that she'd ever felt sorry for the popular psychiatrist.

Before beginning the job, she'd thought it ironic. Like a punch line, the shrink with the crazy spouse. Now she believed much of his wife's current problems were his fault.

Just like yesterday, Sabrina had waited until Dr. Roth had left and then revealed the capsules she had not taken, by flipping back the place mat before her. She'd asked if Emily had taken the powder for testing, and she said she was still looking for a trustworthy place.

"Starbucks?" she asked.

"No." Sabrina tapped the vehicle's touch screen and opened the nav app.

"We're going somewhere special."

TWENTY-FIVE

"Hey, Mercedes, find favorites," said Sabrina, from the passenger seat.

Emily glanced at the console, now issuing a blue ambient light, and was about to admit she didn't know how to do that, when the car interjected. A lovely female voice spoke.

"Your list of favorites..." the voice assistant began, and Sabrina cut it off.

"Four," she said.

A navigation map appeared on the screen but Emily could find nothing familiar about their destination.

"Turn right," said the assistant, guiding them from the driveway, and pointing them in the direction of the closest "residents only" exit.

Emily felt as if she had landed in a space capsule, but turned as instructed, taking them out of the drive and in the opposite direction than her usual route. They glided beside a wide median that could have served as a magazine layout for landscaping. How much did this place spend on tropical plants? She slowed at the gate, which lifted on her approach. No security on the residents' exit if you didn't count the camera aimed at them.

"Beautiful day," Emily said, trying to start a conversation.

"Hey, Mercedes, increase temperature to seventy," Sabrina said, as if Emily were not there or just some bothersome extension of the carputer.

"Temperature seventy degrees," said the disembodied voice.

Sweat beaded on Sabrina's forehead. She pressed her hand in a fist and shoved it against her mouth gripping it with the other. For a moment, she blasted air, her chest moving like a bellows.

Was this a panic attack or something else?

Emily's internal voice whispered a warning, sensing something she could not. This trip was different than any of the ones before it because she had no idea where they were going or why.

"Where are we—"

"Shhhh," said her passenger, holding her index finger before her lips.

Emily closed her mouth and turned her eyes forward but watched her passenger with quick sideward glances as Mrs. Roth's chest continued to heave.

"I can turn us back."

"No!" Her cry was nearly desperate.

The navigation app ordered a right turn.

This wasn't the way to the coffee shop, the nails place, the salon, or the art store. Where were they going?

The unease grew with the steadily increasing thump of her heart. The air conditioner turned Emily's anxiety into a shoulder-shaking shiver. But she gripped the wheel, clamped her teeth, and did as instructed by the vehicle.

This was the route to the hospital and the medical practices that surrounded it and one of the more desirable elementary schools. Beyond that, a city park held a running trail, soccer fields, baseball fields, tennis courts, and a fenced playground.

School was out, so the park was filled with summer sports camps. Kids in matching uniforms, high socks, and cleats attempted to juggle soccer balls, spending most of their efforts running after their ball.

The tennis court was dominated by elderly folks trying to stay young. On the playground, small children ran and spun like small nervous dogs while their parents and caretakers sat still as lounging lionesses in the shade.

"Are we going to the hospital?"

Sabrina lifted her fist from her mouth to bark directions.

"Stop here."

There was no place to stop, but Emily did as instructed, gliding to the shoulder, blocking the bike lane and flipping on her hazards.

This was a quiet street, off the main thoroughfare, one that Emily knew very well. In the parking lot, two helmeted riders lifted their bicycles onto a car rack, the colorful spandex outfits accentuating their bulging thigh muscles.

The only dark spot in the sunny day was the small white sign the size of a salad plate placed by the Florida Department of Traffic to mark the site of a fatality. Those signs, with black lettering, said simply, *Drive Safely*. Below that, in even smaller print, was often a name.

These were the only permanent memorials legally allowed by the state and, long after the flowers died, the teddy bears lolled, and the crosses tipped, they held the name or names of traffic fatality victims.

The city often removed the public tributes but was some-times lenient. The cross of faded plastic flowers and a sagging, sodden teddy bear, strapped to a nearby telephone pole, was proof of that.

Emily recognized the name on the memorial sign. It was of

the woman killed by Sabrina's vehicle in the traffic fatality. She wondered if her passenger knew where they were. Anxiety scampered up her spine as she glanced to Mrs. Roth. But Sabrina seemed blissfully unaware as she sat watching the children with a wistful smile on her face. Was she, perhaps, remembering taking her daughter here?

Her smile was dreamy and her expression unfamiliar. Emily would have described it as contentment.

"Did you bring Taylor here?" she asked, her voice holding a hysterical note of hope laced with panic.

"Don't talk now," said Sabrina, nearly whispering, as if they were in church.

Emily shut up and played with her phone, checking social media and Googling the address where they now sat while ignoring the cars passing and casting her dirty looks for blocking half the lane.

If Sabrina was aware and was this euphoric, well, that wasn't normal. It gave Emily the creeps until she was no longer sure if it was the air vents or her skin that was causing the shivers.

Finally, Sabrina spoke.

"Hey, Mercedes, navigate to favorites number six."

The female navigator directed them to drive straight, and Emily put them in motion. The next stop was a quiet intersection.

"Stop there."

Emily complied. They faced a busy gas station. On the corner, near the crosswalk, a biker zoomed through the intersection in the bike lane. Two elderly women, one with a walker, sat at the bus stop waiting. Before the bus stop was the sign with the route number, a speed limit sign, *Drive Safely* sign, and a cardboard sign advertising AKA golden retriever puppies.

Who buys puppies from a cardboard sign? she wondered.

Sabrina spoke to the vehicle again and directed Emily to

make two more stops. One was at an ordinary intersection before a fast-food chicken place and another before a legal office.

Or were they?

"Is this your attorney?" Emily asked.

"My attorney doesn't paint his building like a flag."

Emily stared at the white *Drive Safely* sign and lifted her phone, Googling the address.

Sabrina folded her arms and stared out the side window.

"Hey, Mercedes, take me to a pharmacy."

The vehicle's computer offered five choices. Sabrina made her pick and off they went. At the store, Sabrina directed her to park in the handicapped spot.

"Stay in the car," she ordered and left Emily with the engine running.

Emily moved the car to the spot right next to the accessible one, waited until Sabrina disappeared into the store, and then followed Sabrina. From the end of the aisle, she watched her boss lift a packet of makeup and drop one into her designer bag. This was followed by three more small items.

By the time Sabrina exited the sliding doors, Emily was already behind the wheel.

Sabrina slid into the passenger seat. "Take me home."

TWENTY-SIX

On Friday, Dr. Roth informed her that he had already seen to his wife's first round of medications and that Sabrina had been up since four in the morning.

"She's too agitated to sleep."

Emily still had not told Dr. Roth that his wife skipped some of her medications. But she did wonder if his wife had digested any of the pills he'd overseen.

He told her to expect a grocery order this morning and not to take Sabrina on any road trips today. Then he was off to his practice, and she was off to find Sabrina.

Mrs. Roth perched on a stool at her drafting table, in her studio, scribbling away. She seemed energized and focused.

Was her frantic activity a side effect of her medications or their absence? Hard to know without learning if Sabrina had ingested her prescriptions.

Emily managed to get her to eat the top of a blueberry muffin with a generous addition of butter and half a glass of grapefruit juice before giving up.

After putting the dirty dishes into the dishwasher and tackling the kitchen mess, she checked to see if the office safe and Dr. Roth's side of the bathroom drawers were locked.

Back in the studio, Emily sat on the love seat behind the drafting table, reading on her phone. Today, Sabrina's creations seemed to be accident-related. If she had to guess, she'd say Sabrina was drawing the objects left as a memorial at crash sites. Amid the scribbles, the flowers were recognizable and part of a teddy bear. A web search of images on her phone for memorials, linked to a particular address, made her stomach pitch. The resemblance was unmistakable.

The subject of Sabrina's creations disturbed on a visceral level, making Emily queasy and her lips purse as if something sour and bitter filled her mouth. The hairs on her arm lifted as the tingle of warning buzzed over her skin.

"You seem well today," she said, probing.

Sabrina stopped drawing and peered back at her.

"I mean, this combination of medication, it's less... sedating."

She flipped back a closed notepad on her left and revealed several colorful pills and capsules.

There was her answer.

Emily sucked in a breath.

"Flush those, will you?"

Emily stepped forward, hesitating as she stared at the pile of untouched medication and Sabrina's expectant expression.

"You're not taking any of them?"

"Obviously. They dull my mind. I can't think or imagine."

Imagine what? Emily wanted to ask, but something stopped her. She wondered, but the possible answers disturbed and she listened to that internal voice that whispered caution.

She had suspected that the medications had made Sabrina docile and easily manipulated, but what was her charge like when she was clearheaded? Dangerous possibilities emerged in her mind, pounding just behind an invisible wall, like captives trying to escape.

Emily collected the pills and tucked them in her pocket, instead of flushing them, wondering if she should reveal his wife's subversion to Dr. Roth or continue to pretend ignorance. She didn't know.

Sabrina's phone alert notified her that a grocery delivery had cleared the main gates.

"Will you get those?" asked Sabrina, still hunched over her drawing, scratching away.

"Absolutely. I'll put away anything that needs refrigerating." Emily would be putting it all away because that was one of her jobs.

"The salmon and Caesar are for tonight."

"Yes, ma'am." She'd put those up front.

Throughout the day, Sabrina seemed increasingly restless, absorbed with her laptop and, again, exercising on Dr. Roth's stationary bike. To Emily, she looked like a woman struggling with withdrawals, like a person who has stopped smoking and needs something to do to keep them from lighting up.

Late in the afternoon, Emily prepared the salad for dinner.

Sabrina would add the extra Parmesan, as she enjoyed the cheese grinder. Emily set the table, arranged the condiments, and preheated the oven for the garlic bread.

An unfamiliar sound made Emily jump. A quicksilver jolt of panic fired her heart rate as she turned her head in the direction of the noise. She set aside the bread knife and cocked her head. There it was again, an animal growl.

She hurried down the hall to find Sabrina in her studio, seated behind her drafting table, using the pointy end of a metal compass on a photo in the open photo album Emily had been unable to find despite repeated searches.

Sabrina scribbled and then stabbed at the photo. When she stabbed, she made a high, strangled shriek. The sound raised the hairs on Emily's arms. It was as if she was restraining her scream, so as not to be heard, but the vicious stabbing at the image, seated on a thick mat of additional pages, gave Emily a chill.

Emily backed up and called, "Mrs. Roth, would you like anything from the kitchen?"

When she reached the doorway, the compass had vanished, and the photo album lay peeking out from under the pages of drawings on her left.

"Bottled water."

"I've got your dinner ready. When should I pop the garlic bread in?"

"You know when he comes home. Figure it out."

"Yes, ma'am."

It no longer seemed that Sabrina trusted her. It appeared she was hiding something from her doctor and her nurse. What was going on?

Emily headed for the kitchen returning with a bottle of cold water. Sabrina accepted it but set it aside, then stood and stretched. Emily headed back toward the kitchen as Sabrina cut across the hall to the bathroom.

Emily reversed course and zipped back into Sabrina's studio. Quick as a cat, she lifted the drawings that had covered the photo album. But it wasn't there.

She turned in a full circle. Sabrina had only had a moment. Where did she hide it? Emily checked the closet but found nothing. Then she scrambled to open the drawers of the map cabinet.

Back at her desk, Emily made another quick search for the album.

Where was it?

"Looking for something?"

Emily spun to find Sabrina watching her from the doorway.

TWENTY-SEVEN

On Saturday night, Jennell met Emily in the hotel bar where she worked. She'd gotten employee of the month and that came with two free appetizers. The appetizers would be dinner, so they scanned the caloric intake numbers looking for the highest ones.

"Kung pao shrimp?" asked Jennell. "It's got protein."

"Artichoke dip. Cheese," said Emily.

"I've had that one. It's great."

They closed the menu and Jennell called their order to her friend behind the bar. The space was part of the lobby, with an elaborate open room divider separating lobby and reception from the bar. Here, blue glass pendant lights hung low over the smattering of tables and the high-end liquor bottles were illuminated from behind with fiber optic lights in ever-changing colors, as if they were rare objects of art.

The music was something jazzy, with a torch singer. Ella Fitzgerald, perhaps.

"How many today?" asked Emily, trailing her finger through the beads of condensation on the outside of her draft beer.

"Seven. One written on a business card."

Emily rolled her eyes. Jennell kept a running count of how many propositions she received each day. Average was five, but more on weekends and evenings.

She was young, pretty, and guests often mistook her welcoming manner as something more than her job. Well, the single men did.

"They never give up, do they?"

"Bless their hearts," said Jennell. It was a high insult in the South. As in, "Bless her heart, she don't know no better" or "Bless her heart, she's doing what she can."

Emily laughed. It felt good to release some of the tension from her shoulders and relax.

"What's new at work?" asked her roommate.

"Nothing. Yesterday was just another long day." And Sabrina was becoming prickly and dangerous as those cacti with the thorns that resemble spears.

"I hear you on that."

"When are you back on nights?"

"Not for a while. Next schedule."

She knew that Jennell didn't mind the overnight shifts at the hotel where the pace was less frantic and more entertaining.

"Still looking for the photo album. She caught me searching for it yesterday."

"What did you do?"

"Well, she asked if I was looking for something and I lied and said I just wanted to find something to put under her water bottle so it didn't sweat all over her drawings." She considered herself a good liar but the look Sabrina had cast her said she wasn't buying what Emily was selling. And that little, devilish smile afterwards, as if this were some kind of game and Sabrina liked her odds. The entire exchange made Emily uneasy and that disquiet clung to her like sand to wet skin.

"Did she buy that?"

"I don't think so."

Emily lifted her beer and took a swallow, enjoying the aftertaste of hops. She didn't spring for the Guinness, opting instead for the darkest they had on tap at the happy hour pricing.

Her gut told her Henry was involved in Sabrina's illness. How involved was the question. He might be helping her, over-medicating her, or even exacerbating her symptoms. Why he would do that last one, though, she couldn't figure.

"I caught her dumping her medication out of the capsules and down the sink."

Jennell's forehead furrowed. "What'd you do?"

"I took one. And some of the powder. It's in my bag. I've been carrying it around for days." She gnawed her lower lip, waiting to see what Jennell would say about that. Would she condemn or lecture or support? Emily had no idea.

"Why?"

Emily leaned across the round high-top table toward Jennell. "What if he is, you know, intentionally overmedicating her?"

Jennell sat back, retreating from the possibility. "Oh, come on."

"I know. It's ridiculous. Isn't it?"

"Probably, but he could be giving her drugs to keep her, you know, at home."

"Yeah. I have a bad feeling." Emily gnawed her lower lip.

"You should listen to those. Intuition is rarely wrong." Jennell glanced at her phone. "I've got to go soon. You going to be all right?"

The brave face was just a mask. Emily wasn't really sure how any of this would play out.

"You think I should give notice and stick it out until they get a replacement?"

"I think you should get out of that madhouse and away from those toxic people as soon as possible."

Emily wouldn't do that. Because she needed to figure out what was happening in that house and to her patient.

"Yeah. Soon as possible. But what about Sabrina's belief? I could get them tested and show her the results."

"You said no amount of evidence changes a delusion, which is why it's a delusion."

"Dr. Roth did say something like that."

"Take her to a doctor. Have them deal with it."

"But what if it's not a delusion and she's right?"

Jennell slowly shook her head, clearly not liking that possibility.

"And taking her to another doctor, I'll get fired and for what? Plus, the blood work will only show what they are testing for and what is in her blood. And she's not taking the capsules anymore. But with the powder and the capsule, Brian could at least let me know what is in these. That her medications are exactly what they should be. You know? And that might not change her delusion, but it would certainly relieve my mind."

"You still seeing him?"

"No. We broke up because I wouldn't ride his Hog," she said, referring to his Harley.

"Why?"

"Because I don't want to end up an organ donor."

Jennell laughed. She sipped her drink, a colorful pink foaming concoction involving frothing an egg white. Then she set down the gorgeous cocktail and turned serious.

"So, why's he going to do you this favor?"

"Because he can. It's just to prove her wrong. You know? For my sake. I'd feel terrible if she was, you know, being mistreated."

Jennell pushed a shrimp around on her plate.

"What do you think?"

"I think you should quit and get the heck out of there."

"I'm going to call Brian."

"Okay, think that through. Her husband is her doctor. He can prescribe anything he wants."

"No. Not if it's contraindicated. Not if he doesn't want this drug to show up on his wife's prescription list."

"Why would he care?"

"Malpractice. Suspended license. And if it comes to the attention of her attorneys, he could lose custody of his wife."

Jennell gave a low whistle.

Emily continued. "And if this is what Sabrina thinks it is, all the things he's trying to prevent might just happen."

"Okay, I get that. But what if, instead of getting peace of mind, Brian tells you that really is the wrong medication?"

"I'll..." Emily dropped her gaze to her lap. "I can't tell her doctor because *he's* her doctor. Call the police?"

Jennell made a sound in her throat, then said, "And get yourself tied up in a criminal case? You crazy?"

Emily made a face. "Geesh, that does sound bad." She thought a moment. "If it's positive, I'll quit."

"What if he won't let you?"

"What's he going to do? Drug me, too?"

"I don't know but he didn't have any trouble getting you to work for him. Did he?"

"He did not."

* * *

Emily texted Brian on Sunday and he agreed to have a look at the powder and pill if she'd run it over to him at the hospital where he worked. He'd consented mostly out of boredom, she thought, because he had the graveyard shift running blood work on emergencies, or possibly to see her again. But upon arrival she'd found the lab deadly quiet.

She stood in the doorway of the phlebotomy department and called a hello. He glanced up from his mobile phone at her arrival and accepted the two sandwich bags, one held the capsule and the other the powder.

"What am I testing for?"

"It is supposed to be a common prescription medication for anxiety. But it might be anything. Talcum powder, sugar, anti-depressants, antipsychotics. Or it could be an opioid or a synthetic opioid."

His brows lifted at that last one. "All right then. I'll have a look."

TWENTY-EIGHT

On Monday, Emily chirped her usual hello on entering the kitchen.

"Is that you, Regan?" she called.

Emily halted in the doorway, blinking in confusion. Sabrina's face fell.

"It's the one from before," said Sabrina to her husband, seated beside her.

Sabrina's usually perfect hair stuck up in the back as if she'd just risen from bed. Without her makeup her eyes seemed smaller, bloodshot, but still that haunting gray. She pinned Emily with a hard look, and she noted the pink creases on her face, as if she'd slept on wrinkled bedding for a long stretch. The sleep of the dead, Emily thought, drug-induced slumber.

"Where's Clare?"

"She's gone. Remember?"

Dr. Roth kept his voice patient as if talking to a child or imbecile. The tone he used on his wife irritated Emily.

"This is Emily. Regan doesn't work here anymore."

"Here. There. Anywhere," said Sabrina and started humming a Beatles song.

Her husband's mouth stretched thin and tight as a bowstring.

Emily paused exactly halfway between the Roths and the exit.

"Is it Monday already?" Sabrina asked.

"Yes. Monday."

Sabrina pushed away her untouched toast with a peevish shove and glared at Emily. "I don't want her here."

"I'm sorry."

"She has green eyes."

Dr. Roth's glance flashed to Emily and then back to his wife.

Emily remained silent during the conversation, which disturbed her on so many levels.

His wife gave a slow shake of her head. "It's not safe for me to drive," she said.

"That's right."

Dr. Roth checked his wife's phone, having no trouble getting past the pin and tapping the calendar app.

"I'm going to work now." He rose, kissed the top of Sabrina's head as if she were a child, and then sauntered toward the garage.

Sabrina sat motionless until his car rolled down the drive.

"I think he knows. He's been watching me take my pills. And he added something new." She turned her head toward Emily, showing red eyes. "He was after me all weekend. I'm exhausted. Had me up last night at three in the morning, walking around the pool. Wouldn't let me stop until I promised never to leave him."

Emily blinked in shock. The jolt of surprise rapidly swirled into outrage. Sedation was one thing. But walking her around to the point of exhaustion sounded like some barbaric form of domestic torture. Oh, no. This had gone far enough.

But had it happened? This was just the reason having an

unreliable memory was so dangerous. Who could believe a word Sabrina said?

She was in a prison fashioned by her father and her husband. Emily thought that must be terrible.

Sabrina deserved her sympathy.

"He kept telling me I can't drive ever again. Made me say it over and over."

"I'm sorry you had a terrible night."

"I shouldn't have told him I want to drive again."

"Probably not."

"Regan?" Sabrina stared at Emily and then dropped her gaze as if her exhaustion and confusion could be solved by staring into a half-empty mug of coffee.

Her heart broke at the glimmer of hope, dashed at seeing Emily, instead of her former housekeeper.

"I'm Emily."

"Well, I *can* drive. He just won't let me." Sabrina sloshed the contents of her cup, watching the waves of brown liquid splash over the lip and to the saucer below. Then she stirred the puddle with one finger. "Funny, a friend once told me I don't have a conscience. But I do. I want my husband to be happy. But I have needs, too."

"I'm so sorry."

"It's not your fault. But he just kept me walking and walking."

* * *

As Emily was making meal preparations, a text chimed on her phone. It was from Brian.

Call me

Now?

Yes

Emily placed the call and Brian picked up on the first ring.

"You were right."

"About?" Her voice held the caution that stilled her body. She knew. Even without his confirmation, she knew what he would tell her.

"The powder, it's baby powder laced with fentanyl!" Brian's voice held a sharp, hysterical edge. "The capsule was plain sugar mixed with traces of fentanyl."

Emily gasped. Fentanyl was a synthetic opioid, a hundred times more potent than morphine and much more dangerous.

She knew exactly where that had come from. And she knew how it had gotten in there.

"I knew it," she said.

"Em, fentanyl, in combination with anything else, like anti-depressants or sleep aids, is super dangerous. If he's lacing her medication with this stuff, you need to call the police. If you don't, I have to."

"This is terrible."

"I'll say, and you dragged me into this. I'm so stupid. I'm going to get fired for running those tests. And if I have to testify..."

"Whoa. No one is testifying. The police can't prove that Dr. Roth put those narcotics in his wife's medication because he'll just deny it or say that his wife bought it. Or... Oh, God, Brian!"

"What?"

"He'll say *I* did it!"

"Oh man! You're right. Of course he will. That's what I'd say."

"What should I do?"

"Call the police. You can't unsee this. You have to report what he's doing to his wife."

Emily began to cry.

"Em?"

"It's a narcotic, Brian."

"Yes."

"I'm scared."

"Of Dr. Roth?"

"Of the police. They don't always get it right, you know?"

She swiped at the tears and sniffed.

"If you don't call, how will you live with yourself?"

Emily got control of her breathing.

"You're right. I'm calling the police now."

"What are you going to say?" he asked.

"That you found fentanyl in her medication."

"You can't do that! I'll get fired."

"You just told me that if I don't, you'll have to."

"But don't drag me into it. Just tell them what Mrs. Roth told you. That she thinks he's switching her medicine. Don't mention the testing."

"You think they'll believe a delusional woman over the doctor they call when they need a disturbed suspect evaluated?"

"Maybe not, but it's worth a try. Cover your ass if nothing else. And if they take her medicine, they can run the same tests. And then they can't claim that you or I tampered with the pills."

"That's smart."

But even as she said it, she knew they might still suspect she was responsible.

"And you'll have a clean conscience. You did what you could. No one needs to know about the testing. All right?"

"Sure, Brian. I don't want to get you in trouble."

He was off the hook and his tone relayed relief.

"Hey, good luck with everything. Let me know how it works out."

"I will. Thank you."

She ended the call.

"Who are you talking to?"

Emily spun around. Sabrina leaned against the entrance to the kitchen, arms folded, fingers restlessly drumming on her biceps.

"Just a friend."

"Are you going to call?"

Emily's mouth was so dry she couldn't even swallow back the dread.

"Call?"

"You just told that person you would call the police because you have evidence my husband is putting narcotics in my medication."

TWENTY-NINE

"Do you know where he'd get fentanyl without a prescription?" asked Sabrina, her eyes suddenly very clear and sharp.

Emily knew but revealing that she knew would be admitting what she'd done. The little key she'd fashioned for Dr. Roth's locked cabinet seemed to be pulsing against her leg. And Dr. Roth's reasons for keeping his bathroom drawers secured became apparent. Had he tried other things to help him sleep before resorting to the Russian roulette of a synthetic opioid? Or had he obtained this deadly drug for something more sinister?

Inside his locked bathroom drawer, below the razor and shaving cream, tucked beside his expensive cologne, were syringes and three types of fentanyl. First was the prescription boxes with the foil card insert holding neat rows of white pills that needed only a push to release. And he had the 29ml bottle, half full. But most damning of all was the baggie of blue pills, like the ones she'd seen during a lecture in her class on substance abuse. Street drugs, made in illegal labs for recreational use. She'd seen them again in person during her practicum in the ER when they'd fallen out of a dealer's pocket while the team struggled to stop the bleeding from the three bullet holes in his chest.

Sabrina sat still, breathing hard, apparently taking in this new blow to her floundering relationship with her husband.

"Fentanyl is a pain reliever, a powerful one. Does he have chronic pain?" asked Emily.

Her patient snorted. "No. Anxiety."

Emily's gaze flicked away as the pieces seemed to settle into place in her mind.

"If he's added opioids to your medications, it explains why you've been so agitated. Why you have no appetite. I think you're going through withdrawals."

Sabrina opened her mouth but was speechless. How much had Sabrina heard of her conversation with Brian?

"You said the police can't prove that Henry put narcotics in my medication. So, you've had it tested?"

"I did."

"Well, we have the drugs. Bottles of them. I know he's putting something in there."

Mrs. Roth held her smile, as if pleased to finally have her suspicions confirmed. The delight did not reach her cold eyes.

Emily hesitated. If they called the police, she might get fired.

It was worth the risk. She knew what was right and she knew what she had to do.

"Mrs. Roth, is there someone else you could call? A relative? Or someone you trust?"

"I trusted my dad and he found Henry. Though he's doing a crap job, obviously."

"What about your daughter?" Emily belatedly recalled that Sabrina had said Taylor hated her. Could that be true?

"Oh, she'll side with Henry. Daddy's little spoiled princess. The first thing she'll do is call him, guaranteed."

"Do you want to call the police?"

"No, because he said there's no statutory limitations. They can arrest me anytime."

"Arrest you? For what?"

Her voice was an angry bark. "Killing that woman!"

This again. Emily forced herself to keep calm.

"You were a passenger. Everyone said so."

"I was driving."

This circular thinking reminded Emily of the dementia patients who couldn't remember their spouse had died and had to hear the news again and again, daily, hourly, until someone figured out an easier, less traumatic narrative.

"Social services can help you leave your husband."

Though she'd never heard of a woman like Sabrina King Roth having to resort to help from a social worker.

"No. I'm not ready for that. Not yet."

"But you were right about him tampering with your prescriptions. And fentanyl is addictive. Mixed with your other medications, it could kill you."

"He'll be so angry if I call."

"But you'll be free."

Sabrina tugged her phone from her front pocket and held it in two hands as if she held a baby bird.

"You think they'll help me?"

"They should."

"But what if they reopen the investigations?"

Emily did not want to dive down that rabbit hole right now. She refocused Mrs. Roth. "This is about the street drugs he's added to your medicine."

"He can't keep me here. If I could just get out and do things, get some relief, instead of..." Sabrina closed her eyes and a look of happiness lifted her features as she tipped her face upward toward the ceiling.

"You don't need to stay away long. This is your house. You can get it back."

"Yes. A short stay. Somewhere I can think and breathe and fantasize. Spa resort. Maybe Colorado or New Mexico. Oh, Taos!" She lifted her phone. With more determination than Emily had seen her do anything other than draw, Mrs. Roth called 911.

"This is Mrs. Sabrina King Roth. I want to leave my husband. I think he's putting something dangerous in my medicine, a narcotic. I need... I need someone to test them."

Emily stood by as Mrs. Roth told them where she lived and her husband's full name.

She remembered what Rosalind had told her, that the police no longer responded to Sabrina's calls. If she was right, the cops wouldn't come, but her husband would.

Emily had kicked a hornets' nest. Things were about to get worse for all of them.

Worse before better, Emily thought, refusing to turn back now.

Sabrina ended by saying. "Yes, I'm at home." Then a pause. "All right. I'll be waiting." She set the phone on the kitchen breakfast counter and Emily watched the other party disconnect.

"Are they coming?"

"I think so. They told me to wait, and they'd send someone to help me."

"Someone?" Emily had a good idea who that someone would be.

In less than a minute, the security camera in the kitchen clicked on.

"Why don't we go sit in the family room?" Emily asked, feeling the glass eye on her.

Sabrina's phone rang. She glanced at it and said, "Henry."

Then she left her mobile, following Emily down the hall.

"Let's have a seat and wait. They're coming. You're safe."

"And soon I'll be free," Sabrina whispered.

They sat waiting. Finally, the chime from the kitchen, and Sabrina's phone, chirped a familiar alert, notifying that the gate was opening.

Emily heard Dr. Roth tear into the driveway and skid to a halt. Next came the slam of the car door. The chime announced he was at the entrance.

Emily's self-preservation kicked in and she did something she was not proud of. She moved to the far side of the family room gaming table.

Playing stupid was her best option. The police were *not* coming. Of course they were not. They'd called him and he'd come home to deal with his delusional wife.

Unfortunately, she had her answer. The police would not investigate. They would not collect samples of her medication and have them analyzed. But they had logged her call and recorded it. That was enough.

Henry Roth charged through the kitchen, halting at the arching entrance to the family room as he spotted his wife seated on the sofa. His gaze darted to Emily.

He crossed the room in two long strides and grasped Emily's elbow in a punishing grip, trying to tug her out of Sabrina's sight. Emily shook him off and glared.

"She called the police." His voice was a low growl, like the warning given by a dog before it bites.

"She told me. I'm sorry."

"I left a patient evaluation because my wife just phoned 911."

Emily dropped her chin but kept her attention on him, and the threat he had become.

"It's your job to keep an eye on her."

Oh, no, she thought, he was not pinning all his problems, mostly of his own making, on her. Emily pursed her lips and scowled. The best way she knew to handle a bully was to stand up to him. She lifted a finger at him.

"You also want me to do light housekeeping, laundry, receive and put away deliveries, and you told me she could be left alone and given her privacy."

Sabrina sat on the sofa facing Emily, a wicked smile curling her lips as if seeing Henry red-faced and panting was the most entertaining sight imaginable.

"She said I poisoned her! Someone from the police is on their way over here now."

Mrs. Roth stared at the huge television with unfocused eyes. The set was off.

"Bree?"

Sabrina turned her head, as if she were underwater, her movements slow. She now had that vapid, placid look on her face. She was either under the influence of the drugs she deigned to ingest, or she was quite a talented actress.

Which was it?

"Henry?" She smiled. "Is there anything on but this?"

Emily glanced from the blank television to Sabrina.

"What don't you like about it?" he asked.

"Too violent. Car chases, crashes, I can't get the sound of breaking glass out of my head. I need to leave," Sabrina told him. "Give me your car keys."

He knelt beside her, taking both her hands. "No, you need to stay where I can keep you safe."

"I'm tired of safe. You can't stop it. Just let me go. I need to be out there." She pointed at the entrance. "I'll come back. I always come back. I promise."

"You can't."

She pouted. "There's nothing wrong with me."

He squeezed her hands. "Darling, there is. You have a disso-ciative condition. It makes you believe things that are not true."

"I was driving."

He tipped his face toward the ceiling and exhaled. Then he drew in a deep breath and tried again.

"You're here in your home. You're safe. And you need your medications to stay calm and stable. They keep you from... Safe. Remember?"

Keep her from...? What had he been about to say before he changed direction?

Sabrina wobbled, suddenly off-balance.

"Someone found narcotics in my pills."

"Who?"

She pointed at Emily. "She knows."

Dr. Roth dropped his wife's hands and turned to Emily. She gripped the chairback like a shield, her heart thrashing so painfully in her throat that she couldn't catch her breath. She opened her mouth, gasping, and unable to pull the necessary oxygen from the air about her. Blood pulsed at her temples as he took a menacing step in her direction.

A text chimed on his and his wife's phone simultaneously. Was that the notice from the gatehouse announcing a visitor?

"They're here," he said.

The police? Jackpot, thought Emily.

He lowered his chin as he aimed a finger at her nose. "You let me handle this."

THIRTY

The police were not allowed inside this walled kingdom unless called by a resident. The gatehouse text informed both Dr. and Mrs. Roth that a Winter Haven police officer was responding to Sabrina's call.

The next alert came from their gate and Dr. Roth used his phone to open the barrier.

The Roths moved to the dining room, with Emily trailing behind. From the large windows, they silently watched. In rolled an officer on a large black and white motorcycle. Not the sort of conveyance the law used to transport detainees, Emily realized. Her stomach did a little shiver that radiated out to her fingers and toes. She didn't know what would happen next and fear pounded in her throat with her heartbeat.

Dr. Roth met the young officer at the door, trailed by his wife. Emily hovered in the dining room just off the foyer, watching. Listening.

The guy didn't look over twenty, had his mirror sunglasses up on the blond stubble covering his scalp. His biceps bulged from beneath the tight sleeves of his polyester uniform and the calf-high black leather boots hugged muscular lower legs. He gripped his helmet with one hand, holding it against his side, leaving his gun hand free.

"Responding to a call from this address." The officer rocked from toe to heel in his shiny black boots.

"I'm Dr. Roth." Henry extended his hand.

"Officer Jake Lewis, sir. We haven't met."

The men shook hands. Dr. Roth motioned to Sabrina.

"This is my wife. She's the one who phoned you. When you've finished speaking to her, I'd appreciate if we could have a private word. And this is our housekeeper, Emily. She's new."

She suppressed her annoyance at being called a house-keeper after a quick twisting of her lips and then nodded a greeting. Officer Lewis swept his gaze over her and then dismissed her, returning his attention to Dr. Roth.

Her heart continued its painful percussive beat in her chest.

When she was a little girl, just the sight of a police car would send both her mother and her sister into absolute panic.

Driving cars that shouldn't be on the road made the possibility of a ticket they couldn't afford a constant threat. Some of their irrational fear had leaked into Emily's DNA, but she fought it.

She glanced at Dr. Roth. If you didn't notice the forced smile, you might see a relaxed man, self-assured and powerful enough to handle this nuisance. But she could see a threat glittering in those cold amber eyes.

This was not the jovial, approachable healthcare provider she'd first met. This was a hunting tiger.

Any trouble with his wife's medicine, anything added or changed, anything removed, would automatically be her fault.

He hadn't hired a nurse. He'd hired a fall guy.

Officer Lewis stepped over the threshold into the foyer, pausing there.

"Mrs. Roth, how are you feeling?" he asked.

"I'm fine." She was now seated on one of the long, low couches beside a multitude of the blue and green pillows.

Lewis continued into the room, his boot heels tapping on the tiles.

"Did you call to say your husband is tampering with your medication?"

"He is."

"I see. And how do you know this?"

"She said so." Sabrina motioned to her.

Emily felt all her muscles tightening as she suppressed the urge to run. But she held her ground. She could do this. She had to.

"And I'm tired all the time when I take them. I can't even paint or drive. I'm stuck here."

Officer Lewis turned to Dr. Roth.

"She's on some prescriptions that make it impossible for her to safely drive. And as for painting, my wife is a talented artist. That's one of hers on the wall."

Emily stared in surprise at the landscape of Florida's natural springs with lush vegetation painted in deep blues and shades of green. Tiny patches of a hazy sky dipped between the tree-tops. The foliage colors melted and blurred across the water in the foreground. Set on the shore was a small, weathered dock that seemed to have been there for decades.

She could hardly believe that this work and the violent, scribbling pencil drawings were ever created by the same person.

"My wife has some mental health challenges. I have the medical records if you feel you need to see them."

"Not necessary. My captain filled me in."

Lewis faced Emily. "Was it your idea to call the police?"

"No. My client believes that her husband is tampering with her medication. She wanted to call you. I was too late to stop her." The lie, told for self-preservation, did not trouble her. Everyone had a right to protect themselves from monsters.

"My wife has a lot of troubling beliefs," Dr. Roth interrupted. Now he turned to his wife, his tone softening. "Bree, what happened to that young mother, Avery?"

"I killed her."

"And your housekeeper, Regan?"

"I killed her, too."

"What about your mother?"

"Killed her."

He turned to Lewis. "Her mother died of natural causes in Lakeland Hospital."

Sabrina shook her head at this information. "No. That's wrong."

Dr. Roth turned to Lewis and gave him an expression that said, *See what I'm dealing with?*

"And why are you taking those medications?" Lewis asked.

"I'm not taking them. Not all of them. Not anymore."

Henry looked startled at this.

"Bree, you need to—"

Officer Lewis lifted a hand to silence him.

Dr. Roth stopped speaking but his face turned red. He was obviously unaccustomed to being silenced, especially by this public servant who hardly looked old enough to shave. Was he about to give him the "I pay your salary" speech?' Emily wondered.

"Mrs. Roth, do you want to leave this house?"

She looked at her husband and then went back to the officer. "Well, sometimes."

"Do you want to leave your husband?"

She thought about that one. "Sometimes. I like to visit her."

"Who?"

"My mother. At all the places."

Confusion wrinkled the officer's brow and he hiked his

helmet farther under his arm.

"All?"

She nodded. He glanced at Henry, who shrugged.

"She visits the favorites in her navigation app," Emily said.

This got a reaction from Dr. Roth. His eyes rounded and his confidence slipped into an expression of shock.

No, fear.

He knew. Emily was certain now. Henry knew about the other traffic accidents. About his wife visiting them.

The officer flicked his gaze to Dr. Roth. "Could you give me a moment alone with your wife?"

Dr. Roth hesitated, then smiled. It was the smile Emily recalled from the hospital, warm and disarming. And disingenuous, she now knew.

"Sure." Dr. Roth motioned her toward the kitchen. "Emily?"

She followed him through the entrance, where they stood out of sight, but not quite out of hearing. Dr. Roth ignored Emily, straining to listen to the conversation happening in the other room.

"Mrs. Roth," said Officer Lewis, "do you feel safe in your home?"

"Yes."

"Do you want to leave your husband?"

"Sometimes. Can you test the medicine?"

"Do you want me to take you to the station? Get you some help?"

There was no reply.

"You have to say it, Mrs. Roth. If you want to go, I'll take you."

On his motorcycle? Emily frowned.

"Where would you take me?"

"The police station. We have people that can help."

"The station. No, thank you. I'll stay. Will you take some of the pills for testing?"

He raised his voice and called, "Dr. Roth?"

Henry retraced his route back to his wife.

"Do I also have your permission to take a sample of your wife's medications?"

There was a long pause here and a frown flickered before he regained his welcoming expression.

"Sure." He turned to her. "Emily, would you?"

She darted to the kitchen to retrieve the bin of medications. When she had it in her hands, Sabrina, Dr. Roth, and the officer appeared from the living room.

Sabrina selected one capsule from a bottle. Officer Lewis held open an evidence bag, and she dropped it inside.

Dr. Roth took hold of Sabrina's elbow. "How about you go and lie down in your room? I'll give you something to help you rest."

She nodded. "They're going to test it."

"Yes. Come along." He turned and spoke over his shoulder to Lewis. "I'll be back shortly."

Emily watched Sabrina shuffle away as if she were an old woman. Was she acting? Emily could not tell.

She tucked the bin back in its place, then followed the officer as far as the living room. She could tell him everything. All the terrible secrets she now knew.

"Poor guy," said Lewis. Then he switched his helmet to the opposite hip and turned his focus to Emily.

"What will you do with that?" she asked, pointing at the bag.

"This? Nothing. File it for now. No budget for this kind of testing." The silence between them stretched. "Shouldn't you be keeping her safe and calm?"

"That's one of my jobs, yes. But she was very insistent."

"You realize calling the police with an emergency that doesn't exist is a crime."

"I didn't call."

"Just keep her away from the phone."

Her neck and face heated and her fingertips were numb from the mix of emotions zigzagging through her nervous system like heat lightning.

The anger simmered but she pressed it down.

Dr. Roth returned. "I'm afraid we've wasted your time. Ask your chief of police about Bree. He knows her, us."

"I'll do that, sir. You have a good evening."

"Thank you. You as well, and if you need anything, her diagnosis or medication list, for your report, I'll be happy to furnish it."

Emily felt as if she had vanished. She took a backwards step into the dining room, resisting the impulse to scuttle away like a crab, knowing that in a moment she'd be alone with Dr. Roth who would have no further reason to wear his public face.

She'd poked the bear.

"I'll walk you out."

"Unnecessary. You have a good evening, Dr. Roth."

The officer stepped out into the heat. The late-day sun sent shadows stretching across the driveway. Emily battled the urge to chase after him as Dr. Roth closed the door and watched from behind the lead glass windows set into one of the pair of impressive double doors. From the dining room windows, she watched Lewis kick his motorcycle to life, startling several white ibis who had been poking their long beaks into the grass in search of a meal. He rumbled out the gap in the high walls, bordered by a colorful hedgerow of tropical plants. Before he was out of sight, the gate swept silently closed, locking Emily in... with Dr. Roth.

He turned toward her, that vague, reassuring smile still on his face. But it morphed into a mask of such rage, Emily backtracked away until she pressed against the stove, gripping the oven handle with her sweaty hands.

THIRTY-ONE

This next part would be tricky because Emily didn't know what Dr. Roth would do now. She'd gotten Sabrina to call the police and, thankfully, they'd responded. Unfortunately, she hadn't agreed to go with them. That left Emily here, alone with her patient and Dr. Roth. Funny that they'd never asked *her* if she felt safe here or if *she* wanted to leave?

But neither had she asked to leave. So now she'd have to deal with this enraged man.

She'd never seen him so angry. Would his survival instinct protect her, or did he believe himself to be untouchable?

She was about to find out.

"You have one job," he growled, stalking through the dining room, tracking her like a lion after a gazelle.

Emily swallowed past the jagged lump in her throat. "I'm sorry. She made the call."

"You didn't stop her. Encouraged her. She said *you* told her I was tampering with her medication."

"I never said that."

"She said you had her medicine tested. Did you?" His expression and posture held menace.

"Yes. I did that." A hot rush of alarm made her ears tingle and her cheeks burn. "Because your wife was worried. I thought a test, a negative test, might help reassure her."

"Why would you think that, when I explained that you can't stop paranoid thinking or rationalize your way out of an organic delusion no matter what the proof?"

"I'm sorry." Sorry at being caught. Not sorry for the testing. Sorry she was now facing this monstrous version of Dr. Roth.

He glared at her through bloodshot eyes, fists clenching as if he gripped a heart in his fingers and was determined to force it to beat. "Why does she think there are narcotics in her prescriptions?"

"She stopped taking the capsules. I was speaking to a friend on the phone about it. She overheard."

"Speaking about my wife. Her condition? Her delusions? You signed an NDA, Emily."

He shoved her hard. The push rocked her back and she lost her grip on the oven handle, sliding across cabinets to the floor. He bared his white teeth, which now looked dangerous and predatory, as he grabbed her with one large hand between the neck and shoulder, hauling her up.

Pain bit around the muscles as his fingers bruised her flesh, bringing a blinding white flash of panic. She struggled and clawed with fingers gone numb and tingling, a wild animal fighting for escape.

"It's your fault she called the police," he bellowed, releasing her roughly and causing her to dance backwards, her arms waving like a tightrope walker about to fall from a dizzying height.

He shoved her again and she stumbled, unbalanced, her torso hitting the edge of the stone countertop before falling into the gap between the kitchen stools and breakfast table. She didn't stop there but flipped to her hands and knees and scampered away until she had the round wooden table between her and this dangerous stranger. Her body quivered as instinct sent her conflicting messages to fight and freeze and run. Her muscles tensed as panic filled her chest like the expanding gases of a supernova.

She was nearly the same height, but he outweighed her and had the benefit of testosterone to fuel his fury and brute strength.

On the breakfast bar sat a wrought-iron fruit bowl filled with colorful blown-glass balls. In an instant the tasteful display turned to a potential weapon. If he took one more step in her direction, she would throw the largest glass ball, like a shot put, at his head and then run for the door to the lanai and pool.

"Don't touch me," she said. Her voice was high and contorted by her squeezing vocal cords, making her sound like a terrified child.

Not far wrong, she thought.

This was more than she'd bargained for.

"Or what?"

"I'll quit. I'll go to the police."

He made a sound of amusement and his shoulders bobbed.

"Do it. And I'll have you arrested for endangering my wife, stealing her prescriptions, and breaking our NDA. Say goodbye to your job, along with your reputation. I can have your license suspended with one phone call. When I'm done, your legal bills will put you in debt for the rest of your life."

Was this the man who had just been lecturing her on professional ethics?

"I—I..." She needed time to think.

"Violating that NDA. I'll sue you. Breach of contract. You'll have to go to court. And I'll collect damages, which you can't afford, plus my legal fees. I'll garner your wages 'til the end of time. Have you ever been to jail, Emily?"

She had been, but only as a visitor. If it was an idle threat, it was an effective one. There were few things that she feared more than the idea of being caged in a tiny, barred cell.

Emily's fury seared through her chest and bolted down her arms and legs, lifting her and making her strong as their stone countertops. "You won't take me to court because you don't want me on that stand telling the world what's happening here."

He hesitated.

She stood now, fists balled, breathing fast, ready to fight. "You just want her money."

"True. But she's not leaving, either. She might want to, but she won't. Because my wife needs my protection as much as I need her money."

"You're a monster."

"I'm a realist."

"If you touch me again, I'll call the police."

He snorted. "Go ahead."

She gripped her phone. Did he believe he'd gotten the better of her?

Emily's back throbbed and the place on her neck where he'd hauled her to her feet burned as if he'd branded her.

He expelled a breath and his tone changed. When he next spoke, he sounded less threatening, his words and tone coaxing. But the threat was there glittering like poison in his eyes.

"Emily, you have nowhere to go. No one to help you, either."

What did that mean?

The aching at the back of her throat became too full to contain. She choked on the sob. Tears and snot ran down her face. Ashamed and confused, she wiped away the moisture.

"Of course. Tears. The coward's last resort. From this instant, you will keep my wife quiet and no more phone calls."

As if on cue, his phone chimed with a ringtone she'd never heard. "Daddy's Little Girl," she realized, the kind of song brides picked for their father-daughter dance at weddings. Was that his mistress?

If so, yuck.

He aimed a finger at her. "Stay right there." Then he took the call, his voice now upbeat and jovial. "Hey, little girl!"

Emily blinked in surprise at the change in tone, from menace to delight.

"What's up, pumpkin?"

Was this the same man who, just a few moments ago, had shoved her to the floor and then threatened her with jail time?

He was listening now and Emily was reevaluating. A man with such an ability to transform was more chameleon than human being. She didn't know a lot about mental disorders. Just the small amount she had been taught to help depressed patients in her care. But she knew what a narcissist was. And she knew that narcissists were dangerous kin to sociopaths.

She glanced out the kitchen sliders at the turquoise waters of the shimmering swimming pool. The screened cage was not locked.

Her legs seemed wooden, unable to move as an animal instinct caused her to remain still as if that would somehow make her invisible. Meanwhile, her heart slammed in her chest, preparing her for the possibility of flight. She repeatedly tapped her index fingers to her thumbs worried about the tingling of her fingertips and knowing she should be worried about the larger threat before her, speaking to his daughter as if he had not just shoved Emily to the floor.

Should she make a run for it?

And go where and do what? He was right. She had no powerful allies, hardly any resources, and a tenuous job here. If he sued her, she'd never be out of debt. He knew it, knew he could get her license suspended, and understood exactly what that would do to her chances of earning a living.

No wonder he thought her no threat.

"Well, he's your husband, Taylor. You should ask him about that." Dr. Roth's words fell off and he glanced at Emily, his face now hard as stone.

Then it changed again, and he smiled as he nodded.

"Yes, I'm sure you do." He chuckled. "No, I'm not. I'm listening. Go ahead."

Emily lifted her phone from her pocket. Keeping it below the counter, she entered the letters "VO" into the search box, and the search engine populated the choices, including *Record Voice Memo*. She opened the app and hit record.

He was listening, eyes turning upward as he appeared to consider whatever his daughter was proposing.

"You're welcome anytime."

Emily could almost hear her, this spoiled, entitled child, turning to her daddy when she had any trouble from her husband.

"Well, I know he's not there a lot. I can hire someone to be there with you. Especially if they think the twins might come early." His mouth went tight at whatever his princess said next. "Yes, I know, but she's not doing well, and I just can't leave right now."

Emily could hear the whine in the woman's voice but could not make out the words.

"Well, that's what a medical residency is and exactly the point. He's going to be away a lot. You are welcome to come here. Just until the babies come. You know that?"

She could hear the voice but not make out the words.

He lifted a hand in surrender. Clearly this girl had Daddy wrapped around her finger.

"I know you can take care of yourself." He wiped his brow. "Yes. Yes. I'm sure it's a wonderful birthing center, but if you feel better having me nearby, then come up and stay here with us. We'd love to see you."

Emily slid her phone, face down, onto the counter between

them and it was lost amid the clutter of food containers on the stone counter.

The silence stretched, marked by the pounding of her heart. It was illegal to record someone without their permission, wasn't it?

Dr. Roth continued his conversation. "No. She's a little worse."

Emily wanted to sit down. The adrenaline was draining away, and her legs were trembling. She needed some water.

She crept around the table. He tracked her motion, turning as she headed for the cupboard for a glass and filled it with the cold water from the refrigerator.

"All right. Well, *I'd* love to see you."

Emily drained the glass. Then she retrieved a paper towel, mopped her face, and blew her nose.

"Don't thank me!" He laughed. "We're happy to do it." He nodded. "Then *I'm* happy to."

Emily put the glass in the dishwasher. Then she stood near the drawer that held the collection of long kitchen knives.

"Okay. Speak to you then." He smiled, clearly in love with his child.

Doting, dangerous dad, she thought.

"Give my best to Seth. I love you, too. Get some rest, baby girl."

He ended the call and tucked away his phone. The smile lingered on his lips.

"We bought my daughter a house in Tampa, but she's pregnant with twins and so they think the babies will come early and Seth is putting in long hours. Residency at the hospital."

His disarming smile was back, and his tone held the congeniality that she'd once found charming. Now it terrified her. How could he go from attacking her to discussing his family, as if none of it had happened? As if there was nothing left of his fury. If anything, his calm further unsettled.

Emily blinked at this change of tone. She was still buzzing with adrenaline at facing a physical threat. Her heart pumped, her breath came in frantic blasts, and her skin sizzled with heat. He might be done fighting, but she wasn't.

Dr. Roth either did not note her upset or ignored it as he continued. "She doesn't like being alone in that big house."

The sensible reply was marred by her frantic breathing. "The one you just bought her?"

"Exactly. We'd just like her closer to home."

Emily nodded her understanding and wrapped her fingers around the handle of the drawer holding the knives.

THIRTY-TWO

"So, where are we leaving this, Emily?" he asked, as if they were discussing a research project instead of his violent attack.

"You knocked me to the floor. You grabbed me." She rubbed the sore muscles at her neck.

He waved a dismissive hand. "Take one of my wife's pain pills, if you need one."

As if she ever would. That would only make it impossible for her to honestly deny that she had ever taken any of his wife's medication.

"I don't think so."

He smiled as if recognizing that she'd spotted the snare he'd left for her.

"Then what *are* your plans, Emily? Shall I bring the police back? You can allege I pushed you while I contend you fell. Or shall I call my attorneys and begin legal proceedings against you?" He lifted his brows and smirked as if the prospect of suing her delighted. "Get your name in the papers. I'll be sure that you get a color photo being served."

She grimaced. Her mouth felt full of cotton as she confronted this threat. Not the physical kind, but the other kind, the ones that ruined lives, ended careers before they began, and put people in prison.

She set her jaw and tried to stop shaking.

"Or shall we move forward? I have my priorities and I know you have yours."

Oh, he had no idea. Emily swiped at the tears dripping down her cheeks and continued to breathe as if she'd just completed a cross-country run.

"What do you want?" he asked.

Her voice was alien and she hated the unfamiliar squeak. "Stop sedating your wife and get her evaluated by an impartial psychologist."

"No. What else?"

She blinked at him. The shock of his reply rendered her speechless. But she drew herself up and tried again.

"You don't touch me again."

"Don't give me a reason. Next?"

She shook her head, baffled.

Emily could either stay and abuse her patient or leave and be charged with that crime. She hated both choices and felt as off-balance as a rock climber watching their anchor line fail.

"Replace that heap beside my garage with a new car?" he asked.

Like he had done for her last nurse?

"More money?" he offered.

As if every problem in the world could be solved with the right amount of cash. She silently fumed, recognizing that he routinely bought his way out of trouble with his wife's money and that it was going to work again.

"Yes."

"Ah, well, now we are down to it. Money for cooperation and loyalty. Just like the mercenaries of old. You understand that a word from me and you won't like what happens next."

He could do it. Every single thing he threatened.

And she hated him for it. He wasn't a good husband, protecting his wife. He was safeguarding his position, and her wealth, for himself.

"What about a Kia? I hear good things. Or a Mini Cooper. They're nice, suitable for the help."

She blinked, realizing he was again offering her a new car—the bribe, a hefty one. But not to him. To him it was nothing. Pocket change.

"A bribe," she said, "for my silence."

"Let's not call it that. The conscience is a pliant thing, Emily. You can make a case for this. It can help you get that education you want."

He knew all about her. Not just her class rank but her ambitions. What else did he know? The possibilities shuddered through her, making the hairs on her neck lift.

"I'd be willing to fund some night classes. Summer session. Start right away. Get you a solid foundation toward becoming a nurse practitioner. Glowing letter of recommendation once you graduate. Useful, right?"

That was very tempting. All she had to do was check any human compassion or traditional sense of right and wrong.

Why should she care about Sabrina or Henry Roth when neither one would turn on the garden hose if she were on fire on their front lawn? Unless it was to save the grass.

Next, he offered her a thousand-dollar cash bonus for each week his wife did not need him to come home early or feel the need to call the police.

"I can get you admitted to USF or UCF. Just a simple phone call to a friend and, with a new car, commuting will be a snap."

She was embarrassed at how much she was tempted.

"This is wrong, you know. Keeping her from getting real help."

"*I'm* real help. I'm the consulting physician on all the

mentally ill patients in the entire county. I'm the first call from our local police and I have a private practice with a five-star rating. I think I know what the best treatment is for my own wife."

The shoemaker's children go shoeless. She thought again about that proverb.

"And as long as she's here, you keep control of her fortune."

"Yes. That too."

He didn't even try to deny it.

Emily forced herself not to glance at her phone and the voice recording that should be in progress.

"But I'm willing to share. So do your job, Emily. Take what I'm offering and keep your mouth shut."

The worst part, the very worst part, was that he left her with two terrible options.

"Are we done?"

She nodded.

"Good. See you in a few hours." He aimed a finger at her. "No more police."

He left her there. Shortly, she heard the revving engine of his sports car. And then, like a nightmare, he was gone.

Emily checked her phone to find the recording app still running. It took only a moment to discover she had captured their conversation. She left it as is, with only the date as a file name. Then she went searching for Sabrina, finding her sleeping in her bed, covers loosely drawn over her and tucked in such a way that she suspected Dr. Roth had done this after sedating her. Had he given her an injection?

In the primary bathroom, Emily stood before the huge wall of mirrors above the double sink. Gingerly, she drew the blouse away from her neck and winced. The muscles throbbed when she turned her head. Angry purple fingerprints marred her skin.

She wondered if she had the guts to go through with this.

Once she threw this gauntlet down, Dr. Henry Roth would be gunning for her with both barrels.

Emily had very little money. But she'd now managed to save enough for her mother's headstone.

He could sue her, but he'd never collect. Blood from a stone, she thought. And there were worse things than debt. Much worse. He wasn't getting away with this because she wouldn't let him.

With her phone in her hand, she snapped a photo of the marks. Then she turned and twisted, dragging up her blouse to expose the long scrape and bruising where she'd struck the edge of the counter and cabinet pull on her way to the tile floor.

Her roommate wasn't allowed to take personal phone calls while at work, but a text usually got through. Emily would send her a video message and Jennell could view the file when she had her break.

Emily set her teeth and tapped on the phone's video app. The recording she made showed herself in the mirror revealing the marks on her neck, then the long welt and bruising on her back, wincing.

"Jennell, I know you can't take calls at work, but I'm in trouble. So, I'm sending you this video message. I hope you get it soon. Sabrina called the police. Dr. Roth found out. I don't know how. I think the cops called him or something. He was there before they even got through the gate. She told them her husband was drugging her. They didn't believe her. Took his word on everything and left. Dr. Roth sedated her and then..." The tears made her vision blurry, but she held the phone steady. "He told me I was working overtime and left. I can't come home, and I'm scared. Jennell, what should I do?"

She AirDropped the two still images and the video to her roommate.

Her phone rang a few moments later.

"Emily, you need to get out of there right now."

"He said if I leave, he'll call the police. I'll get arrested, Jen."

"For what?"

"I broke our non-disclosure agreement. Told Brian what Mrs. Roth said. I told you, too. He said he'll take me to court."

Jennell's heavy breathing sounded in the silence.

"He offered me more money. Said he'd buy me a car."

Her voice rose. "Of course he did. These people! They think money will fix anything. They treat us like shit, like we're beneath them or something. All day I deal with these self-entitled pricks and their spoiled-rotten designer wives."

Emily's tears burned her throat. "Maybe if I just keep my mouth shut and his wife safe, he'll leave me alone."

"He can't hit you, Em. That's not cool."

"It was a shove. Two, actually."

"He tried to strangle you."

She didn't contradict her friend. The marks on her throat spoke louder than she ever could.

"You have proof."

Emily pressed a hand to her forehead.

"Do I? He could say my boyfriend did this to me."

"You don't have a boyfriend."

"Or that I fell."

"And choked yourself on the way down? You should go to the ER and have him charged with assault."

"I can do that. But then what? Do you really think anyone would listen to me? Tonight, when the police came, he got them to just leave. No charges, no report, and they didn't believe anything his wife said. He's a powerful man. He's got powerful friends, knows the chief of police, and, oh, I don't know who all. It would be like accusing Santa Claus."

"So, what? You're just going to stay there and let him hit you?"

"I don't know." Emily choked on a sob.

"So don't go to the police. But just leave. Don't go back."

"I owe you rent. And if I leave, he will one hundred per cent follow through on every threat." And if she stayed, she could sock away some money, use it to escape. She needed to follow the plan and do what she had to, even if it made her uncomfortable and even if the work involved being degraded and belittled. Working for this couple was a terrible means to an end.

"I did something. It could get me in more trouble."

There was a pause. Then Jennell asked the obvious question.

"What did you do?"

"I used my phone. I recorded a voice memo of his trying to bribe me, grabbing me, and admitting he's after her money."

"That's evidence!"

"He doesn't know I recorded him. That's illegal. He could press charges."

"So could you."

She snorted. As if she ever would. Somehow he knew it, too. Was that why he'd hired her? Thought she'd be easy to threaten and cow?

"I'd need a lawyer. I don't have any money for that." Emily gnawed on her lip, thinking.

"Make a copy. Put it on the cloud. If he threatens you again, play it for him. It's insurance."

"I don't know. That sounds risky."

Jennell was silent for a moment. Then she spoke in a quiet voice. "Do you want me to come get you?"

"No. I'll see you at home."

There was a longer pause and then Jennell said, "Be careful. That guy is dangerous."

He was. She knew that. He was a Florida panther, and she was just a little mouse. But even a field mouse had teeth.

THIRTY-THREE

"Why did you send that message to me if we aren't going to report his attack to the police?" asked Jennell. Her roommate had waited up for her, which was incredibly sweet.

Emily pressed her mouth tight for a moment, trying to keep the tears from welling in her eyes. She'd just come back from a terrible ordeal with Dr. Roth and she was spent and aching and her teeth were clattering as if she were out in a howling rainstorm. Only the storm was internal.

"I was scared and in pain."

"He assaulted you."

"Yes, but also, I don't know. It's crazy."

"What?" asked Jennell.

"In case, you know, anything else happens to me."

"Oh geez! Don't say that. You think he'd... what? Kill you?"

"No. Of course not. I wasn't thinking straight. He's a doctor. Doctors don't kill people."

Jennell snorted. They both knew that doctors did kill people. Sometimes on purpose.

"He's just trying to protect his wife."

"His wife's fortune, you mean."

Emily wondered if sharing so much with Jennell had been the right call.

"Either way, having me disappear isn't going to protect anything."

Jennell looked unconvinced.

"You think he can get away with murdering me?" Emily asked.

"Maybe. It happens, you know."

She did know. And sometimes police got it all wrong. They were human, they had their prejudices and made mistakes, just like everybody else.

They often targeted the obvious suspect and, whether from laziness or prejudice, looked no further.

"I haven't given up. I just need to think this through. It's not like Sabrina Roth is a normal woman unhappy in her marriage."

"No, she's a rich, crazy, unhappy woman."

"Mentally ill," corrected Emily. "She hallucinates and needs special care. I can't just drive her to a shelter and wave goodbye."

"What happens if she's off her meds?"

"I don't know, but Brian..." She hesitated. This might be too much because Jennell was not going to sit by, once she knew that Brian had found fentanyl in one of those capsules. And if Emily added that she'd seen Sabrina stabbing one of the photos in her secret album, with the pointy end of her compass, it would be too much.

"What were you about to say about Brian?" Jennell asked.

Emily's hesitation seemed endless. Finally, she said, "I should call him."

Jennell gave her a critical stare, perhaps sensing the half-truth.

"Did he finish the testing?" she asked.

Emily didn't like to do it, but she lied. "Don't know."

"Then I guess you *should* call him."

Emily nodded and the conversation stalled. Jennell picked it up again.

"And you're going back there tomorrow?"

"Yes. Don't you see? If I call the cops, he calls his lawyers. And he wins."

"Well, what else can you do?"

She didn't answer. But there was more than one way to skin a cat. He wanted to call lawyers. Fine.

"I wish I could get her out from under his thumb and somewhere safe. She wouldn't go to the police station. Didn't want to leave her home."

"I can understand that. Can you get the police to remove him?"

"I can't. All I can do is encourage her to do that and so far she won't even agree to call her lawyers."

"Em, this isn't your problem. It's theirs. I think you should quit."

"I can't. I can't leave it like this."

Jennell cradled her chin in her hand, thinking.

"If I could get her out of that house. Somewhere he can't instantly find her and bring her back in a padded car," said Emily. "Then an objective mental health professional could evaluate her condition and make an impartial diagnosis. I mean, I only have his word that her hallucinations and flashbacks are the result of trauma."

"What about my hotel?"

"*Your* hotel? You own that hotel now?"

"No, but weeknights they don't often book the suites. I use them when we have a problem guest whose room isn't ready, or something is wrong with a guest's room."

"So?"

"Call her lawyers or the police. Maybe call her daughter. Or you could bring her there."

"Really?"

Jennell smiled. "Of course. I want to help."

"I appreciate that, but she's delusional. She thinks things that didn't happen are real. She sees people who aren't there. I've seen her talking to someone. And she keeps calling me by someone else's name."

"You could stay with her. You know until you can call her lawyers or a regular doctor." Jennell snapped her fingers. "Hey, what about their daughter?"

"Sabrina says she hates her."

Jennell frowned unable to even process a daughter not loving her mother with everything she had. Emily felt just the same. They were lucky that way.

"Okay. You need to get the heck out of there."

"I need to get her out of there, too."

THIRTY-FOUR

Emily arrived at the Roths' on Tuesday in a newish skirt and blouse, thanks to her local Goodwill. It seemed a lot of new retirees had cleaned out their closets of work clothes. Pencil skirts, blouses, and winter coats filled the racks, abandoned like snakeskins in the spring. The one she wore today was khaki and the blouse a navy blue.

Despite being fifteen minutes early, the laundry room door was open. She called a hello from the kitchen and spotted Sabrina sitting with her husband in the sunny formal dining room.

"Rain let up?" Dr. Roth asked as if the beams of sunlight flooding the room were not answer enough.

"Yes. Just stopped."

He glanced at the soaking hem of her skirt and the puddle forming from her shoes.

Emily held her tight smile and ignored the throbbing in her back that sent an electric jolt of pain down her spine whenever she moved. Why was the muscle soreness worse than yesterday? She hoped she hadn't cracked a rib.

"How are you both today?"

"Everything is fine," he said, in a tone that relayed it was anything but.

Henry collected his satchel and left the table, pausing in the kitchen, right before her. They were nose to nose, close enough for her to smell the stale coffee on his breath.

"You call me if there's anything, I mean *anything*, I need to know about."

"Yes, Dr. Roth."

He aimed a finger at her.

"She stays home today. I'll call to check in. No more screwups."

She nodded her understanding, but he remained, menacing. When she dropped her gaze, he left her trembling and wrapped in the comfort of her own arms.

When the door closed behind him, she waited for the reassuring sound of the garage door opening and then thudding shut. Only then did she clear the table, load the dishwasher, and clean all the surfaces while Sabrina flipped through her newspapers, ignoring Emily entirely.

It was so strange. Except for Dr. Roth's warning, they acted as if the police hadn't even been here yesterday. Was that normal, the rich person's coping method? Or had Sabrina forgotten in her confusion? Just keep on as if everything was fine?

Emily didn't know, but this entire ordeal upset her.

Eventually, Mrs. Roth rose and dropped her napkin beside her dishes, the last remaining portion of the room not tidied, and ambled off toward her bedroom.

By the time she returned, dressed in black capri pants and a yellow-green square-necked smock-top with a boho flare, Emily had the papers in the bin and the dishwasher started. Sabrina had pushed the three-quarter sleeves up above her elbow and, Emily noted with surprise, she wore subtle and expertly applied liner, mascara, and lip stain.

Sabrina looked put together and alert.

Why did that scare her?

Mrs. Roth breezed through the kitchen, treating Emily as if she were a ghost, heading for her studio. Emily decided two could play this game and went about her duties, ignoring Mrs. Roth.

Of course this ended at lunchtime, when Emily had to either alert her that her food was waiting or bring Sabrina her meal, depending on her client's mood.

Emily padded down the hall on her princess flats because Mrs. Roth objected to her sneakers. She found Sabrina in her studio, kneeling in front of the couch. She reached beneath, drawing out her photo album. No wonder Emily hadn't been able to find it.

Emily hovered in the doorway.

Sabrina sat on the rug with her back pressed to the couch and opened the album, starting at the beginning.

Emily cleared her throat and Sabrina glanced up.

"Come in."

Emily crept forward and stared down at the page.

"You can see it now."

She knelt beside Sabrina.

"My family," she said, not looking up again as Emily inched closer. "My mom had some professionally taken. All the Christmas cards. Here's one with my brother, her favorite."

The boy in the photo had similar dark hair as Sabrina's and they sat, side by side, looking like the theater masks of comedy and tragedy. Sabrina's face was wet with tears and her twin glowed with good cheer.

"This was the one she sent to everyone."

"Of you crying?"

"Yes." Sabrina turned the page. "Here's one of her. The best one."

She pointed a long finger at the woman who had both arms

extended toward the camera and, from her open mouth and furrowed brow, appeared to be both enraged and screaming.

"I took that one when I was eight. Really captured her. She made me throw it away. But I retrieved it. Had this printed after her death. It's the only one that shows what she looked like inside."

This disturbing observation made Emily's breathing catch, but like a bystander watching the aftermath of an accident, she couldn't look away.

Sabrina flipped to the next page revealing another Christmas card. "Here's another one she sent to friends and family." She and her brother wore Santa hats and matching pajamas. Her mother wore a velvet green cocktail dress and her father looked trim and handsome in a dark suit and red tie.

But Sabrina's mom's eyes were scratched out. The angry white lines zigzagged from temple to temple and the eyeballs had been replaced with punctures in the image.

Emily recalled the compass she had seen Sabrina wielding.

The unsettling feeling was crushed beneath a mountain of certainty.

Sabrina had taken a compass and put out the eyes of Michelle Horton King.

"I can't stand her smug smile or those blue eyes."

"Did you do that?" Emily pointed.

"On every one. Improvement. Don't you think?"

She thought that Sabrina was a madwoman. Possibly psychotic and definitely dangerous.

"Did you take any of your morning medication?"

"Not today."

"I think you might need it."

"Oh, without a doubt."

Her comment indicated she knew she needed her medication. Then why fail to take it? Sabrina's behavior and her decision to cease taking her meds left Emily wondering if all this time, Dr. Roth was treating his wife, but not for depression or delusions.

If she was correct, Mrs. Roth's condition was both dangerous and incurable.

Sabrina slapped the book closed and shoved it back under the couch. "Enough for today. Let's go for a drive."

"Dr. Roth said you should stay home today."

She frowned. "Oh, poop. And I promised." She grimaced, then smiled. "And he promised."

What had Dr. Roth offered to entice his wife to stay home?

Sabrina's phone chimed an alert and she glanced at the screen.

"Rosalind is here."

* * *

Emily arrived on Wednesday and found the usual mess in the kitchen and both the Roths quietly sipping coffee and reading the newspapers. Dr. Roth sat facing her but did not glance up at her appearance.

He was dressed for work in a perfectly fitted seersucker suit and black dress shirt. Today, his necktie, a pale blue and black plaid, was knotted at his throat. He made the picture of success with his feet planted on the pale Oriental rug, and one finger looped in the handle of his espresso coffee, as he studied the business section.

Beside him, his wife lounged in her nightclothes, her back to Emily and the local paper open before her to the lifestyle page.

"Good morning," Emily said and received no reply from either.

Retreating to the kitchen, she tackled the dishes. Even the slight weight of a serving bowl made her sore muscles twinge.

Though everything appeared a quiet, ordinary morning, Dr.

Roth had checked in with his wife twice yesterday by phone and once with her. All day the cameras were flicking on and off like a live television broadcast. Beneath the surface, everything was not normal.

At his usual time, Dr. Roth kissed his wife and left the table.

When he entered the kitchen, Emily asked, "Will Sabrina still have her golf league?"

"Sabrina is right here," said his wife from her place at the table in the adjoining room. She turned to cast a side-eye at the help, holding that haughty, stretched-neck posture that few women could pull off while dressed in pajamas. Her silky floral robe was open, gaping, and the tie closure draped to the floor. Her eyes were hawk sharp with no hint of that spacy haze Emily attributed to her prescriptions.

"I'm sorry," said Emily. "Will you be golfing today, Mrs. Roth?"

"Yes. She will," said Sabrina, referring to herself in the third person, as if she were royalty. Appropriate, thought Emily.

Henry muttered a farewell and left the house. Sabrina lifted her coffee and drained the contents.

"Would you gather up my things for golf, please?"

Sabrina then headed for her room, without waiting for a reply.

Emily went to the garage to find the door already closed and Dr. Roth's sedan gone. She gathered the pushcart and clubs, loading them into the SUV. Then she collected extra golf balls, adding them to the bag. She found Mrs. Roth's favored visor, checked that the sunscreen and bug spray were still in the side pocket, and added a water bottle. The golf shoes went in beside the bag. Then she loaded up the small portable cooler with ice and more water because Sabrina usually wanted one for the drive home and the temperature was already in the eighties and climbing with the usual blanket of sticky humidity.

When she returned to the house, Sabrina had not yet

appeared, so she checked the studio, mind racing at the disturbing images Sabrina had shown her yesterday. A glance at the camera found the indicator light off.

Down on all fours, she peered under the couch, then reached, and finally used her phone's flashlight app. There was nothing but dust bunnies under there.

Sabrina had moved the album again.

"Emily?" Mrs. Roth's voice came from the direction of the kitchen.

She hurried out to find Sabrina peering out the dining room window in a golf dress with a zipper closure at the neck and decorated with an overly large illustration of dogwood blossoms with blue petals. Perhaps orchids, Emily wondered, cocking her head.

Sabrina turned at Emily's appearance.

"There you are. I thought you'd already gone for the car. Is everything packed?"

"Yes, ma'am."

She glanced at her smartwatch. "Good. Let's go."

Sabrina headed out the front door. Emily locked it behind her and then hurried to the garage, pulling to the landing to collect Mrs. Roth.

It hurt to turn the wheel. But today, she could take a full breath without that sharp, worrisome pain.

When the SUV stopped, Sabrina descended the stairs waiting for Emily to round the grille and open her door. Emily switched off the engine because she was not letting Sabrina get into a running car without being behind the wheel. By the time Emily returned to the driver's seat and started the vehicle, Sabrina was buckled in and staring at her phone.

"How did you sleep?" asked Emily.

"Just fine."

That attempt at conversation died.

She tried again.

"I'm sorry about the police," said Emily, testing the waters and trying to discover what Sabrina remembered and thought about Monday's fiasco.

"Sorry I called or sorry they wouldn't believe me?"

"Both, I guess."

Sabrina chuckled. "You get used to it."

"Did you think any more on the problems we discovered with your medication?"

Sabrina cut her off. "I don't want to talk about it."

"Are you certain?" This was quite a turnabout from her attitude two days ago. The change of heart might give Emily whiplash.

"Henry and I had a talk. We came to an agreement."

Emily waited but she said no more. The frustration built as they neared the private club.

Sabrina scrolled through her favorites in the carputer's navigation app. What was she looking for?

They rolled into the grounds and up the long, elegant drive. Pink impatiens burst from their flowerbeds and onto the pristine lawn, and old, established royal palms waved their fronds in greeting in the gentle breeze.

"Over there," Sabrina directed, pointing to the same spot they always stopped. Emily unloaded the clubs, adding them to the handcart as Sabrina changed into her golf shoes. When she finished, Emily extended Sabrina's visor and gloves.

"Good luck."

Sabrina tipped her clubs onto the wheels of the cart and was off without a word.

Emily watched her go, wondering if she, herself, might be the one with the mental illness.

Back in the running car, Emily pulled up Mrs. Roth's favorites, programed into her navigation app. She tapped her phone's photo app, taking picture after picture. Some of those addresses were familiar. Sabrina had directed her to several just the other day. The reason began to fall into place.

Finally, she used her phone's map program on street view to virtually drive the first three locations. Each one contained a *Drive Safely* sign.

Next, she searched one unfamiliar address paired with the words: *traffic fatality*.

The results populated and her entire body vibrated with the chill of evil.

THIRTY-FIVE

Emily knew that Mrs. Roth's vehicle had been involved in a traffic fatality a decade earlier. But she visited the locations of other fatal crashes, ones where the hit-and-run driver remained at large.

Here they were, all laid out by date, stretching back over a decade, about the time the Roths had purchased that grand house.

Mrs. Roth liked to visit the sight of traffic fatalities. Was this some morbid hobby? A manifestation of her mental illness? Or was she more intimately involved with each of these deaths?

Emily needed to know.

By the time Sabrina's text arrived, Emily had composed herself. But a wild new possibility unfolded before her, like a tight bud blooming from unlikely to conceivable. What if... what if Sabrina had a hand in these? She had been a passenger in one fatality... and Rosalind had told her that Mrs. Roth's last nurse had a sudden replacement for her old car but couldn't afford to do so. Had Dr. Roth bought Clare Eastman a new one as a bribe for her silence or because something had happened to her old one? Emily studied the list. The list of kills? It was horrible.

It was possible.

And if Mrs. Roth did have more connection to these places than a morbid curiosity, then it would mean she was able to understand what she might have done.

Emily drove to the club entrance and held open the door for Sabrina, then retrieved her silver sandals and waited for her to slip out of her golf shoes before loading them and the rest of her gear in the back.

When they were underway, Emily opened the conversation.

"How was the match?"

"Game. This is a golf course, not a tennis court."

"Yes. Sorry."

"I shot four under. Some bad holes, some good. The usual."

Emily turned the wheel and the conversation. The air in the cool interior seemed to buzz with energy and she was glad her hands were tight on the wheel to diminish the outward signs that her mind was reeling and her body tight and coiled like a compressed spring.

"Sabrina, are you taking any of your medications?"

"Not anymore."

"Is that the deal you worked out with your husband?" She pressed her lips together and braced, waiting for Mrs. Roth's response to this bit of impertinence.

"You're out of line, Miss Emily."

She was, and the twisting ache in her stomach told her so. But she wasn't stopping now. "You know we are both prisoners in that house. Right?"

That caused her passenger to smirk.

"Not anymore."

"I want to take you to your attorney so you can explain what you feel your husband is doing."

"Henry is doing his best, as always."

"Will you go?"

"Absolutely not."

"You trust him?"

"Completely."

Emily's shoulders drooped at this defeat.

Sabrina selected one of her favorites from the list for them to swing by on the way home.

Emily knew the place. The unsolved fatality from March of this year. The brown Mazda, just like the one driven by Sabrina's last private nurse.

Rosalind had told her that Henry had purchased Clare a new car, the blue Prius, at about the same time as this latest traffic fatality. Was that because Sabrina had wrecked her old one killing a pedestrian? Henry, her problem solver, would have known that a damaged brown car was too risky to keep around. And he'd changed her medication recently. Had that been after this recent accident? Trying to manage the unmanageable. Or more recently, when the need had reemerged? Then they had "lost" Clare, and Emily had stepped into her shoes.

But being a zombie didn't suit Sabrina. She'd stopped her medication. And not for the first time, if Sabrina was to be believed. Henry noticed a little too late, after the police were called, unfortunately.

Now they'd come to some other arrangement. The possibilities made Emily sick.

"Mrs. Roth, that woman, the one that your assistant hit while you were a passenger? What did she look like?"

Sabrina's expression hardened into a twisted snarl of hatred.

Emily kept her hands tight on the wheel, slowing and then gliding to a stop in the parking lot of a suite of medical offices.

Sabrina did not notice they had stopped because she seemed to be looking backwards in time.

"That woman," she snapped, her tone filled with bitter

loathing. "With her designer handbag and nose in the air. That walk. The red lipstick and so neat. She was perfectly dressed and flawlessly styled. I hated her. Just like—"

"Your mother," finished Emily.

"Yes," she hissed the words, the sound full of venom.

"The airbag broke your wrist."

"Yes."

"Because you had your hand on the wheel."

Sabrina didn't deny it.

"I wasn't even in the driver's seat. Everyone said so."

"But you hit her."

"I did."

And there it was. The admission Emily needed.

"And Henry took care of it. That time. Every time."

Sabrina turned her head, still resting on the seatback.

"You're quicker than my last one. Wasn't until I wrecked her car that she figured it out."

"You're talking about Clare?"

"Eastman. Yes. Top of her class. Just like you. Bright. Inexperienced. Easy to handle. Funny, it used to be years between my excursions. But the need comes quicker now. It's constant."

"You're killing people."

Sabrina smiled, a look of perfect contentment on her face.

"Well, just one person." Emily had read about this, killers having a type. Mrs. Roth's type was any woman who had the misfortune of resembling her mother. If only she could have been like Edmund Kemper, the infamous serial killer who murdered nine people before finally killing his mother and then turning himself over to police. Sabrina's mother was long gone, so she could only settle for a substitute.

Killing her again and again.

Sabrina liked visiting the sites of her kills. Emily remembered Sabrina telling her to hush up. Was that so she could

relive the moment when she used a two-ton automobile to oblit-
erate her mother?

Henry knew. That's why he'd instructed her not to allow his
wife to drive. This had nothing to do with her medications. It
had to do with impulse control. He knew the need was building
and that his wife was moving closer to killing again.

Sabrina gave a vigorous shake, like a dog clearing water
from its coat. Then she drew a full breath and blew it away.

"Why have we stopped?"

"I have to go to the police," said Emily.

Sabrina lowered her dark glasses to stare at her for a
moment. Then she slipped them back in place. "I don't think so.
You signed an NDA, and if you tell anyone what I said, I'll deny
it. I'm crazy, remember. Nothing I say can be trusted. Plus,
there's no evidence implicating me. Henry has seen to that. And
if you are still determined, let me remind you that you are hope-
lessly in debt, need this job and a good recommendation and the
money, none of which you will get if you lose this job and have
to spend every waking moment defending yourself against
charges of defamation, incompetence, patient abuse, theft,
tampering with my medications, and anything else that Henry
and my fleet of attorneys can conjure from the ether."

Head pounding and heart throbbing, Emily choked the
wheel. Every single threat beat against her resolve like a
battering ram. They'd do it. And who knew if the police would
even believe her or bother to investigate? Henry had friends in
high places, like detectives and city councilors and judges?
These were the sort of people the Roths knew. They had power
and influence.

She had accusations. Nothing more.

Defeat dragged at her as her skin continued to burn with
her impotence. Trapped like a goat staked in the pen of two
hungry, capable, rich tigers. They were vicious and bloodthirsty,

and her only chance was to be less trouble than the other fettered goats. Useful goats didn't get butchered.

Emily swallowed back the disgust and the horror.

"Why did you tell me?" asked Emily, in a weak, defeated voice.

Sabrina narrowed her cold eyes on her.

"You won't do anything. You're smart enough to know that. Now be a good nurse and we'll replace your unfortunate vehicle and help you get that student loan under control. Best for everyone. Don't you think?"

Emily found herself nodding. Not because she agreed but because there was no point in objection. Nothing reasonable would work here.

"Besides, they won't believe me. And they *certainly* won't believe *you*."

There was a terrible truth in her words. Sabrina's accounting of events was dismissed because of her diagnoses. Henry had seen to that. And if Emily went to the police, Henry's connections, combined with his wife's condition, would make sure that anything Emily said was hearsay from a mentally ill woman.

Emily now knew what was wrong with this woman.

Psychopath.

Emily silently ticked another box. Sabrina visited her victims and was preparing to kill her mother yet again.

Henry knew.

She had all her answers.

THIRTY-SIX

All right, then, thought Emily—plan B. She was choosing the only path open to her.

"Get me some water," demanded Sabrina.

Emily drew a very specific iced water from the cooler and waited for Sabrina to crack it open. If she knew there were ways to reseal a bottle or if she noticed the difference when turning the cap to break the seal, she did not say.

Did she detect less fizz or a slight aftertaste?

"Let's get moving," said Sabrina, motioning with the bottle before taking several long swallows.

Emily drove in silence, waiting. Mrs. Roth sipped as the bottle beaded with condensation. When it ran down the plastic exterior and dripped onto her lap, she didn't seem to notice.

Sabrina closed her eyes. The drugs Emily had put in her water bottle were now circulating in her bloodstream. Emily waited for Sabrina's head to loll forward. Then she raised her voice to break into her trip.

"Mrs. Roth, are you okay?" Concern prickled over her skin because this had to work.

"Sleepy," Sabrina muttered. She blinked, suddenly bleary-eyed. She pressed a hand to her pale face. "I feel dizzy."

"Do you want me to call Henry?" Emily scanned her patient and then flicked her attention back to the road.

"Yes."

Sabrina wilted back in the seat and passed out.

Emily pulled to the shoulder and patted Sabrina's cheeks. Then she used the rest of the water to moisten a golf towel, pressing it to Mrs. Roth's forehead.

Sabrina blinked blearily at her, tried to speak, and managed only incoherent sounds.

Emily pushed down the panic bubbling up inside her as she lifted her phone and called Henry's office and got the message saying that if this was a medical emergency, she should dial 911.

"I'm calling an ambulance."

She placed the call and gave what details she could. Then she waited, holding the cold compress on Sabrina's forehead and watching her breathing.

The wail of sirens grew louder by the minute.

Emily disconnected and pressed two fingers to Sabrina's neck, feeling a strong, steady pulse.

"Help is on the way." But it wasn't here yet. Emily rocked back and forth, gripping the wheel in a steady rhythm, as time slowed.

The siren scream preceded the appearance of the flashing lights in her rearview.

One of the paramedics approached their vehicle and Emily leapt out to meet him.

"She's in the passenger seat. She had some kind of seizure and then just slumped over."

A crowd was gathering, drawn by the unfolding drama. They inched closer for a better look.

"Move, please. Coming through," said the second paramedic, lugging a huge bag toward the passenger side of the SUV.

Relief flooded through Emily, tempered by the realization that Sabrina was still ill, and her husband would be furious. Emily shrunk, feeling as vulnerable as a nesting bird in a hayfield at the roar of the approaching thrasher. Henry would find out. Henry would want to speak to her alone. A hand went to the back of her neck and the bruised muscles that still ached from their last "discussion."

The paramedics checked Sabrina, who roused to answer a few questions as Emily hovered, wringing her hands and craning her neck for a glimpse of Sabrina.

"Call Henry," she said.

They lifted her from the passenger seat and strapped her to the gurney. Emily explained who Sabrina was and that she had some mental challenges.

"I'll call her husband. Is she going to the hospital?"

"Yes."

Sabrina was panting like a husky on a hot day.

"I'm her private nurse. I have her purse and phone. Can I ride with her?"

The EMT said no.

"Can I speak to her?"

He hesitated, then waved her in. She climbed up into the back of the ambulance.

"Mrs. Roth." She spoke in the sort of voice you'd use to get someone's attention across a room.

Sabrina stared up at her, pupils huge and dark.

"I've called your husband."

Sabrina gasped, her gaze casting about as she seemed to come back to herself. "He'll be so angry."

The EMT climbed aboard and used his stethoscope to listen to Sabrina's breathing.

"Is there anyone else you want me to call?"

Emily leaned in to listen to Sabrina's reply.

"Your lawyer?" asked Emily.

She bent close and listened again as the EMT lifted a blood pressure cuff.

"I don't know the name of your lawyer."

The paramedic looked from her to his patient, performing his check of vitals, listening to the conversation.

"Gabriel Rottach." Sabrina spoke with perfect clarity. Then she cocked her head to stare at Emily. "Regan?" she asked.

"It's Emily. I'm calling Mr. Rottach now."

Sabrina nodded her understanding but now looked more confused than disoriented.

A police officer appeared at the back of the open ambulance.

"You're blocking traffic. What's the holdup?" he asked.

"Out you go," said the paramedic.

Emily scrambled down. The doors closed and Sabrina Roth was whisked away. She retrieved her phone from her back pocket and did a web search for Gabriel Rottach. Then she placed the call, her body's trembling made her voice squeaky and caused her to stumble over her words. But she got it all out.

She explained to the pleasant-sounding woman who answered that she was hired to look after one of their clients, Sabrina Roth, who was having some kind of episode. Mrs. Roth had instructed her to call them. She didn't exactly know why.

"I see. Please hold for Mr. Rottach."

The hold soundtrack played for only a few seconds. She suspected this was the time it took for the receptionist to relay her message and for Sabrina's attorney to scramble to take the call.

"This is Gabriel Rottach."

She explained her circumstances, her spasms now making her stomach squeeze and her muscles twitch as if stimulated by some external electric current.

"Have you tried her husband?"

"Yes. I called his office but got the answering system. The police said they'd notify him. But she asked for you by name."

The ambulance pulled away. The crowd of spectators milled about, speculating, and gossiping, gradually losing interest, and heading off.

"I see. Where is she?" asked Rottach.

"They're going to the hospital in Winter Haven."

"And you are?"

"I'm her private nurse. My name is Emily Lancing."

"Where did this happen?"

She told him.

"I see. Thank you for calling, Ms. Lancing. I'll look into the matter."

He ended the call.

The cop dropped behind the wheel and the cruiser pulled out. She stood in stillness, while her nerves jangled like the coins in an upended piggy bank, shaken by a greedy child.

What had she just done? And what would Dr. Roth do when he discovered she'd failed to keep his wife safe? Dr. Wrath, she thought, and stretched the bruised muscles in her back.

He'd sue her for sure.

She scurried back to the SUV, slipped into the driver's seat, and pulled forward, resisting the irrational urge to simply drive away.

"You're fine. You can do this. Just go to the hospital."

But she didn't want to. Perhaps it would be all right if Dr. Roth didn't get her alone. They'd be in public. If he grabbed her, she could scream and there would be witnesses. It wouldn't be her word against his.

But he wouldn't touch her because he'd be wearing that public-facing mask of calm and compassion. She would lay money on that. But if she went back to their home, then he'd have her alone.

The dread built, filling her stomach with tiny sharp burrs of anxiety. The memory of being shoved to the ground and then hauled to her feet flashed through her mind like black lightning, making her throat burn.

For another moment, she thought about running.

No, she was seeing this through.

She parked in the emergency lot, grabbed Mrs. Roth's empty water bottle, then locked the vehicle.

She should just wait in the SUV. But she was already hurrying across the lot, pitching out the empty in a garbage can on her way through the entrance to the emergency medical area, where a nurse kindly held the door for her.

At reception she asked about Sabrina Roth and was told to have a seat. After a few minutes, she was called to the admissions window, and gave what information she could about Sabrina, which was only her name, address, and her emergency contact.

"I have her purse, but I'm not comfortable rifling through for her medical cards. Her husband has privileges here."

"Dr. Roth. Yes, we're contacting him."

"Thank you."

"You can go back and have a seat."

She did, perching on the edge of the plastic chair with a view of the sliding double doors, palms sweating.

Fourteen minutes later, a man stepped into the lobby.

His gray suit caught her attention and the spring in his step. He was a big man, perhaps fifty, fleshy, balding, with a trimmed reddish beard defining what there was of his jawline. He was heavyset, with sagging jowls and a graying complexion that forecast an upcoming visit to the ER himself. But his suit fit perfectly, and his apparel gave the impression of significance.

"I need to see my client."

"I'm sorry, sir. It's family only beyond this point. If you'll have a seat."

"No. I have her power of attorney and healthcare proxy. That gives me the right to see her."

Was this Rottach? Yes, Emily recognized him from his photo on the legal practice's website. However, this man was older, heavier, and had less hair. How often did they update those professional photos?

Interesting that the attorney, and not Dr. Roth, would have this all-important document. Was that Sabrina's father's hand, meddling in affairs and adding safeguards to protect his surviving child?

How much had her father understood about Sabrina's real problems?

Enough, Emily decided. Everything she'd discovered pointed to a well-orchestrated plan.

"I'm Gabriel Rottach. My client is Sabrina Roth."

The receptionist glanced at the documents Rottach extended.

"May I make a copy?" she asked.

"Go ahead."

"I'll check with her attending physician."

"Great."

The receptionist placed both her broad hands on the desk and hoisted herself upright, then shuffled off with the page, tugging at her sweater and muttering.

When she returned and handed back the healthcare proxy, she buzzed the attorney into the ER. "Exam room four. On your right."

Emily hustled from the waiting area and out of the hospital's sliding glass doors, returning to the vehicle.

Ten minutes later, she was sitting in the SUV, waiting for something to happen. Beside her, Sabrina's purse lay abandoned on the floor, her phone chiming alert after alert.

THIRTY-SEVEN

Dr. Roth sent Emily a text that evening. Sabrina had been released. He expected to meet with her tomorrow morning—regular time. The result of that communication was that she barely slept.

After leaving the hospital, Emily had waited in the running car until Dr. Roth phoned to ask her about her version of what had happened. Then he'd instructed her to drive the SUV back to the garage and head home.

Emily had carried Sabrina's purse inside, finding everything just as she'd left it. She made a quick visit to Dr. Roth's study and then replaced Sabrina's purse in her primary closet.

Jennell's knock on her door startled Emily awake. Had she slept through her alarms? The vertical bars of daylight on her bedroom wall proved that she had slept. She sat up, disoriented and exhausted.

"You okay, kiddo?" asked Jennell.

"I'm up. Thank you."

She closed her eyes and dropped instantly into a deep sleep that was interrupted by a second knock.

"Sleepyhead, second call. It's six-fifteen. Get up or you'll be late."

Emily threw the coverlet aside and staggered to her feet as her blood pressure revolted at the sudden change in altitude. She sagged back to the mattress, her heart pounding.

"Are you up?"

"Yes. I am this time. Be right out."

"Okay. Bathroom is all yours."

She checked her phone and found it dead, so she set it on the charger and left the room.

By the time she reached their tiny kitchen, Jennell was filling her Yeti travel mug with ice and then water.

She cast a long gaze at her roommate. "You look like crap."

"Good morning to you, too."

"Keep your phone handy. You remember how to call 911 without dialing?"

Emily nodded. The prospect worked on her nervous system better than caffeine.

"Good. With luck you won't need to. But until you know, you keep that in your hand."

"Yes, mom." Emily said it in jest, but the glib reply landed hard. She missed her mother so much, especially now when she really didn't know what she was doing or if it was the right thing.

Would her mother be proud or furious at her for working for the Roths?

Jennell pointed a finger at her. "If he touches you, you call the cops."

"All right."

"Promise me."

"I promise. He won't touch me again."

Seemingly satisfied, Jennell capped her mug.

Emily moved mechanically to the coffee maker and saw that

Jennell had poured her a large mug full and left her two slices of buttered wheat toast.

She really was the best roommate ever.

"Hey, Em?" Jennell shifted, as if the topic she raised wasn't easy. "I found a coffee table."

"That's great."

"Yeah, but, um, I need room to bring it in."

The realization of what this conversation was really about dropped like a ball of hot lead.

"I know the stuff in those boxes belonged to your mom, but those bins and the pallet, they need to go. Maybe it's time to sort through them? Or, you know, you can put them in your room. Completely up to you."

"Okay. I'll get them out of the living room and toss the pallet."

The boxes were all the worldly belongings left after Emily had cleared out her mother's apartment. They included keepsakes, costume jewelry, photos, electronics, and all of the pain medication her mom had needed during the short time she was in hospice care at home.

Jennell's shoulders dropped. "Thank you."

The drive to work was the usual chaos and she was cut off at a yield, narrowly missing a collision.

But she reached the gatehouse nearly on time and parked in the Roths' drive as usual, hurrying through the garage and into the house.

"Emily?" It was Dr. Roth's voice.

Fear made her mouth go dry and her voice higher than usual.

"Yes. It's me."

He waited in the kitchen alone.

She drew off her shoulder bag and set it on one of the stools. Then she slid her hand in her back pocket and wrapped it around her phone.

"Where's Mrs. Roth?"

"Resting. She's exhausted from yesterday's ordeal."

"I'm so sorry about everything."

"Yes. Well, you should be."

"Did the hospital discover what happened?"

His scowl deepened. "That's not your concern."

As her nurse, she disagreed, but kept the rest of her questions to herself. She already knew what they'd find—same as the lab found in her blood and Brian found in that powder. Narcotics.

"No outings today. She can have a walk or a swim. I'll be back at the normal time. She can have acetaminophen if she still has a headache when she wakes up. Nothing else. Keep her out of my office."

"Noon medications?"

"Nothing," he said.

So, Sabrina was no longer taking anything. That did not bode well.

Had he seen the open safe, noted the missing keys that Emily had tucked in Sabrina's purse?

"I understand."

He handed her a piece of paper. "My direct number. Add it to your contacts. If you need me, call that, not my office."

She nodded. "Yes. Of course."

"I hope you two have an uneventful day. But if..." His smartwatch interrupted his hopes. He glanced down at the text on his watch.

Whatever he saw made him curse.

"Wait here," he ordered, then left the room.

She didn't, following as far as the juncture between living and dining rooms as he continued to the foyer, stopping under the massive chandelier. There, he raked both hands through his hair, and paused with his fingers laced on the top of his head.

He gave a shout of frustration and dropped his hands.

She watched as he pulled in a long, slow breath, releasing it with the tension at his shoulders.

Then he calmly walked the few steps to the doors, tapping the button to roll back the gate. Beyond the dining room window, Emily watched as a sheriff's cruiser swept into the driveway and rolled to a stop.

He'd ordered her to stay put, but she'd be damned if she'd miss this.

What had him so upset—the interruption or the fact that the sheriff was in his driveway?

He conveyed a near-perfect façade of unflappable confidence. Yet, Emily could see how tightly he gripped the latch.

Out he went. The door clicked shut.

Creeping forward, she slowly turned the latch and cracked open the door. She watched the sheriff step from his cruiser and tug at his utility belt. Emily's attention went to the gun, holstered at his side.

Where were his handcuffs? Would Dr. Roth struggle? Would he run?

Dr. Roth lifted a hand and called a greeting.

"Henry Roth?" asked the sheriff. The guy was six-seven if he was an inch. A brick wall of a man in uniform, he looked like a contestant in a powerlifting competition moonlighting as law enforcement.

"Yes," Dr. Roth said. "I'm Dr. Henry Roth."

The title did not seem to impress the mountain of muscle in the driveway.

"I have a summons and formal complaint to deliver to you."

"Is that right?"

The sheriff folded at the waist and reached back across the bucket seats, straightening with a legal-sized envelope and a clipboard.

"Sign this and this," he said, handing over two documents.

Dr. Roth stepped forward and blocked her view of what was happening. The sheriff ducked back into his cruiser.

Dr. Roth waved and then watched as the sheriff cleared the roundabout and left the driveway to the private road.

He stood there for a long time, hands on hips, loosely holding the forms he'd been delivered.

Then he studied the two pages of the complaint and summons.

All Emily knew from her experience of complaints was that they came certified and usually meant that she and her mother were moving again because they'd been evicted.

It had been such a relief when she could work part-time and add a little cash to the family income.

Dr. Roth looked about the quiet neighborhood. From somewhere nearby a lawnmower engine rumbled. He transferred the pages to his opposite hand and then swung his fist at the air in a vicious half circle. He choked the papers then threw them in the bushes. Finally, he turned toward the house, but Emily had already closed the door and was running to the kitchen. By the time he cleared the foyer, she was busy loading the dishes from the sink to the racks in the dishwasher.

When he came in, she kept her head down and her eyes on her work.

He paused behind her. She could feel him standing there, silent and dangerous. Her heartbeat pulsed in her throat, large as a tennis ball.

She couldn't swallow past the lump.

Finally, he headed out the back door without a word. Emily paused to hear his car door slam and the garage door lift.

She stood there with bubbles and water dripping down her arms to the sink, hardly breathing until there was nothing but silence.

Her head bowed and she squeezed her eyes closed, thankful he was gone.

Once assured he had left the property, she headed outside.

On the sidewalk beyond the wide driveway, a jogger trundled past, a tiny white dog dancing willingly along beside her. Across the street a gardener trimmed a neighbor's hedge as the gate rolled slowly forward, closing them off.

Emily dragged out the hose and prepared to water the plants beside the landing, being sure her back was to the doorbell camera as she retrieved the papers and read.

The complaint was against Henry Roth, demanding that he report to a medical office to have his wife's mental health independently evaluated by a third party. The complainant was Mr. Gabriel Rottach.

No wonder he was enraged. Sabrina's attorney's probing might lead to the demand she be institutionalized and that would shoot his cash cow right between the eyes.

Emily returned the pages to the bushes and coiled up the hose.

Sabrina's attorneys were now aware that not everything in their client's world was as it should be.

It was nice to have *him* be the one under scrutiny for a change. And she had to wonder what would happen next.

THIRTY-EIGHT

Whatever her husband had given her, it had knocked Sabrina out for hours. Mrs. Roth even slept through Rosalind's vacuuming right outside her door. Emily checked on her after the cleaner left but did not disturb her. She did, however, disturb her phone.

The funny thing about that software was that you didn't need to be awake for it to recognize you.

Emily wiped the smudges from her fingers off the screen and set aside the phone. It was nearly noon.

She gave her charge a slight tap on the shoulder. "Mrs. Roth, you need to get up now."

Her eyes blinked open and she frowned at Emily.

"Give me a few more minutes."

"It's noon. Your husband gave you something. You've been out for hours." That news caused Sabrina to force herself upright.

"Oh my God. I remember."

Emily stood beside the bed, acting the good nurse while silently trying to orchestrate her escape. "The sheriff was here."

She spun her legs out from under the covers and draped them over the edge of the bed. They didn't reach the ground.

"The sheriff? Why?"

"He delivered some papers to your husband. Dr. Roth threw them on the ground beside the landing."

Mrs. Roth pushed off the mattress and to her feet, no longer groggy.

"Let's have a look. Shall we?"

Emily didn't know anyone else who used phrases like *shall*, *shall not*, and *shan't*.

But Sabrina came from a family with means, and she and her child had both had easy access to higher education.

Meanwhile, Emily had begun working the very moment she qualified for her work permit. At fourteen, things like sports or clubs hadn't even been an option. It was time to go to work, so she went. And this job was the very first one where she didn't make minimum wage.

So, why was she preparing to toss that all in the toilet and butcher her cash cow?

Because her morality was not for sale and what had happened under this roof was so very wrong.

She couldn't call the cops, but would the Roths really come after her if she just quit and kept her mouth shut? Didn't Sabrina's revelation give her some power over the woman?

No, it just made her more tangled and ensnared and vulnerable. At least that was how Sabrina saw it. Her money protected her and endangered Emily. Was she right?

She walked Mrs. Roth out the front door and watched as Sabrina retrieved the pages, carrying them to the dining room, reading along the way.

"He's received a notice of complaint requesting a judge mandate a psychological evaluation by an outside party."

"Of who?"

"Whom," she corrected without glancing up. "Of me, of

course! Gabriel signed this. He came to see me at the hospital.
I'm not sure how he knew to find me there."

"You asked me to call him."

"What?" She cast an impatient glance at Emily.

Emily held her ground, not out of courage but because her
legs had ceased working and her knees trembled, not actually
knocking but close. She now worked for a psychopath who had
threatened and bribed her nurse into compliance—for now.

"From the ambulance. You asked me to call your lawyer."

"I said *lawyer*?"

She hesitated. Something about the way Sabrina stared
unsettled her.

"Yes..." She thought a moment. "Maybe not your exact
words. But that's what you wanted."

"I would have said *attorney*."

"Oh, maybe you did say 'attorney.'"

Sabrina nodded. "Very likely. In any case, he wants me
examined by someone other than my husband." She dropped
the notice on the table and then read the summons. "This just
tells Henry when and where he is to report."

"Is this good or bad?" asked Emily.

Did Sabrina remember her confession in the car before
she'd passed out or had she been too high?

Emily certainly did. Her entire body had buzzed and shivered with the realization of exactly what this woman truly was.
Beneath that elegant, expensive veneer, she was a stone-cold
killer.

"I'm not sure. Gabriel and my husband got into a shouting
match at the hospital. My attorney wanted me admitted, but
Henry got me released while Gabriel was speaking to an admin-
istrator."

"What happened to you? Did they say?"

"Henry said I fainted. Never done that before."

"Did you speak to the attending doctor or get a diagnosis?"

Sabrina pursed her lips. "No. I did not." She studied the papers in her hands. "Why did I pass out? And why did I have such crazy visions?"

"Some narcotics cause hallucinations," said Emily, then waited. Sabrina was smart. She likely knew that her husband was using and his drug of choice.

Sabrina squeezed her hand to a fist. The papers crackled and submitted to the attack. Lifting them, she glared, as if they were somehow to blame.

"He accused me of stealing his drugs. As if I ever would."

"His drugs?"

"Henry's an addict. Says it's the stress of our marriage, the coward."

Emily widened her eyes as if the admission of her husband's addiction was news.

"Why would he put recreational drugs in your medication?"

"Another clumsy attempt to subdue me." Sabrina turned very animated, gesturing wildly. "Because he sees it coming again. What do they call it? A Hail Mary pass? It won't work. Never works."

Subdue? Now that was an interesting choice of words. Not *treat*, but *subdue*, as if she were an escaped tiger.

Sabrina threw up her hands in disgust. "He can't control me. And that's killing him. Drove him to that damned needle. But I'm not weak. I do as I please and he can't handle that. Never could. And I've been so damned patient, taking all the drugs he said would fix this. It's not fixable, because I'm not broken. And I've had enough of his blind blundering."

"You think he did this to help you?"

"More like help himself. If I go down, so does he, the little phony." Sabrina swept up the front stairs. "Get my suitcases."

"Where are we going?"

"Hotel."

"Should you meet with your attorney first?"

"Hand me my phone."

Emily listened as Sabrina spoke on the phone.

"Gabriel, it's so good to hear your voice."

Sabrina listened and then laughed.

"I understand you sent the sheriff by. I didn't see him because Henry gave me a shot of something. I just woke up a few minutes ago. Actually, I think I'm very lucky to have woken up at all." She stuck her index finger in the ear that did not have her phone pressed to it. "He has a drug habit, Gabe. Fentanyl. I think he tried to make it appear that I overdosed."

More listening and Emily strained to hear what her attorney advised.

"Yes, I know. Did you see my blood work from the hospital?" A pause. "Good. Let me guess. I had narcotics in my blood?" She paused, listening, then continued speaking. "He knows he can't keep me here, so he tried to kill me. Luckily my nurse got me help."

She listened, nodding and scowling.

"No need. I'm leaving right now. My nurse will pack up a few things... I'll bring it along." She paused. "No. I'm not staying here. I'll fight him for the house. Or even better, give it to him. He can't afford it without me."

Emily heard snatches of her attorney's words.

"I'll be gone before he gets home."

More listening as Emily fidgeted, tearing away her thumb-nail with her teeth.

Sabrina listened. "Yes. Tomorrow. I'll be waiting."

She ended the call, then glanced at Emily.

"I have an appointment with a doctor in Orlando. Gabriel needs the hotel address so he can pick me up at seven-thirty tomorrow morning."

Her expression of determination dissolved into a slow boil of panic.

"My roommate works reception at a boutique hotel. She said on weeknights they rarely book the suites. She could get you one. It would be a private place to meet your attorney."

"No. Hilton or Marriott. Largest suite they have."

Emily made the call while Sabrina stood sullen, reviewing the papers the sheriff had delivered.

"All set. You have a suite waiting. Private meeting space, kitchenette. Two bathrooms."

Sabrina folded the papers, ignoring the creases and wrinkles. "Fine."

Of course there was no thanks or show of appreciation. That need was met, and she was on to the next.

She extended her phone. "Use my attorney's private number. Send him the details."

Emily retrieved the number from Sabrina's contacts and sent the information along.

"I'll open the safe. I want you to clean it out. Jewelry, all the paperwork. Load everything in the Mercedes. Gabriel wants it."

"Yes, ma'am."

"Does this hotel have a safe?"

Emily tapped on her phone checking the room's amenities. "Yes, they do." Only it would be the size of a toaster oven, not a refrigerator.

Sabrina waved her away.

"Go, go. Get the luggage out and then we'll clear out the safe. Don't think about taking any of that jewelry. I know exactly what's in there."

Sabrina headed for her husband's office, then met Emily in the bedroom. She watched as Emily gathered the matching luggage set and laid it out, open on the bed. Next, they went to the safe.

It was a big one. Under Sabrina's watchful eye, Emily loaded two plastic bins from the stacks in the garage and heaved them into the back of the SUV. When she came back, Sabrina no longer looked resolute.

She sat on her bed amid the luggage, now strewn with a variety of clothing and shoes. Lots of shoes.

Sabrina stared off into space, her mouth open as if receiving some heavenly message, like the shepherds in their fields or Joan in her garden.

"Mrs. Roth?"

Her body sagged like a wilting flower.

"Gabriel's office phoned. He received your text with the hotel details."

"That's good. And tomorrow, you can get a diagnosis and appropriate care."

Sabrina's tone was brittle as thin ice. "I don't need a diagnosis. I know what's wrong with me." She covered her face in her hands. "I'm afraid."

"Of him?" asked Emily.

"No, not him. Oh, God." She cast her gaze on Emily, and her eyes were so wide the whites showed all around.

Emily worried that without any medication, Sabrina might have a panic attack. Her disturbed thinking and paranoia might resurface if that was even her problem. Really, she didn't trust anything Dr. Roth said. He had too much skin in the game.

"It's safe there. A good hotel."

"You need to take the car keys."

"Why?"

"Are you here to ask questions or help me?"

Emily stiffened at the rebuke delivered with such venom it left fang marks.

Sabrina clutched the coverlet of the king-sized bed, as if that might keep her from tumbling into her personal psychological minefield.

"Are the papers in the car?"

Emily nodded.

"Jewelry?"

"All that was there."

"Grab my box out of the closet. It's got the ones with precious metals."

Emily ducked into her patient's closet and collected the heavy wooden box, returning to find Sabrina, still on the bed, pressing her palm to her forehead as she panted and shook, eyes flashing wild. "I can't. No. He'll be so angry."

"Mrs. Roth, he's keeping you a prisoner. You told me that. And his practice, this house, the cars. It's all yours."

"Malpractice is more like it. Four suits just this year and uninsurable. My father would be so disappointed in him. But he has kept me safe from them."

Emily wanted to ask, but after the reaction to her last question, she kept her mouth closed.

Sabrina wrapped her arms around her knees, pulling them close so she could rest her chin on them.

Emily began folding clothing and carefully packing the designer threads. Sabrina busied herself by staring into space and speaking, it seemed, to herself. A pep talk, Emily thought.

"Gabriel said it's a nice place. A very private facility. Henry won't be allowed to see me. I'll be free."

Was her attorney planning on institutionalizing her?

Mrs. Roth glanced toward the windows as if imagining soaring into a blue sky, like the birds. Then her gaze dropped to the carpet. "But the shadows, they'll follow me. I'll never be free."

Emily hurried to gather the obvious gaps in the collected items. Things like a bathroom bag, makeup, underwear, slippers, a robe, sleepwear, and the container of medicine.

"Absolute pros, he said. Get to the bottom of things. But Papa didn't want that. He made them destroy the records. Dangerous. That's what he called them."

Sabrina clenched her teeth and swung her legs to the ground.

"No way back. No way to fix it. Only forward. Forward and away. I'm not going to sit around and let him inject me with his poison."

It was the strangest one-sided conversation Emily had ever witnessed.

What needed fixing? Did she mean her marriage? Emily didn't know. She did know that Henry Roth would be home at five and they could not be here.

Sabrina paced before the bed.

Emily loaded the luggage, filling the rear seat. At four, she pulled the SUV out into the drive and parked before the entrance because Sabrina did not like to enter or exit through the garage.

She left the running vehicle.

Emily returned to the house to find Sabrina curled in a ball beside the kitchen counter. Above her sat her phone and designer purse.

"Mrs. Roth? You okay?"

"I don't think... I mean, I know what he's doing. But it helped. Keeps me in... Papa said certain necessary safeguards... I know it's bad, but it's the best he can do. After all, he's trying."

Emily had had enough. If they hung around here, she was not only getting fired, but she might get attacked or arrested.

"Mrs. Roth. You said he drugged you with fentanyl. You can make sure he doesn't get away with this. With any of it. Or you can live in denial of what he's doing to you. Have some courage and face this."

That had been harsh, intentionally so.

Indignation filled Sabrina's face and she rose to confront this upstart, this underling. No one spoke to Sabrina King Roth like this.

Emily faced Sabrina, certain what she was doing was right and justified.

She could not stand what Dr. Roth had done or was doing. And Sabrina needed to take ownership of her own life and her actions.

If nothing else, Emily could be certain that criminals were held to account no matter how rich they were. Money couldn't insulate them from this.

Emily lifted Sabrina's purse. Sabrina collected her phone and sailed out the main entrance, leaving it open behind her. Emily exited, then closed and locked the door, and then hurried after Sabrina.

Behind her, the video doorbell recorded their exit, just as it had recorded Emily lugging and loading the heavy bags.

If Emily had to guess, she'd say Dr. Roth was on his way home early today.

THIRTY-NINE

Fear burned down every nerve ending. Dr. Roth had given her reason to be afraid, but his bribes and threats wouldn't stop her. She saw him clearly now. This was too important, and people like this needed to be stopped.

All the way out of the gated community, Emily expected to see Dr. Roth's sedan roaring toward them. But they made it all the way to Lakeland, and she was beginning to believe they'd escaped.

I'll garner your wages 'til the end of time. Have you ever been to jail?

This time her fear wouldn't stop her.

The urge to run tugged, but she continued to drive through the upscale homes, pushing away her fear and holding tight to what she needed to do next.

He held Emily with her terror of losing everything. Not that she had that much. Really, very little, but that made what she had even more precious.

Emily drove them to the hotel. She pulled the SUV into the portico and spoke to the bellman, who went to work loading the luggage and crates onto a dolly.

When Sabrina stepped from the vehicle, Dr. Roth swept thought the automatic doors and charged straight at them.

He roared at Emily.

"Just what the hell do you think you're doing?"

Emily blinked at him, and Sabrina stepped in.

"She's helping me. About time someone did."

"Get in my car, Sabrina. We'll talk about this at home."

Emily gnawed at her lip, uncertain what to do.

"I shan't be going anywhere with *you*."

Henry reached. Sabrina shook him off.

"How did you find me?"

"I know how to find you, Bree."

"How?"

He lifted his chin, defiant, a smug little smile twisting his lips.

"Spying on me! Well, no more."

Emily's head was on a swivel as she searched in vain for some help to get them away from Dr. Roth, who looked dangerous and capable of forcing Sabrina to go with him. Should she let him?

"God, Bree. I'm here to help you."

"You poisoned me. Well, no more. We're finished."

The raised voices had drawn the attention of a couple waiting for their vehicle at the valet station. The pregnant woman cradled her belly and stepped closer to the man who scrutinized them with tight-jawed attention as he gauged the level of threat. They watched as Dr. Roth tried and failed to grab his wife. The mother-to-be drew out her phone and Emily thought she was using it to make a video recording of them. They'd be trending on TikTok and collecting upvotes on Reddit in a matter of minutes.

Emily pulled out her phone and hit the buttons to dial 911. It took only a tap.

Henry Roth had managed to get his struggling wife into his sedan.

Once inside, she was unable to open the door and pounded on the glass. Her husband must have engaged some child-safety feature, turning the back seat of the automobile into a secure detention area.

"You can't do this. She wants to leave you."

"The hell she does," Henry growled. Then he aimed a finger at Emily. "I'll have you arrested. This is kidnapping."

"I agree, Dr. Roth," she said.

The sirens' screams rose to a volume that no one could ignore. Two units arrived, blocking in their vehicles. A young, clean-shaven officer stepped out of the first cruiser, hand on his service pistol.

"What's going on here?" he said.

The valet glanced to Dr. Roth. Two more employees in hotel uniforms arrived from inside the lobby, followed by a security officer in uniform.

"I'm a doctor," said Dr. Roth as a second patrolman stood beside his cruiser covering the officer making the approach.

Inside the rear seat of his sedan, Sabrina continued to scream and pound.

"That's my patient. She's under my care for dissociative thinking. I'm a psychiatrist."

"He's her husband," added Emily. "And his wife wants out of their marriage."

They were no longer in Winter Haven, and Emily hoped that Dr. Roth's connections did not extend to this police force.

"Step back, both of you."

Emily did. Henry hesitated and the officer gripped the handle of his gun. Dr. Roth retreated, hands lifted. The woman at the valet station held her phone out like a handgun, side-stepping to get a clearer shot.

A gray-haired man in a hotel uniform stepped forward

holding only a radio.

"I'm hotel security," he announced. His commanding voice impressed. If she had to guess, Emily would say he was retired law enforcement from up north somewhere.

"Stay back." The officer glanced from the circle of witnesses to the sedan.

"Don't open that," warned Dr. Roth. "She might harm herself."

The clean-shaven officer ignored him, approaching the vehicle.

"I won't be responsible. She's irrational."

The policeman glanced to his colleague. "Watch him," he said, meaning Dr. Roth. Then he stooped beside the rear window. "Ma'am, stop pounding."

She did.

"Sit back."

Sabrina did that as well.

"What's your name?"

"I'm Sabrina King Roth." Her words were muffled by the glass, but she didn't slur or hesitate.

Emily smiled.

"Is that your husband?" He thumbed over his shoulder.

She glanced past her interviewer, narrowing her eyes on Henry.

"For now," she said.

Dr. Roth's face flushed scarlet.

"What's the date today?"

Sabrina repeated a date. She was off by several days but nailed the month and year.

The officer stood. "She seems okay to me."

He tried and failed to open the door. Then he turned to Dr. Roth. "Let her out."

"You don't understand. She's mentally fragile. She could harm herself."

The officer lowered his chin and placed a hand on the weapon on the other side of his utility belt. A Taser, Emily realized.

"Open the door."

Dr. Roth lowered his hand to his jacket pocket. The officer watched him closely. There was a blipping sound and the click of locks releasing.

Sabrina flew out of the car and straight at her husband.

"You put that poison in my meds." Her finger was aimed at his nose.

"What? What poison?"

"You know exactly." She waited as her husband continued to look confused. "Bottom drawer, bathroom?" she prompted.

He flushed. "I never."

She spun away, but Dr. Roth grabbed her and drew her up short.

"Wait just a minute," he said.

"Let her go," ordered the officer.

Henry turned but did not release Sabrina.

The bellhops stepped back away from the conflict.

"I'm taking her home. She's my patient," said Dr. Roth.

The officer drew his Taser.

"Let go. Now."

Henry complied and Sabrina ran right into Emily's arms.

"I got you," Emily whispered.

The officer told Dr. Roth to put his hands on the top of his shiny black sedan.

"You're arresting me?"

"Failure to comply," said the young officer.

Henry put his hands on the vehicle, and was handcuffed, searched, then hustled into the back of the officer's cruiser.

"See how he likes it," muttered Sabrina.

"You got those two," said the officer to his female backup.

"Here or station?" she asked.

"Station. Get a photo of those bruises." He pointed at Sabrina.

Emily then noticed the red marks left on Sabrina's upper arm by her husband.

"Maybe these, too," said Emily, drawing down her collar. "He did this to me on Monday."

The officer nodded and stepped back to his vehicle, rounded his unit, and dropped behind the wheel. From the rear seat, Dr. Roth glared at his wife. But he did not shout.

They'd just gotten the better of him. Emily basked in the glow of satisfaction. Was this feeling of elation just the rush that happened after you were brave enough to jump but before recognizing that your parachute wasn't going to open?

The second officer asked them to come along with her. Emily helped Sabrina into the cruiser and then went to the gawking valet, handing over the key fob.

Beside him, the woman was still recording.

"That vehicle belongs to Sabrina Roth. Could you park the SUV? She has a reservation and we'll be back."

The woman was still filming. She'd probably get a million views before Emily made it back here. Even make a few bucks selling a clip to the local news. Either way, it might help prove that Sabrina's husband was a self-serving monster.

Emily didn't look at the woman but felt her pointing her phone in her direction. In a moment, she was in the back of a police car, just as Dr. Roth had promised, and pulling away from the hotel.

She was fired. But she couldn't help feeling pleased. The attack was now on the record.

* * *

Sabrina had been less coherent at the station than Emily would have liked, but she was clear about wanting to leave her marriage.

"You know he's been drugging me with his fentanyl."

That got their attention and possibly a search warrant, thought Emily.

Sabrina's weeping had triggered the call to the psychologist. That woman had gotten Sabrina calmed down and helped her through the questioning.

Emily was done long before Sabrina and waited for her outside the squad room. She'd allowed them to photograph both her neck and the bruises on her torso. Really, it was all she had to fight the shitstorm that Dr. Roth would rain down on her.

"How long will they hold Henry?" asked Sabrina.

"I'm not sure."

"We can't go back to that hotel," said Sabrina. "He might be waiting."

"There's the boutique hotel where my roommate works. It's very nice. Funky, urban vibe."

Sabrina lifted her head from the cradle of her hands and stared at Emily.

"Fine."

She called Jennell and discovered they had only the third-floor suite available.

"She'll take it."

"See you soon then. Can't wait to get a look at this woman."

Emily called them a ride to the hotel where they'd left Sabrina's vehicle. There, they waited with security while the valet retrieved the SUV. Then Emily drove them to the new hotel and valet parked the vehicle. In the lobby she accepted the keycard from Jennell, who was relaying her scorn for Emily's patient with her eyes. Finally, she took her former employer, and all her luggage, up to her suite.

It was one of the best hotels in Lakeland, but not the Ritz. It had a rooftop bar, a restaurant, exercise room, outdoor pool and offered dry cleaning service.

Sabrina was on floor three, halfway between the bank of elevators and the exit at the end of the hall. The room was a non-smoking king with a sitting area and kitchenette.

"Did you bring my medicine?" Sabrina asked, slouched on the bed and rubbing her arm. "I won't sleep without them."

Emily recovered the sleeping pills and gave her the normal dose. It would have to be enough to help her rest.

"I think you're all set. Pajamas and robe are on the bed." She pointed. "I put your toothbrush and everything else you need in the bathroom."

"You're a dear. I don't know what I'd do without you." She spoke as if Emily was here out of the goodness of her heart or some sense of duty, instead of her human decency and obligation to her patient. Mrs. Roth did not look up as she rummaged through her bags, tossing items onto both bed and floor.

Emily wondered why it still bothered her that no one ever said thank you.

"Where's my eye mask?"

When not on her face, the mask usually resided in the top drawer of her bedside table. Emily had forgotten it.

Sabrina's look morphed to disapproving. "Never mind. I'll use a damp washcloth."

She stood and unbuttoned her blouse.

The haughty, entitled woman was back. All traces of gratitude had vanished, and her eyes were hard as granite.

"You can go now. I'll see you in the morning."

"You want me to come back tomorrow? I thought your attorney was picking you up early."

"You work for me, don't you? You do what I say."

"About that. I think you need to find someone else."

"Oh, really? This from the girl who took some of my pills without permission. Didn't you? Had them tested?"

"Because you asked me to."

"I did no such thing. You stole prescriptions, took them to a friend, I could have you both arrested."

Emily was flabbergasted. "I helped you."

"That's your job, Emily. Helping me. What I pay you for."

Emily stood blinking at this horrible, self-serving woman. Seeing her but hardly believing what she saw.

"Here's the thing. Henry protected me. Helped me clean up afterwards. You know, the detail man. But his inept attempts to suppress my natural instincts, well, it's exhausting. It doesn't work and I'm done with his feeble bungling. That makes you my new best choice. With your help, I'll be free of Henry, since he's going to jail, and getting divorced. And you need a job. Win-win."

"I'm not doing that."

"Oh yes you are. Or I'll call the police and have you charged with oh, I don't know, theft, anything I want to, really."

If Emily had any doubts about whether Sabrina's impulses were beyond her control, they were up in smoke. Henry was bad. Sabrina was worse.

Had she expected these self-serving people to change? People didn't change. They were bad today. They'd be the same tomorrow and the day after that.

"I see my attorney tomorrow, but I need you to keep all this safe." Sabrina motioned to the crates and matching luggage set.

"You mean stay here?"

"Goodness no. Tomorrow, you'll bring it to my attorney's offices. Their people will handle it from there."

Emily stood, so angry she was shaking. "Yes, ma'am."

"Eight o'clock sharp. That will give me a few minutes to speak privately to my attorney."

"Yes, ma'am."

"Oh, and get yourself an Uber home. Right?"

Somehow Emily managed not to slam the door on her way out.

FORTY

I walked about the suite and kicked off my flats, finally alone. It had been years since I'd had the luxury of solitude. My first action was to turn on the television to a British mystery. Then I shrugged out of my clothing and into my robe, kicking the garments on the floor into a semblance of a pile and then moving the suitcase off the bed to the desk. Emily had done a fair job packing, but she'd forgotten my lavender-scented eye mask.

I heaved a sigh of annoyance. Why couldn't anyone do their job properly?

From the satchel, I collected the pill bottles and set them out on the bathroom counter. The length of the line made me melancholy. It was just incredible that anyone who wasn't terminally ill would need so many drugs.

Well, I wasn't taking them. Not anymore.

Had the police released Henry yet? He wouldn't find me. Not in this tiny boho nightmare of a hotel.

Tomorrow, I'd discuss that and divorce with my attorney. How much had my father told Gabriel about my problem?

Once, I'd believed Henry when he said he would protect

me always. And he had gotten me out of a very serious predicament when Regan's testimony and mine conflicted. But had he done so out of love, obligation, or self-interest?

It didn't matter. Everyone looked out for themselves first.

The court case ruined us. The spark that had ignited between us and once roared with passion had died as all fires do, from lack of fuel. Nothing left to burn but my need and his desperation. I was never sure if he loved me or just the idea of me—rich, beautiful, and dangerous as a pit viper. What an irresistible combination. Or, perhaps he thought, with all that education and all those degrees, he could fix me. But I was unfixable. I knew it. My mother was the first to see and later my father, who found me Henry. Papa understood I'd need someone else, a protector.

If I ever loved anyone, it was Dad. Henry, I needed, and I was fond of him in the same way you are fond of a beagle puppy. How can anyone resist those worshipping eyes and the faithfulness of a hound?

Perhaps he thought overmedicating me would make me easier to handle. Maybe he was right.

And that gibberish about my being delusional. He'd put that in my medical records and now no one believed a word I said. Made it illegal for me to drive. Insurance dropped me. Not that I care. I don't have to follow rules because I'm above all that.

Tomorrow, my attorney would begin the process of getting me away from my keeper. Henry would lose everything, and I'd be in control again.

I didn't need a handler anymore. My little helper was right. I was rich enough and smart enough to keep killing people and letting others take the blame.

Bye-bye, Henry. You were lucky I didn't kill you when I had the chance. And there were many chances.

No more husband to hold me back. But also no one to clean up my mess.

That thought gave me a long pause. Freedom, I wanted. Responsibility I did not.

I gnawed on my knuckle for a moment, thinking.

Funny. I thought I'd be fine here alone for a single night, but I wasn't alone. Was I? Because I'd brought that relentless little voice along with me.

The one that wanted to collect my car from the valet and go hunting.

They all looked like her. My lovely mother. They had her walk or that need to be noticed. Dark hair. Red lips. I've killed my mother nearly a dozen times. At first, it was years between accidents. But lately, the need comes back more quickly. The one I killed with Clare's car was in the spring and here I am hunting again, so soon. Henry tried to stop me. He knows the signs.

Julian was the first.

I remember him in the water, thrashing. And I called out, "Mommy! Julian is swimming."

Even without seeing me, she knew I'd pushed him. To this day, I'm not sure if I wanted to see him swim or drown. Probably the latter.

My mother thought so, because he was born with my umbilical cord wrapped around his neck. And blue as glacial ice. That's what Papa said. Momma said I was trying to kill him before we were even born.

Oh, how Momma loved that boy and how she hated me, before and especially after. And I hated her right back. It was years before I could do anything about it. I wish I had, but her death due to natural causes robbed me of any chance to take my car and see that look of surprise and panic on her face. Perhaps a flash of realization before that lovely crunch.

Maybe I'd call room service and order a steak.

I could go out. My conscience wasn't a cricket in a top hat

and tails. Mine was more like a howling storm, filling my head with the evil I'd done. Still needed to do.

Best plan was to check myself into a facility and refuse to allow Henry to visit. Once I'd got the medications worked out and some help with my anxiety and mood swings, I'd file for divorce and turn Henry out on the street. He could sleep in that suite of offices that never quite paid for themselves, resell his fleet of pretentious automobiles, lose his private jet privileges, and cancel his country club membership.

The alarm on my watch beeped. Time to take my medication. Used to be the time. Henry usually sorted these out. But I couldn't trust him. Neither could I trust myself.

I returned to the wet bar and opened the fridge. The water was gratis. The prices of soda, wine, and beer were displayed on the paper collars around the throat of each bottle. On the counter sat a basket of snacks that tempted. My mouth watered as I flicked through the options: popcorn, gummy mangos, a chocolate-drizzled granola bar, pretzel sticks, and smoked almonds.

The water would do for the medications, but not for a celebration of my freedom. So, I phoned room service to order champagne, an entire bottle on ice. The best they had.

By the time I'd downed most of the pills and munched through the bag of smoked almonds, there was a knock on the door. The young man standing in the hallway held a cheap stainless-steel bucket, but it did hold a dark green glass bottle and plenty of ice. I opened the door.

He looked to be in his twenties, with an unfortunate Prince Valiant hairstyle, terrible acne, and one too many piercings on his face. His uniform was ill-fitting and cheap.

"Bedroom, please," I said, pointing, but waiting where I am, as he swept past me, returning a moment later.

My tip was miserly, but he seemed grateful as he thanked

me, bowing his way back out the door and I closed it behind him.

It wasn't until he was gone that I realized that I had never opened a champagne bottle before.

"How hard can it be?" I asked myself as I sauntered into the bedroom, grasped the bottle, and retrieved a hand towel from the bathroom.

Seated on the white coverlet, I carefully peeled off the foil and wire cage, and covered the cork with the towel. The satisfying pop made me laugh.

When was the last time I'd laughed?

Henry and my dreadful marriage had stolen my joy.

No, the aftermath of the criminal trial had done that. Exposed my vulnerabilities. Impulsiveness. Crime of opportunity. That rash decision almost got me caught. Stupid. Can't do that again.

He said another traffic fatality and they'd know for certain.

Was he right? It scared me. But not enough to make the cravings cease. Nothing worked. Not the fear. Not the drugs. It was just time.

The vibration and ringtone of my phone made me jump. I took my mobile from my bag, sure it was Henry, but it was my daughter.

Taylor didn't call me. Only on very rare occasions, like my birthday, and our conversations were strained. My wild child had survived her rebellious years, when she'd vanished to the Arizona desert doing who knew what. I wondered sometimes if she was like me.

When she got back, we both somehow made it through her wedding, though I really remembered very little except that Taylor's husband reminded me of Play-Doh. Squishy and easy to manipulate. It gave me hope for Taylor.

My daughter had a clearer memory of her wedding, because once she came back from her honeymoon, she hadn't taken my calls for a month. Henry wouldn't talk about it, so I knew I'd embarrassed them all.

Hey, he told everyone his wife was crazy and I served up crazy. You got what you paid for.

I took the call, trying for a calm, maternal tone.

"Hi, sweetheart."

There was no reply. A pocket dial? Very possible, I thought. "Taylor?"

There was a definite choking sound coming through the phone.

"Taylor. Are you there?"

My daughter's voice strained with emotion. "Mommy? Daddy called from the police station. He's worried about you."

"He should be worrying about himself."

"Is it true?"

"What, darling?"

"That you had Daddy arrested."

"We're having some issues."

"Issues?" Her voice was that unappealing screech I detested. "He said you claimed he gave you fentanyl."

I straightened, my lethargy gone with the obvious upset in Taylor's voice. Taylor didn't need me. Or hadn't since the accident and Regan's trial. That had been the closest I'd come to getting caught. Stupid to just yank the wheel like that. I'd been lucky and Henry had been scared. And Taylor... she'd been suspicious. After that, my then sixteen-year-old had managed her life with some help from her dad, without her mother.

"Because he did. You know he uses? We both just look the other way."

"So, why now? He's been using for years."

"Because he put some in my prescription."

"I find that hard to believe."

Sabrina changed direction like a reckless driver swerving across three lanes.

"He's got another mistress."

Taylor groaned as I reached for the champagne, tucking the phone between my shoulder and ear to give me two hands to pour. Some of the fizzing liquid spilled on the coverlet, but I dropped the bottle back on ice and lifted the glass, watching the tiny bubbles effervesce inside the glass.

"You're sending him to prison for sleeping around? Mom, that's nothing new, either. You two had an open marriage."

"Well, he did. Maybe his next mistress will be wearing prison stripes instead of jewelry he bought her with my money." My phone was back in one hand, and I held the delicate glass stem in the other.

"I can't talk to you when you're like this."

"You called me. Remember." I took a sip. The bubbles burned down my throat and fizzed in my nasal passages.

"Drop the charges."

I wouldn't. "Let me think about it."

Taylor didn't answer, but I could hear her labored breathing.

"Is the baby all right?" I asked.

"Babies. It's twins. Remember?"

That knocked me back a bit. Had Taylor told me that? She must have, because my daughter was due this month. Or was it next month?

I pictured a pulsing blue-gray umbilical cord drawn tight around a tiny neck.

"And they're fine." Taylor sniffed. "Five pounds already."

Taylor was one of the most self-sufficient, determined people I knew. She didn't let anything stop her from getting her way. Only occasionally in her short life had she faced any real disappointment.

"Can I come up there and talk to you?"

"Why?"

"Because you won't allow Dad near you and you can't be alone."

"Did he tell you that?"

"He didn't have to. So, can I come see you?"

"Not tonight."

When Taylor left to attend college, she had not come back. I had finally had the help throw everything she'd left behind in the garbage. But my act of spite went unnoticed, as Taylor did not come home for the holidays, or summer recess, or after she'd graduated. Her wedding photo with her parents looked like an image taken at a funeral. Both Henry and Taylor looked grim as pallbearers, while I was on fiesta. Such a cliché, the mother who can't keep her shit together on any given day but expected to do so on emotionally charged days, like graduation and her daughter's wedding. Henry never hung that image in a frame.

Of all the things I'd screwed up, my relationship with Taylor was the worst. The fact that she was willing to come see me revealed how desperate she was. Desperate to help her dad.

I locked my teeth together and snorted like a dragon.

"Mom, please."

My calm was counterfeit, as was the appearance of careful control.

"Well, of course you are welcome to drive over here. But I'm not at home right now."

"What do you mean?"

"I'm at a hotel."

Now her voice was full of exasperation. "Which hotel?"

What was the name of this place again? I searched for a notepad or welcome package that would tell me. I hadn't driven, but I should remember where Emily had dropped me.

"I'm not sure. In Lakeland. It's a color name, like The Turquoise or The Azure."

"Oh my God."

"You can come see me. It's a suite. But tomorrow would be better."

This solution was met with a heavy sigh. "In the hotel you don't know the name of?"

Now it was my turn to expel a breath in annoyance. I hated being treated like some feeble-minded nitwit.

"I'll call the front desk and get the address. Will that help?"

"Mom, what about your medications?"

"He's been poisoning me."

"Mom—"

I cut her off. "They said so. He gave me fentanyl. I could have ODed."

"You've... Mom, you can't be there alone."

"Why can't I? Why does everyone think I'm so fragile that I can't be alone? I'm an adult. I'm fully capable of seeing to my own needs."

"What about your medications? Are you taking them?"

My daughter had seen me when I'd stopped taking Henry's prescriptive plan on more than one occasion. Witnessed the building mania, until it was too much. Or was she remembering the times after the trial when my mood was so black that Taylor had called her dad more than once? It had been too much to expect a teenager to keep watch over her mom, so Henry sent her away to boarding school.

And no one had died. Perhaps this apple had rolled far from the tree.

"I'm not like that anymore. I feel..." I couldn't say fine. I never felt fine. In fact, I noticed the tremors in my hands and that itching had started again. The one that made me feel like bugs were crawling over my skin.

I needed to take my medication, at least the ones that stopped the tremors. This was Henry's fault, getting me hooked on drugs that had withdrawal symptoms.

"There's a reason that Dad started hiring private nurses instead of housekeepers. They helped him keep an eye on you."

"He treats me like a prisoner. He doesn't believe a word I say."

"Because you remember things wrong. Just like my wedding!"

"Oh, for goodness' sake, Taylor. Your wedding was perfect."

"Dad had to give you an injection. You frightened our ring bearer's parents half to death. Seth's parents, my friends, everyone, and you think it was perfect."

"Taylor, if I did something..."

I recalled seeing a child. Julian, all dressed in a tiny tuxedo, up on the lip of the fountain. Had that been the ring bearer? After he'd gone in with a little plop, someone in a white shroud had been screaming. Taylor?

"You see? You don't even remember. Do you?"

"Well, no. Are you coming to stay with me?"

"Someone needs to. Will you at least take your medications?"

"I will," I lied.

"Don't go anywhere."

"I love you."

"Oh, God, Mom. I don't need this right now."

Taylor ended the call.

My shoulders sagged. My own daughter could barely stand to speak to me. I hadn't been there for her. I knew that. But after the verdict, the fear just overwhelmed me. Such a narrow escape. The shock at the finger of blame nearly pointed in my direction. No longer untouchable. Vulnerable and a suspect.

She must have known. Had she overheard Henry and me planning for the trial?

Now I felt as if every step was through wet cement. My whole body ached.

My phone rang. It was Henry. I rejected the call. A moment later the phone blipped with a text.

Where are you?

I sent back the poop emoji.

You need to call me right now.

I smiled. Oh, I did, did I? Fat chance. Another message pinged into my feed.

What are you doing?

Leaving you.

This isn't funny.

It is not.

Why are you doing this?

You put your poison in my medicine. Emily said so.

I didn't!!

Lies. Gabriel will be in touch. Phone off.

The three dots indicated he was writing something else, but I put down the phone.

By the time I finished taking the pills with champagne, the hotel phone began ringing. After an eon, it ceased only to start up again.

"Oh, for goodness' sake." I tipped the glass, closed my eyes, and drained the contents. Then I poured a second glass as my phone bleated like a lost lamb in search of its mother.

After two more attempts, the phone went silent.

"Finally," I said.

But a few minutes later, someone pounded on the outer door to the hotel suite.

FORTY-ONE

The next knock on the door was followed by a male voice identifying himself as hotel security. I reached the small entry and opened the door. The man had close-cropped black hair, dark skin, and a concerned expression. He scanned my face through the available crack in the door.

"Mrs. Roth?"

"Yes?"

"I'm with hotel security. My name is Wyatt Guthrie. Your husband is downstairs. He was concerned about your well-being."

That was a laugh. He was concerned about his own. But good for him, he'd found me.

"Please tell him I'm fine."

"He said you could be having a medical emergency."

"Well, as you see, I am not."

"He also said you are under his care for some mental health issues."

"He felt he had the right to share that with you?" I checked his name tag. Wyatt Guthrie, just as he said. There was a gold badge clipped to his belt and he wore a wrinkled dress shirt and ill-fitting synthetic blazer.

"Because he said you might harm yourself."

I scowled at this. He was so determined to have me under his thumb. Well, not tonight.

I met his gray eyes. "Does he know my room number?"

"No, Mrs. Roth. We don't give out that information. But I am allowed to check on a guest who may need assistance."

"I left him today. It's an unhealthy relationship. He'll say anything to get up here. But I don't want him near me."

"I understand. And you have no thoughts of self-harm?"

"No. I certainly do not."

"Then I'll tell him I checked and that you are fine."

"Should I change hotels?"

"That's up to you."

I thought of the disaster of my unpacking in the bedroom area and the absence of my nurse. Why had I sent her home?

"How did he know I was here?"

Wyatt shook his head. "I don't know. Best guess, tracked a charge on your credit card, tracer on your vehicle, or used the Find My Phone app."

Clearly Wyatt had been down this road before.

Then it came to me. Taylor had called him. She knew the hotel or at least the city and that the name was a color. The Cobalt. No, The Sapphire. It didn't matter. But from that, he could find it. My daughter had handed me back to my keeper, the little narc. What a comedy my life had become. No—a farce.

Wyatt's radio blared with a tinny, female voice. The message seemed garbled to me, but Wyatt turned toward the elevators.

"Sabrina?"

I knew that voice, but I could only back farther into my room.

"Dr. Roth, you can't be up here."

"Sabrina, you need to come home." Henry appeared at the door.

I lifted my hands to my throat as he charged forward.

Wyatt grasped Henry's arm and I tried to close the door in his face. But his arm was inside, and his foot blocked my efforts.

The hotel security pulled him back and I slammed the door.

I stood in the entrance between the bathroom and the closet as the two shouted. Henry pounded on my door, yelling my name. I feel like the little pig in the house made of wood. Everyone knows what happened to that little piggy.

Outside the door, Wyatt threatened to have Henry arrested but he tried once more.

"Sabrina, please come out and speak to me."

I would not. Never again. Did he really think that keeping me medicated to the point of catatonia would stop me? We both knew it was never a permanent fix.

How many of my recent problems were caused by that poison he put in my medication? How many were just the inevitable building of my need? And how many by Henry's inventive cocktail of drugs designed to control my bloodlust?

"Go away, Henry. Don't come back."

The male voices came from farther away now.

I pictured Wyatt Guthrie dragging Henry away and smiled.

"I hope they arrest him. Again."

Now all I could hear was my own accelerated breathing. The silence should have been comforting, but instead I was pacing, waiting for him to return.

But all that came next was a gentle rapping.

"Mrs. Roth? It's Wyatt Guthrie again. We've escorted your husband off property."

I spoke through the closed door.

"Thank you."

"Would you like to change rooms?"

The thought of the time it would take to stuff my belongings back in the bags and gather all my medication was daunting. I was exhausted by the prospect.

"No. I'll stay here."

"All right then. I'm sorry for the disturbance. You have a good night, Mrs. Roth."

"Thank you, Wyatt."

I turned my back to the peephole, leaning against the solid comfort of the closed door. I was safe. He couldn't get to me and I'd be rid of him tomorrow.

The need twisted, uncoiling inside me like a waking snake.

I could go out tonight. Find someone careless, stupid. My private nurse checked my vehicle with the valet. It's downstairs in the garage and they have the fob.

But I pushed against the need as I reconsidered my options. Maybe I didn't need to go to a place tomorrow. Maybe I should just leave him in the traditional way. But the trust... My papa still watched over me. Either Henry looked after me or I'd live in one of those places.

It wasn't fair.

Dad had wanted Henry to keep me safe, but if something happened to him, I either checked into a residential facility or I lost the money.

Tomorrow, I'd meet with Gabriel and check into a facility. That would engage the trust and I'd be rid of Henry. Afterwards, I'd see about dismantling that trust. You never know until you try. I mean, a conservatorship. It was draconian. "Free Britney!" and all that.

If Gabriel couldn't do it, I'd hire a different firm and have *them* take apart my father's trust.

Difficult. Not impossible.

I'd read that trust document many times over the years. Perhaps it would be unbreakable, but I'd created a little safety net. If I couldn't get to any more of dear old Dad's money, I'd make do.

All those cars Henry wanted were in my name. The boat, the house, too. And the beach house and the one in the mountains in North Carolina. It was only a few million dollars, but it might be enough. God, the untouched clothing and handbags in my closet had to be worth a hundred thousand. I could make it work.

I headed to the bedroom to take that sleeping pill with more champagne and something for this blooming headache.

"A hot bath," I said to the silence.

I set my half-empty goblet on the fiberglass lip and filled the spa tub, slid into the bath, and closed my eyes. Time slipped as I nestled neck-deep in the hot water when I heard someone behind me.

FORTY-TWO

The next morning, Jennell knocked on Emily's door at the usual time.

"Emily? I'm done in the bathroom. You've got work today. Right?"

Friday morning Jennell was picking up some overtime on the morning shift, and Emily needed to get to the hotel before eight.

Her snoozing alarm aroused, filling the room with a cascading, repetitive trill, and Emily hit the stop button, then dragged herself from bed, exhausted. A few minutes later, she used the steamy bathroom after her roommate.

When she appeared in the kitchen, she found Jennell filling her travel mug with black coffee.

You would think a hotel that gave away coffee to all its guests in the lobby and in their rooms would let the staff have some. But if you had ever worked in the customer service industry you would know they would not.

"Good morning," said Jennell, fixing the lid on her travel mug.

"If you say so." That was her usual response, so she gave it and Jennell chuckled as always.

"Hey, thanks for moving those boxes."

They were mostly still in her room, but she had sorted them and disposed of all her mother's medications and beaten the paperwork back to a reasonable pile.

"No problem. Needed to get done." Emily retrieved a mug and Jennell moved aside, giving her access to the carafe of coffee.

"They had a visitor at the hotel last night after you left."

"Really? Who?" She thought she knew.

"Her husband showed up. Caused a scene in the lobby."

A constricting band of dread squeezed her breath away as uncertainty tingled through her.

"Is she all right?"

Jennell shrugged. "Far as I know."

"How do you know he was there?"

"Got a call from Stacy. She was at the desk."

Emily blinked, her pulse stammering along like an engine with water in the gas tank. "What happened?"

"Stacy said that Wyatt told her, her husband tried to break into her room and was escorted off the property."

"Oh, God, Jennell. I'm so sorry."

Her roommate lifted a hand to wave away her concern. "It's okay. It happens."

"When was this?"

"Don't know." Jennell's voice had a breathy anxious quality that worried Emily.

"He didn't come back?"

"Not that I heard."

"Maybe I'd better go over there now."

"Or call."

"Let me check my phone. See if I missed something. It's on the charger." Emily ducked into her room to retrieve the device.

"Anything?" asked Jennell at her reappearance.

The aroma of toasting bread filled the kitchen.

Emily lifted her gaze from her phone. "No. Just a calendar alert. But she's meeting her lawyer this morning. Told me not to show up until eight."

"Oh gosh! And I got you up so early."

"That's okay. Might be for the best. I can do some yoga or something."

"Really?"

"No. But I will stop by the cemetery and put some flowers on the graves."

"Oh, I forgot. Your sister. Right?"

"Yup. In two more years, I'll be older than she ever was. I can't believe it. It's so strange."

"Got enough for your mom's stone yet?"

Emily grinned. "I do. Finally. It's on order. Takes forever."

The toast popped and Emily quickly lifted each golden slice onto small plates, then placed one on either side of their table.

Jennell slathered jelly on her slice and Emily smeared a little butter on hers, added marmalade, then took that first lovely satisfying crunch, letting the salty, sweet taste fill her mouth.

Her roommate ate the last two bites as she walked her plate to the sink. "I've got to run. Do you mind doing these?"

"No problem."

Jennell grabbed her travel mug and waved. "See you tonight."

Emily set the kitchen back in order, then followed Jennell out. She stopped at a flower center in the grocery store to buy roses, red today, instead of her usual yellow. Since mosquitoes were such a problem in Florida, especially in the rainy season, and because they bred in even the smallest amount of standing water, the vases held flowers but not water. As a result, most visitors left plastic flowers, which Emily hated.

She knew the blooms wouldn't last. She also knew nothing did.

By the time she finished her errand, she struggled to shake off her melancholy and got moving so she'd reach the hotel on time. By then Jennell would have been behind the reception desk for an hour.

She tucked the flowers, now wrapped in colorful purple paper, in the seat beside her and drove to the cemetery. At the grave she broke the bouquet into two small bunches, three roses, one fern, and one stalk of baby's breath each.

Her mobile rang. She tugged the device out of her back pocket and saw Jennell's pretty face on the screen. It was unusual for her roommate to phone during the workday. Something was wrong. There was a tightness in her chest as she took the call.

"Hey there."

Jennell's voice was a strained whisper. "All hell is breaking loose here."

Emily's breath caught and she swallowed past the spiky knot of worry she heard in her roommate's voice. "What do you mean?"

Jennell's breathing was audible and fast. "Her attorney showed up—"

Emily interrupted. "Yeah. He was supposed—"

Jennell cut her off. "Listen, will you? When she wasn't there to meet him, we sent housekeeping up. They found her... Emily, she's dead!"

She didn't need to ask who. The tightness in her throat hardened, dropping into her stomach like a loose brick.

"What happened?"

"How should I know?" Jennell's voice went from whisper to

squeak. "The police are here. Paramedics. Security told me. I think she killed herself or something."

The pause stretched out to the horizon.

"Em? You there?"

"Jennell, I'm in trouble. I helped her leave him."

"That's not your fault."

"Isn't it? I abandoned a mentally ill woman with all her medications. If she overdosed—"

"It wasn't an overdose."

"What?"

"I think she slit her wrists or something. Security said he saw her in the tub. He said there was blood on the floor."

Emily cried out. "Oh, God! What should I do?"

"You should get down here."

She didn't want to. She wanted to drive in the other direction. Then she imagined herself making a daring getaway on a half tank of gas and bald tires.

"This is terrible. I'm so scared."

"Em, this is not your fault. Those two both seem nuts. And you were trying to help her."

"What if they arrest me?"

"For what? Trying to get an unhappy wife out of a bad marriage?"

"You *know* Dr. Roth will blame me. Oh, no! I packed her bags. Drove her over there."

"Emily. Stop it. Just take a breath."

"Okay." She did. And she took another. "I'm coming. Keep your ears open."

"Oh, believe me, I am. See you soon."

Jennell ended the call.

Emily tucked away her phone and placed one bunch of flowers in the vase before her sister's grave and tugged away some of the encroaching grass at the corners of her sister's flat, lawn-level marker. Then she set the second bouquet on the eroding mound of earth before the paper sign that marked her mother's final resting place.

Emily stared at the depression of earth.

"I bought your marker, Mama. Real marble with engravings to match hers." She motioned toward the small stone that marked her sister's grave and checked the date of death—seven years to the day.

Then she rose and walked back to the car.

The familiar aching loss squeezed her heart. She thought that today she'd feel different, that some of the pain would have lessened. But it pulsed as if her skin had been peeled back. Perhaps it had been silly to think that anything would lessen her grief.

Emily drove to the hotel, but the police were so busy she wasn't allowed to go up to Sabrina's floor. So, she told the uniformed police officers stationed in the lobby that she was Mrs. Roth's help. He told her to wait and that was what she did for most of the morning.

But just as her stomach started to growl, and she considered abandoning the lobby for some lunch, a detective showed up.

"Are you Emily Lancing?" he asked.

Just speaking to a law enforcement officer gave her an unwelcome jab of worry.

"Yes. That's me."

"I have some questions."

FORTY-THREE

The detective seemed to be creating a timeline of events, asking her to pin down everything that had happened yesterday, beginning with when she arrived at the Roths' home.

She did her best to remember, not knowing the exact time but generally what had happened when.

Then he turned to getting her opinion of the relationship between Dr. and Mrs. Roth.

"I'm not in a position to judge."

He wasn't letting her off with that. After a few more non-answers, she said, "I'm not a doctor, but I wonder if a husband should be the person treating his wife."

"Why?"

"Because it was mental illness. And well, Mrs. Roth had told me that her husband's business wasn't as lucrative as it appeared. She claimed she was the one with the money."

He nodded. "Hard to be objective. That it?"

Emily's palms were damp and she pressed them against the absorbent fabric of her slacks.

The detective finished scribbling in his pad and flicked his gaze back to her. "Did you see any of the documents she carried to the hotel?"

"Not yesterday. I mean, I did pack them, but I, no, I never read the documents." Just the photographs of the documents, she thought.

"In your opinion, would Mrs. Roth take her life to spite her husband?"

"What?" she asked, the surprise clear in her voice.

"You know, to keep him from getting anything."

"How can anyone answer that? I mean, a person's sense of self-preservation would kick in. So, no. I don't think so."

"What if they divorced?"

Emily wiped her hands back and forth over her thighs. "I think she wanted that. She said so. Or at least a separation."

"What did she say exactly?"

"Exactly? I'm not sure. But something like, 'I'm leaving him.' I think."

"Did you ever witness Dr. Roth abusing his wife?"

She straightened, alarm bells sounding in her mind. "What do you mean?"

"Did he hit her?"

She shook her head and kept her eyes down. But her ears were suddenly so hot.

"But you were both at the station yesterday. She stated that he grabbed her."

Emily nodded. Her mouth was so dry that her tongue stuck to the roof of her mouth.

"You witnessed this?"

"At the other hotel. Yes."

"And he attacked you?"

"He shoved me."

"I've read your statement. Seems more serious than a shove."

She lowered her gaze to her hands which were clenched tight before her.

The detective continued, reading from his little notebook. "Her attorney stated that Sabrina Roth believed that her husband was meddling with her prescriptions."

"She thought that, yes. Dr. Roth told me that she had hallucinations, and Dr. Roth explained they were..." Emily thought and then said, "Organic delusions. He said that's things that she believed no matter what proof there was that it wasn't true."

"I see. What were these delusions?"

Now she laced her fingers together and reminded herself not to fidget. "I don't know all of them. But one was that she thought she killed someone. Said she was driving when she wasn't."

"In an auto accident?"

"Yes. I think so." She squeezed her fingers bloodless.

"She didn't drive?"

"No. That was one of my jobs."

"What else did you do?"

She explained her nursing responsibilities, housekeeping duties, and administrative jobs.

"Did you tell her that Dr. Roth put fentanyl in her medication?"

Emily started to cry. The tears burned down her cheeks and she dashed them away.

Busted, she thought, but nodded.

"I took some of her medication for testing. The results showed fentanyl."

"Why did you do that?"

"Because I thought it would be proof that she was wrong. Which was stupid, because even if she had been wrong, *and* I had proof, her delusions would likely make her not believe it anyway."

"But she wasn't wrong?"

"I never expected..." She looked up at him with watering eyes. "How did you know?"

"Text sent to her husband. She mentioned you in her accusation. Tell me about this test."

She did.

"Why would the technician test this sample without a doctor's orders?"

"We dated. Favor for a friend."

He shook his head, clearly disapproving of her decision-making. She set her jaw against saying something in anger.

His attention went back to his notes. "His name?"

She told him and he jotted it down.

"Do you know how it got into Mrs. Roth's medications?"

Emily shook her head. "I don't."

Here was where they blamed her, she thought.

"Did you put them in her prescriptions?"

Emily gasped at this accusation. "What? No. I didn't."

"All right. One more thing. Where did you go after you left Mrs. Roth?"

Emily sobbed. "I shouldn't have left her."

He leaned forward, pressing in on her personal space. "Why?"

"She was taking a lot of medications. She was upset. I should have stayed."

"Was she upset?"

Emily glanced upward at the dirty acoustic ceiling tiles, thinking. "Well, earlier. Not when she got to her room."

"Not upset?"

"I didn't think so, but she was." Her brow wrinkled. "She must have been."

"Why?"

Exasperated, Emily blurted out the obvious. "Because she killed herself."

"How do you know that?"

Emily flushed. "Um, my roommate works here. She told me."

"How did she know?"

"Security officer who found Mrs. Roth told another employee and he told her, I think."

"I see." He glanced toward the reception area. "Who is your roommate?"

She hesitated just long enough to realize this was the sort of information he could get elsewhere. "Jennell Green."

He wrote it down as her foot drummed relentlessly on the leg of the chair.

"Did Mrs. Roth ask you to stay?"

"No. She told me to go home and be back at eight this morning."

"Why eight?"

"So, she could meet with her attorney alone before that."

He nodded and scribbled in his pad.

"Did she express a desire to harm herself?"

"No. Never." Her vehement expression and shake punctuated her opinion on that question.

"Where did you go after you left the hotel?"

"Back to my apartment."

"Address?"

She told him.

"Anyone see you?"

"I don't know." She puzzled a moment, thinking back over her trip from the hotel to her apartment as she tapped one finger into the indentation above her upper lip. "Maybe."

"Were you alone?"

"No, Jennell came in after work."

"When did you leave the hotel?"

"I left after six."

He consulted his notebook. "Security cameras have you leaving the lobby at 6:43pm." He flipped back to the page where he'd been scribbling down her responses. "Take me through the evening."

She did, relaying that she and Jennell had streamed a movie on her roommate's laptop and then gone to bed a little after ten. He wanted the name of the movie. Was he going to check to see if Jennell was streaming it? That would give him a timeline, she supposed. And if he had the IP address of Jennell's computer, Wi-Fi would verify where they were.

"I went to bed and Jennell woke me up this morning at six."

"You didn't leave your apartment between retiring and rising?"

"After I went to bed? No."

He flipped his notebook closed.

Why was she feeling sick to her stomach?

"I may need to speak to you again. It's possible you'll need to come to the station."

"Am I in trouble?"

He did not offer a smile or say anything reassuring.

"I'll be in touch."

She sat for a time after he left, unsure her legs would support her. That had been much scarier than she'd anticipated, and she'd anticipated it would be terrible.

* * *

Emily did not sleep well that night. Too many worries and doubts. She finally gave up and grabbed her phone before six on Saturday morning, searching the news outlets for details. They reported that Mrs. Sabrina Roth, wife of the local psychiatrist Dr. Henry Roth, had died of an apparent suicide in her room following an altercation with her husband at the hotel where she was staying. Witnesses described Dr. Roth, on the evening of August 10th, as extremely upset, yelling in the lobby. The paper reported that he'd later been escorted out of the building by security.

And that was not a good look for a psychiatrist who was supposed to model calm, control, and mental stability. She wondered how he was feeling today. And was he upset over his wife's welfare or his own?

Either way, Dr. Roth had just lost his place at the trough.

She heard Jennell returning home after pulling a double shift.

Emily carried her laptop out and set it on the table. Jennell stood in the kitchen, swaying with fatigue.

"Good morning," Emily said.

"If you say so." She sank to the seat across from Emily. "Police finally released the scene. They were there all last night."

Emily motioned to her laptop. "It's the lead in the news."

Jennell drew a heavy breath. "Not surprised. You know, housekeeping took one look inside that room and refused to clean it." Jennell thumped her empty insulated bottle on the table, her movements relaying exhaustion. "They had to call some specialists. Specialists, can you believe that? There's a whole business for people who are willing to clean up after murders and suicides."

"But you've had suicides before in the hotel. You told me. And you said that was why the windows don't open all the way."

"True. And the shower curtains are those pressure ones. You would not believe the number of guests who just yank on them like they are their own private guardrail. But they can't hang themselves there or on the towel hooks."

"Towel hooks? On the back of doors?"

She nodded. "It's possible."

"But that's only about six feet up."

"Just need to get their feet off the ground, apparently. So

ours break away. Not intended for that much weight. Suicides are bad for business."

Emily shuddered, knowing she could have lived her entire life without knowing that.

"So, what's your plan for today?" Jennell asked.

"I'm supposed to go to the police station."

That news cut Jennell's yawn short. "What? Do you need a lawyer or something?"

"Why?"

"Well, you know, maybe you're an easy target. Blame it on the help."

Emily made a humming sound of concern in her throat. "The butler did it."

"I'm serious."

"I have no reason to harm her. I'm out of a job because of this. The best-paying job I ever had. Maybe ever will have."

"Don't say that." Jennell drummed her fingers on the table. "You did leave her there."

"Because she told me to."

Emily poured Jennell a glass of cold water from the pitcher they kept in the refrigerator. Then she returned to her seat and the mug of dark, sweet coffee.

"But back to the room. Why won't the housekeepers clean it?"

"Because blood is everywhere. On the walls, towels, and soaked into the grout. Even the ceiling, they said because she cut the arteries of both wrists. Used a double-edged razor. Security said she cut deep, right through the tendons."

"Both?"

"That's what Gary said. He went in with her lawyer, who made the ID."

The body.

Emily shivered at how quickly her employer went from a person of influence, with a fine home and a family, to *the body*.

"How did she cut the other wrist?" asked Emily.

"What do you mean?"

Emily demonstrated with a butter knife. "If I cut here"—she made a slashing motion above her left wrist—"this one first because I'm right-handed." She set the knife on the table and then reached for the knife with her wrist flopping. "If she did cut the tendons, she can't grip the knife. Can she?"

Jennell sat back, eyes wide and tipped up as if studying the ugly, ancient kitchen light with the shadows of dead insects visible in the textured Plexiglas.

At last, she said, "She couldn't." Her gaze dropped to Emily. "She could never have cut that other wrist. Oh, God. That means..." She pressed a hand to her mouth.

"Maybe she cut this way." Emily motioned to a vertical cut.

"I'll ask Gary. Oh, God, I feel sick."

Emily balled her fist before her mouth.

"Should we tell someone? The police?" asked her roommate.

Emily shook her head. "I'm not telling them."

"Why not?"

"They're experts. Professionals."

"The Lakeland police? How many murder investigations do they have a year?" Jennell asked.

"Twelve."

"What? How do you know that?"

"It's why I wanted to leave Lakeland. This apartment is in a safer neighborhood. And the statistics are up there on the web."

An uneasy quiet filled the space between them. Finally, Jennell broke the silence.

"So, when are you going to the station?"

"Eleven."

A text alert had Jennell glancing at her phone. "You mind if I tell that thing about the wrists to Gary?"

"If you make it sound like your idea."

"Sure thing. Good luck with the police."

"Thanks." Emily hoped she wouldn't need it. Her sister had once told her that people with a clean conscience had nothing to fear.

Her experience was that easy targets got fingered, and she had no resources and zero connections.

Jennell rose heavily. "I'm on again tonight."

"Get some sleep."

"Half asleep right now." Jennell shuffled toward her bedroom.

"Did she leave a note?" asked Emily.

"I-I don't know. I'll ask."

Jennell trundled toward her bed and Emily finished her coffee and left their apartment, running some errands, and then heading to the station.

The interview with the police took longer than she had planned. They wanted more information about the Roths' marriage and Dr. Roth's behavior. They spent a lot of time on him. Also Mrs. Roth's moods, routine. Emily did mention the drawings. Those drawings were very disturbing, and she was not easily disturbed.

They questioned her again two days later. Then she heard nothing for the three days except the hearsay Jennell picked up at the hotel and what she saw on the news.

Jennell asked her what her plans were, now that she was unemployed.

"I'll work at the hospital. For a while, at least."

"I thought you didn't like the patient load there."

"I like it better than being unemployed. Also, I'm applying for late admission to Florida Southern College and the University of Tampa. Depends on the financial aid package, though."

"Really? Great. Nurse practitioner program?"

"Yeah. And if I can do it, I'll make more money, have more options."

"Sounds good."

"Yup. Got an appointment this afternoon about a work-study program."

Jennell motioned a finger at her laptop. "When will you know?"

Emily shrugged.

"Good luck."

She made it to the FSC central administration office in plenty of time to speak to a financial aid counselor about her application. Unless they gave her free housing, she was staying put with Jennell.

When she got back to the apartment, she found her room-mate dressed for work and standing at the stove opening a box of mac and cheese.

"Did you hear?" she asked as she stood stirring the macaroni into the boiling water.

"Hear what?"

"They arrested Henry Roth."

FORTY-FOUR

By the end of August, Emily's application was accepted at FSC; the financial aid package was still pending, but looked promising. If she got it, the amount would make school nearly doable. Yesterday, someone from the college called. The housing was full, unfortunately, but she could apply next semester.

She continued working full-time at the hospital before the school year began in September. The patient load was crazy, and being the low man on the floor wasn't ideal, but her job was indoors, in air-conditioning, and didn't involve doing dishes, picking up wet clothing from the floor, or working unpredictable overtime.

Orientation was the day after Labor Day and classes started the following week. The school year kept her very busy, attending classes, and she continued working part-time at the hospital. With her job and the financial aid package, which finally came through, she would be taking on less debt than she'd feared.

And for the next five weeks, Emily juggled work, classes, homework, and the needs of the DA who was preparing the case against her former employer.

Dr. Roth had been arrested less than a week after the murder. It astonished Emily how quickly the news outlets painted him as a monster as the story bloomed to receive national attention. Jennell was not surprised, except to say that people like that so rarely got what they deserved.

The trial began on Tuesday, October 10th, and Emily had made it a point to be in court for opening statements. Dr. Roth's attorney cast a wide net of other possible suspects and her name was mentioned more than once. It was hard to tell what the jury made of that, but she was confident the speculation was not enough to get Henry's head out of the noose. Though all they needed was a reasonable doubt.

At night, in the apartment, as the window unit air conditioner roared like a clogged leaf blower, Emily watched the local news at both six and ten.

Unlike some states, cameras were permitted inside the Florida courts, and news outlets captured every minute to replay the best bits.

Through much of October, she watched the live feed on her phone whenever she could and caught some of Wyatt Guthrie's testimony. The hotel security guard, who had to escort Dr. Roth off the property, told of an angry man. Aggressive, threatening, belligerent. It wasn't flattering.

Mr. Guthrie was uncertain if Dr. Roth had an opportunity to place the duct tape recovered from the lock mechanism on his wife's hotel door but did recall that she had come to the door and opened it and that he had kept her husband from forcing his way inside.

She also caught the live testimony from many of the key witnesses, including staff at the first hotel, the investigating homicide detectives, and several forensic experts.

The evidence against Henry Roth seemed damning.

The bombshell testimony came from a young office assistant with whom Dr. Roth had had a long-standing affair. The prosecution contended that his wish to be rid of his wife, and marry his mistress, made a powerful motive for murder. Testimony that he had siphoned off over nine hundred thousand dollars from his wife's trust, not including their vacation home, his automobiles, boats, jewelry, and watch collection, did not seem to sit well with the jury.

The physical evidence on the base of a hotel lamp, yanked from the wall, had both hair and blood matching Sabrina Roth.

One of the police detectives testified that the double-edged blade, used to cut his wife's wrists, recovered from the bath mat beside her tub, matched the type and brand used by Henry Roth in the razor recovered from his home.

The fingerprint expert returned to the stand to testify that the latents recovered from the razor found in the hotel bathroom belonged to both Sabrina Roth and a partial of her husband. The graphic showed the jury the points of identification to the right thumbprint taken at Dr. Henry Roth's arrest. He also explained that Henry Roth's partial indicated someone had tried to wipe the blade clean and that Sabrina's prints were not in the correct placement for someone holding a razor, and the blood smear, interrupting her print, indicated at least one had been added after its use.

The night before Emily was to testify, Jennell arrived home late.

"How's the star witness?" she asked.

"Nervous." That was true. There were so many details to remember and keep straight. She hoped she could do her part to see that Henry got exactly what he deserved.

"What are you going to wear?"

"It's on my bed."

Jennell ducked her head in. "All white, huh?"

"Seemed to represent purity and innocence."

"Well, you are all that. Still can't believe his attorney's tried to use you as the fall guy."

"I'm not."

"Hey what's this?" she asked, looking at the dark pencil sketch on Emily's bed.

"Abstraction. Charcoal and pencil."

Jennell cocked her head trying to make sense of the spiderwebs of white and the dark patches.

"Gives me the creeps."

"I like it."

Jennell shrugged. "Eye of the beholder, I guess. What about the classes you're missing?"

"I don't have any choice. It's a subpoena."

"Don't I know it. But, boy, was my boss pissed about all this press coverage. Bad for business," said Jennell. "We've had cancelations."

"Maybe you'll get those murder tourists or ghost hunters."

"It's possible. Ghosts are big business for some hotels." Jennell switched topics. "Do you feel ready?"

"I don't think that's possible. It's a murder trial."

Emily said good night early, hoping that she would get some sleep, but it eluded her.

* * *

The next day, Emily was visibly shaking when she took the stand. And her fair skin displayed her nerves for the camera with a spectacular flush. Redheads just couldn't keep those heated cheeks from blazing under pale skin. But the prosecution attorney was calm and assuring and the questions were just as they'd prepared. She explained all that Dr. Roth had said about his wife's condition, what it was like to work in their home, her version of what happened the day Sabrina fainted in the SUV, and how Emily had phoned her attorney at Sabrina's request.

He introduced her communications with Brian and the

defense objected, since they had already had that evidence suppressed.

But the prosecution had still asked the question and she'd had time to say what Brian had found before the judge interceded, telling the jury to ignore that testimony.

And a jury couldn't really un-hear something, could they? Plus, the pathologist who performed the autopsy had already testified that fentanyl had been present in Mrs. Roth's blood.

Meanwhile, the defense pointed out that Emily's mother had been prescribed opioids during her final days. The prosecution countered that script had been for morphine which was not found in Sabrina's blood.

Next, the defense proposed that Emily might additionally have been stealing Sabrina Roth's prescriptions for her own use and switching out the medication with street drugs. Here the judge overruled that being added to the testimony as speculation.

Roth's attorney pointed out that Emily and/or the house cleaner, Rosalind, each had the opportunity to add something to Sabrina's medication but provided no motive for either woman to do so, as the prosecution noted. He did succeed in getting the report thrown out that Dr. Roth's blood also indicated fentanyl use. But photos of the illegal drugs and syringes discovered by police while executing the search warrant on the Roths' home was admitted.

Equally damning was the voice recording Emily had made the day Henry had shoved her into the stove and cabinets because it included an admission of guilt. The prosecution also introduced the photos taken at the police station after the attack.

The court broke for lunch. Afterwards, Emily took the stand again as the prosecution introduced her messages to Jennell after Dr. Roth attacked her.

The judge allowed both the AirDropped video and photos

as evidence, despite objections. If she had to guess, she'd say the jury believed every bit of Dr. Roth being capable of threatening, bribing, and manhandling the help.

The hardest part was when she had to admit that she suspected Dr. Roth was keeping his wife a virtual prisoner, controlling her with drugs meant to subdue her, and that she was unconvinced anything, beyond the potent cocktail of pharmaceuticals, was wrong with Sabrina Roth.

"I'm so ashamed of my part in this. I should have gotten her help that first day. Even then I had suspicions that he kept her a prisoner."

"Objection."

It was those objections and sidebar conversations that ate away most of the afternoon. It gave her time to think and more time to worry. Her stomach spasms sent twisting pain grinding through her middle.

Some of her last testimony was removed. So, on the next question, the district attorney stayed away from speculation.

Through tears she managed to continue.

"I'm not sorry I called the police or helped her get away. I'm only sorry that I couldn't prevent her death."

The cross-examination was brutal. After the defense finished picking apart everything they could and casting doubt wherever it might fall, they insinuated Emily was a thief, a liar, and culpable for leaving Mrs. Roth alone at the hotel.

She was finally dismissed. Exhausted and drained, she left the gallery and plopped down outside in the lower lobby, surprised to have finished her testimony in only one long day. It took only a moment to pull up the livestream of the trial on her phone.

She viewed the proceedings in progress, listening as the defense entered the trust agreement into evidence and called Gabriel Rottach to the stand. He made a compelling figure, in

Emily's opinion. She inserted her earbuds to better hear as Rottach was sworn in and took his place.

"Isn't it true that Dr. Roth would receive nothing upon her death?"

"That's true."

"Then Dr. Roth would have no motivation for killing his wife."

"Except to keep her from exposing abuse, losing his license to practice medicine, and possibly getting arrested."

"No further questions."

* * *

On Thursday, November 2nd, Emily watched the live feed from the courtroom, listening to the expert witness, a psychiatrist, who said fentanyl was not an appropriate medication for a person with Mrs. Roth's diagnoses and was, of course, extremely dangerous when taken in conjunction with her other medications.

Next up was the detective who'd conducted the search of the Roths' home after Mrs. Roth's body was found.

"And what did you find in the laundry area?" asked the prosecution attorney.

"We used luminol to reveal traces of blood on the floor, washing machine, and the bottle of detergent. Also, evidence of cleaning products often used to remove stains."

"Were you able to identify any of the blood?"

"Not from those areas. The bleach used destroyed the evidence. But we did find blood on a pair of Henry Roth's sneakers left in the garage."

"What were your findings on that sample?"

"DNA testing showed a match to Sabrina King Roth."

The question of how Dr. Roth got into the hotel was answered by the head of security at Jennell's place of work. A retired police detective from Yonkers, New York, she was no stranger to a courtroom and easily narrated the surveillance footage of a person, wearing a hoodie and dark trousers, entering the hotel via the employees' entrance and using the stairs to climb to the third floor. There was no footage of the stairs, but the existing video showed the person enter the stairs at ground level and exit to the hallway on the floor where Sabrina was staying, making a beeline to her room, and opening the door. The time stamp showed this individual was inside the room for twenty-one minutes and exited the same way. Footage of the parking lot showed the suspect getting onto an expensive racing bike, exactly like the one belonging to Dr. Henry Roth, and pedaling away.

The prosecution brought in a film analysis expert who concluded the person in the video matched the height of the suspect.

Sensing defeat, the defense asked for a recess. The paper later reported that they had offered to plead guilty if the charges were reduced to manslaughter. The prosecution refused.

During closing arguments, the prosecution alleged that Henry Roth was desperate to cover his spousal abuse and fentanyl addiction by keeping his wife from ruining his reputation and practice. Seeing he could not convince her to return to the marriage, he plotted her murder, attempting to make her death appear to be the suicide of a troubled woman. They then went through every shred of evidence. It made a tasty pile.

The defense's summation was weaker, alleging Henry was home asleep when the murder took place, that he never left his home after returning from the hotel earlier in the evening and did not know of his wife's death until he was notified the following day.

They contended someone else, an unknown individual, for unknown reasons, committed the crime with the intention of making Dr. Roth the fall guy.

But the subpoenaed home security surveillance footage from the doorbell camera showed someone leaving the garage at 2:16 am on a racing bike, leaving the gated community eight minutes later. It also captured someone returning to that residence at 3:46 am.

They offered no explanation as to why the bloody sneakers were in the garage and traces of Sabrina's blood recovered from the garage floor and the doorknob between the garage and laundry room.

Long before the trial wrapped up, the public rendered a guilty verdict. Dr. Henry Roth killed his wife. After a short deliberation, the jury concluded the same. A murder conviction in Florida was subject to the death penalty.

His attorneys could do nothing during the sentencing phase of the trial.

Henry Roth was sentenced to death by lethal injection.

FORTY-FIVE

FLORIDA STATE PRISON, STARKE, FLORIDA

FIFTEEN MONTHS LATER

The February cold snap had brought frost to northern Florida. Strawberry farmers and citrus growers burned smudge pots and used sprinklers to protect their crop.

Emily drove through fog, a rare sight, and reached the prison visitors' lot before nine in the morning. Inside, she presented her ID and cleared security, then followed a family of three down the corridor to the chilly visiting room, glad she wore a fleece jacket.

The prisoners had no such luxury. She saw the first of them as she entered the visiting room. The men were dressed in thin cotton pants and matching pale blue tops that reminded her of the scrubs the nurses wore.

Finally, she had a chance at the education she needed to enroll in a thirty-six-month bridge program taking her from an associate's degree to a master's in nursing. As important, she qualified for financial aid and, next semester, housing. Things were finally looking up and she was ready to move along, just as soon as she wrapped up this last small detail.

Emily paused in the big open room, where inmates and their families mingled, finding it not at all what she'd expected. This was so different than the women's prison. Larger, noisier, and it stank like body odor.

She took a seat near the guards stationed along the wall across from the bank of barred windows. But not too close. Not close enough for them to hear their conversation.

It had taken five weeks to be cleared by the state of Florida to visit. Now she was here to see her old employer one last time before she turned the page.

He entered in the same clothing as everyone incarcerated here, a powder-blue top that showed a white T-shirt at the neck. The pants were elastic at the waist and on his feet were slip-on shoes that fell between sneakers and house slippers.

No more designer duds for this former respected psychiatrist. Gone were his fine watches, luxury automobiles, influential position, and privileged lifestyle.

Emily smiled as the prisoner scanned the room, looking for her.

He'd lost weight, she realized, and his hair had gone powdery on the crown. Had he been dyeing it all along? Yes, she decided that was likely. She wondered what had happened to his fancy cars and the house. Emily suspected Taylor was now very rich and didn't visit. He had no other family except a younger sister who had not even attended the trial.

Henry spotted Emily. She waved from her place at the cafeteria-style table. He headed straight for her.

She could almost see him plotting how best to leverage her visit into some advantage for himself. It was his gift. He needed a win because his initial appeal had been denied.

So went the days on death row.

He smiled, flashing those feline teeth, thinking her glad to see him. Well, he'd misjudged her before.

"Emily, how good of you to come visit me." He sat across from her, his hopeful expression seemed so genuine.

Had she ever really believed that charming veneer?

"Wouldn't have missed it," she said, casting him a tentative smile. She had no idea how this would go, only how she hoped it would unfold. She'd imagined this day so many times.

"I don't have many visitors."

"None, according to the guard who checked me in."

Confusion flashed across his face, and he dropped his gaze.

"No colleagues, former partners... not even your daughter?"

When he lifted his eyes to meet hers, his face was flushed with shame.

"It's been a difficult transition."

She reached into her back pocket to retrieve one of the three things she was permitted to bring inside this facility. Her car fob was in her front pocket and there was no need to bring money because she'd be damned if she'd give him a nickel. The final item allowed by the penal system of Florida was a photograph.

"Yes. Difficult." She nodded at his assessment. "Because you couldn't find someone else to take the fall this time."

"What?"

"As you've done before. Like holding me responsible when your wife called the cops. And for the accident. Or should I say accidents?"

His eyes narrowed.

"You were very good at keeping your wife from accountability. If you weren't so dedicated to covering up her crimes, you wouldn't be here now."

"What are you talking about?"

"I thought it was her. *All* her. And I thought it was just the one fatality. But there were others. And she visited them. Didn't she? All her victims."

"You're not making any sense."

"But she couldn't have done it alone. You cleaned up the

vehicles afterwards, when she came home with blood on the grille and the bumper. Probably had the body shop in your contact favorites. Diverted any suspicion that fell on her as well. Was it three or four before Avery?"

He was sitting straight now. Intent and still, his body leaning forward.

"That one caused you real grief. Because you'd taken precautions. No more driving for her. But she still managed to kill a woman. Couldn't resist. Crime of opportunity. She didn't plan that one. Did she? Wasn't out hunting in one of your vehicles like before. And still she managed to hit her dead-on from the passenger seat, in broad daylight and with witnesses. Just luck it wasn't more than one. And your housekeeper knew what happened. So, you offered her a deal, just like you did with me."

"I don't know what you mean."

"Don't you?"

She slid the photo across the table.

He glanced down. "What's this?"

"Who's this would be a better question."

His brow furrowed as he stared at the photo.

"That looks like Regan."

"Very good. Regan McGrath."

"She worked for my wife."

"I know."

"You knew her?" he asked.

"Not for as long as I would have liked. She was my older sister. Didn't know that. Did you?"

True, Emily had a different last name than her half sister. Different fathers, ages, hair color, and education. But they shared the same vivid green eyes. The eyes that Sabrina must have remembered because she'd called her Regan more than once.

He pushed the photo back. "You got it wrong. Your sister

killed a woman with our car. We had to pay damages to her family."

That wasn't all he'd paid.

"Regan didn't cause the accident."

"What?"

"Your wife did. She grabbed the wheel. Regan told my mother that Sabrina turned them into those people on the sidewalk. And she hit one. Her intended victim, a dead ringer for her mother—again. Sabrina broke her wrist because it was on the wheel."

Unlike the rest of the world, Emily believed Sabrina when she said she'd killed people.

"Well, the victim is dead, Regan is dead, and my wife is dead. I don't know what you expect me to say... sorry?"

He wasn't. But his brows lifted as he glanced from Regan's photo to Emily. She could almost see him casting about for theories.

"Curious? Was it a coincidence, my working for you? I was curious, too. I knew what happened, at least with Avery's death. My big sister told my mother and, a few months before she died, Mom told me. Not on purpose. At the end, she thought I was Regan."

"Your sister lied to police," he said.

Emily ignored this.

"After I figured out your wife's nasty compulsion, I kept wondering if Sabrina understood what she was doing or was she too mentally damaged to comprehend her actions? And did she do all that alone or did she have help? Was she using you or were you complicit?"

"This is bullshit." He placed his hands on the table as if preparing to rise but remained seated.

"Do you remember how you connected with Regan?"

"My father-in-law recommended her."

"Right. A handpicked patsy. My mother worked for the

Kings. It was Sabrina's dad's idea that Regan go to work for his daughter. He knew my mother was a single mom, that money was tight, and that she had a younger daughter. He knew Regan and my mother well enough to realize they'd do anything to protect me. That made them both easy to scare."

He shrugged as if unaffected by this revelation, but his scowl deepened.

"It's from my mother that I know what went on in Sabrina's childhood home. She was there when it happened. You know. The drowning?"

Henry shifted on his seat and his expression went stony.

"Michelle King watched it all on the security camera playback and called her husband. Told him that their daughter pushed her twin in the pool and stood on the deck to watch him die. My mom was right there with Michelle. Heard every word. Sabrina killed someone at college, too, I believe. After they flew her home from school, my mom unpacked her things. Told me the news was full of a coed mowed down on campus. No surprise the Kings wanted their daughter home and safe. Her dad was supposed to drive Sabrina's car home. But, change of plan, he sold it along the way. Cold case now—never solved."

Henry broke eye contact, sitting back and folding his arms across his chest. Emily continued, determined he heard it all.

"Early on, her parents knew what she was. That's when her dad found you. Scrappy poor kid with a brain and no prospects. You boys cut some back-room deal. Met the devil at the crossroads that day. Didn't you?"

"That your little theory?"

She leveled a hard stare at the prisoner before her.

"My theory? Your wife doesn't suffer from organic delusions. And the impulse you were trying to control was her need to kill people, starting with her twin brother. Later, she picked women who looked very much like her dear departed mother."

He said nothing, just lowered his chin and glowered.

"After that impulse murder, the one she pulled off while not even behind the wheel, you got scared. Public accident. Lots of witnesses. Didn't have her in hand, did you? So, you tried sedating her. Bound to fail eventually because Sabrina's biggest trouble wasn't a guilty conscience. It was that she never had one."

"Never prove that."

"That was not my aim. But after my mother told me what Regan told her, about Sabrina seeing that woman, grabbing the wheel, jerking the vehicle, and killing Avery Nell Thomas, I did make some plans."

"If that were true, why didn't Regan come forward, instead of admitting blame?"

"Great question. But you know why. Don't you? When my sister got arrested, you swooped in with offers of using your very expensive, highly qualified attorney. It was that or the public defender. So, she made the obvious choice. But Regan never understood that her defense counsel wasn't working in her best interest, but in yours. By the time she figured that out, it was too late. The deal he suggested was never on the table and her guilty plea got the maximum sentence. You tossed her away like sour milk. When Regan realized what you'd done, she told the public defender. The DA said she changed her story, but guess what? No police records of the accident investigation exist. Computer glitch, they said. They refused to reopen the case. And, what a coincidence, Regan's and Sabrina's medical records following the accident vanished, too. Poof!"

Emily made an exploding gesture with her fingers and then slapped her hands down on the table.

Henry narrowed his eyes. Was he finally seeing something more than a frightened little patsy?

"So, I was thinking," Emily said. "Who made those medical records vanish?"

"You think *I* did that?"

"I know you did. But my sister wouldn't drop her appeal. That's when you had my mom arrested, set up, as a thief. Mom told me before she died that you planted that jewelry the police found in her car and that you told her that if she didn't get Regan to shut up and drop her appeal, you'd prosecute her mother and make sure I went into foster care. She told me what you said. Said you'd send me to an orphanage. Really no surprise Regan took the blame. Such a nasty thing, threatening a person's family."

"She *was* driving."

"Yes. But Sabrina caused the crash, just as she claimed, and then you pressed your cronies with the police to make a quick job of the investigation. Regan was Sabrina's fall guy."

"Disappearing records, bribing police. You give me more credit than I deserve."

She snorted at his weak denial. He actually looked smug, like he'd gotten away with it. As if he didn't recall where he was sitting.

"I saw the bank records. Right after the accident, a twenty-thousand-dollar check to the investigating officer signed by you."

"You're mistaken. There are no records."

There were. He knew it and she had copies. Not that she needed them.

She shrugged. "Your wife's computer didn't have a password. The bank's passwords were autosaved. Banks keep good records. Long histories. Including the purchase of a blue Prius. Found the bill of sale after your wife got into your safe. Copied the VIN number. It cost me ten bucks to discover who owned that car. Not your mistress. My predecessor, Clare Eastman. And what do you know, her old car was missing. Just gone. But she never reported it stolen."

Emily tilted her head to one side to study him. His face was very red.

He met her steady gaze and sneered.

"What are you going to do? Add bribery to my sentence? I'm on death row."

She smiled and nodded. "Yes. You are."

His sneer turned ugly, poisoned by suspicions, into a look of malevolence.

"I don't have to listen to this." He pressed his hands flat on the table and began to rise.

She waved him away. "You don't. But you've got the time, don't you? Nowhere to go for say... ever?"

He sank back into his seat.

"Once I was sure that you were letting this happen... that you were going to keep letting this happen and cover up her murders, I was all in. You two. You think you can do whatever you like. We aren't people to you. Are we?"

"And?"

"Just the help. And you always kept the side door open for the help. 'Come on into the laundry room and wait.'"

He was leaning forward, interest piqued.

"What do you want?"

Emily ignored the question.

"You know you and I are the same size? I had access to all your clothing, there in your walk-in closet. And you have so much, it was hard to notice what went missing. An expensive pair of sneakers with a very distinctive tread, an old hoodie, dark slacks."

And then she saw the puzzle pieces falling into place. The blood vessels in his eyes bulged red. The arteries flanking his throat pulsed. Nostrils flared.

"You!"

"That's right. I murdered a mass-murderer and sent a guilty man to prison. Now *you* can serve a sentence for a crime *you* didn't commit, just like my sister. Until they stick a needle in your arm. So, what do I want? Nothing at all. Your debt is paid. Even Steven. You don't owe me a thing. Not anymore."

He leapt to his feet, roaring as he lunged. "Why, you little—"

The closest guard tackled him, sending him sprawling across the chipped Formica table.

"Roth, you stay down," shouted the guard. Two more guards moved in, and the inmate was dragged to the floor and handcuffed.

The room went silent, watching as this crazy man kicked and spit and flailed.

Emily slowly rose to her feet for a better view of them dragging him away. Just before the door to the inner sanctum closed, she blew him a kiss.

Then she inhaled the stale, clammy air stinking of body odor and mold, as if it held the freshness of spring.

There was such satisfaction in a job well done.

FORTY-SIX

Emily left the prison and returned to her vehicle, just a former employee visiting her former boss. She wondered how he liked an hour in the yard and meals served on a cardboard tray.

Some long-dead Roman said that those seeking revenge should start by digging two graves. Well, she *had* started with two.

Soon there'd be four.

Emily paused to glance back at the high wire fencing topped with spirals of razor wire like a crown of thorns.

It wasn't enough. But would have to do.

Sabrina was a killer. Her husband put an innocent woman in prison.

It seemed just that Sabrina pay with her life, and he be convicted for a crime he didn't commit.

Emily's smile was bitter as the wind nipped at her cheeks. She hurried to her battered old car.

Would her sister and mother be proud of her or ashamed?

Originally, she'd only targeted Mrs. Roth. Oh, she'd had suspicions, but she wasn't a gal to convict a man without evidence.

Her big sister made the tragic mistake of believing the empty promises and vile threats.

Henry's cocktail of medications made his wife confused at times. She'd mistaken Emily for several former employees. But one in particular.

"Regan?" Mrs. Roth had asked, her words slurred, and her eyes still closed as she sprawled on a lounge chair by the pool.

Did they sound alike, too?

She'd dragged down her sunglasses, peering up with blood-shot eyes. "Wait. You're not Regan."

Emily had been patient. "I'm Emily."

"You're the one who was following me."

"No, ma'am."

But she had been, long before planting some of her mom's Oxy in Clare Eastman's car and calling the cops about a woman dealing at her son's school. Her arrest had caused Henry's scramble to find a replacement—her. And got her into the Roths' home.

Behind the wheel now, with the heater sending warm stale air through the chilly compartment, Emily stared back at the prison remembering a different federal facility and a different visit.

At first, they'd gone every Saturday.

Her mother made Emily promise not to tell Regan about the diagnoses. When the treatments and her mother's own ravaged body made it impossible to work cleaning hotel rooms, they fired her. She found work as a clerk at a convenience store in the part of Lakeland that makes folks lock their car doors while just driving through it.

Nights behind the register, days getting chemo, and Saturdays a six-hour drive to see Regan in prison. No surprise that en route to that last visit, August 2016, when Emily was sixteen, their mother dozed off while driving. Emily's shout kept them from hitting the concrete overpass.

It was too much. Their mom finally told Regan about the near crash, and the exhaustion, and her illness, while Regan blinked back tears from yet another black eye.

"We'll call you. Zoom calls on Saturday. Okay?" said their mom.

"No. Mom, no!" Regan howled as if in physical pain.

Emily wished she could go back in time to change her words or forget them. But they rose again like acid from her stomach.

"Mom gets me up in the dark. And we got a speeding ticket. It made Mom cry. When we get home, Mom goes to work, and I have to make my own dinner. I *hate* Saturdays! It's smelly and dirty here. I hate it."

Her sister opened her mouth and then closed it.

"Emily, hush," said her mother.

"I won't. She did this to herself. Didn't she? Killed a woman, a mother. Everyone at school says so. She's a murderer."

Emily leaned her elbows on the steering wheel and pressed her forehead to her arms.

It was the last time she had ever seen her sister because the casket was closed. Her face had been ruined by the ligature she'd tied around her neck before hanging herself in her cell. Her sister had been only twenty-four. One year older than Emily was now.

This was what Sabrina and Henry Roth had done to her sister.

Now Emily had blood on her hands and that felt right. And she *would* forgive Henry Roth, right after his execution.

Emily scrubbed her palms over her face and scowled back at the prison.

Her journey to this moment had been long, starting with her mother's deathbed revelation. Her mother claimed that her sister had been set up and tossed away by the Roths.

Was that true?

She needed answers. Finding out all she could about Dr. Roth, she'd discovered he'd replaced her sister with a licensed practical nurse. When that woman left, he'd hired another, and she'd discovered a common thread. Each nurse was female, a new graduate from the same college, and each was that year's valedictorian.

Did he only want qualified, inexperienced nurses? It seemed so.

Thus, all she needed to do was be that graduate when his current private nurse suddenly quit. Oh, and figure how to get that woman to quit.

Did she feel guilty planting drugs in Clare Eastman's new car and then tipping off the police? Did she regret turning in a woman who she later learned had figured out that Sabrina Roth was a dangerous monster and then decided to take the new car and look the other way?

Not even a little.

Clare was in her path and she had to go. Maybe in that way, she and Sabrina were a bit alike. But she hoped not.

When she'd come to work for the Roths, she didn't know if Sabrina Roth could understand what she was doing or had done. Emily acknowledged that if Sabrina was mentally incompetent, she could not be held accountable for her actions, no matter how vile.

Sabrina answered the question herself. First Emily discovered the list of favorites in her SUV. Easy to connect to the pedestrian fatalities. Most unsolved, except for Avery. She was clever; Sabrina had been. But when the need got too strong, she'd been reckless, impulsively grabbing the wheel while Emily's sister was driving. That one had nearly taken her and Henry down.

After that scare, Sabrina allowed Henry to hire private nurses and to take charge, for a while, until the need became too great again. At those times, she'd take her monstrous SUV and go hunting for a dark-haired woman, of a certain age, with a certain way of walking, and plow her down like a stalk of corn.

That led Emily to Henry. Did he know Sabrina was a psychopath or did he believe she had anxiety, depression, and the laundry list of other less troubling conditions?

In other words, was he a devoted husband treating his troubled wife and helping her navigate an overwhelming world or was Henry her accomplice?

Once Emily learned from Rosalind about Clare's new vehicle and later discovered her old one had been spotted at a hit-and-run fatality, and verifying that Dr. Roth had replaced that missing brown Mazda with the new Prius, Emily had paid Clare a visit. This time in a dark wig, carrying a fake badge and a catcher's chest protector under one of Henry's shirts. Clare had told her about Sabrina taking her employee's car and coming back with the front end crumpled. Both of them knew Sabrina had not hit a deer. Sabrina's favorites proved that. Took Emily right to the site of the March hit-and-run. The single witness saw a late-model brown car. The car that Henry made vanish when he replaced Clare's vehicle with a shiny blue eco-friendly auto.

How nice.

Nice for the environment. Nice for Henry because it made a big problem disappear with Clare's Mazda. Nice for Clare, gifted with a new vehicle. And nice for Emily because Clare later told her everything.

She said that after the "accident with the deer," Henry took her Mazda to an auto body shop, a special one, but he paid with his credit card, the dope. A check of the family's bank records showed this shop had taken care of several body repairs, each coordinating with various hit-and-runs.

Clare had been very clear about her responsibilities when driving Sabrina. She had been ordered by Dr. Roth never to allow his wife to drive and to keep both hands on the wheel, as his wife might have a panic attack and try to force control of the vehicle.

She'd done her job too well. Sabrina couldn't drive and couldn't risk another driver, in her employment, being arrested for vehicular homicide. What's a killer to do?

Steal Clare's car, of course.

Had that fatal accident with Clare's Mazda caused Henry to turn to fentanyl? Or had it been the one before that, or the one before that, or the one before that? Stressful, being responsible for a serial killer to protect everything you held dear.

Emily had her answer. What had been happening was Sabrina's fault and her husband had made sure she took no responsibility for her crimes.

The check to the officer investigating Regan's accident cinched it. Henry's hands were all over this.

Some months after Clare's dismissal and arrest for the planted narcotics, recovered from her Prius, Emily had read that Eastman had not agreed to a search of her vehicle and her case was later thrown out. The new Prius and her willingness to accept the vehicle as a bribe for her silence had cost her more than she'd expected, tarnishing her reputation, and racking up some legal expenses that Emily struggled to feel were less than payment for her Karmic debt.

As if all this were not damning enough, there was Sabrina's photo album. It was old-school style with those clear pages that peel away so photos and newspaper clippings can be inserted. It began innocently enough, with photos of two adorable twin babies and continued right to when Julian died. Then there was a gap of three blank pages. Then, on a black sheet of paper, Sabrina's mother's obituary. Natural causes, but Emily had done some digging. Michelle Horton King liked to drink alone. Cirrhosis.

And then, right there on the very next page were the family photos, each with her mother's eyes scratched away. The final few pages held articles clipped from the local newspapers Sabrina insisted be delivered to her table each morning. The first detailed the death investigation of the coed killed on campus twenty-three years ago. Emily flipped to the accident involving her sister. The articles mentioned Sabrina's driver, Sabrina's car, and a driver who recanted her story, claiming her employer caused the crash. Mrs. Roth had underlined the sentences mentioning her in red. As Emily turned the next few pages, she noted that the articles showed the interval between Mrs. Roth's deadly road trips narrowing. The most recent was dated six months ago, with Clare Eastman's old vehicle described fleeing the scene of a hit-and-run.

Sabrina Roth not only understood she was killing people. She enjoyed it, anticipated snuffing out the lives of any woman who crossed before her automobile while guilty of the crime of resembling her mother. And she kept a trophy book to prove it, filled with clippings of each kill.

Sabrina had known what she was doing and didn't intend to stop. Henry knew what she was doing and was unable to control her or make her stop. He tried. So many medications. Nothing worked.

After confirming the couple's guilt, Emily had set her course, scrambling for a way to drive a public wedge between them. Get some real evidence that the Roths were having marital trouble and that Henry was preventing Sabrina from leaving. Then Sabrina provided the perfect reason. She'd told Emily of her abhorrence of narcotics. Said she'd warned Henry that if he ever prescribed them, she'd leave him.

Emily had dosed the capsule and powder she'd collected from Sabrina, with one of Henry's crushed fentanyl tablets, before delivering it to Brian.

If the evidence had not been thrown out, Brian would have made a good witness, if a reluctant one. But more importantly, it drove a wedge between the pair. It also caused the call to police who registered a domestic dispute at the Roths' perfect home.

Next, Emily made sure Mrs. Roth ingested a tiny amount of the synthetic narcotic, but adequate to make her disoriented and frightened enough to allow Emily to have an excuse to call 911, knowing the ER would order blood tests. And those *were* admissible in court.

Was Henry puzzling how she had pulled this off? She hoped so. Hoped he spent long hours wondering and made countless unanswered calls to his overworked public defender posing unprovable theories.

Once you knew a family's routine, the layout of their house, where they kept the spare key, phone chargers, and private documents, it was just a matter of planning and timing, and some good luck. Oh, and the timeline.

That timeline was so very important. Detectives lived by them. And means and motive, of course.

Over the weeks coming to and from their home, she'd driven the roads through their community, taking various routes and making careful mental notes.

On the night of Sabrina's murder, she'd arrived outside the walls of the gated community after midnight, dressed in her athletic gear under disposable paper coveralls, which she'd purchased with cash from a hardware store, along with a face mask, gloves, and glasses. She wore all this under his clothes and his ball cap. There was no reason to come through the gate. She'd jumped the wall, landing in thick mulch and slipped through the hedgerow, creeping through the neighborhood avoiding doorbell cameras, security cameras, and motion-sensor floodlights.

She'd been just outside his home when the primary bathroom light went on, then off, signaling his retiring for the night. It was such a big house. And just like always, the side door from yard to garage was open.

What a nice coincidence that she and Dr. Roth were the same height. Henry was broader, but the size was close.

On her departure from his garage, she'd used the same side door, lifted the extremely light bike over the wall and ridden on the empty streets, passing several doorbell cameras, from what she gathered in the newspapers' coverage of the trial.

She'd pedaled around the barrier arm and out the owner's entrance and ridden on that fast, sleek racing bike all the way to the boutique hotel.

En route, she'd made sure to pass two banks with ATMs and a convenience store. Those had cameras.

The hotel cameras had picked up the bike entering and leaving the garage and captured her when she exited the stairs, head down, cap down, and moving fast. She'd taped the door lock earlier in the evening. It was the one glitch. How did Henry get in? Why was the door unlocked? The defense contended that he'd placed that tape the night before when Sabrina had opened the door to the hotel security. He had his hand in the door and the security footage was unclear, as were Wyatt's memories.

Emily didn't like to think about the next part. She wasn't feeling guilty. No, just the opposite. She had felt guilty all those years for not doing this.

They'd destroyed her sister. A means to an end. Something to use and then discard. Just a nobody.

In the hotel room, Sabrina lounged in the tub and Emily used the desk lamp on her head. Afterwards, Emily deployed the blade she'd taken from Henry's razor in her gloved hand.

The arterial bleeding went everywhere. She made sure to cut the right wrist first. Then did a fine job on the left. Not the way it would go. Once the tendons were sliced, a person could no longer grip. The pathologist noted that, of course, among other inconsistencies.

Like a massive head wound.

Blood and Sabrina's hair on the base of the lamp, returned to its original place but not plugged in.

The razorblade she'd grabbed from his bathroom drawer, while wearing the food prep gloves he and his wife insisted she wear. That physical evidence, along with a few hairs from his hairbrush, dropped in the hotel bathroom, placed him at the crime scene. His legal team had to confront very damning forensic testimony on the odds of having a fingerprint or DNA match. Astronomical, really.

They'd found evidence of others there as well, Sabrina herself, of course. Several cleaning people and Emily. But she'd been in the room. Staying with Mrs. Roth until she'd been asked to leave.

Afterwards, the blood soaked her sleeve and dripped on her pants—well, on Henry's pants. Sneakers too. Those left a tasty print for the expert in tread marks, provided by the prosecution.

On her exit through the hall, head down, she left more than one bloody footprint. She reached the stairs and jogged to the garage to recover the bike, still stowed between two vehicles. Then she'd ridden Henry's bike back to the Roths' residence.

Back inside the Roths' lovely garage, she returned the bike to its place, then ditched the sneakers under one of the metal racks of his gear. The police had found them while executing their search warrant.

Emily had then walked into the laundry room in her shoe covers, where she stripped out of his clothing, tossed the lot, including the hat, into the washer, added bleach and soap and set the water temperature on hot. So much for any stray bit of her DNA. But she knew what the hot water would do to the bloodstains. Those bloodstains were locked into the fibers of the fabric. And the prosecution had shown that stained hoodie to the jury. According to the news, they'd had to take a recess afterwards.

It was the kind of mistake a man who never did his own

wash might make. No one could blame him, as he had most everything dry cleaned. It didn't matter that they couldn't type the blood. There was some on the bike, the floor of the garage, the steps, the washing machine controls, the bleach bottle.

Back in the garage, she'd used bathroom cleaner to hastily clean the blood from the bike. An intentionally bad job.

She wondered if Henry heard the washing machine buzzer as he slept alone in that big empty bed.

Sneaking back to the hotel to murder his wife didn't sit well with the jury, according to the foreman interviewed on the evening news following the verdict. It was a cowardly, despicable act.

Or an act of vengeful retribution. Depended on your point of view.

Her final challenge was leaving the Roths' property, and neighborhood, undetected. This had been the most dangerous part. She'd stayed off the sidewalks and private streets, hugged the lovely hedges, and cut between columns of finely landscaped property borders of neighbors to reach the wall of the gated community.

Dressed in gloves and a dark gray medical supply disposable protective coverall over a sports bra, spandex running shorts, and the garden clogs Sabrina never used, and no one missed, she paused at the community's final obstacle, the boundary wall. Here she stripped out of the hazmat suit that had made her more difficult to see in the shadows and had protected her from things like blood evidence. But equally important, it kept her from leaving any trace evidence where it did not belong. She turned the cloth-like garment inside-out, wadded it with the gloves and carried them with her over the wall.

Out on the grassy perimeter, Emily dashed across the road to the bushes to retrieve the clothing she'd stashed. No one noticed the homeless lady creeping along in the shadows from the expensive private community of Winter Haven to the earthy side of town. No one reported the trash fire in the metal oil drum where her bloody hazmat coverup and gloves turned to smoke and ash.

The circuitous four-mile trek home took her less than ninety minutes. But she was back in her bed and sound asleep before her phone alarm chimed. It wasn't hard to act exhausted when Jennell knocked on Emily's door a few minutes later.

"Emily? Bathroom is all yours."

She'd emerged from her room in her pajamas, hair mussed, as usual. She'd yawned, anxious to get in the shower. The wet wipes in her room could only be expected to do so much.

After the hot shower, Emily wanted to shout and sing and crow. She'd done it. But, of course, at that time she wasn't certain. There were some loose ends.

But you know, it's always the husband. Isn't it?

"Good morning," said Jennell, already at the coffee maker as Emily entered the kitchen.

"If you say so." That was her usual response, so she gave it and Jennell chuckled as always.

As for Emily's fingerprints, they were where they belonged. In the Roths' house, in the hotel room, but not on the lamp, razor, or his bike. She'd been questioned. Jennell too, who verified Emily had gone to bed at about ten and had emerged from her room the next morning as usual.

Some people hate ground-floor apartments. Less secure, and less privacy from the street. But security works both ways. If it's easy to break into, it's also easy to sneak out of, and Jennell was a sound sleeper.

The bars that covered the window were old, and when Emily moved in, only two rusty screws held it in place. But on the night of the murder, that grate had been leaning against the outside wall. After Jennell left for work, Emily had reattached it with the same two screws.

She put her car in gear and rolled from the lot of the federal prison. The trip cost her a half tank of gas. But it was worth every penny just to see the look on his face when he realized what she'd done.

Likely he thought he didn't deserve it. Those people never did. Entitlement warped their worldview.

Well, if his petitions went to average, he'd be sitting in that cell for about twenty years before they denied his final appeal.

She'd finished with them. It felt funny, not having that responsibility pressing down on her. The lightness in her body was unfamiliar, as if she might float right out of her seat.

She fiddled with the radio. Not much reception up here in Starke, Florida. Not much of anything other than the prison. But that had been destination enough.

Did she worry he would tell his attorneys what she'd revealed?

No.

He had nothing but conjecture. No proof. No smoking gun. And the police had closed the case and moved on. Dr. Roth was simply a desperate man, using a wide brush and hoping to find someone else to take the blame.

Just like always.

Almost.

A LETTER FROM JENNA

Dear Reader,

I want to say a huge thank you for choosing to read *The Nurse*. If you enjoyed Emily's story and want to keep up to date with all my latest releases, just sign up at the following link. Your email address will never be shared, and you can easily unsubscribe.

www.bookouture.com/jenna-kernan

I hope you loved *The Nurse*, and if you did, I would be very grateful if you could write a review because your honest opinion helps new readers discover a book you enjoyed.

As you now know, things are not always what they seem, particularly in domestic thrillers, like *The Nurse*. While researching for this book, I read a great deal of information about antipsychotic medication and the treatment of mental illness. Now my browser ads include queries about whether I need emotional help. Instead of being annoyed, I find it gratifying to know that aid is out there. If you need emotional support, please reach out to family, friends, or professionals. There is never shame in asking for help.

I love hearing from my readers—you can get in touch on my Facebook page, through Twitter, Instagram, or my website.

Be well and happy reading!

KEEP IN TOUCH WITH JENNA

www.jennakernan.com

facebook.com/authorjennakernan

twitter.com/jennakernan

instagram.com/jenna_kernan

bookbub.com/authors/jenna-kernan

ACKNOWLEDGMENTS

This novel would not have reached you without the contribution and support of many talented folks. Here are just a few people who deserve my thanks.

My husband, Jim, offers his full faith and love while the work of building a compelling story occasionally overwhelmed me. Even if I'm unsure about the progress of a story, he has full confidence in my ability.

Thank you to my siblings for making the occasional fuss over me and giving me three voices to say they are proud of me.

Special thanks to my agent, Ann Leslie Tuttle, of Dystel, Goderich & Bourret, for keeping track of my best interests in publishing and for becoming such a good friend.

My editors, Nina Winters and Eve Hall, for their indispensable feedback and the courage to tell me when things are not working. I'm so lucky to have had two talented editors working on this book.

Thank you to the Bookouture team for the stunning cover, promotion campaigns, packaging, and marketing of this book and for your dedication to books, authors, and readers.

The Nurse was available for early reviews, and I need to thank all those reviewers who took the time to read *The Nurse* and offered their honest feedback on the story. These first readers are critically important because they help make books better.

Thank you to these organizations for educating, encouraging, and advocating for writers, including Sisters in Crime, Gulf

Coast Sisters in Crime, Mystery Writers of America, Mystery Writers of Florida, Thrill Writers International, Writers Police Academy, Authors Guild, and Novelist, Inc.

Finally, I am grateful to my readers. This book only comes alive in your hands.

Thank you!

Made in United States
North Haven, CT
15 October 2023

42776632R00240